Blood-Red Goblet

The Glassmaker Series

Book One
The Glass Dagger

Book Two
The Crystal Ship

Book Three
Blood-Red Goblet

Book Four
A Shattered Crystal
To be published later

Blood-Red Goblet

Third Adventure Of The Glassmaker Series

by

Peter Cooke

Petan Publishing

First Edition
Published in Great Britain in 2010

by

Petan Publishing
64 Skipton Road
Ilkley West Yorkshire
LS29 9HA
peter.cooke@petanpublishing.co.uk
www.petanpublishing.co.uk

Paperback ISBN 978-0-9553418-2-3

Printed in the UK by CPI Antony Rowe, Chippenham, Wiltshire

This book is printed on FSC compliant paper stock.

London & Paris

1581 - 1587

Historical Characters

Elizabeth I - (1533 - 1603) Queen of England and Ireland from 17 November, 1558 until her death. Sometimes referred to as The Virgin Queen, Gloriana, or Good Queen Bess, Elizabeth was the fifth and last monarch of the Tudor dynasty, succeeding her half-sister, Mary Tudor.

William Cecil - (1520 - 1598) 1st Baron Burghley Principal Secretary of State (1558-1572) and Lord High Treasurer from 1572.

Sir Francis Walsingham - (1532 - 1590) French Ambassador, Principal Secretary (1572–1590). Head of the spy service.

Admiral Sir John Hawkins - (1532 - 1595) English shipbuilder, naval administrator and commander, merchant, navigator, privateer, slave trader, politician, treasurer (1577) and controller (1589) of the Navy.

Roberto Ridolfi - (1531-1612) Count, of Ridolfi di Piazza family, Florentine banker.

Sir Francis Drake - (1540 - 1596) Vice Admiral, second cousin of Admiral Hawkins, English privateer, navigator, slave trader, politician and civil engineer, first Antarctic explorer, first circumnavigator of the world.

Gilbert Gifford - (1561 - 1590) English Catholic, double agent for Walsingham and Babington plotters..

Sir Henry Babington - (1530 - 1571) of Dethick Hall, Dethick, Derbyshire. Father of Anthony.

Sir Anthony Babington - (1561 - 86) son of Sir Henry. Involved in the plot that bears his name, but did not play a major part in setting up the plot to invade England and put Mary Stuart on the throne. His letters to Mary Stuart, which were intercepted by Walsingham, played a large part in her conviction for treason.

Mary Stuart - (1542–1587) was Queen of Scots (the monarch of the Kingdom of Scotland 1542-1567), daughter of Mary of Guise. Mother of James, who became James VI of Scotland, James I of England and Ireland, succeeding Elizabeth I.

Mary of Guise - (1515–1560) Queen Consort of James V of Scotland and the mother of Mary, Queen of Scots. She was Regent, or Governor, of Scotland 1554–1560.

Thomas Howard - (1535 - 1572) 4th Duke of Norfolk.

Robert Dudley - (1533 – 1588) 1st Earl of Leicester, Master of Horse to Elizabeth I. Elizabeth's favourite for many years.

George Talbot - (1528 - 1590) 6th Earl of Shrewsbury & Waterford, KG. Earl Marshall.

Bess of Hardwick - (1527 – 1608) Elizabeth, Countess of Shrewsbury, built up Chatsworth and the new Hardwick Hall.

Robert Devereux - (1566 – 1601) 2nd Earl of Essex.

Bernadino de Mendoza - (1578 - 1584) Spanish Ambassador to the English Court.

John Lesley - (1527 - 1596) Bishop of Ross, Scottish Roman Catholic supporter of Mary Stuart.

Henri I - **(**1550 - 1588) Prince of Joinville, 3rd Duke of Guise, Count of Eu, sometimes called *Le Balafré* "the scarred". The heroic and charismatic leader and founder of the Catholic League and architect of the massacre of the Huguenots on St. Bartholomew's Day. After leading a rising against the King, he was assassinated at the Château de Blois.

Catherine of Cleves - (1548 - 1633) Wife of Henri I, Duchess of Guise, Countess of Eu, later Dowager Duchess of Guise.

Esmé Stewart - (1542 - 1583) 1st Duke of Lennox, 1st Earl of Lennox, was the son of John Stewart, 5th Lord of Aubigny, Catholic supporter and friend of the Duke of Guise.

Sir Francis Throckmorton - (1554 - 1584) a conspirator against Queen Elizabeth I.

Marquis de Marchaumont - French Diplomat. Chief marriage contract negotiator for the Duke of Alençon.

Claude de l'Aubespine - (1585 - 1606) Baron de Châteauneuf, French Ambassador to England

Michel de Castelnau - (1520 - 1592) Seigneur de Mauvissière, (1575 - 1585) French Ambassador to England

Father Creighton - Scottish Jesuit and messenger for the Pope.

Robert Montgomery - Archbishop of Glasgow, Chancellor of the University of Glasgow, Roman Catholic supporter of Mary, Queen of Scots.

Doctor William Allen - Leader of the English Catholics.

Father Robert Parsons - messenger to the court of Philip II of Spain for the Archbishop of Glasgow.

Sir Christopher Hatton - (1540 - 1591) Educated at Oxford, he became a lawyer and a firm favourite at court. He was a handsome, intelligent man whose elegant dancing soon brought him to the notice of the Queen. As with all her favourites, he was well rewarded and became Lord Chancellor in 1587.

Doctor William Parry - Member of Parliament. Well educated at Chester, but his spendthrift ways led him into difficulties. He was a dubious agent for Walsingham and probably played both sides against each other, for gain. After falling in with Morgan and Paget, he bragged he would kill Queen Elizabeth and received absolution from the Pope. He may or may not have carried out a plan to murder Elizabeth, but if so his courage left him. He was denounced, convicted and executed for high treason.

Cardinal Como - Papal secretary to Pope Gregory XIII.

Pope Gregory XIII - Pope, (1572-1585), probably best known for the Gregorian calender.

William I, Prince of Orange, widely known as William the Silent - (1533-1584) a wealthy nobleman, William originally served the Hapsburg as a member of the court of Margaret of Parma, governor of the Spanish Netherlands. William joined the Dutch uprising and turned against his former masters. He led the Dutch to several successes in the fight against the Spanish. Declared an outlaw by the Spanish king in 1580, he was assassinated by Balthasar Gèrard in Delft four years later.

Francis, Duke of Anjou and Alençon - (1555 - 1584) was the youngest son of Henry II of France and Catherine de' Medici and a suitor of Queen Elizabeth. He courted her in person and she grew fond of him, calling him her 'frog', after a frog-shaped earring he gave her. As with all her suitors, nothing came of the match.

Philip II of Spain - (1527-1598) married to Mary I of England, he ruled with her until her death. He proposed marriage to Elizabeth when she inherited the title, but she was not interested. He became king of Spain in January 1556. He governed Spain in her so-called "Golden Age". However, his reign saw the economic decline of Spain, her bankruptcy and a disastrous decade from 1588 to 1598 which included the disaster of the Spanish Armada.

Giacomo di Grassi - an Italian fencing master who wrote a fencing manual, in 1570. Di Grassi was one of the three première fencing masters known from Elizabethan England.

Thomas Rogers - (alias Nicholas Berden), employed as a secret spy for Walsingham. Active among the dissident Catholics in France. Well acquainted with the Jesuit priests and was undoubtedly taking money from both sides.

George Douglas - Scottish envoy to France in 1581-2. Employed by Esmé Stewart.

Lord Henry Howard - (1540 - 1614) a sympathiser of Mary Stuart, brother of the late Thomas Howard, Duke of Norfolk, who was executed for high treason.

Alexander Farnese, Duke of Parma - (1545 - 1592) a brilliant tactician, he fought at the Battle of Lepanto and later led the Spanish army in a successful campaign in the Netherlands. A skilful diplomat he was the match even of his great antagonist, William the Silent. And, like most of the leading statesmen of his day, he was unscrupulous as to the means he employed so long as he achieved his ends.

William Holt - a Jesuit, working with Father Creighton in Scotland to further the cause of Catholicism.

George More - a messenger carrying letters from Throckmorton to Mary Stuart. Made a full confession without duress and was pardoned.

Charles Paget - Catholic conspirator, involved both in the Throckmorton and Babington plots. Leader of the 'Seculars' in France, much more a leading member of the plots than either Throckmorton, or Babington.

John Ballard - alias Fortescue, educated at Cambridge, ordained priest at the seminary at Rheims, and came to England where he became involved in the Babington plot.

John Savage - a soldier of indifferent quality who had sworn an oath, encouraged by Gilbert Gifford, to kill Queen Elizabeth.

Despite being in England for some considerable time, he lacked the wit and the courage to carry it out.

Thomas Morgan - a catholic conspirator who had fled England to live in France and was Mary Stuart's agent and cipher clerk. He was a major contributor to the Throckmorton, Parry and Babington plots. He stayed in France and was never brought to trial.

Sir Amias Paulet - (1532–1588) an English diplomat, Governor of Jersey, and the gaoler for a period of Mary, Queen of Scots. A zealous Protestant, he opposed everything Mary Stuart stood for.

Sir Drue Drury - assigned to accompany Sir Paulet to Tutbury, Chartley and Fotheringhay Castle and secure Mary, Queen of Scots. He was a witness to her execution.

Thomas Phelippes - (1556–1625) was a forger, intelligence gatherer and important agent under Sir Francis Walsingham. He deciphered the codes of those plotting against Elizabeth I.

Sir Henry Percy, 8th Earl of Northumberland, (1532-1585), implicated in the Throckmorton plot and arrested. He was committed to the Tower by the Privy Council and six months later, on 21 June 1585, he was found dead in his bed in his cell, having been shot through the heart. A jury was at once summoned, and returned a verdict of suicide. There was speculation at the time that he had been murdered, but a Star Chamber enquiry upheld the suicide verdict.

Henry Grey, 6th Earl of Kent - (1541-1615) official witness for the Privy Council to the execution of Mary Stuart

Sir Ralph Sadler - (1507-1587) an English statesman and served as a Secretary of State for King Henry VIII. He was sent to arrest the Duke of Norfolk during the Rising of the Northern Earls, and was unwillingly appointed gaoler of Mary, Queen of Scots. After the Babington Plot, Sadler was also on the council that sentenced Mary to death.

John Somers - secretary to Walsingham and Sir Ralph Sadler's son-in-law.

Gilbert Curle - secretary to Mary Stuart.

Claude de la Boisselière Nau - principal secretary to Mary Stuart.

All other characters depicted in this book are either fictional, and named as such in the *Who's Who*, or are minor characters.
The interlinked Throckmorton and Babington plots occurred substantially as described in the book, but have been simplified. All the events involving Jacob Bell and the other fictional characters outlined in the *Who's Who* are products of the author's imagination.

Who's Who of Fictional Characters

Giacomo (Giam) Bellini, Son of Eduardo Bellini. A Master Glassmaker, Giam changes his name to Jacob Bell in London. Becomes a spy in the service of Walsingham and Glassmaker to Queen Elizabeth of England.

Eduardo Bellini. Murano Noble, Senator to the Grand Council, a widower with one son, Jacob.

Andrea Luciano, Deceased wife of Eduardo Bellini; mother of Jacob and daughter of Antonio Luciano: died from sweating fever when Jacob was only four years old.

Antonio Luciano, Father of Andrea and Jacob's grandfather. Former Grand Master of the Guild of Glassmakers. Master of the Luciano Glass-works, one of the foremost in Murano.

Marco Baffo, Chief Glass-blower of the Luciano Glass-works.

Luca Ridotti, Apprentice, later Capo of the Luciano Glass-works.

Consuela, Serving wench in the Luna Taverna frequented by Jacob. She was his first lover.

Roberto Rosso, (Born 1551) Apprentice at the Luciano Glass-works, becomes Jacob's assistant, confidant and friend. Becomes Junior Partner in the Crouched Friars Glass-works. Skilled knife thrower.

Anna Rosso, Widow, Roberto's mother. Ran Jacob's house in Murano. Becomes Lady Maria's companion after her marriage to Adrian Ragazoni. Later Jacob's housekeeper in London.

Ricardo Morisini, Senator and Avogador of the Grand Council. Very rich and influential. One of the foremost nobles of Venice.

Maria Morisini, Daughter of Senator Ricardo Morisini. Jacob's fiancé and lover. Forced into a loveless marriage by Adrian Ragazoni, until his death. Owner of the Ragazoni empire after the death of Pietro Ragazoni. Later Jacob's wife, Lady Maria Morisini-Bellini (Bell).

Adrian Ragazoni, Senator and son of Secretary Ragazoni. Owner of the Mendoza Glass-works, fierce enemy of Jacob, spurned suitor of Maria Morisini. Special Envoy to English Court. Assassinated with a glass dagger by his own assassin on the orders of Sir William Cecil.

Pietro Ragazoni, Senator and Secretary to the Grand Council of Venice, Rossi of the Three, Inquisitors of the Council of Ten. Father of Adrian.

Enriquo Gomez, Fencing-master of Venice.

Signor Nicolosi, Secretary to the Council of Ten of Venice.

Sigisbei Vercelline, Steward of the Morisini household, advisor, general factotum and chaperone to Maria.

Lunardo Carreras, Childhood friend of Jacob's. Captain of the galleass *Galliano.* Later becomes Commodore of the combined Morisini-Bellini fleet.

Miguel Santini, Former Master gunner of the *Galliano,* latterly gunnery instructor at the Arsenale.

Carlos Basadona, Master gunner of the galleass *Galliano.*

Enzio Carreras, Father of Marcus Antonio; Patroni of a shipwright. Friend of Eduardo Bellini.

Jean Thieré, French, formerly of Antwerp. Original owner of the Crouched Friars Glass-works in London. Unwitting catalyst for Jacob's downfall in Venice. Becomes Jacob's friend and partner. Murdered by order of Sir Richard Urie.

Thomas Pepper, Jacob's lawyer in London.

Sir Richard Urie, Leading member of the London Glass-Sellers Association. Catholic supporter of Mary Queen of Scots. Becomes involved in the Maldini plot.

James McFarlane, Secretary of the London Glass-Sellers Association.

John Isham, Head of the Merchant Adventurers' Guild, moneylender *extraordinaire.* City house, cottage in Tottenham. Owns Lamport Manor in Northampton, which he is rebuilding. Retires at end of 1572 and becomes a magistrate and country gentleman.

Elizabeth Isham, Daughter of John Isham. Aged 16, engaged to and marries Roberto Rosso.

Rebecca Isham, Eldest daughter of John Isham. A widow, her husband died from cholera. Has a brief fling with Jacob before his marriage, but realising he loves only Maria, she marries a local farmer.

Mistress Simpkin, Northumbrian housekeeper at the house in Harte Street, London, shared by Jacob, Jean and Roberto.

Quiff, Named after white lock of hair on forehead. Apprenticed to the glass-works as Roberto's assistant - information gatherer from network of apprentices (The Ring).

John Noble, Servant of Sir Richard Urie at his house in Tottenham. Later Steward to Jacob Bell (Giam Bellini).

Pietro Tiazoni, Venetian from Antwerp - promoted to Senior Glass-blower at the Crutched Friars. Anglicised name to Peter Tyzack.

Colonel Young, Army colonel, in charge of a troop of soldiers who work directly under the instructions of Sir Francis Walsingham. Becomes Jacob's friend.

Count Maldini, Catholic agent for Philip of Spain and the Pope. Mastermind behind the plot to assassinate Queen Elizabeth and put Mary Stuart on the throne.

Jack Petts, Eldest of the two brothers. Entered Jacob's service when he was paralysed. Now runs the house at Mark Street, London.

Bob Petts, Younger brother of Bob. Helps in the Mark Street house.

Ricardo Giacomo (Rico) Bellini (Bell), Known as Rico. Eldest child of Jacob and Maria, b. 18th June, 1570.

Eleanor Elizabeth (Lisa) Bellini (Bell), Eldest sister of Rico, b. 6th May, 1572.

Maria (Jane) Bellini (Bell), b. 12th May, 1574.

Charles (Eduardo) Bellini (Bell), b. 21st December, 1577.

Margaret Anne (Meg) Bellini (Bell), b. 2nd October, 1580, d. 23rd February, 1581.

Caterina Ann (Cate) Bellini (Bell), b. 20th March, 1582.

Jedediah (Jed) Sutton, alias James Stourbridge, Illegitimate son of Count Ridolfi and Agnes Sutton, a distant relative of Robert Dudley, Earl of Leicester.

Patrick Nevison, A highwayman.

Edward Armitage, Tutor to the Bell children.

Doctor Nguyên, Extremely gifted Vietnamese doctor, trained in Chinese Medicine.

Monsieur Dupont, Jacob's business agent in Paris.

Madame Hélène, Proprietress of a fashionable Paris dress salon.

Raoul Laguna, Venetian bead jewellery maker and designer based in the Marais district of Paris.

Toni Laguna, son of Raoul. Gifted bead maker and jewellery designer. Goes to London to design and sell lampwork jewellery.

Jane Tosland, widow of John Tosland a Burton-upon-Trent brewer, murdered by Jed Sutton.

Captain Roberts, former naval frigate captain and now captain of Jacob's ship *The Crystal.*

Harry Heywood, ex-sergeant in Colonel Young's troop of soldiers. Came to work for Jacob as added security.

Brian Walker, ex-soldier who works with Harry Heywood as security and looks after the horses and the coach.

Titus Barr, clerk to the Lord Chancellor, and also to the Commission investigating Mary Stuart, at Fotheringhay Castle.

These characters are all fictitious and bear no relation to any characters either living or dead.

Acknowledgements

This has been the most difficult writing task I have ever undertaken, not least because of the extremely complicated nature of the many facets of what was, in reality, only one continuous series of events. The various plots against Queen Elizabeth I detailed in *Blood-Red Goblet*, are usually portrayed as separate, but are, in truth, part of a single plot. I could not have written this novel, without the unfailing support, encouragement and enthusiasm of my wife Ann.

I must not forget the work of my friends Maureen Blundell and Frank Nightingale. Maureen carried out the editing in her usual no-holds barred style that made sure that my tendency to concentrate on the history did not run away with me. Frank's excellent proof-reading has once more navigated me through the turbulent waters of the complicated events. Any mistakes that remain, are entirely to be laid at my door.

I would also like to thank Sandy Kidd for her wonderful jewellery designs that feature throughout the book. The designs were inspired by the scintillating clothes and jewellery found at the vibrant court of Queen Elizabeth I and now form part of an exclusive range of jewellery, details of which can be found at the end of the book.

Prologue
St. James's Park, London, 1581

Now a mere one hundred yards away, the Queen and her entourage were quickly approaching the dense thicket wherein the watcher lurked. She, as usual, was leading her courtiers a merry dance. Striding out, laughing and joking with Sir Christopher Hatton, that preening, overdressed popinjay, who was her current favourite now that Leicester was away in the Netherlands. The rest of the fawning sycophants and her pensioner guards had been left toiling some way behind. The watchers face contorted with hate as he focussed on the Queen, the Tudor bastard who followed the same path to destruction taken by her dissolute father. His eyes narrowed as, not for the first time, the Queen suddenly changed direction. Fortunately, as on previous occasions, she turned back to the well-trodden path that passed close to his hiding place. Soon, he thought, soon, this serpent who denies the one true religion will be removed forever and the legitimate heir, Mary Stuart will claim her throne.

Behind his tree, Dr William Parry took out the dag he had hidden in his doublet. The steel flintlock pistol was much smaller than most of the usual cumbersome pistols, but far easier to conceal. Of course, it could only be used at short range, but that suited Parry as he was a poor shot. He was sweating profusely and a bead fell from his forehead on to the stock. Snatching the dag away to protect the precious powder, he mopped his brow with his kerchief. Even with the encouragement of the letter from Cardinal Como, Papal Secretary, urging him to put his holy and honourable purpose into effect and granting him plenary absolution from the Pope, the assassination of the Queen was still a horrendous and treasonous act.

The royal party were only about fifty yards away now. Parry cocked the dag, leaned back against the tree and held the pistol in front of his breast with his finger on the guard. He began to count. When he got to forty-five, he thought, he would step out from behind the tree and fire. At five yards' distance he couldn't miss.

Thirty-nine, forty, forty-one. He tensed himself for the act that would liberate the nation and restore the one true religion. Forty-two, forty-three. He prayed for God to give him strength to carry out his purpose - and then froze as he heard the thunder of hooves. There were cries for Her Majesty to hold and, risking another look, he saw the Queen with her back towards him, not more than ten paces away. A messenger had dismounted and was hurrying towards her with a sealed message and she was moving towards him.

You must do it now, thundered the thought in his head. But it's much further away than I planned, his mind answered. What if I miss? He ducked back behind the tree and tried to marshal his courage. He started to shake as if he had the ague. They will hang, draw and quarter me if they catch me, he thought, inhaling deeply and raising the dag again. Then a thought struck. He would carry the dag behind his back, walk forward a few yards and then fire. This would give him a better chance of success than trying a shot from this distance. On three, then. He held the dag behind him and counted. Sweat was almost blinding him and he wiped it away with his sleeve. One, two, three. He stepped from behind the tree and darted back again as he realised, with a sickening jolt in his stomach, that he had missed his chance. The Queen was already moving back the way she had come and the group was closing behind her. There was no possibility of killing her now.

In his lodgings later that afternoon, he pondered the message that had saved the Queen's life. The timing of its delivery could not have been more fortuitous. Was it possible that she was under God's protection? 'Thou shall not kill' was His commandment. Could the Pope have interpreted His message incorrectly? Was it wrong in God's eyes to authorise the Queen's assassination? No, it was unthinkable that His Holiness could be in error. The failure of his mission must be because he was unworthy to undertake it. He slumped in despair - he would have to leave England, but he couldn't go back to Paris. Thomas Morgan, Mary Stuart's agent was there and would want the money back he had paid William to assassinate the Queen. Morgan would probably try to make him carry out his promise, but he would have to get someone else. Anthony Babington, was always proclaiming his destiny to free Mary Stuart, or perhaps John Savage, who was a soldier. They were better suited to the task. William knew, that despite all his bravado, he would never again be able to bring himself to kill the old King's bastard daughter, Elizabeth.

Mary, Mary, quite contrary,
How does your garden grow?
With silver bells and cockle-shells
And pretty maids all in a row.

Children's nursery rhyme relating to Mary Stuart.

Chapter One
London, 1581

The summons to attend a secret meeting at Walsingham's house in Sydon Lane had taken Jacob Bell, the Queen's Glassmaker, by surprise. Heavily cloaked, Jacob, an erstwhile spy of Walsingham's had slipped into the side entrance shortly after dark and on being shown into Walsingham's study, was intrigued to see that Sir William Cecil, Lord Burghley, chief adviser to Queen Elizabeth and now Lord Treasurer, was also present. He was at once on the alert. These two men were undoubtedly the Queen's most influential Privy Councillors along with her favourite, Robert Dudley, Earl of Leicester.

Sir Francis Walsingham, Principal Secretary to the Queen and head of the secret service, thanked him for coming and bade him sit down. 'I imagine you are wondering why I have sent for you,' he said. 'Especially as we have not met for some time.'

'The thought had crossed my mind,' replied Jacob. Indeed, he had been very apprehensive.

'I have intercepted a letter from Henri, Duke of Guise, to the Bishop of Ross, Mary Stuart's chief supporter. The Duke, in what was obviously a reply to a letter sent to him, has recommended you to the Bishop as a trustworthy person to recruit in the quest to free Mary Stuart.'

Jacob sighed. 'I thought they had forgotten about me by now. It is almost ten years since I last had contact with the Duke of Guise.' Just after he married Maria, he had heard that the Duke had written a letter praising him as a devoted supporter of Mary Stuart. Jacob's decision to wait until the Bishop or the Duke made contact, proved to be a wise one. To this day he'd not heard a word, nor had he needed to tell Maria about the letter.

On occasions, Jacob had clandestine meetings with Walsingham. The last one had been almost a year ago. On the matter of the letter, the Secretary counselled Jacob to bide his time and let the plotters contact him.

'I know not when you will get the call to join the League, but rest assured, you will. The Duke of Guise will not allow his cousin to remain in captivity in England without trying to release her. As leader of the Catholic League in France, he commands a large force of men. With the Pope urging him on, he is capable of an invasion which, coupled with a Catholic uprising, would be almost impossible to repulse.'

'How likely is that?'

Walsingham grimaced. 'There are plots aplenty in the air and my spies tell me there is sure to be another attempt to free the Stuart woman in the near future. This might well be the time and place!'

Jacob had been dreading being drawn into another plot. He had been very reluctant to become involved with the Duke of Guise again. Henri was charming, but underneath the smooth veneer lay a ruthless man who would sacrifice all for his faith, his family and his own ambitions, which Jacob suspected even reached as high as the French throne. He counted himself lucky not to have been unmasked as a spy.

Lord Burghley and Walsingham pleaded their case very well. The Duke of Guise had ruthlessly hunted down and removed all of their best spies in Paris and several other parts of France. They were desperate for intelligence and saw Jacob's position of trust with the Duke as a unique opportunity to place an insider who would be privy to all the details of the plot. Lord Burghley, a man Jacob respected, made the final appeal.

'We know we ask much of you, Jacob Bell. England is only your adopted country and you have served it, and my Queen, as well as any true born Englishmen. But we need your help again.' Jacob was not prepared to give them an immediate answer, but promised to consider their request most carefully. He returned home with much on his mind.

‘It’s time the lamps were lit, Bob, it’s nearly dark out there,’ Jack Petts said to his younger brother. ‘Come on sleepy head, stir your bones.’

Dressed in the distinctive black and yellow livery of the Queen’s Glassmaker, they’d been in Jacob Bell's service ever since he’d been paralysed saving the Count Ridolfi’s life some ten years earlier. Fortunately, the paralysis proved to be only temporary, thanks to the acupuncture given by Doctor Nguyên, a friend of Maria's father. After Master Jacob's marriage to Lady Maria Morisini, the Bells moved into the new house at Mark Street and the Petts, together with Mistris Simpkin, ran the household.

Bob grinned sheepishly. He'd been nodding off in his chair. Picking up his lantern and taper he followed Jack out of the front door and up the drive. After lighting the lamps outside the entrance, they closed and bolted the imposing wooden gates and, after lighting lamps at intervals down the drive and those at either side of the carved, solid oak entrance doors, they returned inside.

'You can turn in now, Bob,' said Jack. 'I'll just go and see if Master Jacob needs anything. He's been busy in the study all night since he came home and Lady Maria has already retired.'

'Aye, it's been quiet since Anna got the children off to bed. They fair wear you out chasing around the house and getting into who knows what mischief. I'll bid thee good night then Jack and don't worry about lighting the fires in the morning, I'll see to 'em.'

Jack nodded and made his way to Master Jacob's study. He knocked and opening the double doors entered the study, which doubled as a library and was his master's pride and joy. The oak-panelled library had two walls lined with books from floor to ceiling. Master Jacob had been collecting them since his wedding to Lady Maria nine years ago.

His master was sitting at his desk with books of accounts strewn everywhere. He looked up when Jack came in.

'The lanterns are lit, Master Jacob and everyone's abed.'

Master Jacob looked at the ornate mantle clock in surprise. 'Is it that time already?'

'Yes, Master Jacob. Can I get you anything before I go up?'

'A glass of Mistris Simpkin's fresh lemonade wouldn't go amiss. I'll be off to my bed very soon, I've nearly finished now.'

When Jack had left, Jacob sipped his lemonade and made a few more careful entries to the column of figures. With a final check, he put down his quill and re-opened the letter from Sir Francis Drake that he'd received that morning. It contained a draft on the London Goldsmiths for his share of the booty brought back by Drake from his historic circumnavigation of the globe, which had earned him his recent knighthood.

The draft informed Jacob that the sum of twenty-three thousand five hundred pounds was awaiting his instructions at the London Goldsmiths. Not a bad return on the five hundred pounds he'd invested in backing Drake's expedition.

Sitting back with a sigh, he thought about all that had happened in the past few months. His euphoria at Drake's return in September and the birth of his daughter Margaret Ann shortly afterwards, had given way to despair in February.

Their little Meg, born prematurely, was a small and weakly child. After the birth, Maria was exhausted and the baby needed constant care. They'd spent a very quiet Christmas.

Early in February, Maria and the baby became ill with the sweating fever. Luckily, Jacob and none of their other four children, were infected. Maria soon recovered, but not without a huge toll on her natural reserves of energy. However, despite all their efforts, Margaret Anne died.

For several weeks now Maria had been gripped by a melancholia which resisted all efforts of her family and friends to alleviate it. Jacob was perplexed. Nothing he tried to do to lift her spirits seemed to make any difference. He called in his friend and family physician Doctor Nguyên whose diagnosis was that Maria was suffering from an excess of black bile brought on by the after-effects of childbirth and the fever. Since the heat from the fever had now passed, the doctor prepared a concoction of Chinese ginseng and lotus root. He also suggested that it might be a good idea for Maria to have a change of surroundings. 'Too many bad memories here at moment. Need go away with children, make good memories. Take remedy, soon be feeling better.'

A few days later, Roberto, Jacob's partner and close friend, had informed him that sales in France were tailing off. He wondered if it was due to the lack of a warehouse in the French capital.

'Why don't we open a warehouse and showroom in Paris?' he asked. 'It's bound to boost sales.'

Jacob thought this was an excellent idea. Then it occurred to him, it would also provide the change of scenery that Maria needed. That settled it. He decided he would buy a house in the most affluent neighbourhood in Paris, the Marais, and convert part of the ground floor to a showroom for his glassware, like the one at his father's house, the Casa Da Mula, in Venice,. Not only that, he'd have an opening night to outshine the one held in Venice when he first started as a Fattori, the manager and chief designer of the Luciano Glass-works in Murano.

Surely Maria would be stimulated by the new house, not to mention the chance to explore Paris. Jacob looked at the Goldsmiths' draft again. The timing of its arrival must be an omen. There was more than enough to buy a splendid house and showroom and to have a lavish opening ceremony.

This started another train of thought. What if he met up with the Duke of Guise again, whose château was in the Marais district of Paris? Not that it was a place of fond memories, despite its opulence. Jacob remembered the injury that had led Count Ridolfi to take him to Paris. He would never forget his feelings when he recovered consciousness in the Duke's château and found he was crippled. He rubbed his back distractedly. Although cured of the temporary paralysis, it still gave him a little pain. Especially on cold, damp nights in the winter. And now, with the earlier meeting with Walsingham, all of those painful experiences had been brought home to him again.

Roused from his thoughts, he became aware of a light at the open door. A very pale Maria was standing there holding her night-light. 'Are you coming to bed, Jacob?' she said, in a tremulous voice. 'The children have been asleep for ages.'

Jacob went across to meet her. 'I was just clearing away. You go on up and I'll follow directly.'

She gave him a wan smile. 'I'll wait for you if you don't mind and we can go together.'

Jacob took the night-light from her and placed it on the desk. Taking her in his arms he held her close. 'Why, you're trembling like a leaf, my love. Are you cold?' He took off his cape and placed it round her shoulders. 'There, is that better?'

She nodded. 'I was a little cold, but I'm really upset about the dream I had about our little Meg She was holding her arms out and crying over and over again, "Where are you, mama. Where are you?" '

Her voice broke and she sobbed into Jacob's shoulder. Jacob stroked her hair and murmured words of reassurance. When eventually she quietened a little he blew out the candles on his desk and, picking up her night-light, guided her up the stairs to bed. Once in bed she clung to him and Jacob did his best to calm her. Eventually, her arm over his chest, she fell asleep. But it was a long time before Jacob slept!

Why should he risk everything for England. Maria needed him now, more than at any previous time. There was nothing stopping them from returning to Venice. And yet ... He thought about Venice and what it represented. They both had family there. He was a Senator, the Bellini-Ragazoni empire was extensive and gave him status, but he would always be regarded as an upstart. The Ragazonis might be a spent threat, but the Old Families controlled power in Venice and they would never accept him. And Venice was a fading power. It was stagnating. England was a thriving, thrusting nation with a Queen and her advisers driving it on to greater things. He had built his own new empire here and had gained riches and respect. England accepted him for what he was and what he had achieved. His thoughts seemed clearer now and he sighed and settled down to sleep. Tomorrow was going to be another very busy day.

Chapter Two
White Hart Inn, London, 1581

From where Jed Sutton stood he could see Sumner the ostler aimlessly forking hay from one place to another across the other side of the barn as he waited for Nevison to turn up. Nevison's horse stirred nervously in the stall as it sensed his tension and Jed stroked her nose keeping a tight grip on the reins. As it quietened, Jed heard Sumner speak to someone, obviously Nevison, who had just entered the stable yard. When the unsuspecting highwayman entered the stall he found himself seized in a deadly grip, his arm twisted behind his back and a knife held to his throat.

'Don't try to struggle,' said Jed. 'I only want to talk to you.' He gave a throaty chuckle. 'I'm not a thief-taker. The reward on Patrick Nevison's head is not worth the effort, as yet. I have a business proposition that I think you will find very lucrative.'

He eased the knife from his throat. 'Now, I'm going to let you go, but one false move and it will be your last. Take a look in that pouch hanging on the rail in front of you.'

When he was released, the highwayman stood still for a moment as if debating his next move, then stepped forward and removed the pouch from the rail. He tipped the contents into his hand and stared at the five gold royals that lay in his palm; taking one, he bit it to see if it was really gold, and then, pouring them back into the pouch, slipped it into his doublet.

'I don't like your way of attracting my attention. But you have it now, so what's this proposition and how do you know about me?'

'I'm in the same business as you, my friend. The North has become too hot for me, so I've come down South for the sake of my health.'

'And what's that to do with me?'

'The wealthy are using coaches a lot more these days and most of them have an armed escort or guard. That makes it difficult for one lone "knight of the road". I hear you had a narrow escape last week when you held up a coach in Finchley Wood.'

Nevison gave the ostler an evil look.

'Don't blame him, he didn't like a knife at his throat any more than you did!' Jed said with a laugh and motioned to some nearby bales of hay.

'Either sit down and listen to what I have to say, or go on your way and be none the wiser.' He indicated the cocked dag in his hand. 'If you're thinking of jumping me, I don't fancy your chances. However, if you leave, the pouch and its contents stays here. It's your choice.'

So began the partnership of Jed Sutton, murderer and Catholic militant, and Patrick Nevison, highwayman. Over the next few weeks, they carried out a series of hold-ups at different places on the main routes to the North out of London. They built up a gang of ruffians to carry out Jed's main plan - to rob two houses belonging to wealthy merchants, which his informers at the White Hart and Spaniards Inn had identified as ripe for picking and poorly staffed.

The first robbery went well. The gang swooped on the house of a mercer on the far side of Finchley Wood at first light. Six masked men who burst in and rounded up the servants met with little resistance. The terrified servants were herded into a storeroom and the door barred. They were told to be quiet, or they would be killed.

The mercer himself was away on business and only his wife and children were at home. Jed had only to threaten the children and their near-swooning mother, roused from her bed, told them where to find all the family valuables. The gang stripped everything of value from the house, tied up the wife and made good their escape.

The second raid, some miles away on the far edge of Hackney Common, did not go well. Although only two days after the first, the owner of the mansion had added a couple of armed strong-arm men to keep his house safe. Unaware of this, the gang was met with stern resistance. Two of them were killed and Jed and two others wounded before they were able to overrun the defenders.

Although only a flesh wound in the arm, it sent Jed into a

towering rage. He butchered two servants and raped a maid before Nevison was able to drag him away. They had just ransacked the bedrooms of a considerable amount of money and jewellery when the lookout shouted that a number of men were approaching across the fields from a nearby farm. Armed only with pitchforks and scythes, they outnumbered the surviving members of the gang by three to one. Cursing violently, Jed, Nevison and the others turned tail and fled.

Knowing that a hue and cry was inevitable, they buried most of the larger loot at the far side of a nearby wood, divided the money between them and split up. Jed and Nevison headed for the White Hart in Bishopsgate Without and the others for Spaniards Inn on the edge of Hampstead Heath. When Jed and Nevison reached the White Hart, they led their horses into the stable as arranged with Joe the ostler and left him grooming the horses while they went up to Nevison's room.

Once there, Nevison rounded on Jed. 'What possessed you to start killing and raping?' he raged. 'The hue and cry will be well raised by now and the whole countryside will be looking for us. They're never going to give up until they find us because of you. It's all finished. We'll have to leave the country.'

Jed began to laugh. 'I like killing people, especially if they give me a good reason,' he said, indicating the bandage on his arm. 'Then I repay them ten-fold.' He smirked. 'As for the woman, she was ripe for the plucking.'

When Nevison called him a butcher, an evil influence and said he regretted ever having met him, Jed went very quiet until Nevison's tirade stopped. 'If that's how you feel, we'll divide up now and go our separate ways.'

'That suits me,' said Nevison angrily. 'I had every intention of doing so.' He hurriedly packed his stuff into a saddlebag. 'I'll pay the landlord what I owe and meet you in the stable shortly to collect the rest of the stuff hidden there.'

Jed held out his hand. 'No hard feelings, Patrick,' he said, in a friendly tone. 'I lost my temper badly. It's like a black mist descends on me and I do wild things.' He clapped Patrick on the back and made as if to put an arm round his shoulders. Nevison shrugged it off angrily, but did not notice Jed slip his knife from its sheath as he stormed out.

When he arrived at the stable Jed was already in the stall and the rest of their booty was divided into two piles on a hay bale. 'Where's Sumner?' he asked. 'He wants his share for passing on the information.'

'Don't worry about him,' said Jed quietly. 'I've paid him off.'

'Right,' said Patrick, with a quick glance at the bale. 'Which pile is mine?'

'I don't mind. Take your pick.'

As Nevison bent to check the piles, Jed hefted the club on which had been nailed a horseshoe. As Nevison turned and stood up with his arms full of gold and precious stones, Jed hit him a terrible blow in the face and as he slumped down hit him several more times on his head and body. The horse smelling blood took fright and began to lash out with its back hooves. One of the kicks sent splinters flying from the back of the stall before Jed could control it. After leading it from its stall, he calmed it by stroking its nose and blowing into its nostrils. He looked around to make sure he hadn't been seen. Then he went to the next stall and dragged out the body of the ostler. He propped it outside, but left it in the shadows, so it wouldn't be seen immediately.

Going back into the stall where Nevison's body lay, he examined the scene. The club had done its work well. Anyone would believe the horse responsible for Nevison's injuries, especially as it had trampled on the body smashing both legs, leaving shattered bones protruding through the flesh and partially severing the head. There was blood everywhere and bloody hoof-prints on his clothes, the walls and the straw.

Removing the old doublet he'd been wearing over his own, he wiped his hands with it to remove any signs of blood. Then, leaving most of the highwayman's share of the valuables scattered around the stall, he picked up the saddlebag Nevison had left outside. He went to his own horse, which was already saddled and taking some of the best gems out of the bag, he put them into his own. Nevison's bag he then fastened and slung across the saddle of Nevison's horse.

He then cautiously peered out into the courtyard and saw the gate into Bishopsgate was wide open. Untying the now docile horse, he led it towards the yard and then thrust the blood-stained doublet under its nose. Immediately, the horse rolled its eyes and reared up, whinnying. Letting go of the reins, Jed gave a violent slap across its rump and the horse shot across the yard like an arrow from a bow. Grooms scattered out of the way, some trying to stop the terrified animal. The yard was in chaos. Seeing the open gate, the horse bolted into the street and almost collided with some travellers heading for the city. While their attention was elsewhere, Jed slipped across the yard and came running towards them as if he'd just come out of the inn.

'What's going on?' he said to the landlord, who was shouting for Sumner and trying to get the yard men to pursue the horse.

'A horse has bolted out of the stables. It's a wonder no one was killed.'

The horse reared up, lashing out with its fore hooves as a well-dressed traveller, who had dismounted his own steed, tried to stop it. He fell to the ground and rolled out of the way as the horse bolted again and swerved through a gap in the houses before vanishing from sight.

The crowd, sensing the fun was over, began to drift away. Across the street the traveller picked himself up and began to dust down his clothes. Seeing his face for the first time, Jed gave a start. He seemed familiar, but he wasn't sure where or when he had seen him before. He moved a little closer, staring intently at the tall, black-haired figure. Oblivious to Jed's scrutiny, the man slung his cloak carelessly across his shoulders, exposing its coat of arms. Then Jed recognised him immediately. The arms were those of the Queen's Glassmaker and the man himself, Jed's mortal enemy, Jacob Bell. Rage boiled up in Jed and he struggled to remain calm as, swinging into the saddle with careless ease, Bell began to ride towards London, passing the entrance to the inn and heading towards the city. Bell would never have recognised him, Jed thought. He had changed his appearance since their confrontation in Count Ridolfi's London house after the plot against the Queen had failed. He was clean shaven then and now sported a full beard and moustache and wore a flat hat, popularised by old King Henry. Wearing it pulled it down at one side changed his appearance considerably.

Fortunately, Bell was in no hurry and the road was crowded with early morning arrivals, It was a lively scene, with workers heading for the city, farmers taking their produce to market and wealthy merchants travelling into the Guilds from their spacious homes outside the city walls. There was no time to go for his horse so Jed decided to follow on foot, it would in any case be better if he wasn't at the inn when Nevison's body was found.

Using the lumbering produce carts as cover, Jed was able to follow Bell easily as he headed for Aldgate. He kept him well in sight until eventually he rode through some imposing double oak gates at a large Dutch-gabled house on Mark Street.

Casually walking past the entrance, Jed saw him dismount and hand the reins to a servant. At the door he was embraced by a tall, attractive, golden-haired woman and they entered arm in arm.

Jed sauntered round the high stone wall, topped with spikes, that surrounded the house and grounds. There were only two entrances and at the rear there was a separate block of what appeared to be stables.

Having discovered where Jacob Bell lived, Jed now returned to the White Hart. The place was full of gossip and several people couldn't wait to tell him that Patrick Nevison, the notorious highwayman, was responsible for a dreadful attack on a merchant's home where he had killed two men and raped a servant.

They described how Nevison had killed the ostler and then been kicked and trampled to death by his horse as it bolted in fear. Some of the stolen property had been found in his saddlebags and some with his badly mangled body in the stall.

Later in his room, Jed congratulated himself on his success. Not only had he gained the money needed to effect the next stage of his plan, but also he had disposed of the two men who knew him. The others in the gang had only seen him masked, he'd made sure of that.

However, there had been a development he had not foreseen. The appearance of Jacob Bell. Bell may have convinced Jed's father, Count Roberto Ridolfi, that as a good Catholic he actively supported Mary Stuart, but Jed knew better. Bell was a spy in the pocket of Walsingham and was going to pay for causing Jed's father to disown and disinherit him. With only enough money to get back to England and stay for a few weeks in London, Jed was forced to take odd jobs which did not suit him at all. When his money had nearly run out, he overheard a conversation about highwaymen in the North of England, between two dubious characters in the Inn where he was working. He heard them say that there were plenty of wealthy merchants travelling the road from Darby to Chesterfield and that the pickings were good. The following day, Jed went North to Darbieshire and became a highwayman.

Unfortunately, after a successful run, his luck ran out. He robbed the wrong man. It was an unusually good haul and Jed was delighted. Until the man turned out to be a rent collector for the Earl of Shrewsbury, the Lord Chancellor and jailer of Mary Stuart. The Earl had sent armed men scouring the countryside for the highwayman. Fortunately, they did not know his name. Every inn was being searched and all the ostlers were being questioned. They had hanged two of the other robbers, but Jed, on hearing about the furore, had wisely left the county and escaped to London.

By now, he was sure that things would have quietened down. With considerable wealth at his disposal and having changed his appearance, he could go North again. He would put into effect his plan to release Mary Stuart. But first he would deal with Walsingham's spy, Jacob Bell.

When he returned to the house on Mark Street he had murder in his heart. Checking out of the White Hart, he went to his horse and checked and primed his two matched pistols and thrust them in the covered holsters on either side of his saddle. He entered the city and rode past the house, but the solid oak doors were firmly closed. The story was the same at the rear of the house. All was securely locked. There was a bakery a little way down the street and Jed made some enquiries only to discover that the Bell family and their servants had left for France. The baker knew nothing more. Even the offer of payment could not elicit further information.

Not wishing to stay in London in case his part in the raids was discovered, Jed headed North. But before he left the house at

Mark Street, he vowed that whatever the cost, one day soon, he would return and Bell would pay for his treachery with his life.

Chapter Three
London and Paris, 1581

The morning after her nightmares Maria felt a little better. She'd slept quite well with no more dreams. As they lay in bed cuddling comfortably together, Jacob told her about the money he'd received from Sir Francis Drake and his plans for it.

At first, Maria was loath to contemplate being away from home for so long, but when Jacob explained his scheme in more detail she began to warm to the idea.

'We can take the whole household with us,' he explained, 'including Anna, Mistris Simpkin, Jack and Bob Petts and even Master Armitage.' He smiled as she raised an eyebrow. 'And the children, I suppose.'

'Oh!' said Maria, in feigned disappointment. 'Can't we leave them at home and enjoy ourselves?'

Jacob was delighted with this spark of her old self. 'I'm afraid not, my love,' he said, with a mock frown. 'Still, we'll have to see that it's not just a pleasure trip. I'm sure Master Armitage can come up with an educational programme to keep them busy for some of the time. At the very least they will have a chance to perfect their French. Meanwhile, if we find a nice place to rent, we'll have a base while we have a good look around for the right house to buy.'

Maria began to cheer up. 'It *will* help the children's education. Master Armitage is sure to use the opportunity to good account.'

And so it was that, two weeks later, the whole Bell household crammed themselves into the cabins of *The Crystal* and set off for Paris. As a precaution, Jacob insisted that Doctor Nguyên went along too to keep an eye on Maria.

At Calais, Monsieur Dupont, Jacob's agent in France who was a small, dapper man, prone to extravagant gestures, met them at the quayside. 'Monsieur Bell, it is a pleasure to see you again. Welcome to France all of you, especially you *madame*,' he said, bowing over Maria's hand. 'Since the hour is too late to set off to

Paris, I have arranged accommodation in a delightful coaching inn, *Le Coq d'Or.* It has only recently been completed, but has already gained an excellent reputation. He indicated three coaches waiting by the quayside. 'If your men will load up the luggage, we will proceed immediately.'

The coaching inn lived up to its good reputation and after an excellent meal they all retired to bed so as to be ready for an early start next morning. After a small meal of bread and ale, the convoy of coaches set off for Paris.

Jacob had no memory of his previous trip to Paris with Count Ridolfi, as he had been unconscious. He was surprised therefore, to find it was over a hundred leagues. Although it was possible to reach Paris in one long, dusty, bone-shaking day, highwaymen permitting, they made a more leisurely journey, taking three days and nights.

Fortunately, the weather was not too hot, or the journey would have been intolerable. At first, the children had been excited, exclaiming at each new sight, but as the trip dragged on, Jane and Eduardo began to complain and then, when that produced no sympathy at all, sank into lethargy.

By the time they reached Paris late on the third day, they were exhausted. Even the children had no energy to explore their temporary new home. Fortunately, Monsieur Dupont had arranged for local servants to prepare the house and to make sure all was ready for their arrival. It was with some relief, therefore, that they ate the light meal that had been prepared and staggered wearily off to bed.

The children, of course, shook off their tiredness quickly, especially Eduardo who, with boundless energy, was racing wildly about the large house. Master Armitage quickly had them under control. When Jacob came down, leaving Maria still sleeping soundly, he found that peace had been restored and the children were in the garden with their tutor. He helped himself to the fruit and bread and had just finished when Jack Petts announced that Monsieur Dupont had arrived.

When Jacob joined him in the day room, he bowed. '*Bonjour*, Monsieur Bell, I trust you are recovered from your journey?'

'Indeed,' replied Jacob, 'I slept very soundly.'

'And Madame Bell, she is feeling a little better I trust?'

Jacob smiled. 'I believe so, *merci*. She was sleeping soundly a short while ago and I have given instructions to leave her until she is ready to get up.'

Dupont pulled some sheets from his doublet. Handing them to Jacob he explained, 'I have taken the liberty of compiling a list of those properties which are for sale in this area. I believe it was your intention to seek something in the Marais District.'

'Most certainly,' Jacob replied with a smile. 'I'm given to understand that the area is one with a large number of wealthy aristocratic families, who are most likely to buy my glass.'

'That is true,' said Dupont, nodding vigorously. 'It is also the preferred area for a large number of wealthy merchants who are also likely to be potential customers.'

Scanning quickly through the list, Jacob noticed a familiar address, that of his rented house. 'I see that this house is also for sale.'

'*Oui*. It was originally only for hire, but when I explained your reason for coming to Paris, the owners asked me to include it in the list.'

Jacob made a few notes as Dupont explained his views on each of the properties. Having given Jacob details of where he could be contacted, he was about to take his leave, when he paused and turned back with a quizzical smile. 'Do you by any chance have any interest in glass bead jewellery made by a Venetian craftsman?'

'It's something I was considering a little while ago, but I haven't made any personally, nor have any of my Capos. Why do you ask?'

'There's a craftsman operating a few streets away from here who comes from Venice. My wife bought a pendant from him a few weeks ago and she's never stopped talking about his jewellery ever since.'

'Do you know his name?'

'I'm afraid not, but I can easily find out if you're interested.'

'Do that, please,' said Jacob, 'but there's no hurry. I need to find the property for my warehouse, so that must come first.'

After Dupont had left, Jacob went through the list again and numbered his choices in order of preference. There was a knock on the door and Jack Petts entered and proffered a calling card on a silver platter. 'The gentleman is in the atrium and is enquiring if you are available to receive him?'

Examining the ornate card, Jacob's heart gave a lurch as he saw it was from Henri de Lorraine, the third Duke of Guise. He still had occasional nightmares of the time at the Duke's château when he was paralysed after saving Count Ridolfi's life. He said slowly, 'Show the Duke in please, Jack.'

The Duke was a small stocky man with a heart-shaped face, pitted with battle scars, and elongated by a pointed beard. The scars had earned him the nickname, *Le Balafré*, "the scarred". He embraced Jacob enthusiastically, kissing him on both cheeks. '*Mon cher ami*, I am delighted to see that you have fully recovered from the terrible injuries you suffered in our cause. When I learned you were here, I had my coach bring me here at once in the hope you could receive me.'

Jacob waved the Duke to a chair. 'My dear Henri, you honour me with your words. You will always be welcome in my house. I regret that we are a little disorganised as yet, we have only just begun to get settled after our journey. I confess my visit to your château did not leave me with any pleasant memories except for your kindness when I was indisposed.'

There was a gentle knock on the door and Maria entered and Jacob taking her by the hand led her across to the Duke.

'My dear, allow me to introduce Henri de Lorraine, the Duke of Guise'. As Maria gave a deep curtsey, Jacob completed the introduction. '*Monsieur le duc*, allow me to present my wife, the Lady Maria.'

Maria extended her right hand and the Duke bowed over it.

'Jacob Bell, I declare that your wife is one of the most beautiful women I have seen in many a long day.'

Maria blushed becomingly. 'You are too kind, *Monsieur le duc*.'

'Not at all my dear,' the Duke replied, 'and please, as we are going to be very good friends, you must call me Henri.'

'Thank you, Henri. I only came in for a moment. Please excuse me. I must have a word with the children's tutor. I only agreed they could come to Paris as long as their education was not neglected.'

'How many children have you?' queried the Duke. He did not miss the shadow that passed over Maria's face and the slight hesitation before she answered. 'We have four children. Two boys and two girls. The youngest, Eduardo, is four and the eldest, Rico, is eleven.'

'A beautiful wife and four children.' said the Duke, giving Jacob an admiring glance.

Maria laughed. 'I'm sure that Jacob would be happy to let you have them at times. They are very boisterous and really annoy him sometimes.' She gave him a friendly smile. 'But now, regretfully, I must take my leave.' She held out the back of her hand for the Duke to kiss, then curtseyed and, with a fond smile for Jacob, left the room.

The Duke resumed his seat. 'To what do we owe the pleasure of your visit?'

Jacob explained his idea for buying a house and making part of it a showroom to sell his glass in Paris. And then he explained about the death of their baby daughter and Maria's melancholy. 'I am pleased to say, Henri, that despite the long, exhausting journey, Maria is looking better than she has for some time.'

'I am most pleased to hear that.' Henri thought for a moment. 'I have an idea. I know that you are a supporter of our cause. In three days time, there will be a splendid reception for the members of the Catholic League and their wives. Would you do me the honour of attending? I'm sure your delightful wife will enjoy it immensely.' He gave a sly smile. 'It will also give me the opportunity to introduce you to some of the most influential Catholic families in France. Who, incidentally, will undoubtedly be potential customers for your glass. What do you think, Jacob?'

It was a most generous offer, but Jacob hesitated. The Duke, a charismatic man with a brilliant public reputation was also the leader of the extreme Catholic League. He was also the architect of the abhorrent massacre of the French Huguenots on St. Bartholomew's Day nine years earlier. The Huguenots, Protestant supporters of Calvin, were attacked by the Catholic League, the implacable enemy of all Protestants, including Queen Elizabeth of

England, and thousands were killed.

But despite his loathing of the Huguenots' massacre which had been carried out at Henri's bidding, Jacob could not help liking the man. Henri had gone to considerable expense and trouble to ensure Jacob had the best of treatment for the injuries he had sustained. He could not have received better treatment if he had been the Duke's brother. But now, if he accepted this invitation, he was likely to be recruited into the latest plot against Queen Elizabeth and must either betray Henri, or Walsingham and Queen Elizabeth. Walsingham of course would be apoplectic if he turned down the chance to infiltrate the inner echelons of the Catholic League. But could he betray Henri?

Realising that the Duke was waiting patiently for his answer, Jacob mentally braced himself and said, 'That is a most generous offer Henri and I'm sure I speak for my wife when I say we would be delighted to accept.'

The slight frown that had appeared on the Duke's face was banished by a broad smile. 'That is very good news. I assume you are a little concerned about Lady Maria, but I will ensure that Catherine looks after her. She too lost a child last year. They will have much in common.' He sat forward in his chair and looked intently at Jacob. 'I have lost touch with you in recent years, my friend. Have you any news of my cousin, Mary Stuart?'

'Only what I hear at court. I understand that after Count Ridolfi's plans were discovered, she has been more closely guarded by the Earl of Shrewsbury.'

'Have you been in touch with her?'

'I'm afraid not. It took me nearly two years to recover from my paralysis. I also married Maria. I was forced to keep a very low profile. Even though no one contacted me, after Norfolk was arrested, I was still questioned by Walsingham several times.'

'That man is a devil. His spies are everywhere. Do you think you are still under suspicion?' Henri said pointedly.

Jacob shook his head. 'My questioning stopped some years ago and I have not been in touch with Mary Stuart, nor have any of her supporters contacted me.' Henri smiled and settled back in his chair. Jacob sensed he had relaxed and was no longer suspicious of him. All he had to do now was to decide where his loyalties and principles lay. Henri was fighting for the Catholic cause and Jacob was a Catholic too, albeit, a much more liberal one. His heart told him he couldn't betray this charismatic man who'd been a supportive friend: his head argued Henri was a dangerous and ruthless enemy who would visit war on Jacob's adopted country, England. Henri would kill him in an instant if he suspected Jacob was Walsingham's spy. When he weighed all of the facts there was only one answer and steeling himself he asked, 'Since I am to meet members of the Catholic League, can you tell me a little about them? I believe you were the founder.'

'I was the founder of the league,' said Henri proudly. 'A strong Catholic alliance is the only way to stop that weak, vacillating King of ours, Henry III, from giving away everything we had fought the Huguenots for. His brother, François, duc d'Alençon, sided with the Protestants besieging Paris four years ago and instead of asking for my help, he caved in and granted them too many concessions.' He grimaced. 'Do you know, my friend,' he said angrily, jumping to his feet, 'he even confirmed that Protestant, Henry of Navarre, heir to the throne of France.' He shook his fist violently. *Non! Non!* That cannot be. The Catholics will not allow it. We will raise an army and stop the Protestants, wherever they are!'

Seeing Jacob was looking a little alarmed he became calmer and sat down. 'I am sorry for getting carried away, my friend. I have fought all of my life for the Catholic cause and to see this weak King make so many concessions to heretics makes my blood rise up.'

'You owe me no apology. I certainly understand the Catholic League much better now. I thank you most sincerely for your invitation to the reception and I will be proud to attend.'

Henri came over and brushing aside Jacob's thanks, embraced him. He promised to do all in his power to help Jacob's commercial enterprise and took his leave saying an invitation would be sent the next day.

Left alone, Jacob sat in his chair brooding. Henri's outburst had shown what a powerful and dangerous man he was. He was a zealot, but an intelligent and shrewd leader. There was no doubt that he had high ambitions and undoubtedly he was planning something to do with releasing his cousin, Mary Stuart from her captivity. Whatever the plan was, it was bad news for Elizabeth Tudor.

Some years had gone by since he had last risked his life thwarting the Queen's enemies. After years of comfortable living and a loving relationship with Maria and his children, was he prepared to put all that at risk? When he became involved with Sir William Cecil and Walsingham, when he first arrived in England, it was for personal reasons. His enemy Adrian Ragazoni had forced Maria to marry him and had joined Count Maldini's plot to assassinate Queen Elizabeth. To rescue Maria, he had been forced to throw in his lot with Walsingham.

Brought up in the enlightened society of Venice, which had rejected the Inquisition and the persecution of minorities, Jacob hated the extremists of his own religion. When he was again offered the chance to join Walsingham in the fight against them, he readily agreed. And, he had to admit, during the last few years, he missed the heady excitement of the fight.

Now, he could be in a unique position to help Walsingham. But he had far more responsibilities. Maria must understand the risks if he become involved. Should he be exposed as a spy, both she and the children would be in the gravest danger.

Chapter Four
Château de Lorraine, Paris, France, 1581

Later that day, Henri, Duke of Guise received visitors. His servant announced them as, 'His Grace, the Archbishop of Glasgow, Father Creighton and Doctor William Allen.'

The greetings over, the Duke invited them to sit around the table and, turning to the Archbishop said, 'Perhaps you would like to explain the purpose of this meeting you requested, Your Grace? I assume it has something to do with the continued imprisonment of our cousin Queen Mary.' It was a safe assumption. He recognised Doctor Allen, a Roman Catholic priest and Cardinal, who had refused to take the oath of supremacy and had been forced to flee to France, where he was acknowledged as leader of the English Catholics.

The Archbishop nodded. 'As Queen Mary's ambassador in France, I have been working on the ways and means of her deliverance from her captivity.'

'May that day come soon,' Henri intoned, to murmurs of agreement all round.

Henri had great respect for James Beaton II, the Archbishop of Glasgow, as had his cousin Mary Stuart, who had appointed him when she was Queen of Scots. He had served her faithfully during her reign and continued to be her agent and strongest supporter in captivity, working tirelessly for her release.

'As you well know,' said the Archbishop. 'Esmé Stewart, Seigneur d'Aubigny, nephew of the Duke of Lennox, is devoted to our cause and has been working to win back Scotland to the true faith. He has developed a strong hold over the young King, James VI: the Catholic families support him because his line goes back to the Ancient Kingdom of the Scots. Have you had any correspondence with him of late?'

'We exchanged letters only last week,' Henri said. 'd'Aubigny informs me that his power in Scotland is increasing by the day and that plans are well advanced to throw open the "postern gate" to admit our armies into England. It is the intention that the

Catholic League will work through d'Aubigny to bring about the destruction of the Protestant usurper, Elizabeth, and restore the true faith in England. Of course, there is still much to be agreed before that day comes, but I hope to begin the final discussions no later than the spring of next year.'

'That is good news,' said the Archbishop, 'and very relevant to the information we wish to impart today. Father Creighton has recently been to Rome for discussions with the head of the Jesuit Order and the Pope and has just returned from Scotland after putting our plan to d'Aubigny. I will ask him to explain.'

Father Creighton stood up and with a bow to the Duke began his story. 'The Jesuit Order is convinced that in d'Aubigny we have an instrument for the fulfilment of our ambitions in both Scotland and England. During our discussions with the Pope, we urged him to give his support to d'Aubigny to win back both Scotland and England to the old faith.'

This pleased Henri a great deal. The House of Guise had a deep-rooted hostility towards Elizabeth. From the first, she had exerted her efforts to weaken the power of the Guises in France. In return, the Guises had constantly plotted her destruction. After all, Mary Stuart, the heir-presumptive to the English throne, was the daughter of Mary of Guise and his first cousin.

'What was His Holiness's reaction to your plea?' Henri asked.

'Pope Gregory is enthusiastic and his blessing on our enterprise is one of my reasons for coming to Paris. He has instructed me to assure you that he shares your desire to free Queen Mary and set her in her rightful place as Queen of England. To that end, he wishes to enter into negotiations with you and d'Aubigny as soon as possible to finalise plans for an invasion of Scotland. Once the Catholic lords have rallied to our cause, the invasion of England can begin. Doctor Allen has assured us that when that day comes, the English Catholics will rally to us and the usurper will be swept from power.'

'That is good news indeed,' said Henri, 'but do you believe that d'Aubigny can deliver what he promises?' In truth, he was having doubts himself. Whilst the Catholic Lords were strong supporters of d'Aubigny, the real power lay with the Protestant Lords and the reformed Church in Scotland, inspired by John Knox.

'Yes I do,' said Creighton, but Henri could see he was holding something back.

'I take it from your hesitation that d'Aubigny has made some extravagant requests.'

'Indeed he has. He wants a force of 20,000 men, financed for a year and a half and placed under his command. He also demanded that the Pope should renew the Bull of Excommunication against Elizabeth and that the Catholics in Ireland and England should be stirred to revolt.'

'What say you to this, Doctor Allen?' said Henri. 'Have I your personal assurance that the English Catholics will rise to support the invasion from the north?'

'With my whole heart I give you my word. We have waited long for a real chance to restore the true faith.'

Henri stood up. 'Then it is agreed. We will set the wheels in motion to agree on how the force will be raised. However, I doubt if we can accomplish this without involving the King of Spain. It is imperative therefore that he is advised of the plan and gives it his support.'

'What about the King of France? Shouldn't we inform him too?' asked the Archbishop.

Henri grimaced. 'I think we should not involve that milksop. He will prattle to the wrong people. Better to ensure he knows nothing of this.' He had no intention of letting Henry III into his plans, he and his brother Alençon were too close to the Protestants. 'I am giving a reception for the leading members of the Catholic League in two days time and I will apprise them of these developments. Meanwhile, we must decide who will go to Rome and who to Spain.'

The Archbishop turned to Creighton. 'Are you willing to return to Rome again if I send one of my aides, Father Robert Parsons to Spain?'

Creighton nodded. 'His Holiness instructed me to return to apprise him of the outcome of these discussions.'

'Excellent,' said the Archbishop. 'I will see that Father Robert goes to Spain as soon as possible. He is well acquainted with the Spanish court.'

Henri had been listening to these exchanges only half-heartedly as his mind was weighing up another thought that had come to him. As they stood up to leave, he asked them to wait a moment. 'My friends, it has occurred to me that if we can accomplish our plan for the Scottish invasion and a rising of the Catholics in Ireland and England, I could lead a second army into the south of England. The combination of two invading forces at opposite ends of the country, and insurrection from within and without, would prove an unbeatable combination.'

There was silence for a moment. Then his guests started talking at once, eagerly approving the new plan and agreeing that this was the final step to realising the success of their dreams. The Archbishop promised that Pope Gregory and the King of Spain would be apprised of the offer which he was adamant would receive their approval. Doctor Allen promised that the southern Catholics would rally to the Duke of Guise's army and do all in their power to disrupt any resistance from the authorities.

When they had left, Henri sat down at his desk and began to write a letter. Signing it with a flourish, he scattered some fine sand on the paper and then when it was dry, carefully folded it. Having written the address, he warmed some wax with a candle and dropping it carefully on to the fold impressed his seal.

He then rang a small handbell to summon his servant and instructed him to see that the letter was delivered immediately to Francis Throckmorton. The servant was either to bring back a reply, or escort Throckmorton here to the Château de Lorraine.

Henri had been cultivating the acquaintance of Francis Throckmorton for some weeks now. Throckmorton had been educated at Oxford and had entered the Inner Temple in the city of London. His legal training made him ideal for the Duke's purpose, acting as an intermediary between Mary Queen of Scots, her supporters and the Spanish Ambassador.

Now that his plan for the southern invasion force was being unveiled in Rome by Creighton and the Archbishop's man in Spain, Henri could use him as a messenger without any suspicion being aroused. Throckmorton travelled extensively in Europe, ostensibly for his education, but he was not a rich man. By working for the Duke, he would have all his money worries removed.

Francis Throckmorton was announced about an hour later, having slipped unobtrusively into the back entrance of the château. Henri bade him sit down and studied him shrewdly. His father, Sir John, had close ties to Elizabeth and his brother, Sir Nicholas, served as one of her diplomats. Francis had refused to sign the oath of supremacy, but had been allowed to leave England on the pretext of continuing his education.

'How is your father, Francis?' enquired the Duke. 'I hear things have not gone well for him lately.'

'Indeed not, Henri. He has been removed from his post as Chief Justice of Chester, purely because he is a supporter of the Catholic faith.'

The Duke murmured sympathetic condolences. However, his briefing from his agent in England suggested his demotion had more to do with Throckmorton's harsh actions in the performance of his legal duties than his Papist sympathies.

He spent the next few minutes bringing Francis up to date with the events of the morning, including his plan for the southern invasion, which had Throckmorton's enthusiastic support.

'You must ensure you do not gossip about this to any of your friends at the Wild Boar Tavern,' warned Henri. 'Walsingham has his spies everywhere listening out for snippets of gossip and wild talk. Should he hear any whiff of this venture, he will make it a hazardous business.'

Throckmorton nodded his agreement.

'The only time you may come to the Château de Lorraine in future,' continued Henri, 'will be to the Catholic League reception later this week. There is someone I would like you to meet. Until then, go about your business as usual.' He handed Francis a small card. 'Here is your invitation. I will see you here at the reception.'

When Throckmorton had left, the Duke sat back in his chair with a sigh of contentment. Today had gone very well and everything was falling into place with a smoothness which could only be the will of God at work. Very soon now, the true faith would once more flourish in England and together with France, she would become the supreme power in Europe. Not even the might of Spain would be able to gainsay them.

As the well-dressed man emerged from the side entrance of the château and quickly turned the corner of the street, Mathieu Loren, a spy in the pay of Walsingham, was watching from his hiding place in a dark doorway. Hurrying after him he took a brief look round. His quarry was about twenty paces away on the other side of the street. Keeping a discreet distance between them, and hiding in the shadows, he followed. Through street after street, Mathieu kept him in sight until the man paused at a small guest house and looked around cautiously. Mathieu had already vanished into a dark doorway. Obviously seeing nothing to alarm him the man entered the building.

Mathieu strolled up to the door and noted the address in his notebook. An alleyway ran along the side of the house and after checking all was clear, he passed along it until he could see into the street beyond. With a suitable escape route established, he relaxed and returned the way he had come in order to watch the premises for his quarry's next movements, notebook held in readiness.

Walsingham's letter had stressed that anyone who visited the château by stealth must be reported to him. Mathieu, as one of his secret agents permanently resident in France, knew Walsingham's moods well. He'd worked for him for ... hmm, nearly twenty years now. In truth, he was more than a little afraid of his satanic-looking employer. However, Walsingham was generous with his payments and Mathieu hoped that news of this clandestine visitor would bring a well-earned bonus. The man seemed important and certainly fitted the criteria that Walsingham had given him. It would be easy to find out his name from madame at the guest house.

Just then, he heard the rumble of cart wheels on the cobbled street. A quick glance showed it to be a tradesman's handcart. Shrinking back into the dark shadow of the alley he waited for it to pass, but instead it stopped in the mouth of the alley. Sensing danger, he turned to flee, but it was too late. A second man had crept silently along the alley behind him and, receiving a murderous blow to the head with a cudgel, Mathieu collapsed in a heap.

After kicking the lifeless body to make sure it was dead, the murderer knelt down, removed the notebook and slipped it inside his doublet, patting it fondly. *Le Balafré* will be pleased, he thought, that's the third spy we've removed this week. He's sure to give us an extra reward. Then he summoned his accomplice with a short whistle and the two of them hoisted the body into the cart, covered it with sacking and wheeled it off towards a quiet stretch of river.

Chapter Five
Paris, France, 1581

The invitation from the Duke of Guise was delivered next day along with a letter addressed to Maria from Henri's wife, Catherine. Maria was very touched as Catherine explained that she too had lost a child and understood how Maria must feel. She assumed also, from her husband's explanation of the reasons for the Bells visit to Paris, that Maria had not expected to attend such a lavish function as the Catholic League reception. Therefore, apologising for her forwardness, she had taken the liberty of arranging for her personal dressmaker to fashion Maria a suitable gown in time for the reception. She would call on Maria in a couple of hours and take her to Madame Hélène's salon. The servant who had delivered the two missives was waiting for a reply and Maria, after a hurried word with Jacob, accepted Catherine's kind offer.

With Anna's help, Maria busied herself putting on her best kirtle and gown. When eventually she emerged, Jacob was delighted to see how animated she was. Hugging her, he told her to spare no expense and to take Catherine's advice as to the latest fashion in Paris court circles.

Maria had expected the countess to remain in her coach, but as soon as it stopped outside the entrance, Catherine was helped down by a footman. Maria regarded her with interest. She had an attractive oval face with large luminous wide-set eyes which dominated her face. It was further enhanced by her light brown hair, which was swept up and away from her face to form a roll, and held in place by a jewel-encrusted cap. As she approached Maria she could see that her age, height and build were similar to her own.

Sweeping into the atrium, she embraced the waiting Maria enthusiastically, kissing her on both cheeks. Holding both of Maria's hands at arm's length, she studied her carefully.

'May I call you Maria, my dear? I do so hate to be formal, especially with my friends. And I believe you and I are going to be firm friends.' She paused breathlessly. 'And please forget the formalities and call me Catherine.'

Although a little taken aback by the effusive greeting, Maria responded warmly for, in truth, she felt an affinity towards this delightfully friendly open women. 'You are so kind. I too feel we are going to be friends.' The countess hugged her again. 'Oh, I'm so glad we have met. And now we must hurry to see madame. She has little enough time to prepare as it is..' She linked arms with Maria and together they went to the coach.

When they were settled, Catherine leaned towards Maria. 'I do believe that you and I are of a similar build. This could make things easier.'

'How so, Countess?' Then, blushing a little at her impertinence but emboldened by her companion's raised eyebrow, Maria amended, 'How so, Catherine?'

'There are several court functions coming up in the near future. Two weeks ago I instructed Madame Hélène to make two more dresses for me.' Catherine gave a gentle smile. 'I already have the gown for the reception, so if one of the other gowns is to your liking, it will be easier to alter it to fit than to make a new one.'

Maria was a little doubtful. Dresses were such an individual thing. The countess's taste might be totally opposite to her own. However, in the circumstances, it might be the only option available to her.

After a short drive, they turned into a wide tree-lined avenue and stopped outside an impressive stone building with Italianate decorations and a colonnaded entrance. They were met in the ornately decorated entrance hall with much ceremony by the redoubtable Madame Hélène. She was not tall, slight, immaculately dressed and her black hair showed no sign of grey even though Maria judged her to be in her late sixties. They were shown into the salon and offered refreshments, which the countess declined saying they must waste no time deciding if either of the dresses already ordered was suitable for Maria.

Madame Hélène clapped her hands and at once the salon became a hive of activity. Two assistants modelled the dresses and Maria was surprised at the way they were swept out at the waist by a large hoop, and were lower at the front than the back. She was familiar with the French farthingale, or bum roll, used for a similar purpose, but this was very different.

Madame informed her that the hoop, called a great farthingale, was absolutely the latest fashion at the French court. 'It is unthinkable that milady should appear at the reception in such society without this fashion,' madame tutted.

The countess encouraged her to try on one of the dresses and Madame suggested the pale rose silk would enhance her dark colouring.

The assistants fluttered around her, chattering excitedly in the local patois as they pinned adjustments to the fit of the dress. Although her French was fluent, Maria found it difficult to understand them. When finally it was done to the assistants' satisfaction, they cried, '*C'est magnifique, n'est-ce pas, madame,*' to the approaching proprietress.

Maria examined her image critically in the long mirror. The deep rose of the kirtle showing through the slashed, pale-rose over-skirt at the front, made a beautiful contrast and when she moved, the sway of the farthingale enhanced the shimmering effect of the silk.

Catherine nodded in approval as Maria turned to face her. 'The dress could have been made for you, *c'est parfait.* Are you happy with it, *ma cheri*?'

Maria smiled and nodded. 'Oh yes. I could not have chosen better.'

The countess embraced her warmly.

'To ensure the dress is a perfect fit.' she told madame, 'we must allow time for any small adjustments that may be needed. But it must be completed by the day after tomorrow at the very latest.'

Madame Hélène and her assistants arrived with the altered dress shortly before eleven o'clock the next day. Jacob had already left on another house-hunting foray with Monsieur Dupont. Anna helped Maria to put her hair up into a formal style with entwined strands of pearls and Maria wore the double strand of matching pearls given to her by her father.

Anna then helped her into the new dress, with the two

assistants from the salon fluttering and fussing around as before. Much to Maria's relief, it fitted perfectly. She examined her image in the long mirror then turned to Madame Hélène. who was looking thoughtful. 'Is there a problem with the dress, *madame*?'

'Not at all, the dress is *magnifique*,' she said, kissing her fingertips and exuberantly throwing her arms wide. 'But I regret to say that the pearl necklace is not suitable for this dress. Rubies, *certainemant*. Pearls ...' she shook her head and made a small moue of disapproval. 'I am sorry, milady, but they will not do at all.'

Maria turned to look in the mirror again. 'I see what you mean, *madame*. The pearls are too neutral. Unfortunately, I do not have my ruby necklace with me. I have only brought a small part of my jewellery.' She frowned. 'I will have to see what I have that is more suitable, but my thanks to you for the lovely gown. Please let my husband have your account.'

Madame came over and embraced her, kissing both her cheeks. 'Thank you, milady. Should you require anything else we will be delighted to help.' Gathering her assistants together, they curtseyed and Anna showed them out.

Alone again, Maria looked at her image in the mirror. She noted the high colour of her face and smiled. It was the first time for weeks she had felt so alive. She twirled and laughed as the farthingale followed her movements after a slight delay. Then a thought struck her. 'However am I going to sit down?' she said to her image and then burst out laughing. 'Jacob will be quite sure I have gone mad if he sees me talking to my own reflection.'

When Jacob returned he went straight to his study. He had just sat down when there was a knock on the door and Anna appeared. She curtseyed very formally and then made an announcement.

'Senator Bellini please allow me to present Lady Maria Morisini-Bellini.' Opening the door wide, she stood back and curtseyed again as Maria made a grand entrance wearing her new gown. Then smiling fondly at the two of them, she slipped quietly out of the door.

Jacob who had jumped to his feet at the announcement took one look at the ravishing figure of his wife. Striding over took her proffered hand and kissed it.

'You look very beautiful, my darling wife,' he said, with relief tingeing his voice. 'I am so pleased to see you looking so well.'

Maria looked at Jacob doubtfully. 'Will you promise not to laugh if I tell you something.'

'Of course I will,' said Jacob, very sincerely.

Maria explained to Jacob her fears about sitting down in the farthingale. 'I'm really frightened of making a fool of myself at the ball.'

'What is the problem with the skirt?'

Maria asked him to put one of the chairs in the centre of the room and, with Jacob looking on, tried to sit down. The first attempt was a disaster. As Maria sat down, the farthingale knocked the chair over and it was only Jacob's quick reflexes that saved Maria from a fall.

Finally, after several more attempts, Maria realised that by holding the farthingale a little behind her waist on both sides as she sat down, she could swing the farthingale up to allow enough room to sit down. Jacob applauded enthusiastically as Maria sat back with a self-satisfied smile. He stopped when the smile turned to a frown.

'What's the matter now, my dear?'

Maria looked glum. 'I love the dress, but none of my jewellery is suitable. I thought I might use the pearls, but they are quite wrong for the colour of the dress.'

She sighed. 'If only I had brought my ruby necklace. It would have been absolutely perfect.'

'Is that all?' said Jacob in relief. 'I thought from your expression it was something disastrous.'

Maria gave him a look of exasperation. 'Just like a man,' she said. 'Of course it's a disaster. I can't go to the reception without the right necklace to set off the dress. You wouldn't want me to show you up in front of all those aristocratic women.'

Realising that it wasn't a joke and that Maria was deadly serious, he hurried to make amends. 'Of course you must have the right necklace. And I think I might know where to get it, but it will have to wait until tomorrow.'

He hesitated and Maria spotted the small frown that crossed his face. 'Something is troubling you, Giam. Don't be afraid to tell me, I am my usual self again. You don't need to protect me any longer.'

After a moment's thought, Jacob told her of his fears. 'You must realise that by attending this reception, I will be drawn into whatever the Duke of Guise is planning. I have decided I must again act the spy for Walsingham. I cannot allow the Catholic extremists he leads to plunge England into civil war, if I can prevent it. I will report what I learn to Walsingham.' He searched her face for signs of fear, but there were none. 'I love you and our children and I hesitate to put you all at risk, which undoubtedly you will be if the League discover I am a spy. You must be very careful what you say at the reception, particularly to the Duke and his wife Catherine. I know they seem very kind and attentive, but make no mistake, the Duke is a ruthless and implacable enemy of the Queen.'

'Have no fear for me,' Maria said firmly. 'I grew up with the politics of Venice. My father often gave me a similar warning. It's the price we must pay if we are active participants, rather than onlookers. You must be true to your principles. In any case, I doubt very much that even France can stoop to the depths of corruption we experienced in Venice.'

Chapter Six
Paris, France, 1581

On Jacob's way back from a very disappointing visit to the latest house on the list, Monsieur Dupont pointed out the workshop of Raoul Laguna, the Venetian lampworker he had mentioned earlier. Jacob was curious to know exactly how the glass beads were made. He knew they added layers of coloured glass and metals using spirit lamps, but he had never seen the process.

'Welcome to my workshop, Master Bell.' Laguna, a dark, swarthy Venetian, spoke in Italian-accented French. 'I know of your work at the Crouched Friars in London. Your *façon de Venise* glasses have caused quite a stir here in Paris, not least because they are much cheaper than buying direct from Murano.'

'That may have been true a little while ago,' said Jacob. 'but sales have been falling quite sharply in recent times.'

'Not just for you, Master Bell. All of us are feeling the pinch at the moment. Things have not been the same since so many of the Huguenots were killed.' He looked at Jacob curiously. 'And how does an Englishman come to be making glass to rival Murano?'

'I spent all my formative years in Murano and learned from an early age how to make glass.' Which was only a partial truth. He had not explained the fact that he was actually Italian. His real identity was known to only Queen Elizabeth, Lord Burghley and Walsingham outside his family. This dated back to when he escaped to England from his ten year sentence in the Venetian galleys. He needed to change his name when he became involved in glassmaking. Giacomo Bellini was too well known in Venice and the Venetian assassins might be sent after him if they found he was making glass in England. Although that danger had now passed, it might jeopardise his position as a secret agent if his real name became known.

Laguna gave him a puzzled look. 'So what brings you to Paris?'

Jacob explained his thinking about the showroom.

'I have been to look at some premises this morning, but they were totally unsuitable for converting to a showroom. I have heard about your work and was hoping that you might show me how you make the beads and some examples of your work.' He was thinking that glass jewellery might make a useful addition to his new showroom.

'I'd be delighted. Come on through to the workshop.'

Passing through the door, Jacob was greeted by an unfamiliar scene. He had expected to see a furnace, but instead there were a number of benches arranged around the room occupied mainly by women, who were layering fine threads of coloured glass on top of glass beads with the aid of spirit lamps.

Seeing Jacob's surprised expression, Raoul pointed to another door at the end of the room. 'The furnace is through there,' he said. 'That's where the core of the beads is produced.'

'Do you employ Capos?' Jacob asked. He wasn't sure if the lampworkers called their senior glass-blowers the same as a Murano glass-works.

'They are still called Capos, but there's no glass-blowing involved and we still call their workplace Chairs, as in Murano. We only have two Capos at present, although if we are really busy, I take a Chair myself.'

'So how are the beads made?'

'The core is made from molten glass at furnace temperatures and the beads are solid, except for the hole for threading, made with a needle.' He handed a dark blue bead to Jacob.

Jacob examined it with interest and held it up to the light. 'Is this standard soda glass?'

'It is indeed. We colour it in exactly the same way, but we have a more extensive range of colours than are used for drinking glasses.'

'I presume you have clear cristallino beads as well.'

'We do, but it's the standard Murano type.' He looked at Jacob shrewdly. 'I understand you have a special way of producing cristallino that gives more lustre. I heard that one of the Murano Glass-works had invented a new way of making it. Is yours the same process?'

This was dangerous ground, since the new cristallo was

associated with his alter ego Giacomo Bellini, so Jacob made a non-committal reply and changed the subject.

'What happens to the core beads? I assume they have to be annealed.' With drinking glasses, unless they were cooled slowly, the glass became crizzled, a fine patterning of cracks.

Raoul nodded. 'It's just the same with beads. Once they have been cooled and annealed, they come in here,' he said, indicating the work benches. 'Other colours of glass are added to the surface to create many different effects. Thin foils of gold and silver can also be added,' he said, showing Jacob the tissue-like foils.

'Finally, a transparent layer is laid over the top of the bead and it is fired in a kiln to make it more durable.' Jacob was fascinated by the whole process and thought the finished beads were lovely. Perhaps I should see if Raoul is interested in selling his jewellery through my showroom, he thought.

Raoul led him to a bench where a young man was working. 'This is my son, Toni.' he said proudly. 'He's been my apprentice since he was eleven. He's now sixteen and very knowledgeable about the whole range of processes. Add to that the fact that he has a good eye for design and it makes him my most valuable worker.'

The parallel with his own rise in his grandfather's glass-works was not lost on Jacob. He was even more impressed when he was shown the range of finished jewellery designs that could be achieved with many different beads. There were necklaces, pendants, bracelets and earrings. This clinched the matter as far as Jacob was concerned.

'I believe you have very saleable products, which complement my own. I'd like to explore how we can co-operate in future when I have my new showroom. If you are interested of course.'

'Certainly,' said Raoul. 'I believe your showroom is an excellent idea. It will make a wonderful outlet for displaying our different facets of the glassmaker's art.'

Jacob then explained about Maria's dress and the need for a necklace to match it. 'Could you come to the Villa Saint Germaine in about two hours and bring several necklaces that might be suitable.'

'I will indeed,' promised Raoul.'

'Excellent,' said Jacob and shaking hands with him, left for home.

When Raoul Laguna arrived carrying a plain oak box under his arm, Jacob sent a message to Maria and asked her to join them in the study. 'Allow me to present a countryman of yours, Raoul Laguna.'

The newcomer bowed formally and then at Jacob's suggestion placed the plain oak box on the desk. Maria looked at it curiously. Jacob gestured to Laguna who carefully removed the first drawer from the box and carried it across to Maria. He removed its blue satin cover and Maria saw two beautiful necklaces nestling in the satin lining.

She examined them closely. 'Why, they're made from glass.'

Master Laguna gave a little inclination of the head. 'Indeed, my lady. They are made from the finest Venetian lampwork beads.'

Jacob intervened. 'After visiting Master Laguna's workshop and seeing his work at close quarters, I asked him to bring his most suitable necklaces in the hope that one of them might be right for your dress. He has chosen the colours that are most likely to match.'

Alter studying each exquisite necklace, Maria chose one with a single row of graded rose-red beads. At the front, there were five drops of two, three or four beads with the longest drop at the centre and the two drops either side being progressively shorter in length. There were gold disc spacers between the beads, which lightened the colour, so that they almost matched the kirtle of the dress.

Maria complimented Raoul on his skill and pronounced that she liked them all, but had chosen the most suitable one.

Raoul bowed. 'It is most kind of you to say so, my lady. I hope you will be kind enough to recommend my work.'

'I will indeed,' cried Maria wholeheartedly. 'And perhaps my husband can arrange something at his showroom.'

'Most certainly we can,' Jacob agreed. 'When my new warehouse and showroom is ready, I suggest that Master Laguna has an exhibition of his work to complement my glass.'

Raoul shook Jacob's hand warmly. 'I will begin work on some

suitable exhibits. How big an area did you have in mind?'

'To start with I think a single tier of shelves, about six feet wide, but if the jewellery does well, who knows.'

They talked for a while longer and, when Raoul took his leave, Maria was surprised when he left the box on the desk. 'Master Bell asked me to leave the rest of them,' he said, when she indicated it, 'for you to decide if you would like any, or all of the other pieces.'

'All of them!' she gasped.

'If you like them all,' said Jacob. 'And before you tell me how extravagant I am, it will cost me only a fraction of the price of a new ruby necklace.'

When he returned from seeing his guest out, Maria threw her arms around his neck and kissed him soundly and he responded immediately, his desire rising rapidly. He began to stroke her right breast and Maria placed her hand on his and gently restrained him. 'I'm sorry, my love. I'm not ready yet. Please be patient a little while longer.'

Although it was difficult, Jacob stopped immediately. 'Of course you must have more time.'

Maria looked at Jacob, her eyes filled with love. 'Thank you for being so patient with me. I know I have been a trial these past few weeks. I could not shake off my grief. The dreams kept coming back to haunt me, so I dreaded going to sleep, yet I was so tired.' She laid her head on his shoulder. 'These past two nights have been the first since the funeral I have slept peacefully. I promise that I am well again now and looking forward to the reception.'

'You will eclipse them all, my darling,' said Jacob. 'None will hold a candle to you.'

After Maria had left, he decided to make good his resolve to make sure that Rico had the benefit of his experience with the sword. At eleven years old his eldest son was already showing signs of being a good athlete and showed a natural ability with a rapier. Rico was only too delighted to escape his lesson in French with his tutor and they went in to the large room at the rear of the atrium.

They fenced for a short while and then Jacob called a halt. He had noticed that Rico's grip was not right.

'Your grip must be firm enough to prevent your opponent from knocking the rapier from your hand, but light enough to allow you to move the weapon easily. The sword must become an extension of your arm. Does that make sense to you?'

'Yes, sir. I understand now.'

'Good,' said Jacob, 'but above all, what must you do when you're in a duel?'

'Keep your temper and keep your life,' intoned Rico, but with boredom.

Jacob stepped back and dropped his sword point. 'I know what you're thinking, but I want those words to become second nature to you. When you are facing an opponent who is trying to kill you, and God forbid that it should happen, they could save your life.'

'Have you ever killed anyone?' asked Rico curiously.

For a moment Jacob was nonplussed, but decided that Rico deserved an honest answer.

'I'm afraid I have,' he said seriously, 'and it's not something I like to talk about. It coloured my actions and made me very defensive. Taking another man's life is something that should not be done lightly and only as a last resort. Unfortunately, sometimes you are left with no other choice when your own life is at stake.'

He ruffled his son's hair playfully. 'I think that will do for today. We will continue our lesson tomorrow if I have the time. I will find a fencing-master for you when we return to London. You are coming on well, but need more practice.'

'You will still teach me though, won't you father?' Rico said anxiously. 'I do so look forward to our sessions.'

'I will do my best,' Jacob promised. He was touched by the boy's wistful tone. The demands of his work and his involvement with Walsingham had left him less time for his children, especially his eldest. He was aware that he did not know him as well as he should. Nor had he helped him with his fencing. As soon as he returned to London, Jacob vowed he would arrange for Rico to have lessons with Giacomo di Grassi, the best fencing master in London. Rico must learn how to protect himself if he was in danger and with Jacob once more preparing to play the spy, that likelihood had increased.

Chapter Seven
Château de Lorraine, Paris, France, 1581

When Jacob and Maria arrived at the Château de Lorraine, they were directed to the magnificent horseshoe staircase that led up to the Grand Gallery where the reception was being held. As they slowly ascended the stairs having joined the queue of people halfway up, Jacob looked around and tried to remember if he had been in this part of the château. The staircase was decorated in the Renaissance style now sweeping across Europe and reminded Jacob of some of the palaces in Venice. Indeed, in the grand hall room leading to the staircase were three magnificent Murano glass chandeliers.

Lining the staircase were various House of Guise portraits, including one of the beautiful Catherine of Cleves, commissioned to celebrate her wedding to Henri. At the entrance to the Gallery they were announced by a liveried servant.

Henri greeted Jacob with a great show of friendship and Catherine embraced Maria and whispered that Maria looked wonderful.

'You must be very careful tonight, my dear Maria. Half of the men will be trying to make you their mistress and all the wives will hate you!' Jacob asked why she had burst out laughing, but before she could answer, he realised that the Duke was trying to introduce him to someone.

'Jacob Bell, Francis here is the son of Sir John Throckmorton from Bristol, who is a great admirer of your drinking glasses and has been rather extravagant in buying a large number of them.'

Jacob smiled and bowed to Francis Throckmorton. He had never met either him or his father before, although Sir John was a generous patron. Throckmorton was a slim, wiry fellow, well dressed, but with a slightly superior expression.

'I am delighted to make your acquaintance. I hope your father is pleased with my glass.'

'Most certainly,' said Throckmorton.

'Have you been in Paris long?' asked Jacob.

'Only a few days. I have been visiting Thomas Morgan and Gilbert Gifford who are living in exile here.'

The Duke immediately shot a warning look at Throckmorton and suggested he took Jacob to look at the gallery. As Jacob walked with Throckmorton he made a mental note of the two names. He had not missed Henri's warning look at Throckmorton and the quick change of subject. He must find out more about these two exiles, but now was not the time.

At the far end of the gallery, a twelve piece orchestra, wearing Guise livery, were playing a selection of light airs. The gallery was decorated in the Reconnaissance style, with many ornate embroidered wall hangings and numerous large oil paintings of former members of the Guise family. Jacob estimated it was at least fifty paces long.

'Do you know my father, Sir John, personally?' Throckmorton asked.

'I'm afraid not.'

'He was removed from his post,' said Throckmorton, with some venom, 'for being a Catholic, you know. They claim to treat us equally, but they don't.'

Jacob made a neutral reply. Realising that Maria was still talking to the Countess, he stopped and turned back. Then he spied a familiar face over her shoulder that sent a shiver of recognition down his spine. Advancing towards her was Count Roberto Ridolfi.

Excusing himself to Throckmorton he went to join her.

The Count embraced him with great enthusiasm. 'Jacob Bell,' he cried, his voice breaking with emotion. 'I cannot tell you how good it is to see you looking so fit and well. I thought that with my lack of courage, I had done you great harm to bring you here to Paris.'

Jacob shook his head. 'My dear Count, you mustn't blame yourself. As you yourself said at the time, you are not a soldier, you are a diplomat. See,' he said, throwing his arms wide, 'here I am in Paris again and no harm done. So please, no more guilt. By the way, how is that son of yours, Jedediah was it not?' Jacob knew full well that Jedediah or Jed Sutton, as he was usually known, was the illegitimate son of the count's liaison with Agnes

Sutton, a distant relative of the Earl of Leicester. Since their first meeting about twelve years earlier, they had been at daggers drawn whenever they met.

The Count frowned. 'I was hoping you might have news of him. I have not seen or heard of him for over eight years. We last spoke in Paris, shortly after you had returned to England. He too was about to leave for England, but I'm afraid we did not part on the best of terms.'

'I'm sorry to hear that,' said Jacob, although in truth he wasn't. 'I too have not heard from him since I escorted you to France.' Thank goodness, he thought.

Maria linked arms with Jacob and the Count swept into a deep bow. 'And who is this ravishing creature who has taken such a proprietary hold on your arm? Please introduce me at once.'

Jacob indulged him with a bow. 'Count Ridolfi, allow me to present my wife Lady Maria Bell. Her father is Senator Morisini, a leading member of the Signory of Venice.'

Maria acknowledged the Count's deep bow over her hand with a curtsey and a warm smile. 'It is very kind of you to describe me as ravishing. Every mother of four needs that sort of flattery, my dear Count.'

'I assure you Lady Maria, it was not flattery at all, but sincere admiration.' He smiled and patted Jacob's right arm. 'However, I know enough of this sword arm of your husband's to ensure my admiration is kept at a safe distance.' They both laughed politely.

He indicated Henri who was beckoning him. 'Please excuse me, I see I am summoned.'

'So that's the scheming Count Ridolfi,' Maria whispered as he left.

Jacob nodded. 'Don't let his amiable exterior fool you. He can be a very ruthless enemy and a highly intelligent one at that.'

Henri was talking animatedly to Count Ridolfi and after a short while, the Count bowed and strode purposely up the gallery and headed towards the orchestra. Henri spoke briefly to Catherine and then went towards another group of people who had just been announced. Catherine had been conversing animatedly with a small group of extremely fashionable ladies of about her own age. It seemed likely that Maria was the topic of conversation, since there were numerous glances in her direction. Catherine then led the group of ladies across to Maria and Jacob and after the introductions, one of the ladies, identified by Catherine as Marguerite, Marquise of Elboeuf, enquired if this was Maria's first visit to Paris.

'Yes it is, but as yet I have seen little of your city, except for the short trip to Madame Hélène's salon.'

'Ah,' said Marguerite, 'I thought that might be one of her dresses. It is very becoming.' She turned to Jacob. 'Catherine tells me you are Glassmaker to the English Court,' she said. 'What brings you to Paris?

'I have that honour,' Jacob said, 'and I am in Paris to open a showroom for my glass. I intend to base my Parisian showroom on one I had in Venice.'

Before there were any further questions, Catherine interrupted. 'My husband is signalling for us to join him, please excuse us,' she said to the ladies.

Jacob proffered both arms to Catherine and Maria, who linked theirs through his and they walked across to Henri. 'It's not every day I get to escort two beautiful women,' he laughed.

'Indeed,' Henri agreed. 'But I'm not sure it's desirable, they are such expensive creatures.'

Catherine turned to Maria with a gleam in her eye. 'Are we going to take that insult lying down, Maria?'

'Certainly not,' said Maria, 'I think you and I should go on a shopping expedition tomorrow. A very expensive shopping expedition.'

Jacob groaned. 'Now see what you have done, Henri. Apologise at once.'

'He will have to grovel nicely,' said the Countess, the gleam turning to a wicked smile.

Fortunately, the Duke was saved by the arrival of Count Ridolfi, who had a whispered conversation with him, before hurrying off. Henri then had a word with Catherine. Jacob was intrigued, wondering what it was all about.

'Jacob,' boomed Henri pleasantly, 'Catherine would like to spirit your wife away for a short time to meet some of the wives and allay their suspicions. I hear that she has already captivated

Count Ridolfi, who is enchanted by her.'

'As I recall, the Count was always the ladies' man but I doubt he will do anything rash.'

The Duke laughed. 'I'm sure he won't. However, I would like to introduce you to some of the Catholic League's most influential families. The Count will join us shortly. So if you will excuse us ladies,' he said, with an inclination of his head, 'we will meet up with you again soon.'

About halfway down the gallery Henri led Jacob through a door flanked by two liveried servants. They entered a small ante-chamber where two armed servants straightened respectfully as Henri led Jacob into the large room beyond. The room was probably used for dining, as there was a large table covered with a heavy royal blue embroidered cloth, around which high-backed chairs were arranged.

There were about a dozen people present, standing around in groups. All of them richly dressed, but Jacob recognised only Count Ridolfi and Francis Throckmorton. Leading Jacob towards the head of the table, Henri introduced him to several prominent members of his family. Charles of Lorraine, Duke of Mayenne, was, said Henri, his most trusted lieutenant. Jacob judged him to be in his late twenties. He had a high forehead, with a widow's peak, and a beard and moustache. His black doublet with a simple white cambric collar gave him a sombre look. When Henri mentioned Jacob was Glassmaker to Queen Elizabeth, Charles regarded him suspiciously, but Henri was already introducing Jacob to his cousin, the Duke d'Aumale and Governor of Picardy, a swarthy young man in his mid-twenties.

His companion, a military man of about thirty, with a full beard and moustache, bowed and was introduced as Philippe Emanuel, Duke of Mercouer. 'I hear you saved Roberto Ridolfi's life a few years ago,' he said warmly. 'It is a pleasure to meet an active supporter of our cause from England.' Jacob thanked him and then Henri with his hand on Jacob's arm led him towards the top of the table where they were intercepted by an older man of about forty.

Charles III, Duke of Lorraine, had a long thin face, elongated by his pointed Spanish-style beard. 'Is this the swordsman and glassmaker that Ridolfi's been telling me about?' he asked aggressively.

'Yes,' Henri said firmly. 'He is also a good Catholic, having been brought up in Venice.'

'Humph,' muttered Charles, 'A bunch of appeasers, the Venetians, if you ask me. Refuse to allow the Inquisition. How are you going to weed out the heretics without the Inquisition?'

Henri frowned, obviously displeased that Lorraine had introduced a note of disharmony to his gathering. He signalled to the servant standing behind his chair at the head of the table. 'My lords, please take your seats,' announced the servant, in a ringing voice.

Much to Jacob's surprise, he was invited to sit in the position of honour on Henri's right, with Count Ridolfi on Jacob's right. Sitting immediately opposite, dressed in the robes of a cardinal, was the Archbishop of Glasgow, whom Count Ridolfi introduced to Jacob.

Looking round, Jacob realised for the first time, the full power of the Catholic League. Around the table were seated much of the cream of French nobility and most of them related to Henri of Guise and his cousin Mary Stuart. Collectively, they controlled large sections of France and had scores of thousands of soldiers and supporters at their command. He felt tension rising up in him and struggled to control his nerves. Count Ridolfi must have sensed what he was feeling, but misinterpreted the reason. 'Daunting, aren't they,' he said jovially, 'but don't let them intimidate you.' He indicated Henri, 'We're on your side.'

When they were settled and looking expectantly towards him, Henri stood up, invited Jacob to stand and, holding out his arms, addressed the gathering. 'Esteemed members of the Catholic League, allow me to present Master Glassmaker Jacob Bell of the Crouched Friars Glass-works in London,' he said and Jacob bowed to the gathering. Henri informed the gathering of Jacob's plan to set up a showroom in Paris to display his glass. 'I understand that in the near future you will receive an invitation to a very special opening day,' he announced. There were some puzzled looks around the table at this announcement, but Henri ignored them.

'But that is not the reason for his presence today,' he

continued. 'He is a follower of the true faith and has supported our cause even at a severe cost to his own health. Some of you are aware of the incident when he saved Count Ridolfi's life and was severely injured in the process. Now, by the Grace of God, restored to full health, he joins us again to help us in our fight against the heretics.'

This introduction was greeted with a mixed response. Some applauded enthusiastically, but Charles of Lorraine did not share their sentiments. 'The man is English,' he cried, standing up and confronting Henri. 'He grew up in Venice with those feeble Catholics who appease heretics. Why should we trust him? That damned usurper who rewards him with honours has been supporting the Huguenots for years.'

The Duke held up his arms again, laid his hand on Jacob's shoulder and addressed Charles directly. 'Jacob Bell has risked everything to help our cause. He warned Count Ridolfi that Walsingham's troops were coming to arrest him, having learned about his plot against Queen Elizabeth. He used his own ship to help Ridolfi to escape to France. When they were attacked by assassins, he fought four of them alone to enable Ridolfi to reach safety and was almost killed.' He indicated the cardinal. 'The Archbishop will also confirm that our cousin, Mary Stuart speaks most highly of him in her letters. With his official position at court in London, he is in an ideal position to pass on information that will help us in our fight.' Both Ridolfi and the cardinal were nodding their approval and Charles sat down muttering.

Henri paused, waiting until the murmuring had died down and then addressed the gathering again. 'And now my friends, I have some momentous news. Our plans for the invasion of England with the help of d'Aubigny in Scotland have found favour with the Holy Father in Rome.' He was forced to pause again until loud applause had died down. 'As we speak, representatives of the Archbishop of Glasgow are on their way to Rome and Spain. They seek approval for my additional idea for a Catholic League army to enter the southern part of England simultaneously with the army sweeping down from Scotland. They have further received the assurance of the leader of the

English and Irish Catholics that they will rise in revolt to support our armies. This will form an irresistible invasion that will sweep Elizabeth from power and ensure that our cousin, Mary Queen of Scots, takes her rightful place as Queen of England, restoring the true faith to that blighted realm.' This news was greeted with loud acclaim, but there were some questions.

'How many troops are the League to supply for this venture?' asked the Governor of Picardy.

'About twenty thousand men in all. The rest will come from the Papal army, the Scottish Catholic Lords and mercenaries from Germany.'

'Twenty thousand you say. That could leave us exposed to attack by the Huguenots.'

Heads nodded in agreement at this.

The Duke of Mercouer now stood up. 'I am sure that Henri has not ignored the threat of the Huguenots. Since Saint Bartholomew's Day, they have been fighting a defensive war, where they are fighting at all. As many of you know, I am now Governor of Brittany and I pledge a substantial army to this great cause. The Huguenots will be no threat there.'

'Thank you, Philippe,' Henri said. 'That will be a great help. It is as you say, a great cause. It will place our cousin Mary Stuart on the English throne, restore the true faith to those islands and together, England and France will form an alliance that even the might of Spain will fear. France will become the true leader of the Catholic faith. 'My brothers,' he cried, spreading his arms wide, his face transformed by the intensity of his fervour, 'we have God's work to do. Join me.'

That settled the matter and there were cries of approbation all around the table.

Jacob too sprang to his feet and applauded, but he felt as though there was a heavy stone in his stomach. He must make no mistakes now. England must be warned of this huge threat to her sovereignty. Should this plan go ahead it would almost certainly succeed.

Count Ridolfi turned and embraced Jacob. 'This must be a great day for you, my friend,' he said, his voice shaking with emotion. 'The chance to play a major part, in such a wondrous fight for God's true religion, is not given to many.'

Jacob tried to reply enthusiastically, but in truth he did not agree with the Count at all. Although ostensibly about the restoration of the Catholic faith, it was really about power. Henri's fervour was not religious, it was naked ambition. He saw himself as the leader of this great alliance of England and France. Henri covets the French throne and I must try to find any information that might help Walsingham counter this conspiracy.

'Let us hope,' he said, addressing Count Ridolfi, 'that Philip of Spain does not realise how strong an alliance with England will make France.'

The Count looked at him shrewdly. 'You have hit at the heart of it. Should Philip decide we would become too powerful and challenge Spain's position, he will never agree to provide forces. Without Spain's backing, Pope Gregory will find it difficult to support us. Spain must confirm her agreement in writing. The Holy Father will not move without it after Spain's failure to honour their part in the planned Irish incursion.'

The Archbishop who had joined them agreed. 'We have certainly asked for no less,' he said. 'I made sure Father Robert understood this.'

There might be something in this for Walsingham to exploit, Jacob thought. If he can play on Philip of Spain's fear of an alliance between France and England, he might cause a split in their ranks. I will certainly suggest it.

Henri then took Jacob, Count Ridolfi and Francis Throckmorton to one side. 'Count Ridolfi is returning to Rome shortly,' he informed them, 'and I want Francis to act as a go-between for letters he sends to the Bishop of Ross, the Spanish Ambassador and Mary Queen of Scots in her captivity in England.'

Francis and the Count signified their approval. 'Since Jacob is setting up a showroom here in Paris,' Henri continued, 'it will be ideal for passing messages to him for delivery to Francis when he is in London. He will also be able to keep us apprised on anything he gleans from his visits to the English court.'

Jacob was elated by this news, it would give Walsingham the opportunity to see how matters were progressing in Rome and probably Spain. He would have to ensure that when he returned home, someone the Duke trusted would be available at the showroom to accept messages.

Realising that he had not answered the Duke who was looking at him expectantly, he hurriedly assured him of his agreement. Henri smiled and suggested that Jacob might like to talk to some of the others and then excused himself. 'I must get back to the reception, or my absence will be missed. Please come back to the Grand Gallery when you have finished.'

When Jacob emerged into the gallery again, Maria whispered to him that she was feeling very tired. When Jacob explained to their hosts that Maria was exhausted, Henri summoned one of the servants and instructed him to arrange for the immediate availability of a coach.

'I will be in touch with regard to the matter we discussed,' he said to Jacob. 'The reception has been a great success.'

Back at the villa, Maria went straight to bed and Jacob was glad of the quiet to mull over the events of the evening. The wealth and sheer power that the Guises wielded had been a shock and Henri's tactics, brilliant. Far beyond anything that Walsingham suspected. Their confidence that both Spain and the Pope would approve and be active participants, made this the most dangerous challenge that Elizabeth's rule in England had ever faced. Unless he could help Walsingham to defeat it, thousands could die and his adopted country would be changed beyond all recognition.

Chapter Eight
Paris, France, 1581

In the days following the Catholic League reception, Jacob and Maria concentrated on finding a house that matched their needs. After a thorough look at the three houses that remained after the unsuitable ones had been eliminated, they had at last arrived at a decision.

There was little to choose between two of the houses, but in the end, the house they were already living in became their choice.

'I've become quite attached to it now,' said Maria. 'Can we come and stay here from time to time?'

'I don't see why not, the house is attractive, but it will depend on the political situation in France.'

'It does have everything we need, with good living quarters and an excellent series of rooms on the ground floor for your showroom.'

Jacob agreed. 'It will do very well. The rooms are large and with some relatively minor alterations they can be adapted to my requirements. All that remains now is to arrange the sale and for you to decide what you want in the way of alterations and decorations.'

'Now that you have your premises, how long will it take you to alter them and decide on the stock you need for the opening?'

'About two to three weeks for the alterations and any decorative changes. We will also have a good idea of what stock we will need by then.' He studied her face. 'I know that look, you are about to tell me something I won't want to hear!'

Maria gave a wry smile. 'Was it so obvious? Let me ask you a question first. How long will you need in London to make and ship the glass for the showroom?'

'About a week, that is all. Stock has been building up in London ever since sales in France started to fall. I didn't want to stop production, so I arranged with Roberto that we would continue to allow the build up of stock until it was sufficient for the new showroom.' He went to his desk and came back with some sketches. 'The main problem will be these,' he said handing them to her.

Maria examined the glass designs carefully. 'Oh, you are making a new range of glasses for the opening.'

'I am indeed, but it will take time to ensure the Capos can make the new design to our standards and to complete the stock and pack it for shipment. From previous experience I think it will take at least two weeks in all.' He smiled. 'And you still haven't told me what you were thinking.'

Her enigmatic smile widened. 'Oh you know me too well!'

'I should hope so after ten years. Come on, out with it.'

'Well,' she said, with some hesitation, 'I thought that as you were going to be busy, I could stay here and keep an eye on the alterations and refitting the decorations, while you go to London and organise things at that end. What do you think?'

'Oh no,' said Jacob firmly. 'I'm not going to leave you and the children here while I go home alone. You must forget that idea at once.'

And, of course, Jacob went back to London alone!

In fact, it was almost three weeks before he returned and he was amazed at the changes Maria had made. The house had been redecorated from top to bottom with many new hangings and furniture.

The greatest change was in the showroom. It was already complete and Raoul had moved his jewellery into his section. The regular stock which had been brought over on *The Crystal* ten days earlier by Quiff, who, although he was the controller of the Ring, the apprentices who supplied information to Jacob, was also Roberto's assistant. Quiff had already taken charge of the shipping cases and was busy opening them. The stock was being transferred to display shelves and there was a central stand prominently situated ready to receive the new range of glassware.

Jacob was intrigued by the golden fleur-de-lis design that had been used to decorate the stand for the new glasses. 'Why did you use this design, Maria?'

'It was Catherine's suggestion. The fleur-de-lis is both a symbol of France itself and also appears on the coat of arms of the Île-de-

France, the region for Paris, and on the city coat of arms.'

'Excellent, you have solved two problems in one.'

'How so?' asked Maria.

'Because I didn't have a name for the range and now you have named it for me. Fleur-de-lis it shall be. That is the last link in the chain and we can get ready for the opening quickly now.'

Despite Jacob's confident prediction, it was two more weeks before the opening could be held. There was no time for worrying as he had for his very first opening in Murano. The support of the Duke of Guise and the Catholic League meant that Jacob was forced to disappoint a great number of people, the showroom would have been too crowded. He therefore decided to hold the opening over three days.

Interest was so great that Jacob sent an urgent message to the Crouched Friars to despatch extra stock. He knew it was unlikely to arrive before the opening, but at least orders would not be delayed for long.

Notwithstanding these extra measures, when Jacob sat down to total all the orders, he had badly underestimated the demand for the fleur-de-lis range. The other stock had sold well, but everyone had been astounded by the overwhelming success of the new design. Raoul too was very pleased with the sales of his glass jewellery, which had been sold using the name Morisini Jewellery.

Maria, Quiff, Raoul and Jacob were gathered together in Jacob's study after the doors had closed on the evening of the third day. They sat around drinking wine and discussing their success. It was only the excitement of their achievement that kept them going for, in truth, they were all exhausted.

'Firstly,' Jacob said, raising his glass, 'I want to thank you all for making this new showroom a success. I could not have done it without you all.' They all raised their glasses and drank a toast.

'Secondly, we must make arrangement to keep the showroom open, but I must return to London as soon as possible. I wondered if you would stay on to run the showroom until we can employ someone, Quiff.'

Quiff was shocked. 'You want me to run the showroom, Jacob? That's more than I expected. I'm not sure if I can do it on my own. And I only have a smattering of French.'

'Don't worry,' said Raoul, 'I'll help you. My son can run the bead making for now.'

'Excellent. Then that's settled. Let's have another drink,' said Jacob, reaching for the wine.

It was Quiff who left first. 'Master Jacob,' he said, draining his glass, 'it has been an experience I would not have missed, but if you will excuse me I am now going to bed. I feel as though I could sleep for a week, but I have a showroom to open in the morning.' With that he saluted the others and staggered off. Raoul too went shortly afterwards with a reminder that he must check on the most popular designs and start making stock for the launch of Morisini Jewellery in London.

Maria sat beside Jacob on the new settle she had installed in his study. Leaning her head on his shoulder she gave a sigh of contentment. They sat in companionable silence for some time and then a grin appeared on her face. 'I feel so alive and well,' she whispered in his ear, gently nibbling it.

Jacob, his exhaustion forgotten, responded immediately feeling a desire that had been missing since the death of little Meg. He kissed her passionately and Maria strained against him. When Jacob slid his hand inside her dress and began to fondle her breast, the nipple became hard immediately. Maria gave a groan of pleasure.

'Not here,' she gasped, 'someone might come.' She jumped to her feet and, as Jacob scrambled to follow her, gathered up her skirts and fled up the stairs. Part way up she stopped and looked over her shoulder. Seeing he was bounding after her, she gave him a sultry look and with a girlish giggle raced up the stairs with Jacob in hot pursuit.

Catching her just inside the bedroom, Jacob swept her into his arms and they kissed. Then they were frantically helping each other to get rid of their clothes. Naked, Maria threw her arms around his neck and jumping up wrapped her legs around his waist. Laughing like newly-weds and entwined, Jacob carried her across the bedroom and they tumbled on to the bed.

Maria gasped as she felt Jacob's hardness between her thighs. 'Come in to me now, darling. I can't wait to feel you inside me, it's been too long.' Jacob did not need any urging and she gasped as he entered her and, matching him thrust for thrust, they reached a final peak that left them gasping.

It was some while before Maria opened her eyes. Jacob was lying propped up on one elbow studying her. Their lovemaking had come as a great relief to him. Ever since Maria had asked him to be patient he had been wondering if there was some deeper barrier between them other than the loss of little Meg.

Pulling his mouth to hers, Maria kissed him with an abandonment that quickly wiped away his doubts and brought a lively response. He pulled her across his lap and she leaned back, so that he could plunder her straining breasts with his mouth. His tongue was everywhere as he laid her gently on her back, caressing her breasts and working ever closer to the fine hairs of her womanhood. She arched her back and he stroked her inner thighs as they parted. As his stroking drew ever nearer to her sex, she bit her lips to stop herself from screaming with pleasure.

She lifted her knees, opened her thighs wide and gasped as his probing tongue raised her to a new pitch of pleasure that was almost painful.

'Please, Giam, now!' she panted and wrapped her legs around him, locking them behind his back.

Moving slowly at first, he struggled to control his need to thrust quickly, but as her movements quickened, so did his. Their desire was taking them to heights they had never known before and reached a climax so intense that Maria could not prevent a cry escaping her lips before, totally spent, she collapsed exhausted. Jacob too lay still, breathing unsteadily, face down beside her with his right arm draped across her breasts.

Maria pulled the sheet across them and they slept. When she awoke, the sun was shining brightly against the drapes. There was no sign of Jacob and Maria stretched luxuriantly. Snuggling into the pillow, a smile crossed her face as she remembered the events of the previous night. She sat up and realised she was still naked. Sliding out of bed, she went to fetch her wrap which was draped across the chair beside her dressing table. In the full-length mirror that had cost her a fortune, but was worth every penny, she examined her reflection. Hmm, not bad for an old married woman, she thought as she examined her firm buttocks and slender legs.

Before she had time for any further narcissistic inspection, the door latch was opened. Grabbing her wrap, she held it in front of her. 'Oh, it's you, Giam,' she said.

Jacob, smiled at the tantalising glimpses of his wife's body. Had he not been carrying a tray he would have swept her into his arms. Maria eyed the contents of the tray hungrily. 'Oh you wonderful man. I'm starving.' And you can take that expression off your face. You had your way with me last night. I'm hungry for food now.' She stalked to the bed and sat up, drawing the sheets almost to her chin and gestured imperiously for him to set the tray on her lap.

Jacob set it down with a smile. 'There you are, Your Majesty. Was there anything else?' he said, imitating a servant's ingratiating tone. Try as she might, Maria could not keep he haughtiness up. With a laugh she said, 'Yes there is. Come and kiss me immediately and then let me get on with breaking my fast.'

Jacob obeyed with alacrity, sliding in beside her and then, with a wicked smile, said, 'I thought we did that last night!'

Chapter Nine
Paris and London, 1581

There was only a single candle shining in the downstairs window of the house in the Rue de Rivoli, a quiet cul-de-sac close to the Louvre and the English Embassy. Thomas Rogers, or Nicholas Berden as he was more usually known, was a secret agent for Walsingham. Having newly arrived in Paris from Rome, he had only received the message to go there, two hours earlier. After a careful look around from his vantage point in the shadows across the street, he sidled down the side of the house to the rear door. It was unlocked and going inside, he entered the first room on the left, down the corridor.

Walsingham lowered his cocked pistol and placed it on the table alongside the reports for the Queen.

'You're late.' he said mildly. 'I expected you an hour ago.'

Rogers shrugged. 'I only arrived in Paris about three hours ago and found your message, at my apartment. The journey from Rome was difficult.'

'Never mind, you're here now, what have you to tell me?'

'The Scottish Jesuit, Father Creighton, has put a Catholic League plan before Pope Gregory. An army of twenty thousand men will invade Scotland and then march into England where there will be a Papist uprising in support. The Pope has been informed that the invasion has also received the support of Philip of Spain, but he is waiting for written confirmation.'

'Did you learn any more details?'

'I'm sorry, Mister Secretary, my sources did not know any more. I decided not to risk a letter, the information was too important.'

Walsingham took a bulging pouch from his doublet and tossed it to Rogers. 'You have done well. How soon will you return to Rome?'

Rogers hefted the purse and stowed it away in his doublet. 'It will take me about ten days to conclude my official business in

Paris.' He operated a wine merchant business which allowed him to move freely between Italy, Spain and France. 'Do you have any more instructions for me?'

Walsingham nodded. 'Do you still have contacts in Paris?'

'As far as I know, I have not been in touch with them for some months now. What do you want to know?'

'Someone has been killing my agents off in Paris and elsewhere in France. I'm sure the Duke of Guise is behind it. I need to find out more of this invasion, especially when it will take place.'

'I'll see what I can do. It takes time to assemble an army of twenty thousand men and it will be difficult to keep it secret. Will you remain in Paris for much longer? It will take me a few days to get any useful information.'

'There is also another matter,' said Walsingham, reaching into a drawer and extracting another pouch, which Thomas eyed with interest. 'You mentioned Father Creighton the Jesuit. As I'm sure you are aware, there are two main factions among the exiled Catholics, the Society of Jesus, or Jesuits and the Seculars.'

'I have met William Gifford of the Seculars on several occasions. He has bought wine from me. What do you require me to do?'

Picking up the pouch, Walsingham tossed it to Thomas. 'I want you to try and stir up trouble between them.'

Thomas hefted the pouch. 'Divide and rule, eh? There should be enough here to stir up quite a bit of tension between them.'

Walsingham smiled. 'Excellent, you can add any information you have gleaned on that subject to the report. I leave for London the day after tomorrow. If I haven't heard from you before then, give the letter to Stafford, the English Ambassador in Paris and he will send it on post-haste.'

Sitting in his study at Seething Lane a few days later, Walsingham tried to make sense of the information he'd received from Rogers. His own mission for the Queen, connected with the marriage negotiations with the young Duke of Alençon, had proceeded as expected. Alençon had agreed to come to England to meet the Queen, but unfortunately, little progress had been made with his brother King Henry III, regarding an Anglo-French Treaty. This was a pity, since it would be useful to have such an alliance with Elizabeth's welfare at the heart.

Rogers sources in Paris had informed him that the Duke of Guise had met with a number of Catholic dissidents. Walsingham had not received confirmation of this from his Paris agents since, in the last few weeks, three more had disappeared. The latest being his informer on the Duke of Guise's visitors. There was obviously a concerted effort to remove his spies and it gave credence to the information from Rogers. He also said he had made contact with several Catholics, including Gilbert Gifford, Thomas Morgan and Charles Paget. Morgan and Paget were violent Seculars and already deep in the wrangling of the English Catholics. He also had reason to believe that Gifford was a rapacious man intent on feathering his own nest. He wrote, *Gifford professes deep Catholic convictions, but I believe him to worship money more. I sweetened him with a loan and he told me he was coming to England shortly on a mission for Morgan, who seems to be a very active supporter of Mary Stuart.*

Another snippet reported by Rogers was that the social engagements of the month were a grand reception for the Catholic League at the Château de Lorraine and the opening of a glass showroom in the Marais district, by none other than Jacob Bell, the Queen's Glassmaker. The latter event had been attended by many members of the Catholic League, including its leader the Duke of Guise.

Walsingham mused over this information. It sounded as though Jacob Bell had renewed his contact with the Duke of Guise. Bell had been extremely useful during the Ridolfi plot. However, he had not been an active agent since his serious injury when escorting Ridolfi to France. It was not often Walsingham felt guilt, but the attack on Ridolfi that led to Bell's serious injuries, had been on his instructions. He had disagreed with Lord Burghley's decision to let Ridolfi escape. Unfortunately, he had not been privy to the fact that Jacob Bell was escorting Ridolfi, so his assassins treated him as one of Ridolfi's men. It was ironic that Jacob should have saved Ridolfi and in so doing had made himself a hero with the Catholics.

From intercepted letters to the Archbishop of Glasgow, Walsingham knew that Bell was considered to be a loyal Catholic supporter by the Guises and Mary Stuart. Together with himself, Bell had planned it that way. But what if Bell had been turned by the Duke of Guise - he was Catholic after all? Walsingham stroked his beard distractedly and thought, I don't think he would turn double agent, but I will need to be cautious. But if he was loyal, what a coup, to have my own man at the centre of the Catholic League!

The next step was to arrange a secret meeting with Bell when he returned to London. It would not be prudent for them to be seen together in public. Accordingly, not long after Jacob had returned from Paris, he was picked up at the rear gate of his house after dark and taken in a heavily curtained coach to the safe house in a quiet lane off Three Needle Street, sometimes used by Walsingham for secret meetings with his agents. When they were settled down, each with a glass of Walsingham's favourite malmsey, he enquired of Jacob how the opening of his new showroom had gone.

'It went far better than I expected. In fact, it was an outstanding success.'

'I'm delighted, but of course, as you will already have guessed, this was not my main reason for meeting you.'

Jacob gave an amused laugh. 'My affairs are not that secret. I would guess you are anxious to hear what I was doing with the Catholic League.'

'You are absolutely correct. I don't mind telling you that they have been much in my thoughts of late.'

'And with very good reason,' said Jacob. 'Their plans for an invasion of England are well advanced and far more dangerous than I ever imagined.' Walsingham did not like the sound of this, but at least his fears about Jacob did not seem to be confirmed. However, he would wait a little longer before he was entirely satisfied.

'Then the Duke of Guise did recruit you,' he said, a little more anxiously than he intended. Jacob looked at him sharply, although he made no comment. Oh dear, thought Walsingham, he picked up my relief.

'I could not begin to imagine,' said Jacob, 'what you would have done if I had failed to take the opportunity to become part of the Catholic League's inner cabal. Send me to the Tower at the very least, no doubt!'

Walsingham gave a barking laugh. 'More than likely. So what did you find out?'

Keeping a detailed note of all Jacob had to say, Walsingham listened in silence, other than for a few questions to clarify certain names, or points. Despite his earlier worry, the information checked out in every detail with Rogers' account. By the time Jacob had given him the full details of the plot, Walsingham had few doubts about his loyalty. The detailed list of participants, the involvement of Ridolfi and Throckmorton, were all new. But as Jacob had said, it was a brilliant plan and very likely to succeed unless he, Walsingham, could thwart it. The key was time. Given that, there was every chance he could find a strategy to counter the threat. But was it too late? The next answer was vital.

'How long is it before the planned invasion of Scotland?'

'I'm not sure, but my best estimate is that it will not happen until late Spring or early Summer of next year. There are still points to be negotiated with d'Aubigny and with representatives of the Pope, but none of them will move until Philip of Spain gives his approval to any amendments.' Walsingham was reassured by Jacob's open replies. He could detect no strain or attempts to avoid the question. He prided himself on being difficult to fool, but he was not infallible, as the affair with Count Ridolfi had proved.

'At least that gives me some time to act. I would hazard that Philip has his hands full at the moment in the Low Countries and will not be in a hurry to acquiesce to raising another army so soon. He is not well known for making quick decisions.'

'Then.' said Jacob, 'the Pope will be reluctant to move. According to Count Ridolfi, he is still furious with Philip over his half-hearted approach to the Irish invasion plan a few months ago and will not commit himself without written confirmation that Philip will take part. The Duke of Guise has very grandiose plans for an Anglo-French alliance once Mary Stuart is restored to the throne. I doubt that Philip will welcome that. Perhaps your agents could play on his fears to stop him joining with the French.'

'Exactly my thoughts. I will instruct them accordingly. Anything that buys us a little time is all to the good,' Walsingham said. His mind was working furiously as he absorbed this new information. For too long his agents had failed to get to the heart of what was happening. At least now, there was a chance to do something.

'What of young Throckmorton? You say he will carry letters to the Bishop of Ross, as well as Mary Stuart and her supporters. What did you make of him?'

'He is an intelligent and ardent Catholic. Very influenced by his father's fall from office. He sees it as a sign that the Queen is bent on removing all Catholics from positions in her government. The Duke is keen to use him as a go-between which he will do very well. He will be worth keeping an eye on.'

'You can rely on that,' said Walsingham, with determination. 'We will allow him some rope for the moment. Mayhap he will gather enough of it to hang himself and others in the future.' Jacob simply nodded.

'What is also true,' Walsingham continued, 'is that, because of your help, there is a good chance we can prevent a bloody civil war, where Englishmen will be pitted one against the other. Foreign troops will be trampling on our English soil. Not to mention the cruel reprisals the Inquisition will exact if Mary Stuart should oust our good Protestant Queen. Unfortunately, Guise has laid his plans only too well. This plot has an extremely good chance of succeeding.'

'Henri certainly agrees with that,' Jacob said. 'He is convinced that his plan to lead a strong Catholic League army into southern England, while the Papal and Spanish troops invade from Scotland, will be the final nail in the coffin of Protestant rule.'

'Did you hear any word of the French King being involved?'

Jacob shook his head vigorously. 'On the contrary, the Duke refused to allow any news of the plans to be passed to him and described him as "a milksop".'

'Ah,' said Walsingham. 'That explains why my spies in the French court have been getting nowhere. Those I have left that is. I received word only yesterday that the agent shadowing the Duke of Guise, had been dumped in the Seine with his head staved in.'

He drained his glass and regarded Jacob steadily and then sighed. 'And now I must ask you to put your life on the line for my Queen and country. Will you help me to forestall this plot? I recognise that your circumstances have changed a lot since we worked together ten years ago. I little thought it would be so long before you would be approached by the Duke of Guise to play an active part in their plans.'

There was no hesitation on Jacob's part. 'I decided to be involved the day I accepted the Duke's invitation to the reception of the Catholic League. There was no doubt in my mind that if I did, I would become embroiled in whatever they were plotting.' He raised his own glass that Walsingham had just refilled. 'Here's to confounding the Queen's enemies.'

Walsingham nodded and drank deeply. 'Amen to that. I thank you Jacob. This plot could be the most dangerous one we have ever faced. Should this double invasion come to pass, it will be well nigh impossible to overcome. With the Catholics in revolt, it has every chance of succeeding.'

'I agree,' said Jacob. 'The effect will be catastrophic for this realm. There will be civil war and thousands will lose their lives. It seems to me that the only way to prevail is to ensure that the invasion never takes place.'

'My thoughts exactly, Jacob,' agreed Walsingham. 'I must set my agents in Scotland to stir up the Protestant Lords in undermining d'Aubigny immediately.'

'Is that possible?'

'It should be since d'Aubigny has made plenty of enemies in his rise to prominence. There are many of the nobles who believe he wields far too much influence over the young King. And then there is the Kirk.' At Jacob's frown, he explained, 'The Reformed Church of Scotland. They'll not sit idly by and see Scotland return to Papism.'

There was a pause as Walsingham sat back in his chair, drumming his fingers on its arms. Suddenly he leaned forward and regarded Jacob with a friendly expression. 'I want you to know, Jacob, that while we cannot make public your contributions to the security of the realm, the Queen holds you in the highest esteem. She is well aware that you put yourself at risk to ensure her safety. The fact that you are neither English, nor Protestant, is a matter of great importance to her. Few of her own subjects have done so much without asking for reward.'

'I don't do it for rewards,' retorted Jacob hotly. 'And I am a Catholic it is true. But I cannot support or condone those who would kill thousands of innocent people in order to establish Catholicism in England, or in France for that matter. In my view, religion has little to do with these plots; it is just a convenient label. Power, pure unadulterated power, is what drives these fanatics.'

He paused to gather his thoughts, then went on slowly, 'When I joined you in the fight against Ridolfi, it was because England and the Queen had recognised my efforts, rewarded my skill and restored my trust in my fellow man. I look on England as my country now and I will fight all who seek to destroy her.'

Chapter Ten
London and Burton-upon-Trent, June, 1581

The day after his secret talk with Walsingham, Jacob arranged to meet with his old acquaintance Colonel Paul Young. He was still working directly with Walsingham and was one of the few men who was aware of Jacob's part in both the Count Maldini and the Ridolfi plot.

'So,' said the colonel, with a friendly smile, 'you're getting involved in our intrigues again. Walsingham told me last night. I would have thought you'd have learned your lesson after last time.'

'You'd have thought so, wouldn't you. Anyway, Colonel, I need to protect my family and I want to employ some extra men who know how to fight, what would you advise?'

'First of all, Jacob, please call me Paul, we've been through too much together to be so formal. As to your request, how much does your wife know of your situation?'

'My wife knows everything, but my children nothing. They're really not old enough to be told.'

'I assume that your knife-throwing friend Roberto is in the picture.'

Jacob laughed. 'I'm sure Roberto would be amused by your description, but at the moment he has not been told. I have not seen him since my return from Paris. Nor has Quiff who runs the Ring been told. He's still in Paris running my new showroom.'

'Oh, is the Ring still in operation?'

'Of course. Members of the Ring provide me with valuable information to help my business affairs, as well as working for Walsingham who requires them to report on various people from time to time.' He regarded the colonel with curiosity. 'I'm not sure why you want to know about Roberto and Quiff. How does that help my family?'

The colonel smiled grimly. 'In a city like London, it is very difficult to ensure that your family is kept safe. You should make sure that you have a system to warn your wife of imminent danger. Not only that, but there should be a safe place for them to go and people available to protect them.'

'Can you recommend anyone?'

The colonel looked thoughtful. 'I might know at least one man who could help, but I would need to talk to him first. How many men were you thinking of?'

'It would look odd if I suddenly started employing lots of obvious soldiers. However, a couple of men from the right background, who would be prepared to do other jobs, might make all the difference in a tight situation.'

'That seems sensible to me,' said the colonel. 'Leave it with me for a couple of days and I will see what I can arrange.' He got up to go and then made a final point. 'You should let Roberto and Quiff know what is happening. They are both trustworthy and will not flinch should the worst happen.'

The following day Jacob told Roberto, who was all for moving his family to live at Mark Street. However, there were a number of practical difficulties, not least the overcrowding. In the end, it was agreed that, until Quiff returned from Paris, Roberto would alert all members of the Ring to be on the look-out for any suspicious characters lurking in the vicinity of Mark Street. Also anyone asking questions about Jacob and his family. The Ring now numbered fifty and were readily identified by the numbered copper rings they wore. Over the years, several of the earlier apprentices had become full members of their Guilds, but to a man they still kept in touch with Quiff, even though it was often through an intermediary. Even Walsingham's household had a member of the Ring in residence.

All members of the Ring were told to keep a special eye out for Jacob and his family and any suspicious events were to be reported immediately. Those apprentices who worked near the Crouched Friars Glass-works, the Harte Street showroom and Jacob's house at Mark Street were asked to be especially vigilant and be ready to respond if they received a Clubs message. Every apprentice had a club, similar to the ones carried by the Watch, to defend their master, and a "Clubs, Clubs" cry was the traditional call for apprentices to help a member in trouble. Once the cry was raised, every apprentice must grab his club and rush to help immediately.

In the event, it was nearly three weeks before Jacob saw Colonel Young again, who said he had been on a mission for Walsingham in Scotland, but offered no further explanation. Jacob assumed it was to do with d'Aubigny, but wisely refrained from asking questions.

The colonel had some news. 'Do you remember my sergeant with the clumsy feet?'

Jacob recalled this sergeant, a stocky man with big feet, tripping over a tree branch when they went to arrest Count Maldini and his confederates. 'The one who was shot by Sir Richard Urie?'

'The very one. You met him again when we went to get Ridolfi out of the country.'

'Indeed I did. He was much better in towns than in woods I venture. What of him?'

'He has been talking about retiring for some time. If you are interested, he might be willing to join your household in some capacity. He already knows you are working for Walsingham. I have no hesitation in recommending him.'

So it was that ex-sergeant Harry Heywood came to work for Jacob. Ostensibly to look after the new coach and horses and the family hacks, but in reality, with the help of another ex-soldier George Walker as ostler, they were employed to protect the family, if required. Above the stables at the rear of the house was a room large enough for both of them, since neither of them had married. They'd always followed the old soldier's maxim of loving and leaving the ladies.

Although not told their true role, Maria had a shrewd idea. She was just grateful that once they'd taken up residence, Jacob became more relaxed instead of prowling the house and grounds.

As Jed Sutton turned the dray into the yard at Modven Brewery at Burton-upon-Trent with a clatter of hooves and a rumble of wheels on the cobbles, a woman came bustling out of the house wiping her flour-encrusted hands on her apron. She was of medium height with a ruddy, pleasant face and a well-rounded figure. 'You're very late, John,' she scolded, although there was no trace of the shrew in her voice. 'I expected you more than an hour ...' She broke off in confusion as she realised that it was not her husband driving the dray, but a tall, thin-faced man she did not recognise.

Jed jumped down and steadied the two massive beasts before tying the reins to the hitch post.

'Who are you,' she cried, 'and what are you doing with my husband's dray?'

Jed Sutton took off his hat and made a small bow. 'My name is James Stourbridge and I am afraid I am the bearer of some bad news. Your husband has had an accident just outside Burton, on the Darby road. The nearside wheel went into a ditch and he was thrown out and crushed. He's dead.' He indicated the back of the dray where a pair of feet was protruding from under some sacking. 'Some people who knew your husband helped me to get him out. It was they who directed me here. One of them has gone for the Watch and other to the undertaker.'

As he told his tale, Jane burst into tears and ran sobbing to the dray and its load. 'Oh John,' she cried, 'how often have I warned you about drinking when you drove home? I knew this would happen.' She collapsed in a heap and even Jed's callous heart was touched by her distress. He went over and, lifting her up, carried her to the house at the side of the brewery.

A maid came hurrying towards him alerted by the cries of distress and Jed curtly told her that her master was dead and that her mistress was in shock and needed some smelling salts or brandy. The maid directed him into the parlour where he lay the swooning woman on to the settle. The maid came back with some salts, holding them under the woman's nose and rubbing her wrists.

'Tend to your mistress, while I go and see to the dray,' ordered Jed. As Jed began to unhitch the horses there was a gleam of satisfaction in his eyes. The first part of his plan had gone perfectly. He was certain that neither the Watch nor the widow would suspect that the brewer's death was anything other than an unfortunate accident. Now he must put the second part of the plan into action which was to become part owner of Modven Brewery. In so doing, he would become supplier of beer to the Earl of Shrewsbury whose various houses were used as prisons for

Queen Mary. He had vowed to release the Queen from her captivity and help her to gain the throne of England. This was the first important step in that process.

From then on, Jed went out of his way to be supportive and friendly. Once the funeral was over, he made himself indispensable to the widow and ran the brewery well. After a few weeks, he began to woo her - it was the business he was most interested in, but it was not long before she began to warm to him.

One afternoon, Jed was working in the barn, changing the hay. He was stripped to the waist when the widow came and stood by the door looking at him. Jed dropped the rake and sauntered towards her. 'Do you like what you see?' he asked, going close to her. She didn't reply, but the look in her eye said it all.

Jed put his arm round her waist and pulled her towards him. She resisted at first, but Jed pulled her in close and she gasped as she felt the hardness of his body against hers. Pressing her thigh between his legs, she began to stroke his back. Jed gave a confident smile and with a quick movement pulled the strap of her bodice down over one arm, exposing her breast. She gasped as he fondled her and did not resist as he swung her up into his arms and carried her to a pile of fresh hay. Laying her down, he roughly pulled open her bodice and as his mouth found her stiffening nipples he lifted her skirts and tore off her draws. Pushing her legs open, he immediately drove into her and she cried out in pain. But he was relentless. She began to moan with every violent thrust, getting louder and louder until finally, as he climaxed, she gave a loud cry of pleasure.

Jed was now welcomed into the widow's bed at night and Jane quickly became besotted with him. His rough lovemaking was exciting after the ineffectual gropings of her often drunken husband. Even when Jed had drunk a lot, he still managed to satisfy her. Before many weeks were out, she accepted his offer and sold him a half share in the business.

Over a period of weeks, Jed established the good name of James Stourbridge and Shrewsbury's stewards were happy to accept him as their supplier.. He discovered that Queen Mary was being moved from one house to another, never left too long in one place and closely guarded. So far, he had not been able to get anywhere near her, or any of her servants. He would have to be patient and build up his credibility with the Earl. Fortunately, he was unlikely to meet anyone who would recognise him as Jed Sutton.

This set him thinking about Walsingham's agent, Jacob Bell. He still had a score to settle with him, but for now he must bide his time. Ingratiating himself with Shrewsbury's men came first, so he could get close to Queen Mary. His dream was that he, Jedediah Sutton, bastard son of Count Roberto Ridolfi, would be the instrument of her deliverance. His father had failed her and run away to the safe luxury of Rome, just like he did to his mother. That was not his way. He would rescue his beloved Queen, or die in the attempt. Killing Bell would have to wait, but one day soon, he would have the time to make a trip to London and Walsingham's lapdog, that scheming glassmaker Bell, would pay the ultimate price for his betrayal.

Chapter Eleven
London, July, 1581

During the last week of the month, Raoul Laguna came over from Paris on *The Crystal.* He arrived at the Harte Street showroom with two large cases containing the stock that Jacob had requested. A section of the showroom had been fitted out with large sloping shelves with a ledge running along the front. The jewellery was mounted on velvet-covered trays and displayed on the three tiers of shelves.

Raoul brought with him his eldest son, Toni, the Venetian version of Antonio. He had asked to come to London to look after his father's business. He would look after the warehouse and help with sales and would also be available to make jewellery from beads sent over from Paris.

This being an altogether satisfactory arrangement, Jacob said Toni could stay in one of the vacant rooms at Harte Street. Mistris Simpkin had engaged a housekeeper and maid to keep the house and showroom clean, and the rooms ready in case they were needed.

Once Toni was settled, Jacob called a meeting at Harte Street. Present were Roberto, Toni and Peter Tyzack, the chief Capo. Jacob introduced Toni and then went straight to the matter in hand.

'As you know, the lampwork jewellery proved very popular in Paris. However, we had the advantage of the Catholic League reception when Lady Maria wearing the rose necklace and the Duke of Guise urging the League to support me, had a major impact on sales.'

'I assume you plan to have some sort of Grand Opening?' said Roberto.

'Oh, I think so,' said Jacob. 'After all, they've been very successful in the past. What about you Roberto, you're looking very thoughtful. Have you any ideas?'

'I was just wondering if there was any chance of getting the Queen to wear some of the glass jewellery. That would make a huge impression on the ladies of the court. You know how they like to copy her fashions.'

Jacob had been thinking along the same lines, but once again Roberto had shown his ability to get to the heart of a problem. He clapped him on the back so enthusiastically that Roberto winced.

'Sorry, Roberto,' he apologised, 'but that's a brilliant idea. The only problem is finding the right necklace to attract her approval.'

'Do you know what her favourite colours are?' enquired Toni.

'I'd have to say black and white. She tends to wear them a lot. What had you in mind?'

'Will you excuse me a moment.' So saying, Toni hurried out and returned a few minutes later carrying a wooden box. Opening it, he pulled out a number of drawstring pouches and began to look inside them. At the fourth one he gave a smile of satisfaction and carefully poured its contents on to the table. A cascade of large and small glass beads rolled out. They were all matt black in colour, but had lovely silver and gold foil detailing inside that gave the beads a beautiful shimmering effect. From another pouch, he produced some clear crystal beads over silver foil.

As they examined them, Toni explained that he could make up a single or two strand necklace, with matching earrings, that would look magnificent with a black and white dress. He took out a piece of silk and began to thread the beads, alternating the black and crystal beads, with gold disc spacers in between.

Taking two round discs, one a plain black, the other black with silver and gold, he placed them at the centre like a pendant. He then placed three drops in crystal and silver below them.

'That's only a rough idea of how I see it. What do you think?'

Jacob was fulsome in his praise. 'It looked so simple the way you put it together, but I couldn't have done anything nearly as good without extensive study.'

'I had a good tutor and I've been studying for five years.' He shrugged. 'Making the necklace is a relatively simple task. Getting the Queen to wear it is another matter entirely.'

It was Jacob's turn to look thoughtful. Then a smile lit up his face. 'I know the very person to give it to the Queen and I believe she might well be persuaded to wear it. You make up the necklace and earrings Toni, and leave me to do the rest.'

An opportunity for Maria to visit the Queen came a week later. Maria received a letter from the Queen inviting her go to Greenwich. Having dismissed the ladies-in-waiting so they could talk on intimate terms, Elizabeth welcomed her back to court. 'It is good to have you back. I wish you would take up my offer of a place in my household. I do so enjoy the chance to talk to you. You are like a breath of fresh air. I have not been able to talk so freely with a woman since Kat Ashley, my old governess retired.' Maria had been told the Kat Ashley had been the only mother figure that Elizabeth had known during her formative years. It was a great compliment to be compared to her.

Maria smiled. 'It is very kind of you, Your Majesty. You know I value our friendship. However, I'm not sure that would still be so if I was a member of your household. I would not be free to speak as I do now. In any case, I have too much to do to look after my children and my husband.'

'That rogue of a husband of yours has certainly kept you busy these last few years,' said Elizabeth. Despite these words, her amused tone told Maria that she did not consider Jacob to be a rogue at all. 'What is he up to now? I understand you have been in Paris.'

Maria explained about the new showroom in Paris and its success. She produced a beautifully tooled leather case and gave it to the Queen. 'My husband asked me to present this to you with his compliments. It has been made especially to match your favourite colours.'

The Queen opened the case and gasped when she saw the necklace and matching earrings. 'Why, I do believe they're made of glass.'

'Yes they are. Would you like me to help you to put them on?'

When Elizabeth nodded, Maria unfastened the pearls the Queen was wearing and replaced them with the necklace. When the earrings had been added, she handed the Queen her mirror. 'What do you think, madame?'

The Queen was silent for a while and examined her reflection carefully in the mirror. Turning to Maria with a slight smile she said, 'Your husband is a very clever man. I wish it was possible to have both of you here in my court. You may tell your husband that I will wear the necklace at court tomorrow when the envoy from my little frog arrives.' This was her pet name for Alençon, her French suitor, ever since he had given her a beautiful enamelled brooch in the shape of a frog, with little diamonds for eyes.

'I like the necklace well and it will be no hardship to wear it. No doubt the ladies of the court will be besieging his showroom after tomorrow and I may even visit myself to see what else he has to offer.'

They talked for nearly an hour, mainly about Alençon, who was the youngest son of Henri II of France and Catherine de' Medici. Elizabeth thought she could bring herself to love him, but still had her duty as Queen of England. Even if she was to marry him, France and England must agree an alliance against Spain, to keep England's sovereignty over her own subjects including their religion. This was proving a stumbling block for France and despite the tenderness of her feelings for Alençon, Elizabeth was on the verge of rejecting him.

Apologising for talking so much about her problems, Elizabeth asked about Maria's children and the death of little Meg. The Queen was very sympathetic and Maria found she could talk about it to someone outside the family for the first time without becoming emotional. Of course, the hurt was still there, but death was after all, part of life and life had to go on. With this thought, she abstractedly stroked her stomach.

Eventually, the Queen received a message that obliged her to curtail Maria's visit. But before she left, Elizabeth gave Maria a beautifully illustrated prayer book. The cover was in ivory with an inlaid cross and each page had the most gorgeously illustrated text. On the flyleaf, the Queen had written "To my friend Maria Bell, with great affection, Elizabeth R".

'Please accept this as a token of my regard,' said Elizabeth, embracing Maria warmly. 'You will always be welcome and I look forward to your next visit. Don't forget, you must come when the gardens are in full bloom this year. You have always been either having babies or dashing off to Venice in previous years.'

Maria promised she would do her best to comply and as the ladies-in-waiting returned, gave a deep curtsey and left for home. When she told Jacob that the Queen would wear the necklace next day at court, he was delighted. 'She also said you were a very clever man and that the ladies of the court will be besieging your showroom after tomorrow and that she might pay a visit herself.'

Jacob gasped. 'I'm not sure that's wise! But we may not need to have a grand opening ceremony after all!'

Maria looked at him so seriously he thought there was something wrong. 'What is it, Maria, you look so solemn, is something troubling you?'

'Oh no, nothing like that,' said Maria. 'There's something I want to tell you and I was not sure how you would take it.' Taking his hand she placed it on her stomach. 'I'm with child again.'

Jacob's look of love and delight said it all and her face was radiant.

'Oh, darling,' he said fondly, 'I'm so pleased. You're absolutely sure?'

'I'm sure. I have not had my flux these last two months.'

A huge smile lit up his face. 'Paris,' he breathed. 'Of course. Now that night you broke your fast is even more special. We must call Doctor Nguyên immediately.'

Chapter Twelve
London, December, 1581

Despite Jacob's expectations of his imminent involvement in the Duke of Guise's plot, in fact there had been no contact with Francis Throckmorton, nor had Henri sent any messages. The weeks leading up to Christmas had been very busy, particularly with the new fleur-de-lis range of jewellery. It had proved to be hugely popular, particularly with husbands and lovers, since it was far less expensive. It was popular with the ladies because they could have a necklace made up especially to match their latest new dress. Of course, the black beads were particularly popular since the Queen had worn them as promised.

Two days after the reception for the French envoy, Jacob was in the Harte Street showroom talking to Toni, who was very gratified by the success of the jewellery.

'It was a fortunate day for my family,' he said, 'when you came to our showroom in Paris. You have some wonderful patrons.'

'Patrons are of no use unless you have the right product,' said Jacob seriously. 'It is your designs that are bringing in the sales.' He was about to say more, when a coach pulled up outside. 'It looks as though we have another customer Toni. You'd better make sure the display is ready.'

Elizabeth, Countess of Shrewsbury, or Bess of Hardwick as she was popularly known, swept into the showroom like a tornado. Jacob knew her well from his visits to her beautiful house, Chatsworth, in Darbieshire. She was one of the most prominent women in England after the Queen. She had been a beauty in her youth, but now her figure was rather stout. Her most striking feature was her red hair and the magnificent four strand, matching pearl necklace she always wore. She was rich in her own right, owning property and land thanks to her three previous husbands, each one richer than the last, her present husband the Earl of Shrewsbury, was the guardian of the Scottish Queen. Bess was altogether a very redoubtable woman.

She embraced Jacob, kissing him full on the mouth - an English custom that Jacob still had not become used to. Toni seeing the exchanges, looked at Jacob with an amused expression and raised his eyebrows.

'What can I do for you this time, my lady,' said Jacob, when he had recovered. 'Do you want some more of my drinking glasses?' He had made a set of matching glasses for Bess as well as an armorial goblet for Mary Stuart when she had been held at Chatsworth. Was it really twelve years ago!

Bess smiled archly. 'It's the jewellery I have come to see. I was at court for the visit of the French envoy when the Queen wore your necklace and now all the court are fighting to get one.' Before Jacob could answer, she spied Toni by the jewellery display. 'Ah, is this the young man who makes the jewellery?'

She swept over to the display and imperiously instructed Toni to show her the collection of jewellery. Toni bowed over her extended hand and then began to exhibit his designs. Jacob, seeing the lad was doing very well without him, went into his office.

A little while later, Toni called him over. 'The *contessa* likes the jewellery, but has said she prefers pearls and from the necklace she is wearing, I can see why.' He looked thoughtful and then said to the countess, 'I believe I have an idea how we can combine your love of pearls with our lampwork beads. We have always supplied pearls from Cathay, as they are very popular in Paris, although we have never combined the two.' He excused himself for a short while and went back to his workroom.

Jacob asked Bess how things were at Chatsworth and, knowing that Jacob was a true friend who could be trusted with confidences, she began to complain that keeping Mary Stuart was bankrupting her. 'I've been forced to lend my husband a large sum of money to make up the shortfall between what the Queen pays for her upkeep and what it really costs. He has been forced to mortgage some of his properties as well. If this keeps on we will both be paupers.' Before Jacob could comment, Toni returned carrying a sketch pad and several large beads in different colours. They were either square, or discs. First he showed the Countess the pad on which he had sketched a design for a simple rope of pearls, separated by small garnets, gathered together just above the breast with a single, large, round lampwork bead. Attached to this bead were two short strands, with drops at the end.

Bess pored over the beads and then selected a round, disc-shaped red bead with an attractive pattern of silver and gold foil embedded in it. 'This one,' she announced. 'It will go perfectly with my black and gold fur-trimmed dress. How soon can you make it?'

'Will tomorrow afternoon be satisfactory?'

As she told Jacob before she left, 'This necklace is to cheer me up, but please don't mention what I said about our finances to anyone. They might not understand as you do.'

She collected the necklace the next day, wearing a black and gold dress. 'I'm delighted with it,' she exclaimed in great satisfaction, 'but you haven't told me the price as yet.' When Toni gave her the invoice, she turned to Jacob. 'Why, it is but a fraction of what I paid for my pearls.'

Jacob pretended to look downcast and turned to Toni. 'I told you we were selling the jewellery too cheaply!' he said, mischievously.

Later, in view of the extra trade the jewellery was attracting, Jacob had a word with Quiff. 'I'm thinking of taking on a couple of apprentices. One to work in the showroom, selling drinking glasses, the other to work with Toni. He needs some help both in making the jewellery and doing the running about.'

'That would be good, but its not a simple thing to do,' Quiff told him. 'The law is archaic and applies in very complicated ways.

'I found that out, when I bought out your apprenticeship,' Jacob said, 'goodness knows how many years ago now.' He looked at Quiff remembering the way Quiff's previous master had beaten and starved him. The confident strong man in front of him bore no resemblance to his former cringing apprentice. Except for the white streak in his hair from which he took his name. I'll have a word with Thomas Pepper, our lawyer,' he said. 'He sorted yours out very satisfactorily.'

'It was the best day of my life when I came to work for you,' said Quiff with feeling. 'I'm sure Thomas Pepper will sort it out. Probably charge you a fat fee I don't doubt.'

Which is exactly what happened. Jacob, as the employer of the apprentices, promised in writing: *to teach and instruct them, or cause them to be taught or instructed, finding unto his said apprentices, meat, drink, apparel, lodging and other necessities for seven and a half years or longer according to the custom of the City of London.*

The two new apprentices were both seventeen, and had to give this oath which was formidable:

We will faithfully serve our said master, his secrets keep, his lawful commands everywhere gladly do. We shall not commit fornication nor contract matrimony within the said term of years. We shall not play at dice, cards, tables or other lawful game, nor shall we haunt taverns or playhouses nor absent ourselves from the master's service day or night unlawfully.

The length of the term of apprenticeship was seven and a half years on average, but it could not be terminated until the apprentice reached the age of twenty-four. As well as signing the Article of Agreement with their master, the apprentices were required to write out an oath of loyalty to prove they were literate.

As Quiff remarked to them later, 'You are very fortunate to be in the employ of Master Jacob. He treats you well and you have the chance to grow into good jobs with a thriving company. I've just come back from running our Paris showroom for several weeks.' But he gave a note of warning, 'Master Jacob will not tolerate idleness, or drunkenness and neither will Roberto or I. So mind your step.'

He handed them both a club, a round heavy stick, about five hands long. 'I'm sure you know what these are for. You must guard your master's premises and if you hear the cry, "Clubs! Clubs!" a fellow apprentice is in trouble and you go to his aid. It might be you who needs help one day.'

Christmas was a happy time for the Bell family. Since the apprentices lived a considerable distance away and could not afford to go home so soon into their apprenticeship, they were welcomed into family events organised for all the workers.

After the excitement of Christmas Day had worn off and they were alone, Maria broached a subject with Jacob that she had been mulling over for some time.

'I want to talk to you about Rico.'

Jacob looked puzzled. 'Has he done something wrong?'

'No, nothing like that,' said Maria with a laugh. 'Please just listen without asking questions while I explain.

'A few weeks ago, I was talking to Master Armitage about Rico and he told me what I am about to tell you. Not before,' she added, 'I had a long chat with Rico.'

Jacob was still looking puzzled.

'How strongly do you feel about Rico joining you at the Crouched Friars?'

How did he feel? That was a good question. Jacob had not given the matter a lot of thought, but as Rico was now almost twelve, perhaps he should have done. 'To be honest, I've tried to keep my own preferences out of it. I have to admit though, that Rico has not shown anything other than a polite interest in glassmaking. I'm not sure that he has the feel for it as I did at his age.'

Maria nodded. 'When I talked to him later, I discovered that there is something he's really keen on.'

'What's that?' asked Jacob with interest.

'The sea,' said Maria. 'He wants to be a ship's captain and master of his own ships.'

'I see,' said Jacob thoughtfully, casting his mind back to all the times he'd seen Rico listening intently to Captain Roberts and Admiral Hawkins as they told him stories about their voyages. 'It hadn't occurred to me that he might have more than a passing interest in the navy.'

'It's a lot more than that. His tutor tells me that he's been studying navigation in his spare time and has already achieved a standard well beyond the usual one for his age.'

'Well, I've always had a more than passing interest in the sea,' Jacob shook his head ruefully. He had been all for taking letters of marque from the Queen, becoming a privateer and heading for the Azores to capture a Portuguese carrack laden with jewels and spices, when he thought he'd lost Maria. The nearest he'd come to doing that was the small cog they had captured off Portugal. Still, there had been some nice jewels in the booty, including Maria's engagement ring.

'Not to mention getting involved in galley fights and pitched battles!' laughed Maria.

'That's true,' Jacob chuckled. 'However, going back to Rico. I have no objection at all, if that's what Rico wants. My father allowed me to follow my heart's desire and I can do no less for my son.' Maria hugged him and Jacob promised to speak to Rico soon. 'First, I'll have a word with Captain Roberts when he returns from France. It may be that Rico could serve as an ensign with *The Crystal.*' He could see that Maria was pleased, but wished her to understand that the life at sea was not easy.

'Make no mistake, Maria. Should Rico take this as his career, he will find it's a hard life. Captain Roberts will not give him any special favours just because he's my son. He'll treat him exactly like the other ensigns. But to be fair, life is not quite as bad for a merchant sailor as it is for a naval rating. Ships of the Navy are much more crowded than *The Crystal.*'

'I'm sure that Rico will not look for any special considerations,' Maria said confidently.

'And now my dear,' said Jacob, 'I think it is time you had a rest. You're looking rather tired.'

Maria rubbed her swelling stomach. 'Doctor Nguyên was saying the same thing this morning. It's really good to know he is keeping an eye on me. He's not getting any younger and he's supposed to be easing off.'

'I know,' said Jacob. 'I get his report every visit. His report this morning was excellent, although he did say, "Lady Maria tired. This normal. Make to lie down and rest.".' Maria chuckled at Jacob's imitation of the doctor's accent and promised she would do as she was told.

Chapter Thirteen
London, March, 1582

As the snows of Winter thawed and turned to blustering March winds, Jacob had neither received word from the Duke of Guise, nor heard anything from Walsingham. He decided to stop worrying and deal with some of the problems that were occurring at the Crouched Friars Glass-works.

For some time the supply of beech for the furnace had been an escalating problem. Despite the concessions granted to Jacob by the Queen, all the beech woods for scores of miles around had been totally depleted.

To alleviate the problem, Jacob had been experimenting with the use of coal which was readily available and produced a suitable temperature in the furnace. Unfortunately, the fumes also turned the glass a distinctly yellow colour. He was now experimenting with different sources to eliminate the problem.

About two years earlier, Jacob had acquired a further part of the old Crouched Friars monastery. In it, there was a large room that was used as a temporary warehouse for storing an emergency supply of beech billets. Another smaller room had been converted into an experimental workshop. The furnace, much smaller than a typical furnace, had only two glory holes for melting the glass mixture. New designs could be tried out, without affecting production; indeed at times supplemented it. The separate entrance to the workshop provided Jacob with a degree of privacy, which he valued.

Today, Jacob was trying out a new source of coal brought from Newcastle in the north of England. Taking a pontil, a solid rod slightly thinner than, but similar to a blow pipe, Jacob attached some of the molten glass from his latest experiment and roughly shaped it on the marver, a highly polished flat iron plate. He then allowed the molten glass to cool before detaching it. Examining it against a piece of similarly sized glass produced from the wood-fired furnace he gave an exasperated sigh. Whilst the glass was still better than with the last source of coal from

Nottingham he had tried, it was still tinged with yellow.

Adding the sample to those already on the old table that served as a desk, he sat down and made an entry in his notes. Putting down his quill, he lowered his head to his hands wondering what his next step could be.

There was a knock on the door and Roberto entered.

'Hello Jacob, how did the tests go?'

'Not well I'm afraid,' Jacob grimaced. 'I've run out of samples and ideas at the moment.'

He indicated the table. 'That's the last of the samples and although the result was a lot better, it's still not satisfactory.' He showed Roberto the latest samples of glass.

Roberto shook his head. 'That's really a pity, because we're struggling to get supplies now. Our stock has gone down by over half in the last few weeks. Not only that, but the prices are going up.'

'We need to supplement it somehow. It's a shame we can't use oak.' Oak was reserved for shipbuilding, but it would be a much better fuel for the furnace. 'How did you get on with the other types of wood?'

'Not too badly, but they burn more quickly and make a lot more ash. We'll have to clean out the furnace more often, which will cut down production time and we will need to keep a larger stock of billets.'

'Well, let's try that for now,' said Jacob, although they were likely to have difficulties keeping up with orders if production was slowed down. 'Until I can think of some way we can use coal, or we locate a new source of beechwood, there's little else we can do.' He gave an exasperated sigh. 'There must be a way of using coal, but for the life of me, I can't think how.'

'It couldn't have come at a worse time, with the Paris showroom doing so well. Sales are going well there.' He gave a lop sided smile, 'Any chance of me going with you to Paris next time. I'd love to see it.'

'Jacob returned the smile. 'I don't see why not, so long as everything here is properly organised.'

There was another knock on the door.

Jacob opened it and Quiff entered, producing a letter from his doublet. 'It's from Walsingham,' he said. 'He sent his houseman to deliver it, but as he's a member of the Ring, the cheeky devil brought it to me. He knew he'd get paid for it, even though he should have brought it straight to you.'

'Obviously a young man who's going to do well in the world. Shows he's got a bit of intelligence.'

'Downright animal cunning, I'd call it,' said Quiff, but his smile told Jacob he wasn't serious. 'I'll leave it to you then, Master Jacob.' And off he went with a cheery whistle.

Jacob took the letter to the table and carefully opened the seal. It was a very short note from Walsingham, asking Jacob to meet him at the safe house the following day at ten o'clock.

He looked at Roberto. 'I have to meet Walsingham,' he said. 'I won't be coming in tomorrow morning,'

'Do you want me to come with you?' enquired Roberto.

'No, you're better employed here. He doesn't say what he wants, but things seem to have gone very quiet. I've not seen hide nor hair of Francis Throckmorton, so I assume the Duke of Guise is still in negotiations with Rome and Spain.'

The following morning he was at the safe house punctually at ten o'clock. He was shown into the study where Walsingham was waiting. As soon as Jacob had sat down, Walsingham enquired if he had received any contact from either Throckmorton or the Duke of Guise.

'Nothing I'm afraid.'

Walsingham looked serious. 'I was afraid you would say that. Throckmorton is still in France and one of my remaining agents has been shadowing him for weeks. He has not attempted to make contact with the Guises, or with the Archbishop of Glasgow.'

Walsingham looked frustrated. 'We don't seem to be getting anywhere at the moment. Colonel Young is in Scotland with Sir Robert Bowes, Treasurer of Berwick. They have been stirring up things against d'Aubigny or Lennox as he chooses to be known since King James VI made him the Earl. Unfortunately, the young King will not hear a word against him.' Negotiations with Scotland were proving to be very difficult. Burghley was negotiating with Mary Stuart to effect her return to Scotland in return for giving up her claim to the English throne. He was also negotiating with Mary's son, James VI, to allow her go to Scotland.

'How strong is her claim to the throne in Scotland?' asked Jacob.

'Oh very strong. She is the only surviving legitimate child of James V of Scotland. When he died, she was only six years old, and nine months later she was crowned Queen. She was Queen of France for a short while until her husband Francis II died. When she returned to Scotland she married Henry Stuart, Lord Darnley becoming, not only Queen of Scotland, but also second in succession, after Elizabeth, to the English throne, under the ordinary laws of succession. However, fortunately Henry VIII's will, excluded the Stuarts from succeeding to the English throne, confirmed by the Third Act of Succession.' He saw Jacob's baffled expression and gave a rueful smile. 'Complicated isn't it. Mary Stuart of course was still Queen of Scotland when she was forced to abdicate and flee to England, after a bloody civil war. She evidently thought that Elizabeth, her first cousin once removed, would help her to regain the Scottish throne.' He sighed. 'Instead, she became the biggest threat to Elizabeth she has ever faced. It's a pity her conscience wouldn't allow her to send Mary back to Scotland.'

'How are things going with her son?'

'The young King is adamant she cannot return,' he said in exasperation. 'She would no more give up her claim to the throne than her son would allow her into Scotland. Nor will James VI hear anything against Lennox. However, there is a faction among the Scottish lords who are considerably more amenable. They resent the influence that Lennox has over the King. The Elders of the Kirk are also preaching against Lennox, since they believe his Catholic sympathies will bring the old religion back to Scotland.' Walsingham shook his head sadly. 'Unfortunately, those lords opposing Lennox do not wield enough power to lessen Lennox's influence over James VI. Lennox still managed to get Robert Montgomery, a Catholic very sympathetic to the French, elected as Chancellor of the University of Glasgow. That was despite the combined opposition of the lords, the Kirk and the students.' He turned to Jacob with a deep frown on his face. 'Have you, or the Ring, heard anything of a Scottish Jesuit named William Holt?'

'I'm afraid I've never heard of him. Who is he?'

'He's a priest working with Father Creighton to promote the invasion of England through Scotland. Bowes believes he is already in Scotland and might be connected with George Seton, the seventh Lord Seton.

'Do you want me to ask the Ring if they have heard of them?'

'That would be useful,' said Walsingham, nodding thoughtfully. 'My agents in Scotland informed Colonel Young that they suspect Holt has come to Scotland secretly and is hiding out somewhere.' He frowned and looked very exasperated. 'I must admit to being somewhat frustrated at the lack of progress in thwarting this plot. It is a very serious threat to the realm and yet all of my efforts seem to have come to nought. We are in need of some information, or some development that will allow us to take action to forestall it.'

'I can understand your frustration,' said Jacob. 'Unfortunately, I have no members of the Ring in Scotland, but I will ask Quiff to contact those members with any connections with Catholic families, or Scotland, to find out what they can. If I'm honest, I don't hold out a lot of hope that we will be able to assist you in this matter.'

'I understand, but there is another matter in which you can,' Walsingham said. 'I have, through intermediaries, tried to persuade James VI that an alliance with England would be to the benefit of both countries. However, the influence of Lennox was making that difficult. He obviously favours the French. During the negotiations, the King suggested a pension of five thousand pounds a year from England would ease many of the difficulties but, unfortunately, the Queen would not sanction such a sum and suggested a cheaper alternative.'

'Oh! What sort of alternative?'

'We would like to present King James VI with some of your special glasses.'

'Special glasses?'

'Something similar to the armorial goblet you made for his

mother, Mary Stuart. You could use his new arms as King of the Scots. How long would they take to make?'

'I'm not sure. If I can employ Anthony de Lyle, a diamond point engraver, probably about three weeks. He's a good engraver, but I warn you, he doesn't come cheap.'

'Is *The Crystal* available for a charter, to take them to Berwick.'

'It could be, but I would need to speak to Captain Roberts about fitting in Berwick.'

In the end, they agreed a price of five hundred pounds, which included the hire of the ship and delivery of the glass to Sir Robert Bowes in Berwick. Jacob made the condition that he must deliver some glass to Paris first.

'That would be acceptable,' Walsingham said. 'You could find out why the Duke of Guise hasn't been in touch.'

'I was planning to anyway,' said Jacob. 'I'll be taking Roberto with me to see the Paris showroom.'

Leaving Walsingham to his thoughts, Jacob set off for Harte Street. He needed to check if there were sufficient goblets for James VI. As he walked down the hill he noticed that there was a lot of yellowish smoke coming from many chimneys. Instead of the pleasant pungent smell of beechwood, the air had a distinctly acrid stench of sulphur. More and more households were burning coal on their fires and Jacob missed the aroma of burning beechwood that reminded him of Venice. No wonder the glass was turning yellow when they used coal in the furnace.

Entering the hallway, he went into the kitchen area to warm himself by the fire. There was a delicious smell of cooking coming from a large covered pan on the fire, which was burning coal. The temptation to taste the stew was too great and, seeing the cook was elsewhere, he lifted the lid and dipped in a spoon. The stew was delicious.

Just then the cook entered. She started to scold him, not realising who he was as his back was towards her. 'Get that lid back on the pot before the fumes spoil the taste you silly clod. Oh! Master Jacob, I thought it ...' She broke off in confusion.

Jacob laughed at her expression. 'Caught in the act again!' Then a thought suddenly struck him. 'Does cooking stew over coal really change its taste?'

'Oh yes, Master Jacob,' she said, taking the lid from him. 'You have to keep the lid on or it doesn't taste right. Of course, we also have the lid on to stop it boiling dry.' She took the proffered spoon, gave the mixture a stir and put the lid firmly back on. 'We didn't have any problem when we used beechwood.'

With a muttered apology, Jacob turned on his heel and rushed down to the Crouched Friars. Three hours later he had his answer to his problem. Putting a lid on the fireclay pot when the glass mixture was first melted, totally prevented it from going yellow in the fumes from the burning coal.

Chapter Fourteen
France, March, 1582

The two day ride to Paris had been long, dusty and exhausting and Jacob and Roberto were pleased to see the Villa Saint Germaine. The following morning, after a good night's sleep, Jacob showed Roberto around the showroom. Roberto was admiring the layout and decorations when Michael Peters arrived. Michael was twenty-five, an English Catholic, married to the youngest daughter of the Mayor of Paris and helped, until recently, in her family's import/export business. He had taken over from Quiff and was doing an excellent job at the Villa Saint Germaine.

'I have a message for you from the Duke of Guise,' Peters informed Jacob. 'He wishes to see you as soon as you have settled in.'

'When was this?' said Jacob.

'Yesterday, in the morning, just after we'd opened,' said Peters.

'That's strange. Did you tell him I was on my way to Paris?'

'No, he just sent a message by a servant.' Curious, thought Jacob, he must have been informed of my arrival in Calais and that I had left for Paris. To know about this yesterday morning, his informant must have ridden all the way from Calais in one day. Perhaps he'd set up a chain of messengers: Walsingham used a series of riders to get messages quickly from Scotland and distant parts of England..

When they'd finished, he set off with Roberto for the Château de Lorraine. After a short delay, they were shown into the ornate study, where Henri was seated at the desk writing. The Duke greeted them warmly. 'Thank you for coming so promptly,' he said, 'and welcome to Paris again, *Monsieur Rosso.* In much pleasanter circumstances than when last we met.'

Jacob was surprised that the Duke remembered Roberto, it was almost twelve years since Roberto had traced Jacob to the Château de Lorraine. When they were seated, the Duke enquired why

Jacob was in Paris.

'For three reasons,' explained Jacob. 'Firstly to bring some stock for the showroom. Secondly to show Roberto the fruition of his idea for a Paris showroom and finally to see you.'

'Oh! For what reason?'

'I thought it would be better to tell you personally about a commission I have been given by Queen Elizabeth.' Jacob could see Henri was puzzled. 'She has commissioned me to make and deliver to Berwick a set of armorial glasses for King James VI of Scotland, as a token of her regard. *The Crystal* will go straight to Berwick when we arrive on board.'

Henri gave Roberto a dubious look and Jacob, noticing it, hurried to reassure him. 'You can speak freely in front of Roberto, I vouch for him completely. He is not only my partner, he is my confidant, my friend and my willing helper. I have no secrets from him.'

'Very well then,' said Henri, 'I accept your word on this.' He smiled at Roberto. 'Forgive me for being cautious, Monsieur Rosso, but it doesn't pay to be too trusting in my circumstances.' Roberto acknowledged the apology and Henri then handed Jacob a letter. 'This is for you. I have not sealed it as yet, as I want you to read it first.'

Jacob saw it was addressed to Charles of Lorraine. He remembered him from the Catholic League reception. He was Henri's brother and his trusted lieutenant, commanding the League's army against the Huguenots. The letter instructed Charles to hand over two thousand gold crowns from the funds he had 'liberated' from the Huguenots at Fère in Picardy.

'Two thousand gold crowns! What for?'

'Not what,' said Henri, 'but who. It is to go to Lennox in Scotland.' He smiled. 'It is quite fortunate you are going to Berwick since that is close to the Scottish border. I was going to instruct the Bishop of Ross to arrange its delivery to North Berwick, close to Edinburgh, and ask you to smuggle it into England in one of your crates. Since you are able to take it direct to Scotland, it will remove much of the danger of it being intercepted by Walsingham. It will also arrive much sooner.'

Jacob looked at the letter again. The second page granted

Jacob safe passage through the Catholic lines and instructed all members of the League to offer their full co-operation. 'I have no idea where North Berwick is,' he said, 'apart from your description that it is near Edinburgh.' He was thinking furiously how he could let Walsingham know about this. 'I will have to consult with the captain to confirm that *The Crystal* will be able to dock there.' 'I understand your caution,' Henri said, 'but I am assured by Lennox that there is a deep water channel and anchorage at the dockside.'

The following morning Jacob and Roberto, with their packhorse, headed up the winding Oise valley towards Fère. As they rode along, Jacob thought how fortunate it had been that Rico had asked to stay on *The Crystal* instead of going to Paris with them. This was no jaunt for a young lad. He glanced across at Roberto. It was reassuring to have Roberto at his side again. There was no one he would rather have with him if they landed in a tight spot, as well they might.

Late in the afternoon they reached the fort which was now the headquarters of the League's army. Having shown their credentials, they were conducted with great respect to the refectory where Charles had instructed the servants to set two places on his right, the place of honour. He waved them to sit down, bidding them welcome. Once the courtesies were over, he told Jacob there would be a small delay in arranging the gold.

'The Huguenots have not taken kindly to being ousted from this part of Fère,' he said. 'They seem to resent the fact that we have recaptured it. After all,' he said with a shrug, 'Condé and his men only captured it for the first time in November two years ago.' Jacob thought at first he was being humorous, but he was serious, so Jacob made no comment.

'We have been under attack for two days now,' Charles continued. 'Not that I fear we will be overrun,' he hastened to add. 'It's the civilians I am concerned about. There have been some instances of looting and rape by our army, which I will not tolerate. I will hang those responsible. I just hope that there will not be any reprisals against the Catholic civilians.'

'It certainly won't help matters,' said Jacob. He was aware that large numbers of innocent women and children had been slaughtered by Catholic soldiers and civilians, both during and since Saint Bartholomew's Day almost ten years earlier. In total many thousands of Huguenots had died. Fère was only one more small grievance to add to the many.

Charles nodded. 'I agree. I'm a soldier and war is war. I will happily kill soldiers who oppose me, but civilians should not be treated the same.' He sighed, 'It was finding the gold that started it off. The Huguenots had systematically stripped the town of all its valuables and put them in a strongly defended farmhouse. My army advanced very quickly and cut off their escape and our German mercenaries stormed the farmhouse. Unfortunately, they became incensed because their colonel and a number of their men were killed in the process and they went on the rampage.'

'Did they kill all the people in the farmhouse?' said Jacob.

'Fortunately, I arrived in time to prevent a complete massacre.' He shrugged. 'As it was only the owner of the farmhouse, his wife, his three daughters, two servant girls and six of the defenders were spared. I sent the mercenaries off with their second in command, a captain, to lead them in the attack on the town and left foot soldiers to guard the gold and the prisoners. The Germans were at the forefront of securing the whole of the east bank for us.' He gave a shrug. 'Unfortunately, the west bank of the Oise is still in Huguenot hands, but it is only a matter of time before we oust them.'

They talked until the meal was over and then Charles advised them to have an early night as they would be leaving early to fetch the gold. He signalled for a servant and they were conducted to their chamber. When they were alone, Roberto told Jacob of what he had heard and seen at the table. 'The German captain on my right had the impression that I knew no German, but I knew enough to tell he was not pleased about something. Not only that, but when the Duke of Lorraine was talking about hanging looters and rapists, he seemed frightened and said something about gold and tomorrow to his sergeant. I couldn't catch any more.'

'You did very well,' said Jacob, 'I missed all of that, as my attention was on Charles. We must be on our guard. The Germans might decide to take the gold and run if they were responsible for the rapes and looting.'

The next morning after a frugal meal of watered wine and bread, they collected their horses and went to meet Charles in the courtyard. He was talking to the captain of the mercenaries who was looking far from happy.

Charles rode over and joined them. 'My brother Henri has instructed that you are to take two thousand crowns and deliver them to the Earl of Lennox in Scotland. I assume you have a ship at Calais.'

'Yes, I was already going to Berwick near the Scottish border, so it will be an easy task to combine the two trips.'

'Excellent. Lennox will be able to complete his side of the bargain and our army will soon be in Scotland.' Jacob did his best to look pleased.

Calling over the two leaders, Charles introduced them as Colonel Lefavre of the Light Cavalry and Captain Steiner of the mercenaries. The colonel acknowledged Jacob with a courteous bow, the captain with a nod and a click of his heels.

'Colonel Lefavre will lead the party to fetch the gold,' said Charles briskly, 'and will issue you, Jacob, with the amount arranged by my brother. The remainder he will bring here.' Jacob noted the sour look that Steiner shot at Charles on hearing this news. It was obviously the first time he was aware of the plan. Jacob was even more certain now that Steiner had designs on the gold.

Jacob realised that Charles was looking at him expectantly and muttered an apology. 'Captain Steiner will escort you safely out of the area,' went on Charles, 'and set you on the road to Calais.' Not if I can help it, thought Jacob. It would give them and ideal chance to snatch the gold we have, especially if the rest of it has already been taken away.

Charles handed a letter to Jacob. 'This is your letter of safe passage in case you are stopped by our forces. Fare you well and God speed.'

The ride to the farmhouse on the southern outskirts of Fère took about an hour. As well as the German mercenaries, about fourteen in number, there was a contingent of twenty Light Calvary led by the colonel.

Shortly before they reached their destination, they were confronted by a group of Huguenot foot soldiers. They were no match for the cavalry who easily routed them with heavy casualties. Calling off the pursuit, the colonel urged them on to the farmhouse. It was moated, with a narrow bridge and well-defended entrance. Jacob had no doubt most of the Catholic casualties had happened here.

The colonel took charge at once, sending a squad of defenders to empty the storehouse and distribute the gold between the packhorses. Once this had been completed, he had a word with Jacob. 'I am taking the foot soldiers with me as extra protection in case we meet up with a stronger force of Huguenots on our return. I think it unlikely you will have any trouble on the way to Calais, but if you are in any doubt, Captain Steiner and his Germans will escort you until you are well clear of Fère.'

'They'd be better with you,' said Jacob. He'd no desire to be left alone with the Germans. 'What about the farmhouse and the prisoners?'

'Captain Steiner will give us a half hour start and then release the family, burn the farmhouse and escort the other prisoners to the fort.'

'Burn it?'

'Well,' said Lefavre, 'I can't leave any men here and I don't want it to become a Huguenot stronghold again.' He gave an expressive shrug. 'What else can I do?'

Jacob could see the logic and busied himself storing the gold on the packhorse. When the colonel and his troops had left, Steiner and some of the Germans went to fetch the prisoners and Jacob and Roberto went into the kitchen to top up their water bottles for the ride to Calais. They'd just finished when they heard women screaming and confused shouting coming from the courtyard. Drawing their weapons, they rushed out to find a slaughter going on. The Germans were butchering the Huguenot prisoners and the women were screaming with terror at the murderous scenes. Before they could intervene, they were surrounded by mercenaries and Steiner ordered them to drop their weapons or suffer the same fate as the prisoners. They were then herded over to join Monsieur La Haye, his wife, two daughters and two female servants. Roberto secretly indicated his sleeves, an obvious hint to Jacob that he still had two knives in their concealed sheaths. At least it was a small crumb of comfort and might yet be the means of saving their lives.

Steiner signalled for one of the men to bring Jacob to him. 'If you want to save your neck,' he gloated, 'you'll do as I say. Your French is better than mine, ask La Haye where the rest of his riches are. And tell him not to lie, or there'll be consequences.'

La Haye denied vehemently that there was any more gold and when Jacob conveyed the answer to Steiner, he went over and gave Le Haye an evil smile. 'Not gold, Monsieur, jewels. Your wife and daughters must have had jewels, but only the gold was found.' He held a knife to his throat. 'Now,' he said, in heavily accented French, 'tell me where the jewels are or I will slit your throat.'

Jacob was about to spring forward when he was stopped by two swords pricking into his back and side. He glanced at Roberto and to his mute enquiry gave a slight shake of his head.

Lifting his chin the husband stared unafraid into Steiner's eyes. 'Kill me then and you will never know.'

'So,' said Steiner, stepping back, 'we have a brave one here.'

He turned and smirked at the other mercenaries who were watching with eager anticipation. 'Very well,' he said and made a signal. At once two of his men stepped forward and seizing the prettiest of the two servants began to strip her. The other women began to wail and huddled together, as they realised what was happening. The frightened girl was spread-eagled face down over a large barrel rolled forward by another mercenary.

'Non! Non! Non!' she screamed, at the top of her voice, 'Please I beg you! Oh God, *Non!*' She struggled violently, but to no avail. The two men forced her legs apart and held her helpless as first one man and then another, raped her. Jacob watched in horror, but was helpless. Even the slightest move resulted in the two swords drawing blood. Roberto too was being threatened.

The girl subsided into heartbroken sobs and Steiner held up his hand.

'Enough,' he ordered and turned back to La Haye. 'See what you have forced me to do. Are you still as brave now?' The man said nothing and turned to his wife in mute appeal. Jacob was tensing himself ready to make a move. He just needed a distraction to give Roberto a chance to get his knives out, but it would have to be soon. Once Steiner had their jewels, he would kill them all.

Steiner nodded. 'I thought that might be too easy. He walked in front of the other women. Stopping in front of the wife, he looked her up and down as she cowered away. 'Too old for me,' he said to raucous laughter from his men. He moved in front of the eldest daughter and leered as he examined her well-developed figure. He nodded and the mercenary behind her seized her arms, holding them tightly behind her. Sliding his hands lasciviously over her breasts, Steiner seized her bodice and with a violent wrench, ripped it open exposing her generous breasts. Several of the mercenaries stepped forward for a better look and Jacob felt the sword in his right side ease off as the man craned his head to leer at the girl. Seizing his chance he spun around to his left, lashing out savagely with his left elbow. He gave a grim smile of satisfaction as he felt the man's Adams apple crush under the blow. The man tottered back gasping for breath and, wrenching the sword from his grasp, Jacob ran him through. Turning to meet the expected attack from the other man, he was just in time to see him pitch forward on his face with one of Roberto's knives in his neck.

Picking up his sword, Jacob raced to Roberto's side as, using his second knife, he defended himself desperately against his captor's sword. Jacob, with one violent slash, killed the man, tossed the other sword to Roberto and cried, 'Quickly, Roberto, back to back!'

The next few minutes passed in a desperate blur as they defended against the overwhelming odds ranged against them. Both of them suffered minor cuts and as they tired, it was only a matter of time before one of them was killed. They fought furiously, determined to give a good account of themselves, and already three of their assailants lay dead, but more of the mercenaries came running to finish them.

Suddenly, there was a thunder of hooves and Colonel Lefavre and his cavalry came storming into the courtyard and the mercenaries broke off the attack on the duo to face the new threat.

Panicking, they tried to run, but were cut down before they'd gone a few paces.

Jacob looked around to see what had happened to Steiner. He was holding the frightened daughter in front of him like a shield, his hand fondling her naked breasts, his knife held against her throat. When Jacob strode towards him, he tightened his grip and slid the blade across her throat drawing a little blood. 'Don't come any closer, or she dies,' he roared. Dragging the terrified girl with him, he backed against the wall of the courtyard. Roberto who had been collecting his knives joined Jacob as the cavalry dismounted and formed a semi circle around the desperate German, their heavy cavalry swords at the ready. Two of their number released the servant girl who had mercifully fainted and the other girl cradled her head on her lap, covering her nakedness with her clothes.

Lefavre strode forward and called on Steiner to release the girl. 'You can't get away. Release her. There's been too much blood shed already.'

Steiner sneered. 'Give me your word to let me go free with a head start, or you will be responsible for some more.' He cut a little deeper and blood began trickling down the side of the girl's neck, staining the remnants of her bodice.

Roberto whispered in Jacob's ear. 'I can take him from here Jacob. And I won't be aiming for his arm.'

Jacob stepped alongside Lefavre. 'Let me have a word with him, Lefavre. I have an idea how to end this.' When the colonel agreed, Jacob took a pace forward and Steiner shouted for him to stop or he would disfigure the girl. This drew wails of despair from her mother.

'I will give you a chance to get away with a safe conduct,' said Jacob. 'I have the authority, I hold the Duke of Guise's commission.' He held it up and the colonel gave a small bow in recognition of Jacob's authority.

'And what do you expect me to do in return?' said Steiner, his voice laden with suspicion.

'Release the girl and you will be free to go.'

'Is that all?' Steiner sneered.

Jacob gave a bleak smile. 'Well there is one small condition.'

'I thought as much. What is it?'

'Only that you must kill me first.'

'You would give your life for a piece of Huguenot trash?' Steiner shrugged 'On your head be it then, I will enjoy killing you.' He released the girl and she rushed to her mother who, sobbing, covered her nakedness with a cloak and held her protectively in her arms.

Drawing his sword, Steiner moved towards Jacob, who stood slightly side-on to him with his sword point carelessly lowered. 'Well, Herr Bell. I hope we are going to observe the formalities, I would not like to ...' He didn't complete the sentence, but instead lunged forward with a killing thrust. Unfortunately for him, this was exactly what Jacob had expected him to do. With a contemptuous flick, he parried the thrust and before the German could correct his overextended reach, stepped forward and ran him through. Steiner slumped to his knees, his eyes glazing over. Stepping forward, Jacob placed his foot on Steiner's chest and pulled out his sword. Steiner toppled over, dead before he hit the ground.

Chapter Fifteen
France and Scotland March, 1582

When they were aboard *The Crystal* and the gold was safely stored away, Jacob and Roberto went to the main cabin to see Captain Roberts. When they explained about the gold and the terrible events at Fère, the captain looked puzzled. 'Why did the the Duke of Lorraine return with the cavalry?'

'They never left,' explained Jacob. 'Charles was already suspicious of the German mercenaries. When he left the farmhouse, he went only a short distance leaving a man to keep an eye on things. He only expected them to steal the gold, not to start killing everybody. When he saw what was happening, the man set off to warn the Duke. Unfortunately his horse stepped in a rabbit hole and went lame, so he was forced to leave it and run. By the time the cavalry arrived, we were fighting for our lives. The rest you know.'

'You were taking a chance in challenging the German to kill you.'

Jacob shook his head. 'I didn't think so. The man was a coward and a bully. I was sure he would try to trick me, rather than fight a fair fight and so it proved.' He changed the subject. 'And now if you don't mind, I would like to discuss the change of plan. Have you had time to look at the charts?'

'I have,' said Captain Roberts, 'and the information provided by Lennox is correct. North Berwick is in East Lothian, just around the coast from Berwick, in the Firth of Forth. It's on the south shore, about twenty-five miles from Edinburgh. The harbour is suitable for *The Crystal,* but it's a bit off the beaten track. It's mainly used by pilgrims going to Saint Andrews and by local fishing boats, or so your son tells me. I had him searching through the charts.' Jacob was pleased that Rico was proving useful.

'Sounds ideal for a clandestine meeting with Lennox,' he said. 'How long will it take us to reach Berwick?'

'Assuming we get favourable winds, six to seven days, but it could take twice that if the weather is unkind.'

'Very well then. We'd better leave as soon as possible.'

They arrived in Berwick eight days later and entered at first light with the tide. Jacob was impressed with the way the town was fortified. The ramparts of the town were very high, affording the gunners a clear field of fire at any ship brave enough to attack.

No sooner had they tied up at the quayside, than Sir Robert Bowes, the Treasurer of Berwick came on board. He was shown into the captain's cabin and after the introductions came straight to business. 'King James VI has gone to Perth. It's a long journey by land, is your ship for charter?'

The captain glanced at his chart. 'Perth is on the Tay, north of Edinburgh. I went to Dundee a few years ago, that's only about twenty miles away. From what I remember, the Tay is navigable to Perth.'

'Could *The Crystal* sail right into Perth?' asked Jacob.

'I'm certain it can. I'll check the charts to make sure if you're proposing to go there.'

Jacob then explained about the money he was taking to North Berwick for Lennox from the Duke of Guise. Sir Robert showed no surprise. 'I received a letter from Walsingham advising me you were bringing the glass for the King, but the gold is another matter. This could be the opportunity we've been waiting for.'

'What had you in mind?'

'I know that Lennox is with the King at Perth, so I suspect he will send his man George Douglas to collect the gold. I will get word to the Protestant Lords. They should be able to seize Douglas in Edinburgh, with the gold and any letters sent by the Duke of Guise. This should prove ample proof to the King that Lennox is plotting a Catholic invasion of Scotland. What is more, they will have gold to use judicially in their cause. With that at their disposal, they may even be able to finish Lennox.'

'You will have to make sure that there is no suspicion of my part in all of this.'

'Of course. The information came from Walsingham, and your ship has simply been chartered to deliver the gold.' Sir Robert went ashore shortly afterwards to make the arrangements, returning about an hour later with his men.

Fortunately, the weather was set fair and the winds in their favour, so the voyage went well. They arrived in North Berwick on the high tide and tied up at the quayside just inside the entrance to the small harbour. Sir Robert and his men remained hidden below decks. Shortly after they had arrived, the harbour master came on board and handed Jacob a sealed letter. 'This is for Jacob Bell,' he said, in his strong accent. The letter informed Jacob that Lennox was sending his agent George Douglas to collect the delivery from France.

'Is George Douglas here?' he asked the harbour master.

'He's away to the town, but I've sent my lad to fetch him. He should be here soon, but you'd better be quick, and do your business if you don't want to be here until the morning.' Having said his piece, the harbour master departed and Jacob showed the letter to Sir Robert. 'Ah well then, George Douglas will have to do.'

Douglas and eight men and two packhorses arrived about half an hour later. They were a wild bunch, all wearing tartan trews, with claymores, the Scottish heavy sword with its typical basket hilt, stuck in their belts. The leader also had two dags as well. Captain Roberts was taking no chances and had two swivel guns loaded with canister trained on them and a number of armed sailors at the ready. When they got about ten yards from the gangplank he hailed them. 'That's far enough. Identify yourselves.'

The leader looked at the swivel guns and the heavily armed sailors and held up his hand. Dismounting, he passed his reins to one of the men and handing his weapons to another, swaggered forward a few yards. 'I'm George Douglas,' he called out boldly. 'Call off your men and bring the package you have for me.'

Jacob went down the gangplank and signalled for Douglas to join him. 'You'll forgive our caution,' he said. 'But we're in a strange harbour and when nine heavily armed men come towards you, it's best to take no chances.' He signalled to the captain and two of the sailors carried the package and placed it in front of Douglas, then hurried back on board. Jacob handed Douglas a packet of letters and turning his back, Douglas signalled his men to bring the packhorses.

'I'll leave you to it then,' said Jacob. 'We have to get under way before the tide turns.'

'Aye,' said Douglas and began to examine the packages. He didn't even glance at Jacob as he went on board and the gangplank was raised.

Because of difficulties with the tides and the possibility of Lennox learning of *The Crystal's* involvement with Sir Robert, he and his men were set ashore at Dundee. *The Crystal* then set course for London and as soon as they docked at Somers Key, Jacob and Roberto said farewell and set off for their respective homes. Rico stayed on board to help with re-provisioning.

By the time Jacob arrived at Mark Street it was already getting dark. As he entered, Doctor Nguyên was just about to leave. 'How is Maria?' asked Jacob anxiously.

'She suffering from back pain. All very normal. Mother carrying child near birth time often has same. Have massaged pain away. Wife asleep now, please not to disturb. Expect baby to arrive in two weeks time. I come every day, but you send for me if baby comes before. Have instructed Anna what to do. She very sensible lady.'

Jacob thanked him and Jack Petts helped him on with his cloak. Picking up his bamboo case he bowed to Jacob. 'Please to excuse, Master Bell. Have another patient to see.' He bowed again and hurried off up the drive with Jack Petts.

Jacob watched him leave and when Jack returned asked if the children were in bed. 'Yes, Master Jacob, since about an hour ago.' Jacob was about to go to see if Maria was still sleeping when the bell at the gate rang.

'I wonder what the doctor has forgotten this time? said Jack. 'He's getting quite absent-minded.'

However, when he returned, it was not with the doctor but with a messenger from Walsingham. He informed Jacob that Walsingham wished to see him immediately as the matter was very urgent. Jacob gave a huge sigh. He had not even had a chance to remove his cloak before Walsingham was chasing him. But since

Maria and the children were asleep, he reluctantly agreed.

When he met Walsingham Jacob left him in no doubt how he felt, but Walsingham was unabashed.

'Unfortunately, our enemies are not taking their rest,' he said tartly, 'so we must be eternally vigilant. Please give me your accounts of what transpired with the Duke of Guise and your trip to Scotland.'

He listened in silence and when Jacob had finished, Walsingham leaned back in his chair and studied him for a few moments. Then, pouring Jacob a generous measure of wine, invited Jacob to join him in a toast. 'To the confounding and demise of the Queen's enemies!'

Having drained his glass he sat down and explained. 'Thanks to your information, the Ruthven group of Protestant Lords seized George Douglas and the gold, shortly after he arrived in Edinburgh. It was not long before they had wrung a full confession from him. A copy of his written confession has been received by the Privy Council. In it, he admits that Lennox had sent him to France to deal with the Duke of Guise and he had conspired with Mary Stuart through the Archbishop of Glasgow in France and the French Ambassador in London. He further admitted that Lennox has communicated on a regular basis with the Scottish Queen about the plan to invade England.'

'A lot seems to have happened in the week while we travelled back to London,' said Jacob.

'There's more,' Walsingham said, with an arch smile. 'The Ruthven group then went to Perth, showed King James the confession and persuaded him to go to Ruthven Castle, for his own safety.'

'How is the King taking to that? He's only fifteen and he must feel very threatened.'

Walsingham shrugged. 'I can't say how he feels, but he appears to be making the best of it. Lennox has fallen from grace and has been forced to leave Scotland. We gave him a free passage across England and he has left for France.' He regarded Jacob benignly. 'The splendid glass you took for King James has also smoothed the way for concluding the treaty between England and Scotland. It will be signed at Berwick, ere long.'

Jacob was delighted with the outcome, but a little puzzled. 'The news about Lennox is good, but I'm wondering why there has been no word from the Duke of Guise, nor any contact with Throckmorton.' What if my part in this has been discovered, he thought. He couldn't see how, because even the Ruthven group were unaware of his part. Sir Robert Bowes had been adamant about that and all George Douglas knew was that he had delivered the gold and some letters as arranged with the Duke of Guise.

Walsingham shrugged. 'I don't know, perhaps he has been too busy trying to save Lennox.' It occurred to Jacob that there might be another more likely explanation.

'Perhaps Henri has received forewarning from his agents in Scotland and is trying to find another way to invade England.'

'You don't believe that he will simply abandon his plan?'

'Not at all likely,' Jacob said firmly. 'He is too sure that the dual invasion plan will succeed and he will take a large share of the credit. His army entering from the south will be the first to enter London.'

'Hmm ...' said Walsingham thoughtfully. 'Whilst I was hoping we might have heard the last of this plan, I feared it was not likely.'

'What do you require me to do? said Jacob. 'I'm sure that this meeting is not just to give me the latest news from Scotland.'

Walsingham frowned. 'I do believe you are becoming more cynical.'

Jacob returned the frown. 'I wonder why that should be so? Perhaps I was mistaken.'

The irony of this drew a smile from Walsingham. 'Enough of this fencing with words. Yes, I do wish you to do something. I want you to plan another trip to Paris to see the Duke of Guise.'

'I've only just got back from the last trip. I certainly am not planning another trip so soon,' said Jacob tartly. 'I will think about it, but it won't be for at least a month.'

When Jacob returned home Maria was still asleep. All through carrying the child she had been radiant, even when tired. It was as if she knew that everything with the birth would be normal. And so it was. A few days later, Maria gave birth to a healthy girl, who they named Caterina Ann, Cate for short.

Chapter Sixteen
France and England, April/May,1582

It was two weeks after this happy event before Jacob felt able to leave to visit the Duke of Guise. On arriving in Paris, he went straight to the Château de Lorraine. Henri's greeting was friendly, but subdued and Jacob was certain he already know about Lennox. I must be very careful, he thought, or Henri will start to suspect my part in the fall of Lennox. 'I came as soon as I could,' he said, sitting in the chair indicated by Henri. 'I feared to send a message by Throckmorton, for I have heard that Lennox is betrayed.'

The Duke nodded. 'I heard the news directly from Lennox, he is in Paris now. After Douglas returned to Edinburgh with the gold, he was seized by the Protestants Lords, led by Ruthven. They have tortured a confession out of him and are holding King James a prisoner. They turned the King against Lennox and he was forced to flee for his life. Lennox is a broken man and my physician is attending him every day.'

Jacob gasped. 'So it is true. I thought it must be, but to hear it has been confirmed by Lennox is a very serious blow to our plans.'

'A very serious setback indeed,' confirmed the Duke. 'However, our plans are too well advanced to consider defeat. I am working on ways and means of achieving the same ends without Lennox. Young King James still supports our cause and so far the supporters of the Kirk have not found a way to stop him. He was able to spirit Holt away from his capturers and keep him well hidden from them.'

'And what of Throckmorton?' asked Jacob. 'I have seen nothing of him for many weeks.'

'I'm afraid that was my doing,' said the Duke apologetically. 'There has been a strong suspicion that Walsingham has intercepted letters to the French Embassy in Scotland. Assuming this to be true, Throckmorton could be compromised and watched. Until I am sure he is not, he has been instructed to stay away from you and the Catholic nobles.' This last piece of news was very reassuring to Jacob. I don't seem seem to be under suspicion at all, he thought. I must try to find out if the Duke has made any fresh plans.

'What will you do now?' he asked. 'We need to find another way to get the army into Northern England via Scotland.'

The Duke looked thoughtful. 'I have been giving it some thought. Throckmorton is only a messenger, but unfortunately he knows a number of the Catholics, both in England and France who are the main activists in the planning of the invasion. Walsingham will get their names eventually if he arrests him.'

'Should that happen, you must let them know that my ship is at their disposal. They may need to get out of the country without a warrant. Walsingham has tightened up procedures at the ports and anyone without a travel warrant is being held and questioned.'

'Are you having any difficulty?'

'Not at all,' Jacob said. 'My showroom in Paris gives me a good excuse for visiting Paris and I have an open warrant that allows me to go at any time. It would be a different matter if I wanted to go anywhere else.'

'I see,' said Henri thoughtfully. 'That might prove to be useful.'

'Is there anything I can do? It should be possible to smuggle in quite a lot in my shipments to London. With our own warehouse and dock at Somers Key and the local Excise Office kept well bribed, they will not carry out any searches unless instructed to do so by order of the Privy Council, which is highly unlikely.'

'In the circumstances that would be most helpful. I need to send a large sum of money to ease the way in the south of England. Also, the gold taken from Douglas needs to be replaced. I was planning for Throckmorton to deliver it, but if he is compromised it would be a fatal error.'

'Who is the money to be delivered to?'

'Lord Henry Howard at Audley End in Essex. He will see that it is delivered according to my instructions.'

'I will make arrangements for a crate of jewellery to have a false bottom where we can hide the money and any letters you wish to send. Can you get them to the warehouse in secret by tomorrow night?'

'That should not be difficult. Thank you for your help in this matter. It has solved a problem for me. Now, have you any news or gossip from court?'

Jacob had been well briefed by Walsingham, who hoped that several pieces of misinformation he had included, would lead the Duke to surmise that Walsingham knew less than he did. Eventually, Jacob took his leave and was relieved that it had gone so well.

However, the Duke had one final surprise in store for him. 'Do you think it will be possible for you to arrange to see Queen Mary Stuart?'

Jacob was taken aback. 'I'm not sure how that will be possible,' he said, shaking his head doubtfully. 'As I understand it, Her Majesty is seldom in one place for very long and I believe that all visits have to be arranged through Walsingham.'

'How did you manage to meet the Queen before?'

'Through the Countess of Shrewsbury. She ordered some of my glass and invited me to Chatsworth, where Queen Mary was staying. I managed to see her in private and passed a message to her.'

The Duke was thoughtful for a while and then his face brightened. 'If the Queen was to commission a special glass for her birthday, do you think you might get permission to deliver it to her?'

'When is her birthday?'

'On the eighth of December as far as I recall.'

'I might be able to get permission from Queen Elizabeth. As her Glassmaker, I get commissions from her from time to time. We are working on one at present. If she likes it enough, I might be able to get her permission to visit Queen Mary. However, it might be a difficult journey at that time of year. It would be better if we made it before the bad weather sets in. What do you want me to tell Queen Mary?'

Again the Duke looked thoughtful. 'Should it be confirmed that Throckmorton is compromised, letters to the Queen and replies which she sends will be intercepted by Walsingham. I would like to warn her. It is urgent, but it might be too risky to send you.'

'I doubt that Walsingham would question the visit if the suggestion came from Queen Elizabeth. Should he do so, I could offer to pass on any letters or information I gleaned from the visit, like a loyal Protestant.'

The Duke burst out laughing. 'You are almost as devious as me. It would be very good to arrange for some misdirection from Queen Mary. We might even be able to throw Walsingham completely off the scent.'

He clapped Jacob affectionately on the shoulder. 'I will be in touch with you before you leave for England. For now, fare you well.'

Shortly after *The Crystal* docked at Somers Key, Walsingham's man Phelippes came to the warehouse in secret, to examine the contents of the crate. The letters were opened and copied and some pamphlets of scurrilous stories against the Queen noted and a sample taken. Once they had done this, Jacob arranged for them to be delivered to Lord Henry Howard at Audley. Phelippes arranged that the noble lord was closely watched, until the destination of the money and pamphlets was discovered.

The letters proved to be very interesting once the cipher had been broken by Phelippes. They gave Walsingham a further insight into the disruption that the removal of Lennox had wrought on the Catholic League plans. The Duke was frantically trying to find a new way to introduce the Papal army into Scotland. He also informed Howard that Throckmorton was on his way to England to gather information on possible sites for a landing of his forces in southern England. Walsingham ensured that Throckmorton was allowed into the country without any problem, but had him closely watched. Once he was sure that they had provided enough of an insight into other members of the plot, he would have them arrested and examined.

A few days later, Jacob met with Walsingham at the safe house. Having passed on the details of his discussions with Henri he told Walsingham about Henri's request that he should visit Mary

Stuart. When Jacob explained how he'd suggested to Henri the idea of misdirecting Walsingham, he nearly choked on his glass. 'They think they're misdirecting me, but we are reading all of their correspondence. And I thought I was the devious one,' he spluttered. 'What are you to make for Mary Stuart?'

'I'm not sure, but I believe it will be some sort of coloured goblet.'

He gave Walsingham an innocent look. 'There is, however, a small problem.'

'Oh, and what is that?'

'Do you think you could persuade the Queen to give me a commission for some glass. I don't have one at present, but I told Henri differently.'

'No wonder your business is doing well,' said Walsingham wryly. 'I will see what I can do.'

Chapter Seventeen
London and Sheffield, September, 1582

'Well, what do you think?' Roberto said impatiently as Jacob had been reading the document for several minutes now.

'I've been expecting an order for a coloured glass,' Jacob said slowly, 'but I didn't expect it to be for a red goblet.'

'Have you ever made a goblet in red glass? I don't think it is a very popular colour. And what about the customer, Mary Stuart!'

Jacob couldn't resist the temptation to pull Roberto's leg. 'I know it's an interesting commission,' he said looking puzzled. 'but there are all sorts of difficulties, not least the fact that I've never made a red goblet before.'

'But what about the customer, Jacob!'

'Oh, that. Well, I was expecting a commission from Mary Stuart. It was the Duke of Guise's idea.'

Roberto was getting worried. 'Won't you get into trouble from the Queen, accepting commissions from Mary Stuart? And what is Walsingham going to say? I ...' He broke off as he saw the smile hovering at the corner of Jacob's mouth. 'You've already told them!' he said accusingly. 'And you didn't tell me.' His face was a picture as Jacob burst out laughing and then he too had to laugh. Jacob explained what had transpired. When he said they would also be getting a commission from the Queen, it started Roberto off again.

'Walsingham's right. You're getting very devious in your old age.'

'Less of the old, young Roberto.' He put his hand jokingly on the hilt of his sword. 'I can still teach you a lesson, or two.'

Two knives appeared in Roberto's hands as if by magic and he grinned cheekily at Jacob. 'Not while I've got these. You know how poor you are at stopping a thrown knife.'

It was Jacob's turn to laugh. Roberto was reminding him that he'd been knocked out by a thrown knife, when he first met Walsingham. *'Touché!'* he cried.

The knives disappeared back into the hidden sheaths in the arms of his doublet and Roberto perched himself on the end of the table. 'Are you going to start experimenting on this red glass right away?'

'I was thinking of doing that. Will that cause you a problem?'

'Not really. I want to go over the current order situation with you, but we'd better leave it until we get the order from the Queen. It might be quite large.'

'On the other hand, it might be quite small. I wouldn't put it past Walsingham to pay me back for my cheek.'

When Roberto had left, Jacob went to the cupboard where he kept the notes of all his experiments. He also had an old notebook of his grandfather's which contained some information relating to adding colour to glass. After searching through for a while, he gave a smile of satisfaction as he found a reference to red glass. His grandfather's notes were rather fragmentary, but did describe a method using aqua regia. There was also a postscript that read, *Highly dangerous process and very expensive. Leave well alone.* The words were underlined three times. He could understand his grandfather's warning, aqua regia was a very powerful acid mixture.

Reading on, he came across an entry about using fine gold dust. Apparently, very small quantities produced a deep ruby red. There were also notes about the effect of adding various other metal salts and changes of conditions. He could just make out the name copper, but unfortunately, the rest of the notes were so faded and the paper so brittled by age, as to make them almost unreadable. However, they would save him a lot of experimental work. He would certainly heed his grandfather's warning about dissolving gold in aqua regia. However, the use of small amounts of gold dust seemed a promising starting point.

The first experiments were encouraging, but it was two weeks later before he had enough red glass to make the first goblet. His first try at a Serissima-style glass proved a disaster. The glass was more difficult to work than a conventional mixture. Despite his best efforts, he could not produce a satisfactory shape.

In the end, he changed the design to a very simple flute-shaped bowl, with an inverted baluster stem on a folded foot. This new goblet was darker in colour than the first one. It seemed that reheating the cullet resulted in a deeper tone to the colour. His grandfather's notes had hinted at this, although most of the entry wasn't readable. It took three more tries before he was satisfied. By now the goblet was a very deep ruby colour.

When Roberto saw it for the first time, he immediately christened it the blood-red goblet. Not a description that appealed to Jacob. He preferred to describe it as ruby-coloured. When he showed it to Maria for the first time, her reaction was immediate. She crossed herself and said that the glass had a strangely threatening look to it. 'I don't like it at all. I couldn't bear to drink red wine from it. It would be too much like drinking blood.' She shuddered violently. 'It gives me such a bad feeling. I don't know why, but I wish you hadn't made it. Please take it away. I don't want it in the house.'

Jacob was amazed at Maria's reaction. She was not normally so superstitious about things. She loved her rose-pink necklace, but something about this ruby-coloured goblet seemed to strike a chord with her. A discordant one at that! Jacob wondered if this was because of the death of her daughter, although she seemed to have got over it. Whatever it was, in respect for her feelings, he removed the goblet back to his workshop and stored it in the cupboard.

It also occurred to Jacob that like Queen Elizabeth, Mary Stuart liked to receive gifts. He therefore had Toni make up a double strand necklace and matching earrings in deep red, overlaying gold foil, with gold bead spacers. Placed in a leather case lined with velvet, it certainly looked fit for a Queen.

Having passed the first hurdle, he now had to get permission to visit Mary Stuart.

The order from the Queen arrived a couple of days later and despite his low expectations, it turned out to be a largish one. Fortunately, it was for one of the standard patterns, to extend the set the Queen already possessed. Because of the increased production now they were using coal successfully, they were able to deliver the order from stock.

Jacob was summoned to deliver the glass personally to the

Queen and took along the red goblet. He decided not to mention the necklace. The Queen was delighted with the glass he had brought for her, but detested the red goblet.

'I cannot for the life of me understand why the Scots Queen should prefer this coloured glass to your cristallo,' she said forcefully. 'The cristallo is greatly superior.'

'My wife would certainly agree with Your Majesty on that account,' said Jacob. 'She has taken a violent dislike to it.'

'I have found the Lady Maria to be most sensible and honest in her accounts. She would not tell you false, but give her true feelings.'

Jacob agreed wholeheartedly. 'I have always found her thus. She would not think one thing and tell you another.'

Just then Walsingham entered and bowed to the Queen. 'I came as soon as the committee of the Privy Council had finished their examination of the latest offer from the French King.'

The Queen looked as though someone had produced a foul smell. 'I trust they were as dismissive of it as I was,' she said scornfully. 'Although the King appears to discharge England from all expenses in the Low Countries war against Spain in the event of my marriage to Alençon, the conditions he has added are the same we rejected some twelve months ago.'

'The Privy Council concur,' said Walsingham, 'as do I. The French stand condemned of backsliding in their negotiations and we all question their sincerity.'

'It is difficult to know what to do about the Franco-English Alliance now.' The Queen looked troubled as she paced the floor as she was wont to do when she was thinking. 'I confess to be disappointed with the lack of progress on all fronts. The King of France is backsliding on his promises and Alençon is proving to be no match for the Duke of Parma and his seasoned Spanish troops. I fear that the plight of the Low Countries is worse than ever.'

The Queen turned to Jacob who had been amazed that they should discus such important matters of State in his presence.

'What are your thoughts on this matter, Jacob Bell?'

Jacob was even more astonished that his opinion should be sought and the Queen picked this up immediately. 'You seem surprised, Jacob Bell. I know you are not one of my councillors, but you are privy to many matters relating to the security of this realm. Mister Secretary Walsingham has the utmost respect for your honesty and clear-sightedness, as has my Spirit (her nickname for Lord Burghley).

'What answer have you for me then, Master Bell?'

Gathering his wits together, Jacob thought for a moment before replying. 'Whilst I don't profess to know all the ins and outs of policy, two things occur to me. Firstly, from what I have learned from my meeting with the Catholic League, the French King is not the strongest power in France. The Duke of Guise is both highly popular with the people and a very powerful influence on French policy. I believe he is ambitious enough to covet the throne. Should this occur, then France itself will become a Catholic nation, whose natural ally will be Spain.

'Secondly, in the Low Countries I fear that Alençon will prove no match for Parma. Better to support William of Orange directly. From all the information I have gathered in Antwerp, they fear greatly that despite all of the efforts to support the Huguenots, Parma and Spain will emerge the victors.

'That being the case, then England will to all effects be isolated and must try to find some common ground with Spain. The alternative is to prepare for war, which seems to be the most likely outcome, since the price of friendship with Spain will be too high.'

There was silence for a moment and then the Queen turned to Walsingham. 'Have you by any chance been coaching Master Bell on your foreign policy?'

Walsingham shook his head in denial. 'They do seem to mirror my own intelligence, more than a little, but I have not put any words into his mouth. They are entirely his own thoughts.' He gave a bleak smile. 'I confess his opinion of the Duke of Guise and his ambition goes further than most members of the Privy Council believe, but I think that Bell has it from the horse's mouth, so to speak.'

The Queen turned back to Jacob. 'Thank you for your thoughts and information. I wish more of my advisers were as well informed and as succinct. I do believe that the best policy will be to wait and see what happens in the Low Countries. I have kept the realm at peace for all of my reign and I do not wish to see us at war with Spain.'

She regarded Jacob with a friendly look. 'We are once more in your debt Jacob Bell. I would dearly love to reward you as you deserve, but to do so would, I fear, put your life in yet more jeopardy.' She extended her hand and Jacob bowed over it. 'Do not doubt Jacob Bell,' she continued, 'that I hold both you and your wife in the highest esteem and one day soon, that will become apparent.' As Jacob was about to protest, she put a finger to her lips. 'You need not tell me you do not put your lives at risk for reward. I have ample evidence over a number of years that this is so. Nevertheless, in due time, reward you I shall.'

Walsingham nodded his agreement and passed a letter and a pouch of gold sovereigns to Jacob. 'This contains your permission to visit Mary Stuart and your expenses for the trip. We cannot issue a warrant to travel post-haste as that would be too suspicious. I suggest you start tomorrow as the weather seems set fair for the moment.'

It was almost the end of the month before Jacob reached Sheffield Castle. On showing his authorisation at the gatehouse, he was informed that Mary Stuart was currently housed in the nearby Manor House. This was a luxurious lodge, situated about a mile away and set in a very extensive deer park.

At first the steward was reluctant to allow Jacob in, even with the letter from Walsingham. He explained that the earl was away visiting a relative. Jacob thought it was probably his mistress. The relations between the earl and Bess, the countess, had been strained for some time. It was common gossip at court that Bess had complained to the Queen that the earl was having an affair with Mary Stuart. It was not believed, because the earl was known to have a mistress living near to Sheffield Castle. In fact, even the Queen delighted in ridiculing Bess and her stories. Not only that, but Mary Stuart had sent a letter to the Queen claiming that Bess had defamed the Queen on many occasions and went on to give a long list of instances.

She even twisted the knife by suggesting that when Elizabeth was ill, Bess had prophesied her death based on the reports of an astrologer who, *in an old book, predicted a violent death for you and the succession of another Queen, which she interpreted as myself.* In yet another attempt to meet her rival face to face, she offered to disclose more of Bess's infamy at a personal interview. As in all her other attempts, this too fell on deaf ears.

Despite the steward's reluctance, Jacob insisted and much to his surprise, was shown in to the Queen's presence chamber and then the steward withdrew. Looking around at the rich hangings and embroideries, not to mention the throne with the cipher of the Stuart arms over it, Jacob could see that, even here, Mary had all the trappings of a Queen.

When Mary Stuart entered from her privy chamber, he was shocked at the changes that prolonged captivity had wrought over the last ten years. Mary had put on weight and could barely walk without the assistance of her ladies-in-waiting. Her dress was much more severe than when they last met, being largely black, except for the French-style ruff.

However, it was soon readily apparent that the Queen had lost none of her charisma and good looks. Once she was settled on the throne, with her maids sitting on stools around her, she greeted Jacob most courteously. Bidding him welcome, she chided him for not visiting her for so long.

'I see you have an interesting packet with you, Master Bell. I hope this is the goblet I ordered.' Seeing that Jacob was ill at ease and reluctant to speak, she reassured him. 'You may speak freely without fear of being overheard. When the earl is away, the steward leaves me alone with the few visitors that call.'

Jacob was surprised, but bowed and opening the package, carried the goblet across to the Queen. 'I hope this goblet meets your expectations, Your Majesty. I have no previous experience of this type of coloured glass and without any comparison colour, I have done my best to anticipate your requirements.'

Taking the goblet from him, Mary held it up to the light. 'It is just perfect and exactly what I had in mind. Red is the colour of the Catholic martyrs and no one can deny that I am a martyr for my faith.' She gave a sad little smile. 'I do hope that my sister Queen will not insist that I die a martyr's death.'

Before Jacob could frame a reply, the Queen's mood changed and she became at once the vivacious woman that Jacob remembered from Chatsworth.

'And how has the last ten years fared you, Master Bell?' she said, flashing her wonderful smile. 'I trust you have fully recovered from the terrible injury you suffered in my cause. Both the Duke of Guise and Count Ridolfi have informed me of your bravery in saving the count's life.'

The soft Scottish lilt in her voice still had the power to bind men to her and Jacob wondered again at the fortitude of this remarkable woman. Despite knowing what a dangerous woman she was, he couldn't help but admire her.

He told Mary of his recovery, how he came to marry his love and of the children she had borne for him. He also spoke a little of his business. For a while Mary became a little maudlin as she spoke of her own son.

'He has refused to allow me to go back to Scotland, you know. I believe he fears I will rule instead of him. But he's still a young boy with little experience of kingship. I could be of so much help and he would learn from me. How can he hope to rule against the Protestant lords. They are too strong for him, but I know how to prevail against them.' She brightened up a little. 'I do not believe he understands what I want for him. By ensuring that my rights to the English throne are not given away. I will be the natural successor to Elizabeth and he will follow me.'

When she had finished, Jacob thought it was an appropriate time to present the necklace. 'I have a small gift for you, Your Majesty,' he said, presenting her with the leather case. 'It is another example of the glassmaker's art, made by a Venetian jeweller I'm sponsoring.'

Mary gave a little cry of delight when she opened the box. She insisted that her ladies remove the pearls she was wearing and replace them with the necklace and earrings. One of the ladies ran to get her mirror and Mary sat admiring them from every angle. Her ladies chattered excitedly and were obviously entranced by the gift.

Suddenly, Mary waved them all back to their stools and turned to Jacob, who had been waiting patiently.

'It was most kind and thoughtful of you to bring this lovely gift. It has brightened my day. You may inform your Venetian friend that I approve most heartily of his skill. No doubt,' she said teasingly, 'the ladies of London will have a further reason to come flocking to your door.'

This quip sent her ladies into fits of giggles behind their hands. The whispered comments were obviously of a ribald nature and a stern look from Mary made then sit up quietly.

'I apologise for my ladies, Master Bell. They behave like low bred servants at times. And now, we must get on. I fear we may not be allowed to be without a chaperone for much longer. What can you tell me of my relatives in France? Have you brought any word from them?'

'The Duke has asked me to warn you not to send letters via Throckmorton. There is a strong possibility that Walsingham has intercepted letters delivered by him. We fear he is compromised and his actions are being watched.' He could see the Queen was worried. 'I am ready to be of service and will faithfully deliver to the Duke of Guise any message you entrust to me.' Jacob had a stab of conscience. It didn't sit well with him that he was deceiving Mary, but he had made his choice and must carry it through.

'That is very good of you. I was however, worried for the More family who get the letters from Throckmorton and deliver them to me when I am at Chatsworth. If Throckmorton is compromised, he may lead Walsingham to George More, which will cut me off from any source of news.'

'If I can be of any help on that score,' replied Jacob, 'please let George More know and I will try to assist him and his family.'

Mary thanked him, but she was becoming very downcast by these revelations. Jacob went on to say how Walsingham had made it a condition of his permission to visit her, that any letters given to him must be handed over. When he told her the Duke's suggestion of misdirection, Mary brightened up at once. Intrigue was the very essence of life to her.

Jacob then described the broad scope of the Duke's plan to invade England. Mary was very interested and asked numerous questions. Jacob answered cautiously as he was not sure what

Mary already knew. It was obvious from her questions that she was well aware of the involvement of the Spanish Ambassador and events in Scotland.

Eventually, the questions ran out and Mary turned to the letters. She thanked him for his offer to deliver them to the Duke of Guise and promised to have the letters ready within the hour. She then excused herself. Retiring to her privy chamber with her ladies fussing around her, she left Jacob to wait in the presence chamber.

Shortly after she'd left, two of her ladies came back bearing a small table and a tray. There was some light ale, which the maid explained was brewed especially for the Queen at Burton-upon-Trent, a town renowned for its breweries. There was also some fruit and a tray of sweetmeats.

As time wore on, Jacob was glad that he had made arrangements for the night at a local coaching inn. It was unlikely that he would be able to get far before nightfall. To set out across the trackless, dangerous moors in the dark was not to be contemplated. It was difficult enough to find the bridleway and the stone markers in full daylight!

Time dragged on. Nearly two hours elapsed before, finally, the ladies reappeared and presented Jacob with a small package of letters. There was also a separate letter. A lady-in-waiting explained that the package was for handing to Walsingham and the single letter was for the Duke of Guise. They also presented him with a beautifully stitched embroidery for his wife.

'Her Majesty,' the lady explained, 'has spent many hours on this embroidery. Please accept it as a token of her gratitude.'

On examining it, Jacob noticed that in one corner, Mary had embroidered her coat of arms with a phoenix and the motto *In my end, my beginning.* This, as he knew from his previous encounter with Mary, was that of her mother, Mary of Guise. It had come to represent how Mary viewed her future and that of her son.

Asking the ladies to convey his thanks to the Queen, Jacob took his leave. He was amazed when there was no attempt to search him as he left. The lack of security would alarm Walsingham, if and when he told him. He was uncertain at present if he would; Mary Stuart had much to bear already and it would lead to further restrictions. When these plots came to a head would be soon enough.

Making his way back to the inn, he got a good night's sleep to prepare him for the long journey home. It took him five days of hard riding, but he was fortunate enough to meet a group of merchants heading for London and enjoyed some convivial company on the way.

He arrived back in London late in the afternoon. Maria greeted him with great enthusiasm and after a light meal and a warn drink, they retired to bed. Cuddling up close to him, Maria looked at him lovingly. 'Tell me all about your visit to Mary Stuart. Did she like the goblet and what did she think of the necklace?'

As Jacob told Maria about Mary's delight for both of them, he couldn't help but contrast the two women. Mary was always using her wiles to bind people to her in furtherance of her own ambitions. Maria was so straight forward and trustworthy and not afraid to speak the truth. He would trust Maria with his life, but he never could with Mary Stuart. As Jacob started to say something more, Maria placed her finger on his lips and made a gentle shushing noise. Jacob stopped immediately and sliding his arm under her pulled her close. She gave him a beautiful smile. 'I am so pleased to have you safely home, my dear husband. I miss you when you are away.' She leaned over and kissed him and Jacob responded immediately, showing her just how much he'd missed her too.

Chapter Eighteen
London and The Tower, November, 1582

'Are those the reports from the agents sent to arrest Throckmorton?' asked Walsingham eagerly as his secretary brought in a number of folded and sealed vellum letter-sheets.

'They are, Sir Francis and also a further missive from Sir Robert Bowes and Davison his assistant, from Berwick.'

'Excellent. I will read these before I leave for Greenwich.'

By the time he'd read the reports Walsingham was less happy. The arrest of Francis Throckmorton and Sir Henry Howard had been effected with little problem. Among the papers seized were a list of Catholic noblemen, a plan showing all the harbours in the south of England suitable for landing foreign forces and a number of scurrilous pamphlets against the Queen. The two men were being brought to the Tower, where Walsingham would make sure he learned everything they knew. They had both been watched for the last six months and he had gathered enough evidence against them to convince the Queen they should be arrested and put to a full examination.

It was the news from Bowes and Davison, his agents in Scotland, that was the cause for concern. They reported that there was still no sign of William Holt despite extensive searches of all his known haunts. Although he had been arrested earlier in the year and had admitted there was a plot against Elizabeth, the details he had supplied were already common knowledge to Walsingham. They threw absolutely no new light on the situation regarding the invasion from Scotland. Worse still, after sending instructions that Holt was to be tortured using the crushing boot to obtain everything he knew, he had escaped, with the connivance of young King James and Lord Seton.

In their latest report, his agents could find no trace of Holt and concluded he had fled the country. However, they had learned that he was an agent for the Spanish Ambassador in London, Bernadino de Mendoza - not, as previously thought, Mauvissière, the French Ambassador.

This put a different complexion on things. Walsingham had been concentrating on the wrong ambassador, a situation he must remedy at the earliest opportunity. The removal of Lennox, who was now seriously ill he had been informed, had made no difference to the situation. The Duke of Guise had not abandoned his plans, but was looking for another way for an invasion of England via Scotland. The fact that the Spanish Ambassador was involved seemed to point to the fact that Philip of Spain was now an active participant in the plot.

Meanwhile, the questioning of Throckmorton needed immediate attention. Accordingly, later that afternoon Throckmorton was brought before a committee of the Privy Council at the Star Camber in the Palace of Westminster. When Walsingham confronted him with the incriminating documents he denied all knowledge of them.

'They must have been introduced into my house by those who searched it,' he insisted.

Walsingham regarded him sadly. 'Do you really believe that we will be convinced by such a pathetic story,' he said.

'Of course,' said Throckmorton. 'It is the truth.'

Walsingham gave a sigh. 'Very well then. I had hoped you would not persist in this lame story, but I will call witnesses.'

Witness after witness, confirmed the papers were already in his house. Throckmorton began to perspire heavily and became more and more agitated as he tried to deny their testimony. Eventually, after repeated questioning following each testimony, he changed his story.

'Very well then,' he declared loudly, 'it was a man called George Nutby who left them in my rooms.' He could see that Walsingham was about to question this and announced hurriedly, 'and before you ask, I did not want to get him into trouble, but I didn't read the documents, nor did I wish to incriminate Nutby.'

'And where is this mysterious Nutby now?' Walsingham's voice was heavy with sarcasm.

'He has fled the country,' Throckmorton said defiantly.

Walsingham turned to face the councillors and threw his arms up in disgust. 'My lords, Throckmorton wastes our time. I suggest we try a little less gentle persuasion to get at the truth of the matter. What say you, my lords?'

Several Councillors agreed, but Leicester who had been whispering to Christopher Hatton, stood up and addressed Throckmorton. 'It is clear from the letters that you are not the instigator of this plot, but simply acted as a messenger. I believe therefore, I could persuade my fellow members of the Council to offer you a full pardon. Of course we would require a full confession and the details of all of your dealings with the conspirators.'

Throckmorton would have none of it. 'I thank you for your offer, my lord, but I know nothing more than I have already told you.' Despite repeated questioning, he just folded his arms and stubbornly continued to deny everything. Eventually, Walsingham held up his hand. 'My lords, I suggest we waste no further time while the prisoner continues to insult our intelligence by repeating this ludicrous story. We will see how much of this silly tale remains after the sterner persuasion of the rack for a while.'

There was no dissension this time and Throckmorton was sent to the Tower.

When Walsingham went down to the dungeons and stopped outside the racking room, he could hear Throckmorton sobbing. 'I will not say what is not true,' Throckmorton protested in an agonised voice. 'Do your worst. I will not tell you any different.'

'You will tell me all I want to know,' said the Rackmaster. 'We have only just started on you.' There was a clanking of metal against metal and the Rackmaster said, 'Put these irons in the brazier. Meanwhile, we will see if a little more stretching will persuade him.'

As Walsingham listened, there came the ominous creak as the spoked wheel of the rack was turned and the pressure on the tortured limbs increased. Throckmorton gave a long scream and then there was silence.

Walsingham knocked on the door and showed his face at the grille. The Rackmaster came out and Walsingham just looked at him and said, 'Well?'

'Nothing, my lord. He has withstood the trial well, but he has fainted again.'

'Very well. Revive him and take him back to his cell for now.' He regarded the torturer grimly. 'And send for Mister Norton and Thomas Wilkes.' Norton was the most notorious Rackmaster of his day and Wilkes his assistant. 'Tell them I want a second trial of Throckmorton in the morning, but not before I've had a chance to speak to him.'

As the man turned to go, Walsingham had another thought. 'When you take Throckmorton to his cell, clean him up and see that he has food and drink and salve for the rope-burns on his wrists and ankles.' He smiled grimly at the Rackmaster's startled look. 'And, in the morning, give him some wine and bread and I will visit him at eight.'

When Walsingham entered the cell next morning, Throckmorton was sitting on some straw leaning against the wall. Seeing Throckmorton's hopeful look, Walsingham was quietly elated. I have him now, he thought. Looking down at Throckmorton, he put on a sad expression. 'Francis, Francis.' he said sorrowfully. 'Why have you put yourself through such a trial? You could have told us everything and had a pardon. The conspirators will not blame you. They know you will tell us everything, eventually.'

When Throckmorton started to protest, Walsingham put a finger to his lips. 'Shush,' he said quietly, 'and listen to what I have to say. What has been done to you so far, is but a nothing. A mere trifle. You have made a great show of Roman resolution, but now it is over. I have sent for Mister Norton, the well-known Rackmaster.' Throckmorton turned pale and gasped.

Walsingham gave a terrible smile. 'I see you have heard of Mr Norton. This is your last chance before I send you to him. Please,' Walsingham pleaded, 'spare yourself from any more of this terrible pain. It will be far worse than yesterday.'

'Do your worst, you sanctimonious bastard,' said Throckmorton and spat at Walsingham. 'Do your worst, I will tell you nothing.'

Walsingham turned round abruptly and signalled to the waiting jailers. They came and placed Throckmorton on the rack and when he was secure, Norton came round and tested the ropes. 'Take up the strain, Wilkes.' he called and watched

Throckmorton's face intently as the spoked wheel creaked ominously round. When he saw the first expression of pain on Throckmorton's face, he held up his hand and the turning stopped. Thrusting his face close to Throckmorton's, he put his right hand on the taut rope stretching Throckmorton's left arm and plucked it like playing a lute string. The vibrations passing into the prisoner's strained shoulder set off a spasm of pain that wrenched a scream from his clenched teeth. Walking round to the other side, Norton did the same to the other shoulder. Another scream echoed round the room and tears began to stream down Throckmorton's face as he sobbed. 'No more. Please no more, I will tell you everything.'

Much of what Throckmorton revealed was already known to Walsingham from his meetings with Jacob Bell. He pleaded with Walsingham to grant him the pardon the Council had offered, but it was too late for that. However, the news that the Duke of Guise had fixed upon the port of Arundel in Sussex and had sent Charles Paget, a dissident Catholic, to survey the port and to sound out the Catholic families living nearby, came as a shocking revelation. It confirmed beyond any doubt the scale of the mistake he had made in setting spies in the French Ambassador's household and intercepting his mail. In spite of all this, the surveillance had disclosed little or nothing of importance. No wonder Walsingham had found out little of the details of this plot, Throckmorton had been dealing with the Spanish Ambassador, Mendoza!

He should have realised this when Jacob Bell told him how the Duke of Guise had dismissed the French King as a "milksop". Guise never had any intention of using the French Ambassador to keep the King informed of progress.

Throckmorton's confession showed quite clearly the extent of Bernadino de Mendoza's involvement. It was he who had sent William Holt, the English Jesuit, to Scotland. He who had sent Mary Stuart's letters abroad, kept in touch with disaffected English Catholics and through Throckmorton, had stirred up rebellion in England to further the Duke of Guise's cause. Throckmorton had even sent most of his incriminating letters to the Spanish Ambassador, when he realised he was about to be arrested.

Undoubtedly, Throckmorton would take the blame for the plot and would pay the ultimate penalty for his crimes, all Walsingham had been able to promise him was a quick death. But what of the others he had implicated to a greater or lesser extent? In the days following Throckmorton's arrest, most of those named by him fled the country, confirming their guilt. Of course, the name of Jacob Bell was included, but Walsingham removed this from the written records that were sent to the Privy Council. He did not want Jacob to be interviewed, since he would have to reveal he was Walsingham's agent. The news would certainly leak out and put the whole counter-plot in jeopardy.

Chapter Nineteen
London, 1583

About this time, Jacob received a visit from George More. At first he could not remember where he had heard the name, but the man had stressed to Jack Petts to tell his master that he was a friend of Francis Throckmorton, and to impress this on Jacob. Thinking back to his interview with Mary Stuart, Jacob recalled that she had expressed her concern for George More, who delivered letters to her from Throckmorton. He had assured the Scottish Queen that he would try to help him and his family if Throckmorton was arrested.

More was a small, frail man with a very thin and world-weary face. When Jacob asked him to state his business, he looked around warily. 'There's no chance of us being overheard is there?'

When Jacob assured him there wasn't he began to talk, hesitatingly at first and then the words came flooding out. 'I take it you've heard of Throckmorton's arrest?' Jacob told him he had, but did not elaborate.

'You need not be coy with me,' said More. 'I am aware that you are an agent for the Duke of Guise.' Not being sure that George More was genuine, having never met him, Jacob decided to be cautious.

More smiled bleakly when Jacob denied any involvement with the Duke of Guise. 'Do not fear on my account, Master Bell. I have been involved in passing letters to the Queen of Scots for over four years. I have come to ask for your advice. The Queen sent me a message that I could trust you if Throckmorton was arrested. Do you think that Throckmorton will incriminate us?'

Jacob looked at him thoughtfully before replying. 'I'm not sure,' he said, deciding to take More at face value. "I know from friends at court, that he was offered a pardon by the Privy Councillors if he confessed, but he refused. I also understand that so far, he has not revealed anything, even though he has been tortured.'

More gave a sigh. 'It is only a matter of time then. Walsingham will not desist until he learns all. When Throckmorton was arrested, his servants were told that they had been watched for months and that Walsingham had proof of their master's treason. They couldn't wait to tell everything they knew.'

Jacob pretended to look worried. 'Fortunately, I have never visited Throckmorton's house and have had no contact with him in England.'

More nodded. 'Neither have I. I was recruited by Charles Paget, some four years ago. He paid me the two hundred pounds owed to my father by Mary Stuart.' Jacob thought furiously. Who was Paget? He must be another of the planners who were behind the plot.

'I don't know this man Paget. Who is he?'

'He is the younger brother of Thomas, Lord Paget and secretary to the Archbishop of Glasgow, Mary Stuart's agent in France,' explained George More. 'In return, for the money owed to my father, I have passed letters from Charles Paget and, only indirectly, from Throckmorton, to Mary Stuart. They go through my uncle who lives only four miles from Sheffield. Paget also gave me your name as an agent of the Duke in case I was ever in trouble. He said you have your own ships and the means to smuggle people out of the country.'

As he was speaking, Jacob was considering what was the best thing to do. He didn't want to betray another person to Walsingham's torturers if there was any possibility of avoiding it.

'Is that what you are asking me to do for you?'

'It depends whether I am betrayed. Although I'm a Catholic, I don't wish to be exiled from my own country. I've no desire to live in France, or Spain, for that matter.'

'Have you anywhere safe to stay in London?'

'I have a room at the Saracen's Head, hard by Aldgate. I'm not sure it would be safe if Walsingham's men are looking for me, they would be sure to search the inns, but I had nowhere else to go in London. Why do you ask?'

'In order to help you,' said Jacob, 'I will need a little time. I have friends at court who can find out if I am under suspicion and mayhap if you are being sought.' He made a suggestion.

'Since you have only acted as a messenger, you might be looked on leniently if you went to the Privy Council voluntarily and made a full confession. Particularly if you can give them some useful information.'

More reacted angrily. 'I'll not betray anyone.'

'You wouldn't need to. Walsingham has already questioned Throckmorton, so it will not harm him if you give his name and confirm any others that Walsingham already knows.' When More looked doubtful, Jacob tried another tack. 'Have you any letters still in your possession?'

'There are a couple I received from my uncle a few days ago. I have not been able to give them to Charles Paget because he has fled the country, along with his brother and Charles Arundel.'

'Did Paget send you a warning?' said Jacob, guessing that Paget might be more concerned about his own skin.

'No he didn't,' said More angrily. 'He obviously believed Throckmorton would tell all and made a run for it. It was only by chance I heard the news about Throckmorton's arrest. I overheard two merchants gossiping about it on the next table last night.'

'Perhaps you could use the letters as your bargaining point.' But he saw More was unimpressed with this idea. 'Paget wasn't bothered that they should be destroyed,' he reminded More, 'or he would have contacted you with a warning.'

'That's true,' said More, but he still looked concerned. 'But what if I'm detained in the meantime?'

Jacob debated his next step. More had put him in a difficult position. He had only two options, turn him in to Walsingham without another thought, or try to negotiate a deal with Walsingham on his behalf. It all came down to his judgement of More, who had impressed him with his straightforward answers and loyalty. He reached a decision. 'I have a house in Harte Street nearby. I use it mainly as a showroom and store. I can arrange for you to stay there, without anyone being the wiser, except my housekeeper of course. She will see to your meals. You will have to stay in your room, though,' he warned. 'There will be people in and out of the showroom and the apprentices live there. But at least you'll be safe.'

More was nodding agreement, so Jacob pressed home with the real point of his idea. 'Do you have the letters nearby and are you willing to trust them to my care? I promise I will only use them in your interest to try to secure a pardon.'

More looked concerned, so Jacob tried another argument. 'From what I've heard of him, Walsingham will only agree if you are straight with him. Some years ago, several members of the Ridolfi plot were given free pardons by confessing all they knew. You were only a messenger and knew nothing of what was in the letters, so he'll probably do the same for you, but only if you give him something of value.'

More was convinced. He handed the letters to Jacob, who arranged with Jack Petts that after dark, More would go in the coach to pick up his belongings and then be taken to Harte Street. He gave Jack strict instructions that More was to be watched by the apprentices and that he was not to leave his room. After More had left, he sent a note to Walsingham.

The following morning Colonel Young arrived with four of his men and had a word with Jacob in private.

'I gather,' he said, confidentially, 'we are here on the pretext of taking you to be examined by Walsingham.' He gave a broad grin. 'That should make for an interesting meeting.'

Jacob raised his eyebrows at this information, but followed the colonel and his men to the waiting coach without any comment. When he was shown in to the study, Walsingham looked up from his desk. 'Well Jacob Bell, what is this all about?'

Jacob produced the two letters given to him by More, handed them over and then sat down. Walsingham gave them a cursory glance at first and then examined them more closely. He gave Jacob a look of surprise, picked up the handbell and rang it vigorously.

When the letters were safely on the way to his cipher expert Phelippes, he sat back in his chair and regarded Jacob steadily. 'Tell me how you came by these letters.'

'Before I do, will you tell me how seriously you regard the threat to the Queen from Mary Stuart.'

Walsingham stared at Jacob for some time with narrowed eyes, until Jacob was beginning to think he had gone too far. Suddenly, Walsingham's face lightened and the furrows on his brow lifted.

'You have a great deal of gall, Jacob Bell,' he said, but there was no edge to his words. 'You come here into my study and calmly ask a Privy Councillor to reveal his thoughts on important issues of the realm.'

Jacob gave an apologetic smile, but said nothing, keeping his face neutral.

Walsingham sighed in exasperation. 'Oh very well, I will tell you.'

He leaned back. 'Over the last few years I have, at the request of the Queen, been negotiating to effect the release of Mary Stuart back to Scotland. In return for a number of assurances as to her future behaviour towards this realm, as you would expect.' His weary expression left no doubt that these discussions had been difficult.

'The talks have been long and protracted, but they have foundered on two rocky problems. Firstly, her own son has no desire for his mother to resume a position of power in Scotland. He has rejected every proposal out of hand.

'Secondly, there have been many reasons to believe that the Scottish Queen has no intention of giving up her claim to the English throne and the restoration of Catholicism to this Protestant country.

'She stands condemned by her own words,' he said vehemently. 'I have seen the letters and have read them. She has actively encouraged the enemies of this country to invade us. I cannot therefore entertain any other belief than that the lady in question is a threat to my Queen, now and for the foreseeable future.'

There was hate in his eyes as he spat out his final message. 'Mary Stuart is a bosom serpent,' he said viciously, 'and while she remains in this realm, she will always be a threat. A threat that must be eliminated. Does that answer your question?' he finished aggressively.

Jacob nodded mutely a little taken aback by the force of Walsingham's answer. He waited while Walsingham took a drink and then, when he looked at Jacob enquiringly, explained about

George More and the letters. He pleaded with Walsingham to allow More a free pardon if he would confess his dealings with Charles Paget.

Before Walsingham could reply, Colonel Young came in and handed to Walsingham the translations of the letters. Walsingham read the letters and then calling Jacob over, pointed out a paragraph in the second letter addressed to Mauvissière.

Mary had written, *If you can, get access directly or indirectly to Throckmorton, Lord Henry Howard, or for the third, Northumberland, who I have never dealt directly with; assure them in my name that I shall never forget their affections for me and their great suffering in my cause.*

'This confirms everything you suspected,' said Jacob. 'Doesn't it?'

'It does. Throckmorton has admitted that the plot was designed to release Mary Stuart and that the Spanish Ambassador was one of its principal promoters. George More has said that he carried many letters between Mary and the Spanish Ambassador. Now this,' he said, indicating the letter, 'sends thanks to Throckmorton for suffering in her cause. I cannot believe other than that she was a party to this plot.'

He sighed heavily again. 'This is the second time she has been caught in conspiracy against the State. Many of these conspirators will die, but the Scottish Queen will not stop until she succeeds, or fails in the attempt. I grow weary of her intrigues at the expense of others.'

He was silent for a while, then he gave Jacob a promise. 'Tell George More that he can have a free pardon in return for signing a full confession of his dealings with Charles Paget. You may also tell him that his uncle will be safe as well.'

He added a warning. 'He must assure me that the letters were passed to Mary Stuart without the help of Shrewsbury's servants, mind you. Should they be involved I will have their names.'

Jacob thanked him on behalf of More and then saw that Walsingham was regarding him with an amused expression. Motioning Jacob to sit down in the chair in front of the desk, he sent for Colonel Young.

'Sit alongside me, Colonel,' he said, handing him some paper and a quill. 'I wish you to record the answers to some questions I will ask the prisoner, Jacob Bell.'

They both looked at Walsingham sharply at this description, but wisely said nothing. Walsingham cleared his throat and then, regarding Jacob with a stern expression, began to read from his notes.

'Master Glassmaker Bell, it has come to my attention that a number of prominent Catholic League supporters, including the Duke of Guise, were present at a function at your house in Paris, in July of 1581. Do you deny this?'

Jacob shook his head. 'Not at all.'

'Why were these people at your house and did you conspire with them against the Queen?'

Jacob vigorously denied the accusation. 'My house in Paris contains a showroom for my glass and a new range of jewellery. Many prominent citizens of Paris were present at the opening, both Catholic and Protestant. They all came as customers and nothing else. I am the Queen's Glassmaker. It was simply a commercial occasion.'

'I understand you and your wife were also present at a reception given for the Catholic League at the Duke of Guise's château. Was this also a commercial occasion, as you put it?' There was irony in his voice and a tiny smile at the corner of his mouth.

Colonel Young, who seemed to have a permanently amused expression, looked at Walsingham as if to say something. Walsingham frowned and the colonel put his head down and busied himself writing down questions and answers.

Jacob watched this little sideshow, but did not change his expression as he answered.

'Not at all. It was purely a social occasion and mainly for my wife's benefit. She had been unwell since the death of our daughter and it was a chance for her to socialise.'

Walsingham turned to Colonel Young. 'Have you got all that down, Colonel?'

'Every word,' said the colonel solemnly.

'Good,' said Walsingham. 'Then that concludes my examination of the Queen's Glassmaker, Jacob Bell. For the record, Colonel, I find that Jacob Bell's answers have satisfied me that he has not conspired against the State.'

He gave them both a cheerful smile. 'Now, let's have a drink of wine to celebrate. And that's definitely not for the record, of course, Colonel. I learned only this morning that Lennox has died. Apparently he has been progressively ill throughout the winter. At least that ends any influence he might bring to bear on King James VI.' Not only that, but thanks to the Throckmorton Plot, the main document of the Bond of Association, written by Lord Burghley and myself, has been approved by Parliament. It has received the Queen's authorisation and it now has statutory authority.'

'What does that mean?' asked Jacob.

'The document obliges all signatories to execute any person that attempts to, or succeeds in usurping the throne, or makes an attempt to, or successfully assassinates Elizabeth. In the latter case, it also makes it obligatory for the signatories to hunt down the killer. We will all be signatories, including Mary Stuart.'

He raised his glass. 'To the demise of all the Queen's enemies.'

As the colonel remarked later. 'Walsingham was in a strangely playful mood. You must have given him some good news.'

'I suppose I must have,' said Jacob. 'But I doubt it will last!'

Chapter Twenty
Sheffield and London, 1584

The news that Mary Stuart was being moved to Wingfield Manor and that the Earl of Shrewsbury would no longer be her jailer, came as a huge shock to Jed Sutton. Hammond, the steward at Sheffield Castle, assured him that since the Manor was a property belonging to the earl, Jed would still be able to deliver ale.

'It's better for you anyway,' he said. 'It's much nearer to Burton.'

'That's true,' said Jed. 'I don't make much profit trailing all the way up here to Sheffield. I suppose it won't be long before she's back though. They're always moving her about.'

'Not this time,' said Hammond. 'From what the earl said, she will only be at Wingfield for a while. Then she'll be moved to Tutbury, in Staffordshire, but I don't know how long she will be there.'

Jed was astonished by the news. 'Tutbury!' he exclaimed. 'The castle was really run down the last time I went there for the earl. It stank. It's no place to keep a Queen.'

Hammond looked at him strangely and for a moment Jed feared the man was getting suspicious. 'I don't know what you're complaining about,' he said, shrugging. 'You don't have to live there.'

Jed wisely said nothing more and went off to unload the dray. On the long drive home he thought about the implications of what he'd been told. He'd heard about the Throckmorton plot and obviously Walsingham had decided to take no chances with Mary Stuart. Tutbury might be unhealthy, but it was a fortress compared to the manors at Sheffield and Wingfield. However, they wouldn't be able to keep her there for ever. They had to clean it all up after full occupation for a while, or the stench became unbearable. He was going to have to revise his plans and find some way to smuggle letters in to Queen Mary, or be able to contact her servants.

It would be at least two weeks before he would have to go to

Wingfield for the next delivery. Since the Manor was new to him, he decided to go and see the steward in charge on the grounds he was checking out their needs. He also decided to take a look at Tutbury. It was only a few miles from Burton. It might be useful to check the layout and how he might get word to the Queen.

His thoughts then turned to Jacob Bell. Perhaps when they moved Queen Mary to Tutbury, he might get the chance to go to London again. The long trips to Chatsworth and Sheffield didn't leave him enough time between deliveries. Next time, if he had the opportunity, he would make sure that Bell didn't betray anyone ever again.

One of the legacies of his time as a highwayman was that he was a very good shot with his pistols. He had a fine pair of snaphaunce pistols he had stolen from a wealthy merchant and had practised a lot with them. He found them easier to use than the wheel-lock pistols, although there was still a delay in firing. He had never used them during his highwayman days, as the mere sight of two pistols pointed at travellers was enough to cower the bravest of them. But he would try to get a shot at Bell with the pistols. Perhaps he could hold up the coach if the opportunity presented itself!

By the time he arrived at Burton it was late in the evening and Jed was in a foul mood. He had been drinking a lot recently. A necessity of his trade was to drink with landlords and stewards, and if a brewer drank his own ale, so they thought, it must be satisfactory. By now Jed was a seasoned drinker and, having downed several pints, went to bed. He dreamed about his father, Count Ridolfi and the life he could have had in Rome if it wasn't for the accursed Bell.

The opportunity to carry out his threat came sooner than he had expected. The following morning he was awakened early by a messenger from Shrewsbury's steward at Wingfield advising him that no ale was required for two weeks, as supplies had been transferred from Sheffield. Since he was now at a loose end, he decided to go to London.

The journey did little to ease his foul mood, it rained for much of the way. He decided to rest and headed for the Staples Inn in Holborn, outside the city. He did not want to go near the

White Hart in case anyone remembered him.

The following morning he entered the city and made his way towards Bell's house at Mark Street. To his disappointment the front gates were securely closed and he was unable to see anything. Going round to the back gates, they were wide open and he stopped his horse a few moments while he familiarised himself with the layout. As he watched, a stout man dressed in livery came out of the stables and seeing the horseman at the gate hurried towards him. Jed simply turned his head and rode off around the corner.

By the time Harry Heywood arrived at the gate, there was no sign of the man on the chestnut horse. Closing and barring the gate, Harry went to see Jacob. 'I'm not entirely sure, Master Jacob, but I have a strong suspicion that a man was watching the house.

'Did you get a good look at him?'

'I'm afraid I didn't see his face,' he said, with a grimace. 'George was grooming the horses and I'd gone down to see him. As I came out of the stables, there was a man on a chestnut mare at the back gates, just sitting there and staring at the stable block. Unfortunately, the gate hadn't been closed when the coach came back. As soon as he saw me, the man turned his head away and rode off. By the time I got to the gate there was no sign of him.'

'Did George see anyone when he came in with the coach?'

Henry shook his head. 'No he didn't. The only reason I paid any attention was because it was a very handsome chestnut mare and the man was dressed in working clothes. It was rather too good a horse for a working man to be riding.'

'He may have been going somewhere for his master, like a smith, I suppose,' said Jacob. 'However, it's best not to take chances. In future, I want the two of you armed and on the coach every time anyone goes out. Both gates are to be shut immediately after leaving and entering.'

Jacob was not overly concerned at the incident, but it would be foolish to ignore it. He couldn't help wondering who might be watching him. Friend or foe?

Jed was now faced with a dilemma. Mark Street was not a broad thoroughfare and although there was a steady flow of people, it would be difficult to keep watch without his presence being noted. After his close shave at the rear gates, he needed somewhere safe as a vantage point.

He rode past the house to the bottom of Mark Street, but there was nothing there that would make a secure hiding place. Going up the hill again, just before the junction with Harte Street, there was a lane between the houses which led across some open ground. He could see a church in the distance and by following the lane he came to the churchyard belonging to St. Olave's. Another lane joined the path and led behind the church into Sydon Lane.

Retracing his path, he noticed that the house at the end of the lane was empty. At the rear a gate led into the lane from a yard with a tumbledown shed that might once have been a stable. After a cautious look around, he forced open the gate and led his horse into the yard. The shed was not quite as dilapidated as it looked from the lane. Only one end was falling down, the other had sufficient room to take his horse so that it could not be seen. There was even some hay which, although it looked a bit mouldy, the horse seemed happy to eat. The back door of the house proved to be little problem either and after kicking it open, Jed had a careful look around.

The previous occupants had obviously left in a hurry as there were still a few dusty pieces of cheap furniture and signs of a hasty exit. Making his way upstairs, he went into the room at the front, the windows of which were so dirty they barely let any light through. From what Jed could see, the overhang of the house gave a good view of the right-hand side of Bell's house. A perfect place to keep watch.

There was a battered old chair in the room which looked as though it would hold his weight. Dusting it off, Jed sat down at the window and cleaned a small patch of glass. Sure enough he had a good view of the house, stables and both gates. Unfortunately, it was too far away to fire the pistols with any degree of accuracy.

Returning downstairs, he noticed that one of the panes of the front window had a large piece missing at the corner. He checked to see what field of view he had from there. A man on a horse was passing by and Jed was sure that he would have a clean shot at anyone passing at a similar distance. Being inside the cottage would also make it difficult for the gunman to be observed. He would be able to run out of the back door and ride down at the side of St. Olave's before anyone could come looking for him.

Jed realised that he was getting hungry. He decided to head back to Holborn and make the necessary arrangements for an early start tomorrow. He would inform the innkeeper that he was leaving and pay his dues. He told him he was heading north-east in case anyone enquired. That way, if he was lucky enough to kill Bell, he could head out of the city in the opposite direction and be well away before the hue and cry was raised.

The following morning he was at the cottage very early. He had brought some provisions for himself and the horse and settled down to wait. Taking up his position in the upstairs room, he kept watch on Bell's premises. Apart from the servants, there was little activity at the house, until about eight o'clock. Two servants appeared and began to prepare Bell's coach for a journey. About three quarters of an hour later, Jacob Bell and a tall, dark-haired boy, probably his eldest son, came out of the house and climbed into the coach. The coach left by the back gate and proceeded into the city. The gates were only opened sufficiently to allow the coach out and were then immediately closed. Obviously, security had been tightened up since his last visit. It was a shame he'd been spotted by that thickset servant. Not only were they now closing the gates, but there had been two men on the coach. One was the same man who had seen him and the other a tall thin man. They were both armed with a couple of pistols, which made an attack on the coach a very risky business, especially for one lone highwayman.

About an hour after the coach had left, two women accompanied by two small children came out of the house and walked in the formal garden for some time. They sat for a while in a bower, but Jed could only just see them. He assumed it was Bell's wife and two more children with a nurse, or servant. Bell had been very busy in the last few years.

Just then, the coach returned and once more the gates were closed immediately. Bell went into the house and the young man went to join his mother. There was little further action that day, other than some comings and goings of servants, so Jed was forced to spend another night in an inn. On this occasion he chose the Saracen's Head, hard by Aldgate, since it was much nearer to Bell's house.

The following day Jed was once more at the cottage early. About an hour after he had arrived, the stocky groom and the tall thin man, who had ridden on the coach, brought out two horses and saddled them. They led the horses to the front of the house and Bell came out dressed for riding. Jed's lips curled with hate as there was a tender farewell at the door for the wife and children. With any luck, it would be Bell's last goodbye.

As soon as he was sure that Bell and the tall thin man were using the front gate, Jed rushed downstairs and cocked both of the already loaded pistols. He waited with bated breath to see if Bell was riding past the house. With a sharp intake of breath he saw he was. There was only going to be one chance. So, taking aim at the point where a rider would be, after the pistol's delay, he waited, heart pounding in anticipation of killing the hated Jacob Bell.

The horsemen came into view moving slowly. Jed snarled in triumph. Bell was in the lead. He would have a clear shot. They were almost in range now and Jed saw Bell turn to say something to the other man, who spurred his horse to catch up. Realising he would be too late if he waited any longer, Jed fired.

The smoke from the discharge billowing up in the confined space obscured his view for a moment, but he could hear horses neighing in terror. He flapped at the smoke to clear it away and frantically rubbed the window to get a better view of what was happening. The other horseman had caught up with Bell and both horses were rearing up, hooves flailing. For a moment Jed's heart sank and then he saw Bell struggling to maintain control of his mount. The horses collided, reeled over and unseated their riders. There was confusion in the street as the horses struggled to gain their footing; but, after they had, Jed saw two figures lying still on the ground. People were rushing to hold the horses' reins and Jed's view was blocked by jostling bodies. He dashed upstairs to get a better view and, through a gap in the gathering crowd, he could just make out Bell's face covered in blood and deathly pale.

There was no sign of movement and a large pool of blood was oozing around his head Jed crossed himself fervently, exultant. Bell was dead, for sure.

Then he heard shouts of 'Murder! Murder!' and realised his peril. Gathering his wits, he rushed downstairs and out into the yard. Mounting his already saddled horse, he opened the back gate very cautiously. There was no one in the lane, so he rode slowly at first and then, reaching the fields, spurred his horse across the field towards St. Olave's.

On reaching the churchyard, he gave a smile of satisfaction as he saw that there was no pursuit behind him. Carrying on into Sydon Lane, he rode down into Tower Street and crossed the city to Newgate, taking his time like any normal traveller. By late afternoon, the city was well behind him and he rested for the night in a country inn. He celebrated his victory that night and despite being rather drunk, slept soundly.

Chapter Twenty-One
London, 1584

Harry Heywood watched as Jacob and George Walker rode away along Mark Street. When the shot rang out, he drew his pistol and ran towards them as they were thrown from their horses and lay still. Bystanders were trying to hold the horses which threatened to trample the still bodies and women were screaming that both men had been murdered.

Harry rammed his pistol in his belt and ran into the crowd milling around the prone figures. 'Let me through to my master!' he roared and forced his way through. Jacob was lying immobile with his face covered in blood. George, close by to him, had been shot through the neck. He was deathly pale and a rapidly widening pool of blood had reached as far as Jacob.

One quick glance was enough to tell Harry there was nothing further that could be done for George. The ex-sergeant had seen too many deaths in his career. Kneeling down beside Jacob he examined him quickly and expertly. There was no obvious sign of a wound. However, he didn't appear to be breathing.

Ripping off Jacob's blood-stained ruff, Harry laid his fingers at the top of his neck, midway between his chin and his ear. At first he could feel nothing. He moved his fingers a little and gave a sigh of relief. He felt a pulse. Rather thin and ragged, it was true, but a pulse nevertheless.

Standing up, he was just about to ask for help when Jack and Bob Petts rushed to his side. 'Is he ...' Jack's voice broke off and Harry was quick to reassure them he wasn't dead.

'You must help me to get him to the house. He must have some medical attention.'

Jack indicated Walker's body. 'What about George?'

Harry shook his head. 'There's nothing more we can do for him. Take Master Jacob's cloak and cover him for now. You can get him after we've moved the master to the house and sent for Doctor Nguyên.'

He turned to the nearest bystander. 'Keep an eye on the body for me until my men can come back for him and the horses. Tell someone to go for the Watch.'

Alerted by the commotion as they carried Jacob into the house, Maria rushed downstairs. When she saw her husband's blood-covered face and his limp body, arms hanging lifelessly as they carried him into the study, she put her hand over her mouth to stifle a scream. Taking a deep breath, she composed herself and dashed into the kitchen to fetch a bowl of water and a clean cloth. When she hastened into the study, Harry hurriedly assured her that Jacob was still alive.

Maria knelt down beside Jacob who was lying on the settle. She gently wiped the blood from his otherwise ashen face.

'It's not his blood,' said Harry. 'It's George's. He's been shot dead.'

'Dead!' said Maria, disbelief in her voice. 'Dead! Who can have shot him?'

Harry shook his head. 'We don't know. Nobody saw anything as far as we can tell. I should have been guarding Master Jacob,' he said grimly. 'I've more experience than George, but Master Jacob insisted I stay to look after you and the children.' Pulling himself together, he went towards the door. 'I'll go and see to George now and send Jack to fetch Doctor Nguyên.'

Maria nodded abstractedly as Harry went out. She examined Jacob carefully. She'd wiped all the blood away and whilst there was only a slight graze on his temple, a large bruise was already blooming. She was also pleased to see that his colour was improving and so was his breathing which had been very shallow at first.

She gently brushed a lock of hair away from his face and looked up as Anna came rushing in.

'Oh, Maria!' she exclaimed. 'I've just heard what happened. Don't worry about the children, the tutor and the maid are looking after them. They don't know the master has been hurt.' She held out a small bottle. 'I brought some sal volatile in case you needed it.'

Maria took the proffered bottle and, uncorking it, waved it gently under Jacob's nose. After a short while he gave a jerk and moved his head to one side. His eyelids fluttered and he gave a groan and tried to sit up. Maria stopped him and lowered his head on to the cushions. 'Lie still, Jacob. You've had a very heavy fall.' She handed the bottle to Anna and, rinsing out the cloth, she wiped his face.

He raised himself up, giving her a weak smile. 'What happened? All I remember is getting a bang on the head.' He sank back with a groan and rubbed his temple.

Maria put her finger on his mouth. 'Sssh ...' she soothed. 'Just lie still now and rest.'

It was some while before Doctor Nguyên arrived. By that time Jacob had been taken upstairs and put to bed. When the doctor saw all his bruises he tutted to himself and then, having finished his examination, gave his verdict.

'Jacob Bell in wars again. Only heavy bruises though.' He shook his head. 'Very lucky. Ball from pistol not go through armour.' When the doctor had removed the brigandine, the ball had almost penetrated right through. 'I prepare lotion for skin only,' Doctor Nguyên continued, 'and potion for pain. Where pain bad,' he said, indicating the large bruise in Jacob's ribs, 'will use needles in *ashi* point where *qi* has stagnated.'

Jacob, who had been lying back with his eyes closed, patiently allowing the doctor to examine him, suddenly opened his eyes wide in shock. 'George!' he muttered, through gritted teeth. 'What about George? I've just remembered what happened in the street. It was me who was the target,' he said guiltily. 'Poor George got in the way. What's happened to him?'

Doctor Nguyên gently encouraged him to lie down again. 'Time enough for servant when master better. Now must use needles for pain.' He rummaged in his large case and grunted in satisfaction. 'Ah! Have some potion left.' Taking out a bottle, he took a glass measure from his case and pouring a careful dose, gave it to Maria.

'Husband must take this now. Help stop pain while I prepare needles.'

He busied himself unpacking the needles while Maria helped Jacob to swallow the potion. By the time the doctor was ready, Jacob was lying quietly and breathing steadily.

The doctor smiled and turned to Maria. 'Potion contained

sedative. Will insert needles in *ashi* points while sleeping. Husband wake up, one hour, maybe two. Give new potion I mix. Feel much better.'

When Jacob awoke nearly two hours later the doctor had left. When he tried to sit up he found the sharp pain had also gone. He ached all over, but it was a dull pain he could cope with. When the door opened he was surprised to see Colonel Young with Maria.

The colonel smiled happily at him. 'I see the reports of your death are somewhat exaggerated. I'm told you are likely to be causing problems for some time yet.'

'My death? Where did you hear about that?'

'From Walsingham of course. I was at his house in Sydon Lane when he received a report from the Watch that you'd been killed. He sent me straight round with my men to find out what was going on.'

'Well as you can see, I'm bloody but unbowed. Courtesy of the Queen's brigandine.' He frowned. 'Not that it was any use to poor George. The ball tore his throat out before it hit me.'

Maria shuddered and crossed herself and addressed the colonel, 'I don't know how you can joke about death. It's the wives and children who have to suffer.' She busied herself fluffing up the pillows behind Jacob so he could sit up more comfortably.

The colonel bowed to Maria. 'My apologies, Lady Maria. I should have been more conscious of your feelings. We face death on a regular basis and flippant words are our way of coping. We must never let our enemies think we are frightened. Or our friends either.' He turned to Jacob. 'I must get back to my men and see how the search for the assassin is progressing.' As he turned to go there was a knock on the door. Maria opened it and a sergeant asked if the colonel was there. Maria let him in and then excused herself to tell the children that their father was on the mend.

'Begging your pardon, sir,' the sergeant said, 'but we've found where the assassin was hiding.'

'Any sign of him?'

'I'm afraid not, sir. It looks as though he's long gone.'

'Very well, Sergeant. Well done. I will join you shortly to have a look at the villain's bolt hole. Are the rest of the men still there?'

'Yes sir.'

'Carry on then, Sergeant.' When the sergeant had left, the colonel saw that Jacob was sitting on the side of the bed reaching for his clothes.

'Stay where you are, Jacob. It would be better for now if no one knows you are alive.' Jacob was about to argue, but the colonel forestalled him.

'For all we know, the assassin may have an accomplice hanging around to find out if he succeeded in killing you. Better you stay here and keep him guessing. In fact, it would be better if you are seen in public as little as possible for as long as you can. Use the coach for travelling and keep the blinds down.'

Reluctantly Jacob promised he would do as the colonel asked. He was secretly rather relieved to let the colonel take charge. The fall had been bone-shaking and some more rest would be welcome.

'Let me know what you find out. I want to know who the attempted assassin is.'

'Have you any idea who it might have been?'

'If the Duke of Guise believes I've betrayed him, he would certainly be a candidate. The only other person I know for sure hates me is Jed Sutton. However, nothing has been heard of him for ten years, so why now?' Jacob shrugged. 'The last time Sutton was seen he was in France. He could be anywhere.'

'It doesn't seem like a long list. Are you sure you've no business enemies?'

Jacob shook his head vehemently. 'No, it's not about business. My former rivals are now the last people who would want me killed. I make them too much money.'

The colonel grinned. 'Money will even make your enemies into friends.' He gave Jacob a comradely pat on the shoulder. 'I'd better go and see what the sergeant has found. I'll come back later to report.'

When he had left, Jacob sent for Harry Heywood. 'Has George's body been brought in?'

'Yes, Master Jacob. We've put him in the small room over the coach house.'

'I want you to cast your mind back to the man on a chestnut horse you saw at the gate yesterday. Close your eyes and try to picture the scene.' This was a little trick his grandfather had taught him. He always found it useful when he was trying to remember something.

Harry closed his eyes and Jacob asked him to describe what he could see. 'I'm just coming out of the stable and looking towards the gate, there is a man on a chestnut horse just sitting in the entrance staring at me.

'Try to describe what you see.'

Harry's brow furrowed as he concentrated on the figure. 'It's a large chestnut horse, I'd guess about sixteen hands. The man fairly tall, wiry and dressed in brown working clothes. He's seen me and is starting to turn away, but he has a slightly hooked nose. Oh, he's riding off, but I do believe he has a short pointed beard. He's a very good horseman he handles the horse very easily. Must have strong wrists for a wiry man. He's gone now and by the time I reach the gate he is out of sight.'

'Very well done, Harry,' said Jacob. Then a thought struck him. Jed Sutton was a very good horseman with strong wrists, but he didn't have a beard. 'What colour was his hair, do you know, Harry?'

'Light brown, I think, but I wouldn't be absolutely sure.'

'I want you to along to Aldgate,' Jacob said, handing Harry a heavy purse. 'A few coins in the right places should ensure you get co-operation. There are two inns, the Saracen, just inside Aldgate and the other The White Hart, outside the gate. Do you know them?'

Harry said he did and Jacob continued. 'Go to both inns and speak to the landlords and have a word with the gate-men at Aldgate. See if they remember a man and a chestnut horse in the last two days, or even for a longer period. A big chestnut horse or mare is not that common.'

Harry was away for about two hours and when he returned, he had some news. 'The man I described, stayed at the Saracen Inn last night, but left saying he was heading north for Cambridge. Interestingly, the tollgate men swear that they have not seen hide nor hair of a chestnut horse for some considerable time.'

'So.' said Jacob, 'our man didn't leave by Aldgate today. Did you get the name he gave at the Inn?'

'Jack Southern is the name he gave.'

The name meant nothing, but the man did have a chestnut mare and they were not that common.

'What about the White Hart?'

'The only time the landlord could remember anyone staying with a horse like that, was the day that Jack Nevison, the highwayman, was killed. It wasn't the same man though, although he had a beard, his name was James Sumner.'

Jacob remembered the day very well. He'd been passing the inn on his way into the city, when Nevison's horse had bolted out of the inn yard. Again the name James Sumner was unfamiliar even though the description was similar. It was too much of a coincidence.

He thanked Harry and when he had left, leaned back on the pillows. Jack Southern, James Sumner, Jed Sutton. Suddenly, he sat bolt upright. JS! they all had the initials JS. Three men all with the same initials, two of them excellent riders and all on chestnut horses. Jed Sutton was an excellent horseman and although he didn't have a beard the last time Jacob saw him, it was not difficult to grow one. What if he was right and it was Jed Sutton? Jed could have seen him when he tried to stop the runaway horse. There was a crowd of onlookers at the entrance to the the White Hart Inn. Maybe he followed me home. Jacob rubbed his aching ribs. But why wait until now to shoot him? And then he remembered. Shortly after the incident at the inn, the whole family had gone to France. Jed had missed his chance and this was the first time he had been able to come back. He was sure now that he had Jed Sutton to thank for the shooting. Another score to be paid back, with interest!

Chapter Twenty-Two
London, 1584

Anyone entering into Walsingham's study who knew him well, would be astonished at the sight of him leaning back in his chair chortling with glee. 'By George,' he crowed, 'Berden has excelled himself this time.' He read the line in the letter that had animated him for about the fifth time. Mary Stuart had written to Charles Arundel in Paris, *I commend Morgan, Paget and your good self for all that you have done on my behalf. I cannot wait for the invasion from Scotland to begin. I weary of the long years I have spent in dreary places and long for the time you and my good cousin, Henri of Guise release me from my jailers and set me on the throne of England. Together with my son in Scotland and Henri in France, we will forge an alliance that will turn back the tide of the Protestant Reformation and forge a new Catholicism that will earn even Spain's respect.*

Walsingham sighed. It most certainly would. Should such an alliance come to pass, the Reformation would be finished. At least, when Mary wrote this letter, she was not aware of the ousting of Lennox from Scotland. That had put a severe dent in their plans. However, it was unlikely that Henri of Guise would simply forget about the invasion. He must find a way to discover what he was up to now.

Undoubtedly, the fortunate position of Jacob Bell at the heart of the Guise plans, was a huge step towards that, but if the news of his death was correct, it would be a disaster. Henri of Guise trusted Bell, unless that is, he had received word that he was one of Walsingham's agents. That seemed unlikely. The position of Bell was unique. He was a highly intelligent, intuitive and talented agent, as well as a brilliant swordsman, who could be ruthless when needed, but only in what he considered to be fair circumstances. Torture to obtain information, was not on that list.

Bell was something of a rarity in that he did not fit into the normal order of precedence in England. Walsingham had to admit, he found Bell rather impertinent in his assumption that he was the equal of a Privy Councillor and treated him as such. Even to the point of being critical. Despite this, he liked Jacob Bell and hoped the report of his death was ill-founded.

He started to read the letter again when there was a knock at the door. Walsingham looked up from the letter and regarded Colonel Young with some trepidation. 'What news of Jacob Bell, Colonel?'

'I'm pleased to say, Sir Francis, that Jacob Bell is bloody, but unbowed. Apart from numerous bruises, which make such a gesture difficult.'

'Ah! Good. So the report was wrong.'

The colonel gave a grimace of distaste. 'Unfortunately, in the case of George Walker, one of the men I recommended to Bell, the report was only too well-founded. The pair of them were shot at while riding towards Harte Street and George was killed.'

'I doubt he was the target?'

The colonel agreed. 'I am certain he wasn't. It appears that the shot was aimed at Bell from a nearby house. Fortunately, Bell was wearing his brigandine and it stopped the shot.' He gave a grim smile. 'Only just, I have to say. The ball had almost gone through the plates. Bell was knocked off his horse and has a huge bruise on his chest, as well as numerous other places after the fall.'

'It sounds as though he was lucky,' commented Walsingham. 'Was there any clue to the identity of the assassin?'

'I'm afraid not. The only thing we know for sure is that he rides a chestnut horse and has a full beard. If this is our man, and I'm fairly sure it is, he rode through St. Olave's churchyard and passed this house to get away.'

'I wonder why he didn't go out through Aldgate? It's the nearest exit from the city.'

'I don't know. no one at the toll remembers seeing a chestnut horse all day.'

Hmm ...' Walsingham looked thoughtful. 'Either he's gone to ground somewhere, or he doubled back to leave the city by Newgate or Ludgate. It doesn't look like a spur of the moment attempt. Has Bell any idea who it might be?'

'It could have been the Duke of Guise's man, if Bell has been betrayed to the Catholics. The only other possibility is Jed Sutton.'

'Ah,' said Walsingham, with interest, 'he seems a very good candidate. He has not been heard of for some considerable time, but he could have been in hiding in England. I'm fairly sure that he's not with his father in Rome. My spies keep a good watch on the count. Anyway,' Walsingham shrugged, 'at least we can forget about Bell for the time being. Let's get back to the matter we were discussing before we were so rudely interrupted by news of that impertinent glassmaker.'

He picked up the letter again. 'There is no doubt now that Mary Stuart has been passing letters through her secretary Curle, to Baldwin, a servant of the Earl of Shrewsbury. Even now we have moved her to Wingfield,' he said, waving the letter. 'This is certain proof.' He sighed. 'I instructed Sadler and Somers to watch her closely and still she gets letters to Mauvissière, the French Ambassador!'

'I'm afraid,' the colonel said, apologetically, 'it's Wingfield itself that's the problem. The very nature of the place defies a strict watch. I checked out what had been done to keep Mary Stuart safe and concluded that her jailers had done all they could to stop letters getting in or out.'

'Very well,' Walsingham said reluctantly, 'what would you recommend, Colonel?'

'We must send her to Tutbury Castle. I also suggest Sir Amias Paulet should be in charge of her. There is little chance of the Scottish Queen corrupting him.'

'No chance at all,' Walsingham said, with a grim smile. Paulet was not only a friend, but a staunch Protestant and declared enemy of all the political and religious ideals that Mary Stuart represented. A good choice. 'She will not wrap him around her little finger like she did with Shrewsbury. I will approach him directly.'

'What of the Queen? It will mean a huge change in the way that Mary Stuart is held. Paulet will not stand for all the trappings of a Queen of Scots in exile.'

'Leave her to me. There is every reason to believe that after the Ridolfi and Throckmorton plots and now this,' he said, tapping the letter, 'that the Queen will agree to instituting a much stricter regime for controlling the ambitions of her wayward cousin.'

'Will you need me to go to Wingfield when you move Mary Stuart?'

Walsingham nodded. 'Of course. You can escort Sir Amias to Wingfield and then assist him to move Mary Stuart to Tutbury. I want you to be in charge of the security of the move. I will give you orders accordingly.'

'You're sure Sir Amias will not refuse? It will be an onerous task.'

'It will be an order from the Queen. He will go gladly.' Walsingham straightened the papers on his desk and the colonel got to his feet. 'I will make all of the arrangements and await your further instructions, Sir Francis,' he said and, with a bow, left the room.

A short while later Walsingham rang the handbell and when his secretary answered, asked if Gilbert Gifford had arrived. When told he had, he instructed his secretary to show him in. When Gifford sat down, Walsingham studied him carefully. He was a cousin of William Gifford who was the leader of the Catholic recusants. Gilbert, a seminary trained priest, was suspected of travelling around the Catholic families in England, sounding them out if they would support a rebellion against Elizabeth and saying mass. Gilbert had been arrested on entering the country and sent to the Tower of London.

'Please accept my apologies for keeping you waiting. An urgent matter needed my attention. Will you take a glass of Madeira?'

'Certainly,' he said in surprise. 'It is infinitely preferable to the rack I was expecting.'

Once they had settled down with their drinks Walsingham explained why he had invited Gifford to meet him. 'It is my understanding that the Seculars have no great love for the Jesuits and the supporters of the Scottish Queen.'

Gifford nodded. 'Many of us consider that the Jesuits are a much greater danger to the Seculars than Queen Elizabeth, who was pursuing a policy of religious tolerance. However, Morgan and Paget are much more militant. They want England to become a Catholic nation again and are even prepared to consider the assassination of Queen Elizabeth to achieve this goal.'

'What can you tell me of this?'

'I will tell you what I know to demonstrate my good faith, but nothing more ... for free.'

Walsingham settled back in his chair. He was sure now that he had read Gifford correctly.

'Do you know of a man called William Parry?' asked Gifford.

Walsingham knew very well who Parry was, he was a spendthrift and profligate who had done enough evil to deserve hanging, but had somehow persuaded the Queen to pardon him. He had been enlisted as a spy by Lord Burghley and had been sent to France to spy on Thomas Morgan. In January he had returned to England and sought an audience with the Queen. He confessed he had had dealings with the Pope and Morgan, Mary Stuart's agent in France and had been recruited to make an attempt on her life. He declared, that there was no treasonable intent, but to discover what they were planning. He showed the Queen a letter from Cardinal Como that seemed to confirm his story. He was forgiven his past crimes and given a seat in Parliament.

He had no intention of confirming his knowledge, so simply said. 'It is a fairly common name. What of this gentleman.'

'The last time I saw Morgan, he was extremely annoyed at Parry to whom he had paid a large sum of money to shoot Queen Elizabeth. Apparently Parry had sworn an oath to do it and received absolution from Cardinal Como. When it came to it, Parry went to shoot the Queen as she walked in Saint James's Park. But as he was about to do it, a messenger called the Queen away. Parry has refused to try again, saying it was divine intervention and God had found him wanting.'

Walsingham was startled by this story. Parry did not strike him as a brave enough man to do a deed like this, but he would certainly investigate. Doctor William Parry, if indeed it was he, would receive no pardon this time if it proved to be true. He regarded Gifford steadily. 'I will look into this. Should you hear anything else on this matter, especially if it is proof, I will reward you handsomely. As to other things, I believe we are well placed to help each other.'

'How so?' queried Gifford.

Walsingham collected his thoughts and outlined his plan. 'What I am about to tell you is not known outside of these walls as yet. Because of the various plots against our sovereign Queen, Mary Stuart will no longer be treated as a Queen in exile. She will be moved to Tutbury and there she will be held incommunicado except through me. Sir Amias Paulet and his assistant Sir Drue Drury will be in charge of keeping her safe and she will be subjected to a very strict control.'

Gifford looked startled at this news and was obviously mulling over the implications before he replied. 'That will certainly ruffle a lot of feathers on the Continent. They must keep in touch with Mary Stuart since they will not be able proceed in her name without her written approval.'

'Exactly so,' said Walsingham smugly. 'And you, my dear Gifford, are going to go and inform your old contacts, Morgan and Paget, what has happened. Before you go, we will devise a method, which you control, whereby they can get all the letters they desire to Mary Stuart, with total security.'

Gifford gave an ingratiating smile. 'And, of course, I will ensure that you receive copies of all of the letters, both in and out.'

'Of course,' said Walsingham. Whilst there were still some delicate negotiations relating to remuneration for services rendered to be conducted, Walsingham could see from the avaricious gleam in his eye, that Gifford was eager to become his new double agent.

Chapter Twenty-Three
London, 1585

The presence chamber in the Palace of Greenwich was in a festive mood as the cream of the Court awaited the arrival of Châteauneuf, the new French Ambassador. Even Burghley was there, despite his recent attack of gout. He had advised the Queen that since Châteauneuf was known to be friendly to Mary Stuart's cause, a show of *entente cordiale* would be appropriate, so she had ordered that the chamber should be decorated with the finest embroidered silk hangings and furnishings. Jacob, still walking rather stiffly from his bruises, nodded to several of his acquaintances as he wandered along the arched cloister that ran down three sides of the chamber. Turning the corner, he saw a magnificently attired Leicester and his gaudy entourage of sycophants heading towards him. 'Ah, Master Bell, there you are,' Leicester said, stopping in front of Jacob.

Jacob bowed. 'My lord.'

Leicester came straight to the point. 'I am planning a great masque later this year and there will be a large banquet. I desire you to design a new set of glasses for me.'

'Certainly, My lord,' said a delighted Jacob. 'Have you any idea what sort of glass you would like?'

Leicester laughed heartily. 'Bless you, Master Bell. I have no thoughts in my head for designing glasses. Horses, now that would be different. I know about them. I leave designing work to those who have the gift, like yourself.' His fawning entourage joined in his laughter. 'Send me some designs and I will choose. I will be here in London for at least two weeks.' With that, he gave a friendly wave and a small bow of acknowledgement and swept off.

A small group of young men standing nearby had watched this exchange with interest. When Leicester departed, a handsome young man in his twenties approached Jacob and bowed.

'Pardon my forwardness, but I believe you are Jacob Bell, the Queen's Glassmaker.'

When Jacob admitted he was, the young man smiled. 'I can see you do not recognise me, Master Bell, but that is not surprising. I was but a very young boy when you visited my father's house at Dethick in Darbieshire.'

Jacob cast his mind back to his stay at Sir Henry Babington's house on his way to Chatsworth. For a moment he was puzzled and then he remembered the ardent young man of about ten years old, reverently handling the armorial glass he had made for Mary Stuart and informing him he intended to seek service in Mary Stuart's household when he was older.

'Of course, Anthony Babington. Your father kindly put me up for the night.'

'That is correct. My father died, you know, and I inherited the title.'

'I'm sorry, Sir Anthony, I had not heard. My condolences.'

Babington gave a little bow of recognition and then after a careful look around to see who was in earshot, lowered his head so he was close and asked Jacob a question. 'Do you remember Gilbert Gifford? He was at my father's house that night.'

The name sent alarm bells ringing in Jacob's mind. That was where he had first met Gilbert Gifford. He had been suspicious of Jacob, but he had managed to convince him he was a sympathiser.

Walsingham had recently informed him that Gilbert Gifford had agreed to work for him, while acting as a go-between for the recusants living on the Continent, Mary Stuart and the new French Ambassador, Châteauneuf. With his help, Walsingham hoped to be privy to everything that was happening. The departure of Mauvissière had left a hole in his intelligence network, since he could not expect to infiltrate a spy into the new ambassador's household for some time. Gifford's agreement to pass to Walsingham every letter he carried would fill that gap and might prove even more effective.

'Of course, I remember now, he is related to William Gifford, is he not?'

'The very man.'

'I must confess, I had forgotten for the moment, it was a long time ago.'

Babington nodded. 'It was indeed, nearly fourteen years.

Much has happened to both of us since then.'

'Indeed,' agreed Jacob, feeling on safer ground. 'I have married and now have five children.' He looked at Babington shrewdly. 'Forgive me for being so blunt, but this is not the place to discuss such as Gifford. Was there something else you wanted of me?'

Again, Babington looked around carefully before answering. 'May I call on you? As you quite rightly say, this is not the place to discuss matters of importance.'

'I will be going to the Crouched Friars Glass-works this afternoon, but if that is too soon, I will be at my Harte Street showroom the day after tomorrow. Do you know it?'

'No, but I'm sure I'll be able to find it. I know of Harte Street. The day after tomorrow you say? May I call on you about ten o'clock?'

'That would be most suitable,' said Jacob and then, having exchanged courtesies, they went their separate ways. They had hardly passed out of sight, when Walsingham came up to him. 'Who was the young man engaging you in conversation? He is familiar, but I cannot bring his name to mind.'

'Sir Anthony Babington of Dethick in Darbieshire,' said Jacob, 'I met him many years ago.'

'Ah, yes.' said Walsingham, 'his father died a short while ago. What did he want?'

'He wants to meet me, to talk about Gilbert Gifford.'

Walsingham's surprise was evident. 'Does he now. That is interesting. I wonder what connection he has to Gifford. Nothing innocent, I'll be bound.'

'I may find out the day after tomorrow. He's coming to see me at Harte Street. I advised him to be cautious here, there are too many people watching your every move,' he said pointedly.

Walsingham ignored the comment. 'Keep me informed,' he said and with a small bow went across to join Lord Burghley.

The French Ambassador arrived a short while later and presented his credentials and although Jacob had seen several such events before, he watched the proceedings with interest. You never knew if the Queen would react to something and then things could get very interesting. But not today. The Queen wanted to make a good impression, so everything went very smoothly.

Later that day after the evening meal, Maria suggested they retired early as she wanted to talk to him.

'That sounds ominous,' said Jacob lightly, but he quickly became serious.

'So how are your bruises now, Giam?' Maria asked sarcastically. 'Did they cause you any trouble today?'

Jacob was taken aback by her tone. 'Not really.'

'It's not something we can ignore, you know. We haven't talked about the shooting at all.' She sat on the bed beside him looking strained.

'Don't worry, Maria, I'm absolutely fine now,' he said, trying to sound as reassuring as possible. Maria however did not react as he had expected.

'You were *very* lucky, you know,' she said forcefully. 'The ball almost went through the brigandine and if it had, you would have been killed.'

Jacob again tried to reassure her, taking her hand. 'It was nothing. It was the fall that caused all of the injuries.'

Maria would not be placated. 'Don't try and fob me off, Jacob,' she cried angrily, snatching her hand away. 'You know it was not nothing. For the first time since I came to London, I'm really frightened for you and the children.'

He had never seen Maria so agitated since the day they were first reunited in London. This went much deeper than he'd realised. 'I know it might have been worse, but it *is* only bruises.'

'You really don't understand how I feel, do you?' she said in a strained voice. 'I'm not just being silly. I gave up everything to be with you and have your children and now you seem set on a course to throw it all away.' She took his hands in hers. 'You don't have to endanger your life for a country that's not yours. We can go back to Venice and live very comfortably.'

'I *do* understand how you feel, Maria,' Jacob said earnestly, 'but we both know that running away to Venice at the first sign of trouble is not the answer. I told you in Paris that getting involved with the Duke of Guise would be dangerous. And as for England, it's my country now.' He moved closer and put his arm round her waist pulling her towards him. There was a little resistance at first and then she relented and put her head on his shoulder. 'You know how I feel about Venice and the old families.' The old families had never accepted him as a noble, because his mother was a commoner. They had betrayed him before and they would do it again if it suited their purposes.

'It didn't seem so bad in Paris,' Maria said, almost as though she was trying to persuade herself it was true. 'It was more like a game we were playing, but now ...' She broke off searching for the right words. 'Now, it's real. You had a close escape and poor George is dead. It's only too real now! It could be you lying there, or one of the children.'

Tears began to fill her eyes, but she shook them off angrily. 'I lost a child not long ago, but that was part of life. Now we have our lovely little Cate and life goes on. But if you were dead ...'

She didn't finish the sentence, but Jacob could read in her face what she was thinking. 'I'm sorry for putting you through this, especially after the death of Meg.'

'I'm sorry too for bringing this up, but it needed to be aired.'

Jacob would have none of it. 'Apologise be damned. You have nothing to apologise for. Why should you? You are showing your love and fears for your husband and children. If anyone needs to apologise it's me. I alone have put you in this position. As you rightly said, it's not as if I need to do it.'

'No, that's true,' Maria said fondly, 'but it's a part of your character I love you for. Despite the risks, you do it, because it's right.'

Jacob was about to say something, but Maria put her finger across his lips and shook her head. 'Don't say anything else, Giam. I just needed to talk about it. I'm over it now.' She shuddered. 'I went cold when they brought you in covered in blood and unconscious. I was sure you were dead.' She put her hand on his cheek. 'Queen Elizabeth is my friend and I know that what you do is important. Walsingham is no fool. On two occasions now, you've helped to defeat men who would have killed Elizabeth. He knows how important it is that you continue to do so. All I ask is that you take no more risks than are absolutely necessary.'

Jacob made a solemn promise and hoped that it was one he could keep. Sometimes, in the heat of violent action, the line became blurred and decisions could not be weighed and rationalised, but had to be made in split seconds.

Chapter Twenty-Four
London, 1585

Babington arrived at the Harte Street showroom promptly at ten o'clock. Jacob took him straight upstairs and offered some refreshments which he declined with thanks. Having given instructions to the housekeeper that they were not to be disturbed, he asked Babington how he could be of service.

Babington leaned forward and regarded Jacob earnestly, his face alight with fervour. 'What I am about to tell you is of great importance to our common cause. Namely the restoration of Queen Mary to her rightful place as Queen of England and the re-establishment of the true faith in this realm of ours. I believe that I am the chosen instrument of Queen Mary's deliverance and I am asking you to join with me to bring about a new and glorious era in England.'

Jacob was taken aback by the burning passion in Babington's rhetoric and the fanatical expression on his face. In his experience, people with such deep zealous beliefs in their own destiny had to be treated with extreme caution. Such beliefs often led them into acts that defied logic, bringing grief to themselves and all associated with them.

'I must confess, Sir Anthony,' Jacob said, 'your invitation has come as a very great surprise. What you ask of me is to commit treason against the Queen whose office I hold.'

A confident smile crossed Babington's face. 'Of course I am aware of your position. The penalty for high treason in the Bond of Association, is execution. You forget that Mary Stuart is a sovereign Queen in her own right. Even this Protestant Queen would never condone the execution of another monarch. It would have too many implications for her own rule.'

He sat back in his chair and regarded Jacob expectantly. Jacob, however, sat still and said nothing.

Eventually, Babington shrugged and went on, 'I can see that you are being rather cagey with me. I realise now that I should have explained why I have made this approach.'

Jacob still said nothing and Babington looked at him quizzically, until realising he was not going to comment, began his explanation. 'As you know,' said Sir Anthony, 'it was my ambition to enter the service of Queen Mary. Six years ago I served as page for the Earl of Shrewsbury and regularly attended on Her Majesty. She was gracious enough to befriend me and when she learned I was going to the Continent to further my education, she asked me to convey a message to her friends.'

He cleared his throat. 'During my stay in Paris I met with a number of Queen Mary's friends, including Thomas Morgan, Gilbert Gifford and the Archbishop of Glasgow, who is the Queen's representative in France. I also met with the Duke of Guise, who you know well. The Archbishop told me of your part in saving the life of Count Ridolfi and the fact that you were actively assisting the Duke and the Catholic League.'

Jacob was forced to revise his opinion of Babington. Zealot he might be, but an extremely well informed one. He must have access to the inner circle of the plotters in order to have obtained this knowledge. It was going to be necessary to play along with Babington. 'You are very well informed, Sir Anthony. But do not underestimate Walsingham. He has come very close to me already and I was fortunate to convince him that I was not a spy for the Guises.'

Babington laughed. 'I was most amused to hear how you turned the tables on Walsingham when you took the goblet to Her Majesty at Sheffield. It was a brilliant ploy to give Walsingham fake letters.'

'How did you learn of that?' asked Jacob in amazement.

'I too was at Sheffield. I visited Queen Mary the following day with some letters from France. She told me all about your visit.' He sighed. 'It will be doubly difficult to deliver her necessary papers now she has been moved to Wingfield.'

On the spur of the moment, Jacob decided to mention the later move to Tutbury. It would be common knowledge soon and it would enhance his reputation as a source of useful information. 'I don't know if you've heard the rumour, but I heard from Leicester that Queen Elizabeth has appointed Sir Amias Paulet to be Queen Mary's new jailer, at Tutbury Castle.'

Babington's face fell. 'That is very bad news if it is true. I knew from Hammond, the steward at Sheffield Castle, that another move was on the cards. Perhaps they have realised I have been smuggling letters to Her Majesty for over two years now. It was more difficult to do this at Wingfield, but Tutbury is a very different proposition. Do you know it?'

'Not at all,' Jacob said, shaking his head.

Babington went on to explain about Tutbury Castle. 'It is obvious that the gloves are off as far as Walsingham is concerned. They have abandoned the charade that Queen Mary is a guest of her cousin, they are confirming what most people know, namely that she's her prisoner.' He became quite agitated. 'We are going to have to rethink our whole strategy. Tutbury is a fortress and very easy to seal off from the outside world and to monitor visitors. We will have to find another way to make contact.'

He got to his feet and went to the window, staring out over the jumble of houses towards the Tower. It was just possible to see Tower Hill, where so many Catholic martyrs had met their end. There was silence for several minutes and Jacob waited patiently for him to continue. Having obviously reached a decision, Babington turned round.

'This new information shows how useful you would be to me.' He paused for a moment, then said thoughtfully, 'Did you learn if they planned to take Mary Stuart direct to Tutbury?'

Jacob knew the details from the letter he'd received from Walsingham detailing what he'd discussed with Gifford. He obviously couldn't admit that, so he used Leicester's name again. Babington knew he had met Leicester and was meeting him again.

'Leicester said that Sir Amias was not available to take up his post immediately,' Jacob informed him, 'so Sir Ralph Sadler has been instructed to take her to Wingfield Manor, until Sir Amias can go to prepare Tutbury Castle for the Queen's person.'

Babington took the information at face value. 'Excellent. I know Wingfield Manor very well. Perhaps we might have a chance to smuggle in a letter to her before the Queen is moved. Do you know when that will take place?'

'I'm afraid I've told you all I know.'

Babington gave a warm smile. 'No matter. Your contacts at

court have already proved their worth - and then there's your ship, *The Crystal.* We could use it to go over to France, without going through the usual scrutiny at the ports.'

'I can certainly arrange that,' agreed Jacob. Providing Walsingham agrees, he thought. 'My agents keep the customs well oiled and they do not inspect my cargo either when we leave or return.'

'That will be very useful. Every time we come into England we run the risk of being stopped by the port watchers.'

When Jacob just returned the smile he obviously thought Jacob was agreeing. 'I will be in touch from time to time and I will let you know if we require any help with shipping letters or people.' He pursed his lips and gave a frustrated frown. 'I must go now and confer with Gilbert Gifford and John Ballard. We must overcome the problem of getting letters to Her Majesty.'

'Ballard?' queried Jacob, suspiciously. 'Who is he?'

'Don't be alarmed. He is well known to me. He trained as a Jesuit priest at the seminary at Rheims and has been very actively encouraging the exiles in France. He is working with Gilbert Gifford, Thomas Morgan, Queen Mary's chief cipher clerk in France and the Archbishop, her agent. He has come to England on many occasions. This time he's brought letters from France to give to Gifford and the new French Ambassador. I have already taken letters to Her Majesty, Queen Mary, at Sheffield, to keep her informed of events, but now we must seek another way to contact her.' He regarded Jacob quizzically. 'You must realise that, on our short acquaintance, I had to be cautious. There are a number of my friends you know nothing about, but you will in fullness of time.'

They talked a little longer and then, as Babington prepared to take his leave, Jacob suggested that he should take some glass items from the showroom when he left. 'Should anyone enquire, it will be a good explanation for your visit.'

'An excellent idea, Master Bell. I will enjoy working with you. You have a talent for intrigue.' He reached into his doublet and took out a well filled purse. 'I believe that should be sufficient for the glass.'

Jacob tried to refuse, but Babington would not hear of it.

'This is your livelihood and I am a wealthy man,' he said arrogantly. 'It would not do to have you out of pocket when it is but a trifle to me.' Normally, Jacob would have insisted, but Babington's tone had been so patronising that he took the purse without further argument.

When Babington had left, Jacob went to see Thomas Pepper, his solicitor. He arranged with him to buy the empty house in Mark Street, used for the shooting by Jed Sutton, and also to let him know if any other houses became available in the street in which he could put some of his apprentices to act as additional lookouts.

On his return to Mark Street, he wrote a letter to Walsingham and set out in it all he had learned from Babington. Walsingham would be shocked to learn of the ease with which Babington had gained access to Mary Stuart. No doubt he would be doubly pleased that she was no longer being cared for by the corrupt household of the Earl of Shrewsbury.

He received a reply from Walsingham the next day. He requested Jacob to ask the members of the Ring to find the lodgings of John Ballard. *I confess, Sir Francis wrote, that my spies have no knowledge of his whereabouts in London. I received some intelligence from France that he was agitating among the recusants, but that is all. Now I will of course have my agents keep an eye out for both Ballard and Babington.*

In the event, it took less than a day for the Ring to find Ballard. He was lodging at a common inn, the Windmill Tavern, in Old Jewry. When Walsingham was informed, he was in a good position to keep an eye on all of the main plotters. He had spies on Ballard, and Jacob was in touch with Babington. For good measure, Babington was also watched by one of Walsingham's spies.

In addition, there was Gilbert Gifford, acting for Thomas Morgan and Charles Paget, as the English courier for letters from France. He ensured that Walsingham received copies of any letters or instructions to the captive Queen from the Catholic League, so the spy-master knew the contents of everything that was being sent to her. Gifford was working with Phelippes, the cipher breaker, to arrange a means of getting Mary Stuart's letters in and out of

Tutbury. Walsingham would receive copies of all of the letters. With this quality of information, Walsingham should soon be able to nullify the threat of an invasion and bring an end to Mary Stuart's plotting.

Chapter Twenty-Five
Tutbury Castle, 1585

From the moment she entered the gates of Tutbury Castle, Mary Stuart and her staff were treated with great rigour. It was soon apparent that she was no longer a royal guest, but a royal prisoner. When Mary heard that Paulet had insisted her maids were searched both going out and coming in to the apartments, she was appalled. Sending one of her ladies for Claude Nau, her secretary, she paced about restlessly until he arrived.

'I will send two letters,' she instructed him imperiously, 'one to the French Ambassador in London, and one to my cousin Elizabeth.' For the next hour she had Nau making notes, correcting sentences while she poured out her complaints. When at last she was done, she sent Nau away to write the letters out, then bring them for her signature.

The French Ambassador replied that he had interceded with Lord Burghley who had promised to have a word with Queen Elizabeth. When this had not worked, he requested an interview with Elizabeth, but she was away on progress and he got nowhere. Elizabeth herself did not reply to Mary's letter and Mary was not sure that she had even seen it. Sir Amias Paulet, having read the letters, simply devised a stricter regime and Mary was told she could not correspond with her friends.

On Paulet's first visit to Mary's apartments, she tried to charm him. 'Sir Amias,' she said, giving him her warmest smile, as though he was a close friend. 'I am so pleased to meet you at last. We must get to know each other better and I am sure that we will become friends.'

'I have no wish to be your friend, madame,' said Paulet sourly, 'but we do have a number of things we must discuss.'

'By all means,' said Mary. She was in truth, a little taken aback by his lack of response. This is not going to be an easy task, she thought. She gave him her most winsome smile. 'Please join me in to my presence chamber where we can sit in comfort and have our discussion.' However, when they entered the chamber, matters came to a head. Mary sat down on her chair as usual, with the cipher of her mother, Mary of Guise, hanging above it. Paulet took one look and reading the sentence embroidered on it, *En ma fin est mon commencement" - In my end is my beginning,* his face darkened with rage. He strode towards her and Mary cowered away, thinking that he intended to attack her. Reaching the chair, he tore down the cipher and threw it on to the floor. 'There is only one Queen in this Protestant realm,' he roared, 'and that is Queen Elizabeth. You will never again put up that cipher, while I am your keeper.'

And so began a battle of wills. Mary was in tears, but no sooner had Paulet stormed out of the room, than Mary instructed her ladies to put the cipher back. The next time Paulet saw it, it was torn down again, but Mary thought he feared to confiscate it since it was a Queen's cipher and she was the cousin of his sovereign.

For the first time since she had fled from Scotland, Mary found herself totally isolated from her friends in the outside world. She was also forced to reduce the size of her household and eat a much more restricted diet. Even when Paulet was temporarily away, Mary found that Sir Drue Drury was also immune to her charms and blandishments. Matters simply carried on as before.

Despondent she may have been, but she never forgot she was a Queen. 'We will behave with the correct protocol at all times,' she instructed her staff. ' Her mealtimes had all the trappings of a royal household and despite the changed food, she still ate well. Her 'diets' were recorded assiduously in her household accounts by her secretaries and she still ate two courses. Her presence chamber doubled as a dining room and her staff served Mary at her own table, using the silver dishes and crystal glassware she had brought with her.

It was inevitable she would put on more weight. She was not allowed to ride and the lack of exercise combined with her overeating, led to her health to deteriorate. As her weight increased, her shoulders became more rounded and she had a slight stoop. As she said to her remaining ladies, 'I am still the prisoner I have always been, but now the trappings of deceit that created an impression of being a guest of Queen Elizabeth have been removed. Now, the whole world will be able to see how I suffer for my religion.'

But Paulet made it very difficult for the outside world to have any contact with Mary Stuart. She was forbidden to write to her friends and could only send letters to the French Ambassador, Châteauneuf. These letters were opened surreptitiously by Phelippes, passed to Walsingham for reading and then copied before they were sent on.

Of course, Mary's friends made attempts to smuggle letters in to her. When Mary ordered some new shoes, they hid letters in the soles and heels. The first Mary knew of their attempt was when Sir Amias walked in to her apartment unannounced. 'Here are the shoes you ordered,' he said mockingly, throwing two pairs of expensive shoes, minus soles and heels, on to the floor in front of her. 'The letters hidden in the soles and heels have been destroyed,' he said with great satisfaction.

'But the shoes are completely ruined and they were very expensive,' complained Mary, 'I demand compensation for them.'

Sir Amias shrugged. 'Demand away. It will do you no good. Ask your friends who hid the letters to pay. I will sanction no compensation. It is up to you, madame. Any further attempts will meet a similar fate.' Not that he expected that his words would stop them from trying. However, he was sure that if they did, the system he had put in place would be able to cope.

Sure enough, a couple of weeks later a crate of expensive silks sent from London was dismantled and letters were discovered hidden in a false bottom. The silks were thrown on the muddy floor and trampled on.

'My beautiful silks,' moaned Mary despondently. 'you have ruined them.'

'I warned you,' said Sir Amias.

The following day, Paulet tightened the ring around her so that even a mouse would have had difficulty getting through to her. The Tutbury servants were forbidden to speak to her, or her servants, unless Sir Amias was present. None of the servants were allowed to leave the castle without a guard and all of them were to be stripped down to their smocks and searched, both leaving and entering the castle. Nothing could come in, or go out, without Paulet or his men knowing about it. Everyone was vetted and Mary could not speak to any of the castle servants, except in Paulet's presence. The searches were so thorough that Mary was reluctant to send anything except the most innocuous of letters.

After this, there were no further tries to smuggle in letters, as it was obvious that Paulet would destroy anything in his search and the letters would all be passed to Walsingham, since Paulet had informed Mary that in future, he had been instructed to open and read letters before passing them to the prisoner. With visitors restricted to those very few approved by Walsingham, Mary's isolation was almost complete.

Mary became despondent and her health began to suffer. As the days wore on, Mary became depressed. 'What will become of us?' she moaned to her ladies. 'They are doing their best to make an end of me.'

When next she saw Paulet she launched into a plaintive complaint. 'The nauseous smell from the sanitary arrangements is making me ill.' She fluttered her fan which she now carried everywhere and tears appeared in her eyes. 'Is it your plan to kill me by exposing me and my household to this vile stench? I would as soon you put poison in my food.' Paulet noted that her delightful Scottish accent had become more pronounced and she looked up at him from a downcast head and regarded him with a sad, tear-stained face. It was a beautiful performance, but her tears had no more success than her smiles and friendly approaches. Paulet was immune to them all. As he wrote to Walsingham in his weekly report, *The Queen of Scots does try her wiles, but I will never ask pardon if she should escape by any treacherous means, or cunning device. It cannot come to pass without some gross negligence or traitorous carelessness on my part. I will not be beholden to traitors for my life and my allegiance to the Queen my sovereign will never be compromised, so will I be assured by the grace of God, that the Scottish Queen shall die before me.*

Walsingham's reply assured Paulet that he had every confidence in his friend. He also instructed him to inform Mary of his latest instruction. The following day, having torn down the cipher in the presence chamber, a task that had become something of a ritual, Paulet informed Mary of Walsingham's new instruction. 'In future, any packets you send to France must be sent to Mister Secretary and not to the new French Ambassador, Châteauneuf. Sir Francis has also given orders to your agent in France, the Archbishop of Glasgow, that any letters he sends from France must be delivered to Mister Stafford, the English Ambassador in Paris.'

For once, Mary forgot all about trying to charm Paulet and raged at Walsingham with a mixture of Scottish and French oaths that, as Paulet reported to his master, "would have made a sailor blush!"

As the weeks wore on, the stench of the castle sewers became so bad that even Paulet was finding it difficult and Mary's health was giving him cause for concern. She had been given some pills by her physician, when she was at Chatsworth, to ease her abdominal pains. Having complained again about the pains, she took some pills and at once vomited up all her food and swooned. Her physician gave her whisky to revive her and she became more comfortable. She continued to take her pills, but with little sign of improvement.

Mary complained of an incessant desire to vomit and of severe abdominal pains in her left side under the short ribs. Paulet was sure some of her illnesses were either exaggerated or psychosomatic, since they certainly increased as the stricter regime unfolded. When he told her this, her reply was simple. 'No one can cure this malady as well as the Queen of England,' she said. Even Paulet had to admit she was not without justification.

When Paulet reported this conversation, Walsingham realised that something would have to be done. He had no wish for the Scottish Queen to die in captivity even though that might stop the plotting. He reported to Elizabeth, who became concerned. 'I have no desire to see my cousin die from the coldness and foul air of Tutbury. No matter if her death should be from natural causes, we will be accused of having her poisoned.' Walsingham nodded his agreement and she continued. 'Despite this new French Ambassador, Châteauneuf being a supporter of the Scottish

Queen, I have been trying to further good relations with France. Her death would certainly lead to serious trouble with France, and Spain would probably use her death as an excuse to go to war.'

Paulet finally advised Walsingham that Chartley Manor, with its moat, castellated battlements, drawbridge and portcullis entry, was the only suitable choice as a safe haven for Mary Stuart, so Chartley Manor in Staffordshire became Mary's latest prison.

Chapter Twenty-Six
London, 1585

September was a glorious month with the weather set fair day after day, but towards the end it changed for the worse. Late in the month, Jacob received a note from Anthony Babington requesting that they meet. He also indicated that he would bring both John Ballard and Gilbert Gifford. Jacob arranged to meet them at The Swan. When Quiff came back from arranging the meeting, he had a warning for Jacob. 'Be careful going in and coming out of The Swan. Particularly, if you've had a few drinks.'

'What's the problem?' Jacob asked.

'There's a group of cutpurses frequenting the area. There have been several thefts in the past week. They work together and will use violence if they meet with any resistance.'

'In that case, I'll be on my guard.' Jacob gave a resigned smile. 'I suppose a gold sovereign for the landlord is in order.'

'Of course,' said Quiff, with an answering smile. 'Your patronage ensures his loyalty. In fact, when I meet the apprentices there, he goes out of his way to see we're not bothered by any of his dubious customers. As landlords go, he is very honest.'

Jacob, wearing his working clothes and hooded black cape, was the first to arrive for the meeting and settled his dues with the landlord, who brought him a tot of good French brandy to "keep out the cold". It was very welcome as the weather had been unseasonably cold and there was a biting wind coming from the north.

When Babington and his companions arrived they accepted Jacob's offer of a brandy with alacrity. 'I see the landlord has a good line in French brandy,' said Gifford, quaffing it with relish. 'Smuggled no doubt.'

'The Swan may not be the most salubrious of places, but it does provide us with a private meeting place away from prying eyes.'

'Indeed it does,' agreed Babington. 'Shall we get to the point of this meeting.' When the others nodded, he addressed Jacob directly. 'Firstly, I would like to thank you for your information relating to the transfer of Mary Stuart to Tutbury. I believe that had I not been aware of the situation, I might have been arrested in possession of letters to Queen Mary.' Ballard added his own thanks to that.

He then took up the story. 'Gilbert has, at some peril to himself, brought a number of letters to Châteauneuf, the new French Ambassador, from sympathisers in France and beyond. Normally, we would have sent them in the diplomatic bag, but we didn't trust security at the Embassy. His predecessor, Mauvissière's letters had been intercepted by someone in his employ, so we held them back.

'Together with the letters we were already holding in England, we have a real log jam. The crux of the matter is that we need to find a way of getting letters to Queen Mary, and soon, without any chance of Walsingham or Paulet being any the wiser.'

Gifford added his voice. 'The point that should be made is the vital importance of obtaining Her Majesty's signature on the decisions already taken. We must make sure all three parts of the plan have been fully disclosed to the Queen, and her countersignature is on all documents.'

Jacob wondered what these three parts were, but before he could ask, Gilbert Gifford had gone on.

'Without Mary Stuart's approval, there can be no further action. The situation in France is critical. The Duke of Guise is obsessed with fighting for the French throne and is no longer pursuing his plan to invade England. He is planning to use the Catholic League army to attack King Henry III's forces.' He looked around to see if there were any comments, but receiving none, he continued. 'I have told Mendoza, Spain's Ambassador to France, that his master must send the Duke of Parma and his forces from the Low Countries, but as yet I have received no reply.'

Jacob was not impressed with Gifford's manner, he appeared to be lecturing them and greatly inflating his influence and importance to the Spanish court. Not even the Pope had that much influence over Philip of Spain. Jacob's initial feeling of unease had deepened during Gifford's speech, and he had learned the hard way not to ignore such doubts. He had begun to wonder whether Walsingham was right in putting too much faith in using Gifford as a double agent.

Ballard too looked sceptical, but he made no comment. He did, however, make a suggestion how they might proceed in making contact with Mary Stuart. 'I have been speaking to people who know Tutbury well. It is most unlikely that all the troops and servants necessary to keep Queen Mary can remain there for too long. It is common knowledge that the sewers will cause problems before long. Apparently, the smell becomes most noisome when the wind is from the north. The key to how we might get to communicate with Her Majesty lies in where she would be held if Tutbury has to be abandoned while it is cleaned.'

'I cannot imagine they will return Queen Mary to Wingfield,' said Jacob.

'I concur with that,' said Babington. 'It was obvious that correspondence was getting through. The same is true for any other of Shrewsbury's properties.'

'Exactly my point,' agreed Ballard. 'My own feeling is that they will go for Chartley Manor, in Staffordshire. It is a moated house and belongs to the Earl of Essex. There is far more chance of them securing it, but we have already identified a way of getting letters safely into the house'

'They might go to my father's house which is also nearby,' Gifford said.

'What good will that do us,' said Babington angrily. 'We don't have any means of getting letters in there.'

'Babington has a point,' agreed Gifford. 'Far better for us, if your father's house was unavailable, it will increase the chance of Chartley being chosen. We can then organise the letter drop before Paulet has a chance to get organised.'

'In that case,' Ballard said, 'I will leave it to the three of you to find something out, since I must return to France. I am meeting the Papal representative in a week's time.'

In the end, it was agreed that the remaining three would see what they could find out and meet again in one week's time at The Swan.

When they left by the back door and turned into the dark alley to reach the main street, Jacob, the last to emerge, noticed two men hanging about near the mouth of the alley. Recalling Quiff's warning. it made him suspicious immediately, so he hung back, keeping to the shadows.

The others were also suspicious, possibly thinking the loungers might be Walsingham's men. They approached the group of men warily, with their hands on their swords. The men lounging against the wall waited until they had nearly reached the end of the alley then one of them gave a loud whistle. Immediately, they were joined by two other men who had been hiding around the corner. Fingering their cudgels threateningly their leader demanded money to let them pass. Just behind them, unseen in the deep shadow of a doorway, two more robbers lurked. Taking the opportunity while their victims were distracted, they pulled out a knifes and one of them grabbed Ballard and held a knife at his throat. The leader of the robbers called on them to drop their swords, or their friend would be killed, while the other man behind them cut the strings of Babington's purse.

Meanwhile, keeping to the shadows, Jacob drew his sword and quietly crept up behind the two robbers menacing Ballard. Hearing a slight noise, the cutpurse turned round. Jacob immediately felled him with a thunderous blow from his sword hilt and in one fluid movement slid the point of his sword under the chin of the man menacing Ballard.

'Drop the dagger or you'll be spitted like a turkey,' Jacob hissed menacingly. 'And tell your friends to step back, or I'll kill you.'

The robber did so immediately and moved back towards the wall. While the other robbers hesitated, Babington, Ballard and Gifford drew their swords. Seeing that their erstwhile victims had turned the tables, the robbers fled, leaving their companion teetering on his toes with Jacob's sword pricking his throat. Babington gave chase as they ran down the street and seeing two members of the Watch talking to some apprentices outside a shop, he pointed to the fleeing robbers and shouted, 'Stop thieves! Stop them!'

The watchmen gave chase immediately and the robbers darted into an alley with the Watch after them. Babington returned to the alley where the others had disarmed the man and were holding him. Seeing his purse on the floor by the robber, he retrieved it.

The robber was pleading with Jacob to let him go. 'There's no 'arm done, sir,' he whined. 'You've got your purse back.'

Gifford was all for killing him, but Jacob wouldn't hear of it. 'The Watchmen could be back any minute and we don't want any trouble.'

'What, for one measly guttersnipe?' snarled Gifford, preparing to run him through.

Taking a quick step forward, Jacob locked blades with Gifford. 'Don't be a fool, the last thing we want to do is draw attention to ourselves.'

Babington stepped forward and grabbed Gifford's arm and Ballard, who was none the worse for his ordeal, remonstrated with Gifford and told him to put away his sword. Gifford reluctantly complied and seeing that his captors had forgotten him for the moment, the robber began to sidle away. He froze, as Jacob flicked out his sword in front of the man's eyes, shaking his head in disapproval Before the others could seize him again, a watchman, blowing hard, entered the alley.

'I'm sorry sir,' he said to Babington, 'the robbers got away in the maze of alleys.' He looked at the robber pinned against the wall and the other man lying on the floor groaning. 'Now then, sir, who have we here?' he cried.

Jacob indicated the man on the floor. 'I caught that one cutting a purse and stopped him,' he said matter-of-factly.

'And what about the other fellow?'

'He had a knife at that gentleman's throat,' Jacob said, indicating Ballard. 'I persuaded him to stop.'

The watchman gave a crooked smile and grabbed the man in an armlock. 'They seem to have bitten off more than they can chew this time,' he said, and started to march him away. Babington and Ballard grabbed the other man who was staggering to his feet and were about to follow him, when another watchman appeared.

'Take a hold of that fellow from the gentlemen,' cried the first watchman, 'and let's get them both down to the jail. We should be able to sort out the rest of the gang once we've had a quiet word in private with these two.' Jacob gave a grim smile. He had no doubt that the quiet word would involve fists and a lump or two for the robbers. It then occurred to him that the Watch might want to know their names, so sheathing his sword, he turned to the others and bowed.

'You'll be fine now the Watch has them, sirs, so I'll be on my way.'

For the watchmen's benefit, Babington thanked Jacob profusely. 'It's lucky you happened to be leaving The Swan shortly after us. But for you, things might not have turned out as well as they did. Will you accept a reward, sir?'

Jacob thanked him, but refused. He said he'd done little to deserve a reward and was just pleased to help. He then hurried quickly away, before the watchmen should think to ask for his name.

Chapter Twenty-Seven
London, 1585

Shortly after the meeting at The Swan, Jacob met Walsingham in secret at the safe house he often used for meeting his agents. Walsingham informed him that he had already spoken to Gifford and arrangements were in hand for Mary Stuart to be transferred to Chartley Manor.

'Mary Stuart's health has deteriorated alarmingly in recent weeks,' Walsingham said, 'and it would not do for her to die from an illness. I have to admit,' Walsingham said contritely, 'at the time of the Stuart woman's complaints, I was not in favour of Chartley and Essex was not happy about us using it. Having spoken to Gifford, however, I have changed my mind. It would be very advantageous to see all letters to and from Mary Stuart. Gifford believes it is ideal for that purpose and he has an idea how he can get letters to the Scottish Queen and receive her replies. I would, of course, be able to copy all of them.

'How does he propose to achieve that?'

'Well apparently, Chartley Manor buys its ale from a brewer in Burton, which is nearby to the house. Gifford plans to smuggle in letters in a watertight container, small enough to be inserted into a cask through the bung hole, but large enough to take a bulky packet. Babington will see Mary Stuart gets instructions how to find the container in the barrel, before she leaves Wingfield.'

'Will the brewer agree to this plan?'

Walsingham gave a wintry smile. 'Gifford has assured me that it is so. Through Gifford, I'm paying him a tidy sum to do it, so I would be rather upset if he refuses.'

The implication of Walsingham's words did not escape Jacob. Walsingham was ruthless if he was betrayed. He hoped for both of their sakes that Gifford and the brewer delivered what was promised.

Walsingham then had a question for Jacob. 'What part is Babington expecting you to play? Does he want you to be part of the inner circle of conspirators?'

'I'm not entirely sure,' said Jacob cautiously. 'Whilst I've met most of the major plotters now, I don't know much about Babington's secret society.' He tried to recall that first meeting at court. Babington had dominated the conversation and the others had stayed well back - probably six, besides Babington.

'Unfortunately, I took little notice of them when I met Babington at court, they stayed well back. As far as I could tell, they were all young, possibly about twenty I would say, but I wouldn't recognise any of them again.'

'Did Babington mention any names?'

'No, none. The whole conversation only lasted a few minutes. They're possibly friends from Darbieshire.'

'No matter,' said Walsingham, 'I'm certain to find out now I'm looking into his affairs. What did you find out at the meeting with Anthony Babington at The Swan?'

Jacob gave him an outline of what was discussed until he reached the part where Gifford had commented on the role of Mary Stuart. 'Has Gifford mentioned anything to you about their being three parts to the plot?'

When Walsingham said he had not, Jacob explained what Gifford had let slip.

After a moment's thought, while he stroked his beard, Walsingham became animated. 'It is strange that Gifford has not told me this. It could be vital in our understanding of what is going on around that damned witch.' He smiled at Jacob. 'Fortunately, Gifford has not been made aware of your part in all this. It will be interesting to see what else he tells you and not me. I am going to have to be careful with Gilbert Gifford. He may be playing more of a double game than I first thought.'

'I confess to a doubt about Gifford's intentions.' Jacob said. 'I have learned to trust these gut feelings.'

He waited as Walsingham searched through various papers on his desk. 'I cannot see anything in my notes that Gifford has mentioned there are three parts to the plot,' said Walsingham thoughtfully. 'Again the question I ask is, why? From what we already know, one part is almost certainly the invasion, by the Duke of Parma's Spanish troops from the Low Countries, accompanied by an uprising from the Catholics here. But what of the others? One could be to rescue Mary Stuart and something more sinister like a plan to assassinate the Queen.'

'I will do my best to find out,' Jacob promised. 'I will also ask the Ring to keep an eye on Gifford and Babington. We can leave Ballard for now as he is going to France.'

'My spies will keep him in their sights in France, never fear. For now I will wait and see what happens.'

Jacob promised to do the same and returned to the Crouched Friars Glass-works.

There was still a lot of work to do on the new designs for the Earl of Leicester, so for several days Jacob became totally immersed in the technicalities of glass design. When at last he was satisfied, he sent a note to Leicester informing him the designs were ready and requesting a meeting at his convenience. The earl arranged for Jacob to bring the designs to him the following morning.

Later that day he received a message that there was a customer at the Harte Street showroom who desired to speak to him personally. He was surprised to see Babington waiting in the showroom office. Quiff, who had been about to leave for The Swan, was attending him.

When Jacob arrived, Quiff left them alone and Jacob closed the door. There was no one in the showroom, but should they become involved in deep conversation, a new arrival might hear something they should not.

Babington was looking very serious and Jacob wondered if he had discovered he was being watched. He need not have worried, since it was another matter he wanted to discuss.

'We have only been acquainted for a short time,' Babington said, 'but I was impressed by your manner and quick thought at The Swan. Your swordplay too was most impressive.'

Jacob gave a deprecating shrug. 'It was really nothing. The cutpurse had his attention solely on you and it was easy to hold him to account.'

'Perhaps, but I was very grateful. However, it was not that which I wished to discuss with you. I think it only fair to acquaint you with the full extent of our plans. Many of my friends have joined me in this affair and we are determined that this time we will bring an end to Protestant rule in England.'

As he talked, the timbre of his voice began to rise and he became more agitated. 'I have done much for the Catholic cause,' he bragged. 'Even Pope Gregory has commended me for the way my secret society has helped the seminary priests.'

He really is a dangerous man, thought Jacob. And the force of his fervour could easily lead him into indiscretions. 'I was unaware of your secret society. It has not been mentioned before.'

Babington smiled smugly. 'There was no reason you should. After I abandoned my law studies at Lincoln's Inn, I settled into the social life in London, aided by my relatives Lady Babington of Whitefriars and Lady Foljambe in Darbieshire. They are my brothers' widows.'

Jacob could see that Babington was full of pride in his part and tried to encourage him to say more. 'I suppose that you came into contact with many young Catholic men of a similar age.'

'Indeed,' said Babington proudly. 'They flocked to join me. My dream was to ride to her rescue and make her the Queen of England. We were all in love with the beautiful Queen Mary and wanted to further her cause. We frequently dine together and attend mass with one or other of the seminary priests we keep safe. Despite the efforts of the Protestant usurpers to stop us.' He gave a frown. 'It is a great pity that I have never been shown the same favour by Queen Mary, bestowed so liberally on others less worthy, despite all I have done in her cause. It makes me wonder sometimes if it is worth all the trouble when my part goes unnoticed.'

Babington was sounding more and more like a spoiled child - vain and callow, with a very inflated idea of his own importance. He is obviously very jealous of Ballard and some of the others - perhaps we can use this for our own ends, thought Jacob.

'Mayhap, the others are wanting to keep the credit for themselves and Queen Mary is not aware of what you have suffered in her cause.'

Babington favoured him with a generous smile. 'I do believe you are right. I have not been able to read the letters I have smuggled in to the Queen.'

'At great danger to yourself,' Jacob flattered.

'That is so true. I must see how this can be remedied.' He frowned. 'Although before that can take place, we must develop a foolproof way of getting messages to the Queen.' He put a friendly arm on Jacob's shoulder and his handsome face broke into a warm smile. 'I told Ballard I thought you would be a wonderful asset for our group and, before he left for France,' Babington continued, 'he suggested that I explained our plans to you. He feels you might help us more if you are fully aware of their extent.'

Jacob looked encouraging and waited for him to continue.

'When I first discussed the matter of Mary Stuart with Ballard, he told me that there was already planned a great Catholic League army of sixty thousand men ready to strike against England. I must confess that I did feel somewhat sceptical as this seemed like an exaggeration. However, Ballard had a ready answer for all of the objections that I raised.'

Jacob also thought this was optimistic, but didn't comment.

'Ballard then went on to talk about the Catholics in England rising to join the invading army. He further proposed that there should be a concerted attack against the Government.' He gave a short derisive laugh. 'As I told him at the time, I see very little chance of that succeeding while Elizabeth still lives.'

Jacob managed to conceal his true thoughts as the killing of the Queen was discussed so openly.

'And what did Ballard have to say to that?'

'He agreed, but the recent arrest and trial of William Parry has left us with no alternative but to try another route.'

'William Parry? That is another name I do not know.'

Babington gave an exasperated sigh. 'Unfortunately, you will hear soon enough. Parry, a Member of Parliament, vowed to the papal representative he would shoot Elizabeth. Ballard paid him a large sum of money and the Pope sent plenary absolution, but, unfortunately, his nerve deserted him. Finally, he tried to recruit a fellow Member of Parliament to help him, but was betrayed by the man. The trial has already been held and he was found guilty of high treason.'

'I'm surprised this has not been made public, I've heard nothing about it.'

'He was tried in Westminster by a special court in the Star Chamber,' said Babington, his lips curling in distaste. 'One of our supporters was at the farce of a trial. Burghley said the Queen had asked for the matter to be kept secret in case it alarmed the public.'

'I suppose Parry named a number of people.'

'Yes, he did. But fortunately, all the people were already known to Walsingham, having flown the country after the arrest of Throckmorton.'

'What will you do now?'

Babington gave a barking laugh. 'My society will carry on as before, of course. We had no high expectations of Parry, he was just a windbag. But if he *had* succeeded ...' He shrugged. 'No matter, we simply carried on formulating our own plans to kill the usurper.'

Jacob was shocked that plans were so advanced. At least now they knew what the third part was that Gifford had referred to. He must find out as much as he could. Vain and callow he may be, but Babington was a very dangerous man.

'How do you and your friends feel about an assassination?' he asked, not wishing to ask a direct question. 'It goes against my beliefs to kill someone by stealth. A killing in the throes of a fight, I can square with my conscience, but deliberate murder ...'

He broke off and Babington nodded in agreement. 'I know how you feel. I must admit that I too, was troubled. However, I was assured personally, by the Pope's representative in Paris last year, that such an act would receive absolution under the terms of the Bull issued by His Holiness. It is a matter of God's will. Should we succeed it will be because He wishes it.'

Jacob could not accept such a jaundiced view of God, having been brought up in the tolerant and enlightened atmosphere of Venice, where even the Jews were tolerated and the Inquisition had no place. Murder was still murder. However justified, it was to be abhorred.

Unfortunately, before he could learn any more of Babington's plans, Roberto came in to the showroom, indicating he needed to have a word with Jacob. Excusing himself, Jacob left the office and shut the door.

'I'm sorry to interrupt,' said Roberto, 'but the Earl of Leicester is at the Crouched Friars. He says he has to leave London tomorrow morning and wants to know if he can have the new designs now. Apparently, he wishes to take them with him to discuss with his wife.'

'They're locked up in my cupboard at the glass-works,' Jacob explained. 'I managed to finish them, so there is not any difficulty. I'd better come though. Tell the earl I will be with him directly and apologise Nicely mind you,' he said with a smile. 'Tell him I'm sorry I was not there to greet him. I will just acquaint my visitor with the facts and then I will join you.'

When he explained about Leicester, Babington smiled. 'He was ever one for the impulsive gesture. You never know, he might let slip some more useful information. I will leave you to him, but I will keep you apprised of any developments. I believe that we will soon be sending letters to Mary Stuart now she has moved to Chartley Manor. Hopefully, this will lead to a big change in our fortunes and prove an important step forward in our plans.'

He handed Jacob a piece of paper on which was written John, the cobbler, Philips Street, Cripplegate, close by the Sun Inn. 'Should you need to contact me, you can send a message to this address. The cobbler is a supporter of ours and he will keep any letters addressed to me until they are collected. One of my colleagues calls in every day at four.'

It has certainly proved to be an interesting meeting, thought Jacob, as he hurried off to the Crouched Friars. I must acquaint Walsingham as soon as possible about Babington's plans to assassinate the Queen. We need to identify all of Babington's friends and keep a strict watch on them.

Once he had dealt with Leicester, he sent for Quiff. He explained about Babington and asked him to instruct the members of the Ring to find out all they could about Babington and his friends.

When Quiff had gone, he sat down and wrote a detailed report for Walsingham, setting out everything he had learned and what he had asked the Ring to discover. They must stop Babington and his inner circle before they could carry out there evil intent of assassinating Queen Elizabeth.

Chapter Twenty-Eight
Burton-upon-Trent & London, 1586

When Gilbert Gifford rode into the brewer's yard at Burton, Jed Sutton, alias James Stourbridge, was cleaning the dray. Even though there was a chill in the air, Jed was stripped to the waist. Gifford swung down easily from his horse and tied the reins to a ring set in the wall.

Walking over to Jed, he watched as he continued to clean the dray, ignoring his visitor. Gifford laughed. 'I see your manners have not improved since we last met, Stourbridge.' He took a bulging pouch from his doublet and hefted it in his hands making the coins jangle. 'Perhaps this might get your attention?'

Jed wiped his hands on a rag. 'It depends,' he said surlily.

Gifford laughed. 'On what, may I ask?'

He tossed the pouch to Jed who caught it deftly. Opening the drawstring, he poured a few of the gold coins into the palm of his hand and examined them carefully, selecting one and biting it. He then examined the edges of the coins, looking to see if they had been clipped. With a sniff he put them back in the pouch. 'They seem to be genuine,' he said grudgingly. 'What can I do for you this time?'

'You can get rid of the surly attitude for a start,' Gifford said tartly. He was getting a little tired of Jed's little games. 'I'm paying enough for your services to expect a modicum of civility.'

Jed shrugged. 'You can always go somewhere else.'

Gifford shook his head in mock sorrow. 'I think that we both know it wouldn't work so easily. However, if you don't want my little job, you can give me back the pouch and I will make other arrangements. Of course, that will mean you losing the right to deliver ale to Chartley Manor and probably to the Earl of Shrewsbury.' He had no intention of doing any such thing, but Jed was not to know that.

Fortunately, Jed did not call his bluff and gave an ingratiating smile. 'I've got a bad head this morning, so how many letters are there this time?'

'Before we go into that,' said Gifford tartly, 'I want to see what you brought back from Chartley with the last delivery. Did you have any problems?'

'None at all. The first two times I went, that Paulet fellow was watching every move I made to see I didn't pass anything on. I wasn't even allowed to speak to the maids.'

He wiped his nose on his sleeve. 'He didn't bother himself last time, but one of the guards never left my side. I still wasn't allowed to speak.' His face became more animated. 'I did see Queen Mary briefly, when I carried her special keg into her quarters.' His face lit up. 'She even smiled and nodded to me.'

'Good, good,' said Gifford, a little impatiently. 'Was there any reply in the empty keg?'

Jed nodded, picked up his shirt and putting it on, tucked it into his breeches before walking into the house. He returned shortly and handed a couple of letters to Gifford. 'That's all there was this time.'

Gifford examined the seals and, seeing they were intact, went to his saddlebag and brought out a packet of letters. He handed them to Jed. 'Will you be able to get all of them into the waterproof container?'

'I'll have to squash them up a bit. They might get a bit crumpled and creased.'

Gifford pulled a face. 'So long as the seals aren't broken or damaged. Should that prove impossible, you must take them in two lots.'

He lowered his voice conspiratorially. 'The first letters you took were not of great consequence, but these are important to the Queen's cause. I know you are a supporter of the true faith. You have it in your power to render her a great service. When the Queen is returned to her rightful place on the throne of England, you will be well rewarded both in this life and the next.'

Jed's face lightened at Gifford's words. He would make his father very proud that he had helped Her Majesty to achieve her destiny. 'I will see the Queen gets her letters,' he said proudly. 'It is an honour to serve her.'

'You will go on Saturday, as usual?'

'Of course,' said Jed, with a sniff. 'You have to be regular on these deliveries. The men get very belligerent if they run out of ale. Come rain, hail or shine, they expect their delivery.'

When Gifford left the brewer's yard he only went as far as an isolated cottage on the outskirts of Burton. Once inside he handed over the letters to Thomas Phelippes to be deciphered and copied before sending on to Walsingham; and from him to their destination.

'How long will it take you to copy these?' he asked Phelippes.

Phelippes examined the letters carefully. 'Not too long by the looks of it.' He looked at the seals and sniffed. 'The only thing that might hold me up is if they are in a new cipher. I don't think that's likely though.'

He indicated the table. 'There's some bread and a very nice local cheese. The farmer down the lane makes it. Help yourself and I'll be as quick as I can. I know you want to get off.'

Although the sun was shining brightly, there was a chill breeze and Walsingham drew his cloak more tightly round him. The gout that had kept him in bed for several days had now subsided and, despite the breeze, he was enjoying the chance to walk in the fresh air. The garden was past it best now, but in the autumn sunlight it lifted Walsingham's spirits. He was just about to go into the rose arbour, when Frances Milles, his secretary, came hurrying in to the garden. 'What now, Frances? Can't I get a little peace?' he growled, frowning fiercely at him.

'I'm sorry, Sir Francis, but you did ask me to inform you the minute Phelippes arrived with the letters.'

When Walsingham opened the first letter, it was simply a request to the Bishop of Ross to send Mary Stuart some money. She complained that under Paulet, anything she requested to be added such as food, or clothes, had to be paid for.

The Earl of Shrewsbury would not have considered for one moment that I should pay, she wrote. Walsingham smiled in amusement. Paulet was obviously taking his task very much to heart.

When he read the second copy letter, he sat forward and read it again with mounting excitement. Mary had written a note to Babington expressing her eternal gratitude for all the work he had done in conveying letters to her. She commended his efforts and apologised for not having written sooner. It was exactly the letter Walsingham was hoping she would write when he sent on the intercepted letter from Thomas Morgan, Queen Mary's chief cipher clerk in France, suggesting Mary should write to Babington.

Morgan informed Mary that Babington was becoming suspicious and jealous that he had not heard from her for some considerable time, whilst others had. He told her it was advisable to write a friendly letter to show that Babington was not forgotten and enclosed a draft of his suggestion.

Mary's response was only a short letter but, to Walsingham's fertile mind, it represented the means by which he could entangle her firmly into the heart of this plot. So long as she was sure that the means of getting the letters out of Chartley were safe, there was every chance she would commit herself to condoning the assassination of Elizabeth.

That would be a fatal error on her part. The Bond of Association she had signed provided the death sentence for anyone party to a plan to kill the Queen. Now all he had to do was to get Mary Stuart to make that commitment in writing! He scribbled a note and after sealing it rang the handbell vigorously. When the servant entered he instructed him to arrange for the note to be delivered to Jacob Bell with the utmost urgency.

Jacob was fencing with Rico when he received the letter late in the afternoon. With an apology to Rico for cutting short the lesson, he hurriedly changed and having made the necessary arrangements, arrived at the safe house in Three Needle Street shortly after Walsingham. When they were seated, Walsingham handed Jacob the copy of the letter from Mary to Babington and asked him to read it.

'What do you think?' he asked, when Jacob had finished.

Jacob was in no hurry to reply. His mind was going through the implications. He knew from his discussion with Babington, that Morgan was right. Babington was very jealous. 'It would appear that Mary Stuart does not know the full extent of what Babington is planning.' Then he noticed the slight smile at the corner of Walsingham's mouth. 'And of course,' he said, 'neither do we. Ergo, if Babington writes back telling all, we will know too.'

This time the smile was real. 'Exactly. We will know too. The most important question is, of course, what will Mary Stuart reply?' He gave a sigh. 'But we are getting ahead of ourselves. The problem we have now is to ensure that Babington writes as full an account of the plot as possible.'

Jacob gave a sigh of resignation. 'And that's where I come in, hence this meeting.'

'Right again, Jacob. I want you to have a meeting with Babington on another matter. Chances are, having just received the letter, he will talk to you about it. Persuade him that the right course of action is to tell Mary Stuart everything. He wants her to see him as her knight in shining armour. Telling her the full extent to which he is prepared to risk his life in her cause is a sure way of getting it.'

'Have you any idea what I can use as an excuse for seeing Babington?'

'Of course,' Walsingham said, with a straight face. 'You are about to give him some important information which is not commonly known, as yet. This will prove that your court connections are of great use to them.'

Jacob was intrigued. 'What is this information and where did I obtain it?'

'As to the who, from Leicester. Babington knows you are talking to him about making some glass. What you will tell him is that Leicester told you he was a witness to the Queen and James VI of Scotland, Mary's son, signing a Treaty of mutual defence at Berwick.'

'Is this a real treaty?'

'Indeed it is,' Walsingham said solemnly. 'The gift of your glass from Elizabeth to King James helped to smooth the way, but, for now, both parties are keeping the treaty quiet.'

'It sounds like something I should not disclose,' Jacob said, looking concerned. He remembered the trip to Berwick well, but should I be telling an enemy of England such secret information, he wondered warily?

Walsingham was quick to reassure him. 'Do not fear the disclosure to Babington will cause any damage,' he said. 'It will become common tittle-tattle, ere long. Long enough for it to convince Babington that you are a person privy to important court affairs. Of more consequence to us, since you have passed secret information to him, Babington will see you as a person he can trust with details of their secret plans.'

Chapter Twenty-Nine
London, 1586

In his hired thatched cottage in Whitecross Street a short ride outside Cripplegate, Anthony Babington was sitting warming himself by the roaring fire in the living room when Jerome Bellamy arrived. 'Any letters today, Jerome?' he asked eagerly. Jerome was his regular messenger and went to the cobbler's shop near the Sun Inn every day at four o'clock.

Reaching into his doublet, Jerome produced two letters and handed them over. 'That one looks a bit strange,' he said, indicating a small folded note that had been carefully sealed with red wax. 'It's a very big seal for a little letter.'

Babington examined the letter and his heart began to pound. He recognised the seal of Mary Stuart immediately and carefully detaching it, he unfolded the note and read it with mounting excitement. At last, he thought. Queen Mary has written to me at last and in very friendly terms. She had commended him for all he had done in her cause and asked him to let her know how matters stood. She even said how much she had missed him when he had ceased to be her page all those years ago.

He had been longing to hear something like this from his Queen. In recent months, he had become dispirited at the lack of any word from her, but he knew from John Ballard that it had been impossible to get letters to her safely. It looks as though Gilbert Gifford has kept his word about beating that bloodhound Paulet. The brewer's secret compartment must be working for this to get through.

Putting the letter aside for a moment he opened the other one. It was from Jacob Bell, the glassmaker. The letter requested a meeting at The Swan Inn in two days time, as he had some important information. I wonder what he has heard this time, he thought. His contacts at court are most useful. Being the Queen's glassmaker and an excellent one at that, his customers were the cream of the court, including the Queen herself. What a pity he had such scruples about assassinating the Queen, he had regular access to her. Still no matter, he was proving to be very useful.

Going over to his desk, he took some fresh paper from the drawer and scribbled a note to Bell agreeing to the meeting. When Jerome came in with some fresh logs, he asked him to deliver the note to Harte Street. After he had left, he picked up the letter from his Queen again. It presented him with a huge dilemma. Putting details of his plans in a letter to Mary Stuart would place him in great danger if Walsingham intercepted it. Maybe it was time to think about going to safety in France. It was one thing to talk about plots, but the arrest of Throckmorton and now Parry, had resulted in penalties that were even more draconian. He had no wish to be hung, drawn and quartered, the thought of it made his blood run cold.

In the next couple of days, he turned the matter in his mind, over and over again. Dare he risk sending the reply his Queen expected from him? When he went to The Swan to meet Jacob Bell, he had still not decided.

When Jacob recounted the details of the Treaty of Berwick he had learned from Leicester, Babington was impressed. 'You have done very well,' he said and then lapsed into silence.

This is very worrying news, he thought. It will cause a great deal of difficulty for our invasion plans. They depend on sending a substantial army into Scotland, without any interference from the Scots, for the attack across the border.

'I must confess,' he said eventually, with a worried frown, 'that this is very disturbing news.'

'What will you do now?' Jacob asked.

'Nothing for the moment,' he replied. 'I'm expecting Ballard to return today. I must consult with him about our next move.'

'I assume,' Jacob said, 'that you will need to inform the Duke of Guise. I can get a message to him if that is of any help. I assume he is still planning to lead an army into southern England.' He looked worried. 'I confess I have heard nothing from him since last year. And, from what I hear from my people in Paris, the war between the Catholics and the Huguenots has flared up again. The Duke will be in the thick of it, as the Catholic League are besieging the Huguenots in Paris.'

Babington regarded him with respect. 'You are well informed, Jacob. Ballard is putting no reliance on the Catholic League forces for that very reason. Spanish troops under Alexander Farnese, Prince of Parma, the Spanish governor-general in the Low Countries, will make up the bulk of the army. They are seasoned campaigners fresh from fighting the Dutch Protestants.'

Babington's mind was working overtime as he mulled over this new information. Jacob was a man with fantastic contacts. He was also very shrewd. He wanted to discuss the letter from Mary Stuart with Ballard, but he wasn't here and anyway he would just tell him to do it. It was not as simple as that, there were a lot of implications. He made up his mind to ask Jacob what he thought.

'There is another matter, Jacob,' he said finally. 'I would welcome your advice.'

'I will do my best,' said Jacob, 'what is this matter?'

'I have received a letter from Mary Stuart,' Babington said, taking it out of his doublet and passing it to Jacob. 'You may read it.'

Reading the short note carefully, Jacob handed it back. 'Queen Mary obviously has a high regard for you and what you are doing on her behalf.'

Babington knew that, but he was not totally happy. He put the letter back into his doublet and gave a sigh.

'I think,' he said, choosing his words carefully, 'that the Queen does not know anything like the full extent of what I have done, or what I am planning to do on her behalf. Up until now it has been impossible to risk telling her.'

'Would you want to commit that sort of information to a letter anyway?' said Jacob.

That's the crux of it, Babington thought. He had thought about little else since receiving the letter.

'Only if I could be certain that only the Queen will see it.'

Jacob was silent for a while and then he straightened up and his face brightened. 'Now that we have established a sure way to get past that bloodhound, Paulet, perhaps it might be safe.'

'Exactly my thought,' Babington said. 'I believe it is only right I should let the Queen know the full extent to which my friends and I have gone and, are prepared to go in the future, to further her cause.'

Seeing Jacob was looking askance at this, he hurried to reassure him. 'Don't worry, I would not name anyone.' He shrugged. 'Other than myself of course, as the author of the letter. It would be worth the risk to let the Queen know how I have served her.'

'Are you certain that the letters will get to Mary Stuart without being intercepted? Jacob asked. 'A letter such as you propose, in the wrong hands, could do untold damage.'

Babington sought to convince Jacob and explained how letters were being smuggled into Mary Stuart. During this explanation, Jacob looked impressed, but seemed anxious about something.

'How trustworthy is this brewer?' he asked.

'Gifford is paying him well for his services,' said Babington, 'but in any case, he is a supporter of the Queen and is taking the risks willingly.' He looked at Jacob expectantly waiting for his reply.

'Since you are sure of that,' Jacob said, with a reassuring smile, 'it should be safe to let Queen Mary know of your efforts on her behalf. Besides, as Gifford said, it is important to get Mary Stuart's agreement to the plans before they are carried out. What if she doesn't agree with assassinating Elizabeth?'

'I had not thought of that, you are right,' agreed Babington. 'I will give the matter some more thought. I appreciate your help and I will let you know what I decide. For now, I will take my leave of you.'

By the time he reached Whitecross Street, he had decided to reply to his Queen. Sitting at his desk, he worked on the letter. It took a number of drafts before he was satisfied. When the final copy had been made, he folded it and sealed it carefully. Putting it to one side, he leaned back in his chair. It was done. And then a little worm of doubt appeared in his mind. What if ...? Stop right there, he commanded himself, you can have doubts, but you know the letter is the only way you will achieve the things you have desired all these years. I must send it, he decided and shouted for Jerome to come down. Once the letter was on its way to Gifford, the worm returned to plague him. This time, there was no shaking it off. Eventually, after much debate, he decided to play safe and seek a travel warrant from Walsingham.

The meeting took place the following day and Babington came straight to the point. 'Mister Secretary, I have asked for this meeting in order to obtain your assistance in securing permission to travel to France. It is my intention to carry on with the education that was interrupted on the death of my father.' When Walsingham regarded him in silence, he continued. 'In return for a licence to travel, it occurred to me that I might be of some assistance to you. I am sure to meet with other Englishmen on my travels and it is conceivable that some of them may be people you wish to receive news about.'

Walsingham nodded. 'Well Sir Anthony, there are certainly a number of people who left the country after the Throckmorton plot that I would like to hear news about.' He regarded Babington seriously. 'What you are suggesting certainly has merit and I will see Her Majesty is aware of your patriotic offer. As I am sure you know, only the Queen can grant the licence.'

Babington was listening carefully to every nuance of Walsingham's reply, but could detect no trace of irony or insincerity in his voice. 'Off course,' he replied, 'but I also know that your word carries great weight with Her Majesty.'

Walsingham acknowledged the compliment and then rising to his feet, rang the bell for his secretary. 'I will apprise the Queen of your offer at the earliest opportunity but, as the Queen is on progress, it may be some little time before I am able to discuss this matter with her. Meanwhile I beg you to have patience.'

Turning to his secretary, he asked him to show Sir Anthony out. 'Until we meet again, Sir Anthony.'

'Thank you for your time, Sir Francis.'

When Babington had left, Walsingham shouted for Colonel Young to come in.

'What was all that about?' said the colonel, coming in from the adjoining room.

Walsingham looked puzzled. 'I'm not sure,' he said. 'I get the feeling that Sir Anthony may be having second thoughts about this plot. Perchance Jacob Bell has done too good a job of playing devil's advocate over the letter to Mary Stuart. Babington may be thinking that such a letter would put him at huge risk if it ever came into my hands.'

'He'd be quite right on that score,' agreed the colonel. 'Do you want me to arrest him? He might try to get to France without a licence.'

'Not yet,' said Walsingham. 'We must give him every chance to write the letter to Mary Stuart. It may be he is just playing safe, hoping to have a licence so that he could leave England speedily if things go wrong.'

'Wouldn't he just go to Jacob Bell and ask him to smuggle him out on *The Crystal*?'

'There is that possibility,' agreed Walsingham, 'but should he do so, Bell will surely let me know. We must hold our nerve and give Babington time to send the letter to Mary Stuart. Once we have her reply we can arrest him. I have him well watched, so unless he makes a dash for it, we will continue to be patient.'

Chapter Thirty
London & Burton-upon-Trent, 1586

Mary Stuart was trying to keep her mind occupied by sewing, as she often did. She had always found embroidery very comforting. But time was weighing heavily on her shoulders today. The regime instituted by Sir Amias Paulet, her jailer, had closed in on her completely, separating her from her friends and the outside world. Unfortunately, embroidery was not giving her any peace of mind today and in a fit of anger, she threw it across the room. As her ladies scurried to pick it up, she sat, shoulders slumped despondently, staring out of the window of her retiring room with unseeing eyes.

In the storeroom, close by Mary's rooms, a new delivery of the special ale for the Scottish Queen had been received from the brewer. When Paulet's men had left, the barrel was broached and Curle, Mary's secretary, removed the cork and opened the secret container attached to it. Sure enough, it contained a letter. Hurriedly sealing the container and returning it to the barrel, he hastened to the reception room.

When Curle brought her the letter, Mary brightened up immediately when she saw it was from Babington. Here was news at last. Ever since her son, James, had forbidden her to return to Scotland, she had been forced to look for help elsewhere. Her French relatives led by Henry, Duke of Guise where busy fighting their own battles with King Henry III of France. She could expect no help from that direction. That left Spain and Mary, ever the pragmatist, had no hesitation in pinning her hopes of salvation on the Spanish backed plot led by Babington.

And now Babington had written to tell her all the details of what he planned to do and how a Spanish army, accompanied by an uprising of English Catholics, would sweep away the Protestant armies of Elizabeth. Furthermore, he promised to effect her own release during the confusion that would follow his assassination of Queen Elizabeth. Babington wrote that, *for the dispatch of the usurper ... there be six noble gentlemen, all my private friends, who for the zeal they bear for the Catholic cause and your Majesty's service will undertake that tragic execution.*

Mary was in a quandary and for a week she tried to weigh up her options. In truth, when she tried to list them, it was a very short list. They were very limited indeed. Her moods swung from despair to euphoria and through anguish back to despair. One thought kept playing on her mind. Ever since Paulet's regime had severed her from the outside world, she feared that she would be killed and they would say she had died of sickness. At last after a week, her despondency led to recklessness and she decided to endorse Babington's plan. The change in her was enormous. From being withdrawn and apathetic, she became excited and animated.

Mary read the letter again, then sitting at her table in her study, she worked out her reply in her head, noting down headings on a piece of paper. Calling for her secretaries, Nau and Curle, she discussed her reply with them. When she explained the letter she intended to write, Nau was horrified. 'Please, Your Majesty, have nothing to do with this Babington, I believe he is a dreamer.' Curle also begged her not to answer Babington. 'The letter you propose would be fatal in the wrong hands.'

Mary would brook no interference, her mind was made up. 'Silence the pair of you. I did not ask for your opinions, I simply want your obedience.' She gestured to the draft she had prepared. 'Now, Monsieur Nau, you will take notes while I read and then you will draft a letter in French for my approval.'

Claude Nau, realising that his mistress was adamant, did as he was told and drafted the letter. Once this had been approved, he translated the letter into English, since the cipher used by Babington was in that language. The letter was finished late in the evening and placed in the empty beer keg early next morning. Included with the letter was an instruction to Babington to burn the letter once he had read the contents, *lest it fall into the wrong hands.*

When Jed returned to Burton from Chartley with the empty casks he found Barnaby waiting impatiently for his return. 'What are you doing here today, I wasn't expecting you until tomorrow?'

'I have to get back to London as soon as possible,' said Barnaby. 'There might be a letter to be delivered to France.'

Jed looked at him sharply. His already suspicious mind was alerted by the slight pause before Barnaby had answered, as if the question had caught him unaware. Jed thought about Barnaby's first visit. Despite the letter from Gifford explaining that he had to go to France and that Barnaby, his cousin, would come in his place, Jed's suspicions had been aroused. Not even the satisfyingly full purse that Barnaby had given him had changed that feeling. Taking the letter that Barnaby had brought from London, Jed had promised to deliver it the next day, which was Saturday, and Barnaby left, saying he was bound for London again.

As soon as Barnaby had left the yard, Jed rushed to the gate to see which direction he was taking. Hurriedly saddling his chestnut mare, he set off in pursuit. Fortunately, Barnaby was in no hurry and Jed quickly had him in sight, still heading for the road south. Jed followed him until he was satisfied that he was indeed heading for London. On his way back to the brewery, Jed tried to justify the feeling of suspicion which was still strong in his mind. But he was unable to do so. Something was wrong, but he didn't know what. He vowed to follow Barnaby every time he came and only if nothing untoward happened might he be able he put his sense of foreboding to rest. And now Barnaby was here again and the suspicion was as strong as ever.

'Why don't you go and wait in the kitchen. I'll be a little while as I have to see to the horses. The maid will get you some refreshment.' He turned away before Barnaby could object and when he looked back, and pointed to the kitchen, Barnaby gave a shrug and went inside.

Leading the horses into the barn, Jed quickly unharnessed them and led them into their stalls. He then saddled up his horse and only when it was ready did he scrutinise the empty kegs. A quick check showed that the one from the Queen's apartments contained a letter in the secret box. Jed hefted it carefully, wondering if there was some problem and he should destroy it. One glance and he could see that the Queen's seal was intact. He must do his duty and carry out his part as he had promised.

Having received the letter from Jed, Barnaby handed over the usual purse and got up to go. He refused all offers of more refreshments and Jed was struck by his hurry to be off. As soon as he had left, Jed followed him at a discreet distance. As before, Barnaby headed south and just when Jed was thinking he was heading for London as usual, he turned off down a lane just outside Burton and rode to the rear of a small cottage.

Leaving his horse tied up in a nearby thicket, well concealed from the bridle path, Jed crept up to the house and circled round to the rear. As well as Barnaby's horse there were two others. Creeping closer, he could hear low voices, but could not make out what they were saying. Doing his best to be silent, he moved towards the window. Risking a quick look, he was just in time to see Barnaby and the back of another man as they went into a room at the front of the cottage.

The garden at the front was very overgrown and provided some cover as Jed tried to get a vantage point. Sidling nearer to the front window, he risked a quick glimpse and slumped back in utter bewilderment, his whole body shaking, when he recognised the man talking to Barnaby. His mind was reeling uncontrollably. Bell! What trick of the devil was this? It couldn't be Bell, he'd seen him lying dead.

Summoning his legs to obey, he risked another look. The glance told him that his eyes were not playing tricks. There was no doubt it was Jacob Bell. Somehow he had survived Jed's attempt on his life.

Jed slipped his pistol from his doublet and made ready to rectify his mistake. He was not bothered about Barnaby, he was frightened of his own shadow. The third man he had seen on his last look seemed to be some sort of clerk, so Jacob Bell was the only one that mattered.

His hands had been busy while he'd been making his calculations and pistol at the ready, Jed began to edge forward again, all senses alert as he made ready to rectify his mistake. He became aware of a faint drumming noise. His head reached the window ledge. He was almost in a position and was preparing to stand up and fire, when he realised the drumming was getting louder - a large group of horses being ridden hard. The sound stopped him in his tracks. Retiring to the side of the house he looked up the track towards the bend about forty paces away. Riding hell for leather, a troop of soldiers led by an officer came racing round the bend.

Jed wasted no time. He was out in the back garden and lying concealed in a ditch under the hedgerow before the troop came to a halt outside the front of the cottage.

The officer began to shout instructions and ten of the troopers rode round the side of the house passing within feet of Jed's hiding place. Shrinking down, Jed pulled some of the branches in front of him and the unsuspecting troops rode past.

Unable to move, Jed could hear a muted conversation between the officer and someone who had come out of the front door of the cottage. He thought it might be Bell, but he wasn't sure.

From Jed's initial look, there appeared to be about thirty troopers and they now threw a protective ring around the cottage. There was only one thing Jed could do. He couldn't take on the troopers to get at Bell, that would be suicide. When the nearest troopers moved a short distance away from his hiding place, Jed squirmed through the hedge and taking advantage of every piece of cover worked his way back to his horse. Putting a hand over its muzzle he led it quietly away. Once he was certain he was out of earshot, he mounted and spurred away, heading for Modven Brewery.

On the way he tried to make sense of what he'd seen. The news that Jacob Bell was alive was a stunning blow. He had been so sure that his shot had killed him. However, there was a more important consideration. He knew where Bell was to be found in London, but first he must try to discover what he was doing with the letter from Queen Mary.

Jed's blood ran cold as he realised the implications. The letter must be very important for a troop of soldiers to be despatched to protect it. That meant that the authorities knew about it. Walsingham was behind this. He'd long suspected that Bell was one of his spies and this was all the proof he needed.

Then a terrifying thought came to him. What if he'd been duped by Gilbert Gifford into betraying his Queen?

Chapter Thirty-One
Burton-upon-Trent & London, 1586

The light from the candles left deep pools of shadow in the room where Walsingham was sitting slumped in the high-backed leather upholstered chair. He passed a weary hand across his eyes, which were red-rimmed from lack of sleep. When he had first received the copy of Mary's letter to Babington, with its token of Phelippes black humour - a gallows, on the outside, Walsingham was astonished. Even though he had hoped for it, Mary had been recklessly indiscreet. After advising Babington not to go ahead with rescuing her until preparations for the invasion from outside and the revolt of Catholics from inside the country were complete, a later paragraph stood out.

When your preparations are complete, let the six gentlemen complete their task and then come and set me free ... but do not take any steps towards my liberation until you are in such force as you can liberate me even if I have been put in some inaccessible place.

Although, strictly, she had not specified the task that these six gentlemen were to carry out, when taken together with Babington's letter, to which she was replying, Mary's meaning was perfectly clear. These six gentlemen were to despatch the usurper, namely Queen Elizabeth. Phelippes was right to draw a gallows, thought Walsingham, there is enough in the two letters to convince even Queen Elizabeth, let alone the Privy Council, that Mary Stuart must be dealt with.

Phelippes also advised Walsingham that he had forged a postscript to Mary's original letter in the English cipher used between Mary and Babington. It was short and to the point.

I would be glad to know the names and qualities of the six gentlemen which are to accomplish the task. Upon knowledge of the parties, I can give you some further advice necessary to be followed and also, from time to time, instructions how to proceed. As soon as possible, let me know who is ready and how far every one is privy to the details of the affair.

Walsingham was now faced with a dilemma. Should he wait in the hope that Babington would reply, but risk the destruction of the letter? Or should he arrest him immediately and recover the letter? After a great deal of deliberation he decided to wait.

As he remarked to Jacob later, 'The opportunity to have the names of the conspirators confirmed in Babington's own hand is too good a prize to miss. However, I will watch Babington most carefully and I want you to ensure that *The Crystal* is not available to spirit him away to France.'

'What will you do with Mary Stuart?' asked Jacob.

'Nothing for now. She is not going anywhere and I have moved troops into the area should the conspirators jump the gun and try to release her.'

'What of Queen Elizabeth? The six gentlemen might try to carry out their assignment to assassinate her.'

'The Queen is indisposed and the court is closed for the time being. Only a few of her closest advisers will have access to Her Majesty.'

Jacob sighed. 'You seem to have thought of everything, but God help the poor fools caught up in this endeavour.'

'Amen to that, Jacob. At the risk of repeating myself, I grow weary of the many who pay the price for the Scottish Queen's intrigue, while she escapes the retribution of her pride and folly.' He gave a long sigh. 'God willing, we might see an end of it when this affair comes to a conclusion.'

He stood up and Jacob did so too. Putting a friendly arm on Jacob's shoulder, Walsingham regarded him with a gentle smile that Jacob had never seen him use before. 'Go home to your wife and children, Jacob Bell. I wish to God that I could do the same but I fear that, until this tragedy is played out, I will be sleeping here, or not at all.'

When Jacob had left, Walsingham rang the handbell for his secretary. He handed Walsingham another letter from Phelippes and one from Gilbert Gifford. Instructing the secretary to send for Colonel Young, Walsingham settled down to read the letters.

Phelippes was asking yet again for the warrants to arrest Ballard. They had determined that this should be done some weeks previously. However, Walsingham again decided to defer the arrest for a little longer as he did not wish to alert Babington and the other conspirators. The letter from Gifford informed him that he had returned from France and had met with Ballard. Gifford promised to keep an eye on him and advised that no attempt should be made to arrest him until the net had closed on Mary Stuart.

Colonel Young arrived a little while later and Walsingham instructed him to keep a close watch on Ballard. 'I believe that he has obtained a warrant to leave the country and this must be prevented at all costs. Should you have any thought that he is intending to flee, he must be arrested at once.'

A few days later, Walsingham received a letter from Gifford, informing him of a second meeting with the Jesuit priest, Ballard. Walsingham became alarmed when Gifford wrote that Ballard was aware of his tampering with the packets sent to the Scottish Queen. He could delay no longer and accordingly, sent instructions to Gifford to find where Ballard was staying and report to Frances Milles, Walsingham's secretary.

Gifford sent a report to Miles that he had been unable to find Ballard and he thought he might have fled the country. In reality it was Gifford who was fleeing. Now that Walsingham was making arrests, he feared that his double game might be exposed when the others came to trial. Accordingly, he obtained passage from the French Ambassador and slipped over to France.

Whilst all this activity was taking place, Babington continued to approach Walsingham through his secretary in a vain attempt to obtain a warrant to leave the country. He again offered his services to spy on known Catholic extremists and even informed Walsingham of two priests who had recently entered the country. Walsingham continued to encourage him, hoping to inspire him to write to Mary Stuart.

On the last day of July, Babington informed Walsingham he was aware of a conspiracy against the State. Walsingham arranged to meet him next day, but was forced to rearrange the meeting. In the meantime, Ballard had not escaped. Colonel Young discovered him in London and arrested him immediately.

Walsingham sent Babington his grateful thanks for the information and arranged a new meeting for the coming Saturday. Babington wrote a letter of complaint to Walsingham as soon as he learned of Ballard's arrest. In reply, Walsingham informed Babington that Ballard had been arrested as a seminary priest and that Babington was in serious danger of arrest for harbouring priests unless he took refuge in Walsingham's house. Babington did not accept this offer and an order was issued for the his arrest along with his conspirators.

Unfortunately, Babington had made good his escape. When the colonel reported back, Walsingham instructed him to have a word with Jacob Bell. 'He might have an idea where he may be holed up, but if not, ask him to ask the Ring to find him. I'm surprised the agent who was watching him, hasn't reported in.'

The reason for that became obvious about two hours later when the agent was found by the watch, unconscious on a waste site close by Babington's address. He was unable to shed any light on who had attacked him, except that his purse strings had been cut and the purse stolen as well as his rings and shoes. The watch reported it as a robbery, but Walsingham thought differently. 'Our birds knew they were being watched, so they disposed of the watcher making it look like a robbery. Where they are now, heaven alone knows, but they won't get far. I have already alerted the Watch in and around London and the watchers at the ports.'

A message was also despatched to the Earl of Shrewsbury in Darbieshire and he sent a strong force of men to search Dethick Hall, not far from his manor house at Wingfield. The house was almost empty except for Babington's sisters, Madeleine and Ellen and his two year old daughter. His wife had fled. After repeated questioning it became apparent that they had not seen Sir Anthony for many weeks. The only address they had for him in London, was the one that had already been raided. As instructed, all Babington's goods and papers were seized and sent to Walsingham. The sisters and Babington's daughter were forced to seek refuge with Lady Foljambe at Walton about twelve miles away.

The only thing of real interest that was found, was an oil painting hanging over the fireplace in the masters study. When this was shown to Shrewsbury, he identified Anthony Babington sitting in the centre of a group of six young men. He also recognised two of the young men as the sons of local Catholic families. Realising this might be a painting of the Babington conspirators, he had it parcelled up and, together with a covering letter, sent it post-haste to Walsingham.

Chapter Thirty-Two
London, 1586

The oak panelled room with its comfortable leather chairs that Walsingham used as a study, had a new addition on the wall opposite his desk. Walsingham regarded the portrait of Babington and his friends that had been sent from Dethick Manor with an intense stare. Where are you, he thought? Despite the raising of a hue and cry, there was still no sign of Babington. Walsingham examined the portrait again and shook his head in astonishment Its existence was typical of the dream world that Babington inhabited. To have their portrait painted before their plot had succeeded defied all logic. It was as if they wanted to be caught! All of the men had now been identified and it was only a matter of time before they were brought to justice.

For once, the Ring, had failed to find Babington and after two days, he decided to see if Jacob Bell had any other thoughts on how they might locate Babington. In answer to the colonel's query Jacob said he might be able to discover where Babington was holed up.

'Wait for me here and I will join you shortly.' Going into his office, he retrieved the note with the address of Babington's cobbler friend from his locked cupboard. He then wrote a short note, folded and sealed it, and then put it in his doublet. He was still in his working clothes and putting on the plain, black hooded cape, he wore as a disguise, he joined the Colonel.

'Do you know this area?' he said, showing the address to the colonel.

'I know the Sun Inn well, I have been there many a time.'

'Good. This is what I want you to do.' For the next few minutes he explained his plan and although the colonel was obviously unhappy with some points, he finally agreed. Jacob set off to Mark Street to fetch his horse, while the colonel led his troops to Aldgate and out of the city.

It was well after three o'clock when Jacob arrived at the cobbler's shop and left the letter addressed to Babington. In answer to his query, he was pleased to learn that Babington's messenger had not arrived. Going outside, Jacob saw that the yard at the rear of the Sun Inn offered a good view of the cobbler's shop. A small coin sufficed to pay the ostler to look to his horse, while he took up a vantage point to watch.

By a quarter after four, Jacob was beginning to think the messenger was not coming. However, a few minutes later, a man on a piebald mare came to the shop and the apprentice held his horse while he went in. Strolling casually past the shop, Jacob saw the cobbler hand him the letter he had left earlier. Jacob sauntered casually across to the Sun Inn and retrieved his horse. When the man set off, keeping a discreet distance behind, Jacob followed.

With its distinctive mottling in brown and white, the piebald mare was easily followed, so Jacob stayed well back as he followed the man out of Cripplegate. Turning left towards the castellated conduit that stored water for the area, the man passed the soldiers watering their horses and turned right into Whitecross Street.

As Jacob passed the conduit, he nodded to Colonel Young, who, with his troop, had circled round the outside of the city walls to the Cripplegate conduit. Cripplegate was the nearest city gate to the Sun Inn. As Jacob turned into Whitecross Street, the troop mounted up and followed him.

The houses became more infrequent as they rode along and just when Jacob was thinking they were in for a long ride, the rider turned a corner of the lane and when Jacob arrived there, he had disappeared. There were cottages on the left, but only shrubbery and an open field leading to a wood, on the right. By the time he had checked the cottages, without success, he was some way down the lane. He would have seen the mare if it had gone so far, so he turned back, scrutinising the shrubbery. He had almost reached the corner again, before he found what he was looking for. A narrow path leading through the shrubs. He dismounted and cautiously edged his way down the path keeping a sharp lookout. A short way along he came upon some steaming horse droppings. At least I'm on the right path, he thought.

The bushes ended a few yards further on. A cautious look revealed a small cottage, about fifty paces away, set in a clearing at the edge of the wood, with a piebald horse tied up in front. Retracing his steps, he found Colonel Young and his men searching the lane. They too had missed the path. After a quick word, the colonel, sent half of his men to circle round and secure the rear and sides of the cottage. Once they were in place, the colonel and his remaining men rode up to the house. Jacob stayed behind in the lane where he could see the cottage, but could not be seen.

Babington and three of his conspirators, were heavily outnumbered, but put up a very stern resistance. They had been hurriedly packing to leave, alerted by Jacob's note. In it he said that the cobbler by the Sun Inn was known to Walsingham and that the messenger might be followed. One of the men fled out of the back and after a brief fight, was overcome. The others on hearing the horses approaching the cottage boiled out of the door and tried to fight their way clear. Somehow in the melee, Ballard managed to mount the piebald mare and escape towards the lane, with two of the troopers in close pursuit. Pulling his hood over his face, Jacob waited until the piebald mare turned the corner where he was hiding and then sprang out and dragged Ballard out of his saddle, sending him crashing to the ground. As he lay senseless, the troopers secured him, draped him over the mare and, with a nod of approval to Jacob, led him back to the cottage.

Once Jacob was sure that the colonel had Babington, he returned to London. His thoughts were sombre as he rode home. More young men to add to the mounting total of those who had paid the ultimate penalty for trying to further Mary Stuart's vain search for glory and power. For the first time since he had known her, Jacob hoped that this time she would reap the rewards of her blind folly.

Even before Babington's arrest, news of the plot had spread through the population. Rumour fed on rumour and by the time the conspirators were captured, the outcry had reached the dimensions of a second St. Bartholomew's Day when the Huguenots had been massacred in France.

Over the next few days, more and more of Babington's associates were captured.

Popular excitement was high and when the conspirators were

escorted through the streets of London to the Tower, the Londoners rang the church bells and lit bonfires in the street to show their joy at the escape of their beloved Queen.

Walsingham was delighted when he was informed of the arrests. He was pondering on the matter of the Scottish Queen, when Burghley informed him that the Queen was advocating that all of the plotters, except Mary Stuart, should be dealt with first. Not only that, but the Queen insisted that matters pertaining to Mary's part should not be divulged at the trial. The Queen was at Windsor and Walsingham realised that she thought she was still in peril. She hardly ever used Windsor, unless she felt herself to be in great danger. Obviously, this was colouring her judgement and she was trying to avoid the consequences that might follow if Mary was put on trial. Burghley indicated that he would speak with the commissioners appointed for the trial and on the following day he handed the Queen a protest signed by virtually all of them.

When Walsingham was apprised of this, Burghley wrote that although he had won the argument, he was disturbed by Elizabeth's wavering attitude. As Burghley remarked to Hatton later, 'I fear that, given the Queen's propensity to procrastinate when she has a difficult decision, even if we convict the Scottish Queen, it will be difficult to get Elizabeth to agree to the ultimate penalty.'

Matters dragged on for weeks with many different opinions as to how to handle the matter. On various occasions during August and on into September, Babington, his fellow conspirators and Mary's secretaries Nau and Curle were examined by members of the Privy Council. Despite the fact that Babington was not tortured, although it was threatened, he confessed all, but placed all the blame on Ballard, who graciously admitted that he wished the spilling of his blood could save his young friend.

Babington made no attempt to protect his six fellow conspirators, seemingly believing that his dealings with Walsingham and the information he provided just before his arrest, would win him a pardon if he disclosed everything and everybody. He even provided a detailed summary of the letter written by Mary Stuart endorsing his actions in the plot, including the postscript forged and added by Phelippes.

On the basis of this confession, he was questioned on further occasions and cross-examined on both his confession and his replies to questions. Both questions and answers were recorded in reports. Faced with Babington's detailed confessions, the other conspirators also confessed their parts.

When Nau and Curle were examined, Nau, in the mistaken belief that copies of the original letter from Mary in French and the English translation had been seized with Mary's papers, confirmed the contents of the letter. Except of course, the postscript, which was added by Phelippes, unknown to Nau. He had translated the letter into French from Mary's minutes and Curle had translated it into English and put it into the cipher for Babington. Both servants were quick to dissociate themselves from the plot. They were simply obeying their mistress's orders!

Burghley took no part in the trial. Babington, Savage and Ballard pleaded guilty so no evidence was required to convict them. Abington and Tilney both pleaded not guilty and Babington's confession was presented as evidence against them and they were both convicted. Convicted of high treason, there could be only one verdict, they were to be hung, drawn and quartered. As soon as the trial was over, Babington wrote to Elizabeth begging her to have mercy and spare him. He even offered a thousand pounds in return for his freedom. All to no avail.

On the following day, Jacob, putting on his work clothes and hooded cape, made his way towards Tyburn. The first seven of the conspirators were taken from Tower Hill to Tyburn, tied head down on hurdles and dragged through the streets of London. As they neared Newgate, the crowd had become very large and volatile. Jacob stayed well to the rear of the crowd, as they pelted the unfortunate men with rotten vegetables. He followed the procession of carts along as they passed through Newgate and up Holborn Hill, until they reached Tyburn.

By now the crowd had swelled enormously until there were many hundreds taking up any vantage point they could. Finding a place on a small knoll to the side of the triangular gallows tree, Jacob could see a number of Privy Councillors including

Walsingham in a seated area set on the opposite side.

Babington was the first to be selected. He was led under the tree where a ladder had been placed and ropes slung over all three arms of the frame. He was offered a black hood, but declined and tried to say something, but it was drowned out by the roar of the crowd as the noose was placed around his neck. The other end of the rope was attached to the horses that had drawn the hurdle and at a signal from the executioner, they plunged away, hoisting Babington high, kicking and jerking his life away as he was throttled.

Again the crowd gave a great roar, but Jacob felt only a great sadness. He knew the barbarity had only just begun. The executioner who had never taken his eyes off Babington, gave another signal and the rope was lowered. Carrying him to the side of the tree, where there was a large wooden block with a fire burning brightly beside it, they laid Babington on the block. Having revived him by dashing a bucket of water in his face. They tore off his clothes and spread-eagled him over the block and his bowels voided, as gibbering in terror they began the torture.

Scream after scream echoed over the crowd's baying, as first the body was slit open and his entrails cut out. He was then castrated and the entrails and genitals held up to his dulling eyes, before they were cast into the fire, to a bestial roar from the crowd. Only then were his heart and lungs hacked out and poor Babington's suffering was at an end. The lifeless body was finally decapitated and the trunk hacked into four pieces to be hung on London Bridge as a warning to others.

This harrowing death was a far cry from the youthful vanities and fantasies that Babington had woven as he played the hero for his beautiful Queen. Even the crowd that had reacted so primitively a short while ago were silent, perhaps shocked by their earlier behaviour.

When the whimpering and wailing Ballard suffered the same fate, followed by the other conspirators, even the most hardened among the crowd were shocked at the barbarity of it all. The crowd lapsed into disturbed murmuring and many women in the crowd were being sick, or fainting.

During the battle of Lepanto, Jacob had seen many terrible

sights when *The Crystal* decimated Ottoman galley crews with its massive fire power. But nothing he had seen came even close to the sheer cruelty of this barbarous execution. Although it was intended as the ultimate deterrent to any other would-be plotters, he could not stomach the brutality. Pushing his way through the crowd, he stood in front of the Privy Councillors, who in fairness were also looking sick, and shouted his protest at the uncivilised scenes. The crowd surged forward, as a large section of them echoed his protest and Jacob was swallowed up in the crowd.

On hearing of the terrible scenes and the protests, the Queen ordered that the remaining conspirators must be hanged until they were dead, before disembowelling took place, and not in plain view of the crowd. So ended the Babington plot, but there still remained the matter of the Scottish Queen.

Chapter Thirty-Three
Chartley, 1586

About a mile from Chartley and out of sight of the manor house, Sir Amias Paulet waited patiently in the middle of an open field for Walsingham's messenger to arrive. The meeting with William Waad, Clerk of the Privy Council, had been arranged in secret. Only Walsingham and the Queen were aware of it. The subject, of course, was what should be done with the Scottish Queen.

When Waad arrived he informed Paulet that the first step must be to seize all of her papers before news of the arrests reached Chartley. It was imperative to ensure she did not destroy them. They talked for some time and then Waad returned to London with a memorandum from Paulet.

Paulet had suggested that Mary might be invited to go hunting and while she was away, her rooms could be entered, her secretaries arrested and all her papers confiscated. When the plan was discussed by Walsingham and Elizabeth, it was agreed that it was an excellent plan. The following day, instructions for it to be carried out were sent to Paulet.

When Mary was offered the chance to hunt deer in Sir Walter Aston's estate nearby, she accepted with alacrity. It was the first time in many months that she felt well enough to ride a horse. All went well with the hunt, but when they stopped at Sir Walter's house at Tixall, Paulet detained her. Despite her tears, protestations and threats, she was locked up in a room in the house, with guards at the doors and only her personal maids to attend her.

As soon as the hunting party was out of sight of Chartley Manor, William Waad, accompanied by three loyal gentleman from the neighbourhood, entered her apartments, arrested her secretaries and seized all of the papers they could find. Secretaries and papers were together sent up to London.

On the Saturday following his narrow escape from the cottage at Burton, Jed was going to Chartley Manor as usual. There were no messages from Barnaby, so Jed went into the office and after much thought composed the following short note:

Your majesty

Be on your guard and send no further messages in the beer cask as they are being intercepted by Walsingham and his men.

A true friend and loyal servant.

Folding it carefully, he sealed it and placing it in the secret compartment of the cask, he carefully sealed it. On his journey to Chartley he was in a high state of anticipation, but his arrival proved to be a huge anticlimax. When he reported to the sergeant-at-arms as usual, he greeted him in his usual friendly manner. 'Good day Master Stourbridge. You can put the casks in their usual place, but don't bother with anything for the Scottish Queen. She's been allowed to go hunting at Tixall and will stay there for at least two weeks. While she's away, her people are cleaning and redecorating her apartments.'

There was nothing in the sergeant-at-arms manner that Jed could find suspicious, even though the timing of the event seemed to be something rather sinister.

'That's a turn up for the book,' he remarked. 'Paulet must be going soft, letting the Scottish Queen out of his sight.'

The sergeant-at-arms laughed heartily. 'Don't you believe it. He's just the same as usual. However, the only reason it's not been granted before is that the Scottish Queen hasn't been able to ride a horse. In fact when she came from Sheffield, she could barely walk. Sir Walter has invited her often enough.'

Jed was confused. There was certainly no hesitation on the sergeant's part. His manner was no different than at any other time Jed had met him. He put the casks in the store and then indicated the Queen's special cask. 'Shall I take this to Mary Stuart's apartments, so it's there when she returns?'

The sergeant-at-arms gave this suggestion some thought. 'Perhaps it would be better in the cool store. It would keep better in there.'

This was the last thing Jed wanted, since if the messages were being intercepted as he believed, they would find his note to Mary Stuart. 'I think it might be best to bring a new cask back when she returns. The ale will probably be flat in two weeks.'

'That's true,' said the sergeant. 'Suit yourself. So long as we have our beer, that's the most important thing. I'll let you know next Saturday when we expect her back. Assuming I know, of course.'

When Jed had left, Paulet emerged from the guardroom where he'd been listening to the conversation with Jed.

'Well done Sergeant, you were very convincing.' He gave a faint smile.

'I'll have to remember that the next time you're up in front of me on a charge.'

'Very good, sir,' said the sergeant, with a grin.

As matters turned out, there was no chance for Jed to pass on his message as the news of the arrest of the plotters spread throughout the nation amid general rejoicing, which of course Jed didn't share. Understanding only too well the implications of these arrests, Jed decided it was time for James Stourbridge to disappear. It could only be a matter of time before he too was arrested for passing messages to Mary Stuart. He'd not left Gifford in any doubt where his sympathies lay. He had no doubt that Gifford would tell Walsingham everything. He struck Jed as a man who was only looking out for himself. He might even be one of Walsingham's men for all he knew!

Fortunately, he'd not spent any of the money that Gifford had paid him and it added up to quite a formidable total. In addition, much to her surprise, he accepted the widow's offer to buy out his share of the Modven Brewery, she had made some weeks earlier. Having acquired a packhorse, Jed left Burton immediately. He stopped overnight in an inn where he learned that Mary Stuart had come back to Chartley Manor House. The following day he scouted the area around Chartley.

A little way from Chartley Manor there was a cottage for hire for which he paid a month's rent. It was in a secluded spot, but handily placed to keep an eye on the comings and goings. The cottage was rather run-down, but it would suffice. Before settling in, he made sure he had ample supplies for at least two weeks. He was consumed with a burning desire for revenge on Walsingham and his spy, Jacob Bell, but first he must find out what was to be done with Queen Mary. Walsingham would probably move her further south if they intended to put her on trial. His biggest fear was that Walsingham would have her poisoned and say that she had died of a protracted illness despite her physician's best efforts.

As the weeks had passed without any news of Mary Stuart, Jed had been forced to seek supplies. He had gambled that should the Scottish Queen be moved it would be to the south, so he had headed in that direction and bought enough supplies for several more weeks. Keeping an anxious look out for signs of the passage of a large party of horses, Jed rode northwards towards his rented cottage on the outskirts of Chartley.

Reaching the cottage and having unloaded the packhorse, Jed set off to survey the roads around Chartley. Finding a vantage place he examined the manor house. Unfortunately, since the house was moated, it was not possible to approach closely. However, he was able to get a view of the windows of Mary Stuart's apartments and he could see people at the window showing that the rooms were occupied.

While buying his supplies, the whole village was buzzing with news of the execution of the Babington plotters. The full gory details were being bandied about and Jed was sickened by the general euphoria that the plot had failed and Queen Elizabeth was safe. Jed had struggled to avoid betraying his true feelings. Everyone was condemning Mary Stuart for orchestrating the plot. There were many voices calling for her to share the fate of the other plotters. Not wishing to be drawn into those discussions, Jed left as soon as he could.

In fact, it was not until early on the twenty-fifth of September that Mary Stuart was moved. At a discreet distance, Jed followed the procession from Chartley. Progress was very slow due to Mary's ill-health. The severe abdominal pains had returned and she was suffering from rheumatism and swollen legs. It took the better part of four days to cover the relatively short distance. Each night Jed was forced to track back to the nearest inn. Fortunately, it took a long time for the entourage to get moving each morning, so Jed simply left the inn early.

Eventually they reached the village of Fotheringhay, in

Northamptonshire. The entourage went right into the village centre and Jed was forced to stay well back for fear of being discovered. When most of the riders had disappeared, Jed followed cautiously. At the far end of the village was a bridge over the River Nene which led to a large fortress. Judicious enquiries at the local inn, revealed that the fortress was Fotheringhay Castle. Built in Norman times, it had a wide wet ditch partly surrounding the bailey wall and a large, polygonal stone keep that contained the Great Hall could be seen on top of the motte. With its drawbridge and entrance towers, it was formidable. Walsingham and his damned lackeys were obviously taking all precautions against a rescue attempt. Even a large invading army would find it difficult to breach the castle walls.

The village inn was, as usual, a hotbed of gossip. Two of the landlord's daughters worked in the castle, as did many of the locals. It was common knowledge that Mary Stuart had been brought there and was to be tried for treason. Some members of the Privy Council had arrived the previous day to prepare for the arraignment.

On the day following Jed's arrival, he took the opportunity to have a look around the village. It was not large, but he took a chance and wandered past the main entrance to the castle. He'd been informed by the landlord that the garrison had been strengthened and it was soon apparent that entry into the castle would be impossible without going through the main gatehouse.

Although he had not loitered, he was already being scrutinised by one of the guards placed at the entrance to the drawbridge. Jed moved on, taking care not to hurry and arouse suspicions. A quick glance reassured him that the guard had resumed his duties and Jed was no longer of interest.

Back in his room at the inn, he pondered his next move. He needed to know how long it would be before anything serious happened. The inn was the only one in the village and was sure to be a haunt of off-duty castle retainers. Sure enough, that evening a number of soldiers from Mary Stuart's escort whom Jed recognised were roistering in the inn. Over a few drinks, Jed found out that the members of the Privy Council had returned to London, having been summoned by Queen Elizabeth. The best he could discover was that any trial would not take place until the second or third week in October. He decided to find somewhere in the local area to stay and then returned to Chartley to settle up his affairs.

The meeting of the Privy Council took place at the end of September in the Star Chamber in the Palace of Westminster. Lord Burghley, who had spent many hours studying the incriminating evidence against the Scottish Queen, laid it all before the councillors. It was agreed that there was sufficient evidence to convict her and that she should be brought to trial on the fourteenth of October at Fotheringhay Castle.

When Burghley reported the findings to the Queen, it quickly became apparent that she was not happy with this outcome. She found fault with just about every decision. 'Where is Walsingham? she cried angrily. 'Why is he not here?' '

'I'm afraid he is indisposed, Your Majesty. He is suffering very badly from the gout.' Burghley could see from her reaction, that her temper was not improved by Walsingham's absence and he hurried to placate her.

'Truth to tell, Your Majesty,' he said warily, 'Walsingham is in need of an assistant, what with the trial and the pressing Scottish and Dutch problems.'

'Then why in heaven's name has this not been mentioned before?' she rounded on him savagely. 'This is a critical time and I cannot be without my Principal Secretary. Well, my lord,' she said impatiently, hands on hips with her head thrust forward and her eyes glaring, 'who would you recommend?'

'I know of no better equipped man for the task at hand than William Davison,' he told her evenly. 'He is an ardent Protestant and, although he was temporarily out of sorts with my Lord Leicester, he was hand in glove with Walsingham, who would welcome his appointment I am certain.'

The Queen thought for a moment and then said more calmly. 'Leave Leicester to me. If Davison is the right man for the job, then I will appoint him immediately. I will send his warrant today and he may attend me on the morrow if Walsingham is still indisposed.'

When Burghley, Walsingham and Davison met about a week later, there were still many outstanding matters to be settled with the Queen.

Burghley complained about the lack of progress. 'What do you feel about this, Walsingham? Is she trying to delay the trial?'

'I'm not sure,' he replied, 'but I would to God that Her Majesty would refer these things to those who are the best judges of them, as other princes do. What think you, Davison?'

'I fear she will keep the same course she held with the Duke of Norfolk, which is not to take Mary Stuart's life without extreme fear compel her.'

'I fear you are right,' said Burghley, gloomily. 'She has always found it difficult to make the really hard decisions. She requires people to like her too much.'

Burghley was even more gloomy a few days later. He had just returned from a very uncomfortable session with the Queen resulting from his forcing of her hand over Mary Stuart's trial. It had nearly proved to be his undoing. He could see that the Queen was in a bad humour from the moment he entered her retiring room. Before he had even straightened up from his bow, she was waving a wad of letters at him.

'What say you to these copied letters that Walsingham has obtained from his spy in the French Ambassador's household? she cried angrily. 'Speak up, sir, or by my oath, I will send you to the Tower where you can be more closely interrogated.'

She glared at him angrily, but Burghley refused to be intimidated. He found that it was usually his best defence. He took the letters from her, and with a polite inclination of his head, began to read them carefully. Mary had written to Mauvissière, shortly before he left for France, to intercede on her behalf with Burghley, who she still believed was well disposed towards her.

'Well,' cried the Queen impatiently, 'Speak up, my lord. It was no idle threat I made, you know me better.'

This was the first time Burghley was aware of these letters and it was clear that the Queen had been dealing directly with Walsingham over Mary Stuart, without his knowledge. Burghley was surprised that she had not keep her chief advisor informed, but as he knew to his cost, Elizabeth was somewhat irrational in her dealings with her wayward cousin, Mary. He also knew that he would need to choose his words carefully.

'I am sorry that after our long association, you feel the need to threaten me in order to obtain the truth. I have always been truthful with you, even to my own detriment. And forgive me, Your Majesty, but you know it well.'

The Queen glowered at him, but he could see that she was not as angry as at first.

'I have never shown Mary Stuart any favours,' he protested. 'All through her captivity, I have dealt with the Scottish Queen in the best interests of Your Majesty and never favoured her. Throughout the negotiations, at your behest, I adopted a friendly manner in order to retain her good opinion so as to further our ends. However, at all times, your wishes and the needs of this realm were uppermost in my mind. Even now, I am here today to entreat Your Majesty to allow the Privy Council to bring Mary Stuart to trial on a charge of high treason. How can this be showing her favour?'

Elizabeth was suspicious of anything she saw as disloyalty, but his powers of persuasion and his long relationship with her saved him and her displeasure did not last.

'My dear Spirit,' she said in a conciliatory tone, 'you must forgive me for doubting you. But to see my scheming cousin suggesting you were well-disposed to her made me very angry. I accept your explanations and I will consider carefully the request from my councillors.'

On the following day she sent him a letter detailing her formal instructions both to him and to Walsingham, for setting up the commission to examine the Scottish Queen on the fourteenth of October. She also authorised them to designate two to four commissioners, including themselves, to confer privately with Mary, if she so wished it. The letter left it to their discretion whether the trial should be public or private and whether Mary's secretaries Nau and Curle should be called to give evidence.

All was now set for the trial and on the sixth of October the Queen wrote to Mary Stuart informing her of her coming trial.

And so began the extraordinary events that were to place a sovereign Queen on trial for her life, on a charge of high treason against the Queen of England. There could be only one penalty for this crime if she was found guilty. Death by beheading.

Chapter Thirty-Four
Fotheringhay Castle, October, 1586

Burghley arrived at Fotheringhay early on the morning of the twelfth. Most of the other members of the commission had arrived the previous day. On consulting the list of members present, he discovered that eight were missing. The Earl of Leicester was the most prominent, but he had not been recalled from the Netherlands campaign so that was expected. Several of the missing commissioners had sent word that they could not attend due to illness. Burghley shook his head. The Queen was going to be most displeased with them unless they could produce proof they could not possibly have made the journey.

In her apartment, Mary was completing preparations for what might prove to be the most important day of her life. Her main defence was that as an anointed Queen of another country, the Common laws of England did not apply to her. Therefore, come what may, she must look and act like an anointed Queen and ignore the pain in her joints and swollen legs. Accordingly, she had maids cleaning and ironing her ruffs and best gown and she wore all of her jewellery including the pearls given to her by the Dauphin as a wedding present.

The proceedings opened when Sir Amias Paulet and Edward Barker, present in his official role of *rapporteur* of the whole trial, handed Mary a letter from Queen Elizabeth.

Mary's initial response was to refuse to plead before the commission. Having expected this, Burghley had set up a special system of post riders to carry letters to Queen Elizabeth. He immediately despatched a letter to the Queen informing her of Mary's refusal and his intention to proceed with the commission in accordance with their terms of reference. Despite the fact that it was seventy-five miles to Windsor and the letter was not sent until shortly after noon, the Queen's approval was scribbled at midnight of the same day. Thanks to the team of riders, the

Queen's reply was received by Burghley late the following day.

Having spent most of Thursday in a vain attempt to change Mary's mind, Burghley led a small committee to meet with her. 'We have,' Burghley informed her, 'come to ask you if you have changed your mind about appearing before the commission appointed for your trial. We must inform you that, should you again refuse, we have been authorised to examine the case in your absence and reach a verdict as to your guilt or otherwise.'

Mary was not impressed. 'I am a sovereign Queen and I am not answerable to any English court.' She indicated the members of the commission with a gesture of her arm. 'This commission has, I am sure, already condemned me. However, I would be prepared, under protest, to answer anything before a free parliament.'

She then broke out into a recital of all her previous grievances, but Burghley interrupted her.

'I speak not as a member of this commission, but as a Queen's Councillor, when I say that you have received many favours since your arrival in England. Your presumptive right to the English throne has been defended by the Queen, even to the extent of punishing those who questioned it. Even after your part in the Ridolfi plot was discovered, the Queen protected you when Parliament was demanding your execution.'

Mary simply brushed these aside as no favours at all, but her rights as a sovereign Queen. 'I require you to supply me with a list of the commissioners and a copy of the commission. When I have studied them I will give you a reply this afternoon.' Having made her stance, she regally gave them permission to leave.

Later that day a further small committee, including the Lord Treasurer, then met with Mary.

'I have no quarrel with the members of the commission,' she told them, 'but I protest that the law upon which the commission is based is directed specifically against me. Further, I dispute the competency of the commission to try me by civil law, so by what law will you try me?'

'By the Common Law of England,' replied the Lord Treasurer and when she started to recite her complaints again, he stopped her immediately.

'Enough of these complaints, we have heard them many times before. Will you appear before the commission if we promise to record your protest without allowance?' When she refused, he then informed her that the meeting was at an end.

'The commission,' threatened the Lord Treasurer, 'will proceed to examine the evidence against you on the fourteenth, with or without your presence. If, as you say, you are innocent of these charges, you wrong your reputation in avoiding a trial.'

The morning of the fourteenth was misty and dismal as the commission assembled in the large presence chamber on the first floor. The full commission consisting of Privy Councillors, judges, attorneys and clerks, numbered over forty. Burghley had chosen the first-floor former presence chamber of the old state apartments, dating back to the early thirteenth century, when William Marshall, Earl of Pembroke, co-regent of England held the castle. The room was the largest after the great hall and was divided by a waist-high oak rail.

At the far end of the chamber, a throne-like chair had been placed on a small dais, with a cloth of state above emblazoned with the Royal Arms of England. This was purely symbolic, since Elizabeth would not be attending the trial. On the right of it, for Mary Stuart, was a high-backed chair with a red velvet cushion. It was set behind the senior judges and in front of the nobles. On the other three sides were the benches for the nobles and Privy Councillors, whilst in the centre were benches and a large oak table for the judges, lawyers and notaries. Behind the dividing rail, the smaller space was standing room for any of the local knights and gentlemen of Northamptonshire who had a warrant, to attend.

Since dawn, the single street of forty houses, dominated by the castle and the distinctive lantern tower of St. Mary and All Saints church, had been swarming with activity. All available accommodation in the village had been filled by the commissioners and their retinues. Everyone entering the castle was carefully vetted and all horsemen were obliged to tether their horses on the banks of the River Nene. Only members of the commission, or those with warrants, were allowed to enter and their official papers were scrutinised very carefully both at the drawbridge and at the gatehouse. Jacob, having obtained a warrant from Walsingham, lined up to be vetted and took his place behind the dividing rail. It was standing room only and there was quite a crush. Fortunately, with his height, he could see quite well over the crowd from the back wall, which was not too cramped. As the commissioners filed in, the tension in the room became palpable.

Shortly after nine o'clock when the commissioners had taken their places, there was a momentary hush as Mary entered the room. Jacob was shocked at the change in her. She seemed to have aged twenty years since he last saw her at Sheffield. Moving slowly, Mary made her way purposefully to the high-backed chair. In respect for her status, the commissioners removed their hats and Mary acknowledged them gracefully and then sat down. She was wearing a black velvet gown, with her usual white cambric cap and around her neck Jacob was astounded to see the twin strands of the red Murano bead necklace. He later found out that the commission had forbidden her a rosary, so she had worn the red necklace as a symbol of her martyrdom.

The Lord Treasurer brought the court to order. 'This commission,' he explained, 'is assembled and constituted as authorised according to the provisions of the Act for the Queen's Safety.' He then turned, bowed to Mary and indicated the floor was hers.

Mary stood up and began by explaining her position and the members of the commission listened carefully. The commission was then read and Mary, looking around at the commissioners, said in a loud proud voice, 'I hereby register my protest against the law authorising this commission. The Act for the Queen's Safety is aimed directly at me, a sovereign Queen. The first part concerns a claimant to the throne who is involved in invasion, rebellion, or plot. I alone have a legitimate claim to the English throne and the Privy Council and Parliament has falsely accused me on many occasions of plotting the very things this part of the Act names as high treason. The second part relates to an assassination of Queen Elizabeth, in which the beneficiary is once more proscribed, hunted down and killed. I cannot from my prison, be responsible for an assassination, but this act gives the commission the right to have me killed if they so decide.'

She was answered by the Lord Treasurer. 'The law is the law. Every person in this realm is bound by the laws, whether newly made or not. You may not speak against them.' He looked around. 'This is the time and place authorised for this commission and we will proceed to review the evidence against you. You may hear and answer if you will, but we will carry out our charge.'

Whereupon, Mary said, 'Under protest, I will listen to what you have to say concerning any act against the Queen of England's person. I reserve the right to answer as occasion serves.'

The Queen's Sergeant now rose from his seat and laid the case before the commission. He described the Babington plot in detail, as given in Babington's confession. He concluded by saying that Babington had confirmed that Mary Stuart knew of it, assented to it, promised her assistance and showed ways and means by which it should be carried out.

Mary stood up and flatly denied the charge. 'I do not know this Babington, nor do I know of his enterprise. Unless you can prove that this is not the case by my own words or in my own writing, you have no case.' Jacob had to admire her bluff. She had obviously decided to deny everything and defy them to prove it. The crowd in front of him was obviously not impressed and began murmuring quite audibly. Jacob feared she was in for a shock, which was not long in coming.

In answer to this statement, her correspondence with Babington was read out and her face registered her dismay. Mary must realise now that she has been greatly overconfident, thought Jacob. She knew now the extent to which Walsingham had intercepted her mail.

At first, she gave no other outward sign of her distress, but her thoughts must have been in turmoil. The prosecuting counsel now built up what he believed to be a watertight case against Mary. He produced piece after piece of damning evidence and Mary could no longer control he emotions. She burst into tears of despair. There were some loud cries from the watchers now and one or two were shaking their fists at her while calling for her to be executed. The Queen's Sergeant immediately stood up and called for order, threatening to have anyone interrupting the Commission's business ejected from the castle. The shouts and threats died down, but Jacob could hear angry muttering all around.

The interruption had given Mary time to regain control. She must have realised that unless she kept her wits about her, all would be lost. There was only one course she could take. When the Queen's Sergeant sat down, she stood up, wiping her eyes with great show. She apologised for showing her emotions, but explained her tears were because of the catalogue of lies that had just been placed before them. 'I deny categorically having written the letters. Since I did not, it is obvious that someone has forged them with the help of a copy of Babington's cipher.'

Looking directly at Walsingham, she accused him of being behind the forgeries out of malice. 'I have never,' she said, looking as sincere as possible, 'and never will, plot against Queen Elizabeth's life, although I would do almost anything else to deliver the English Catholics from their oppression.'

At this point, Lord Burghley intervened. 'There is no man in this realm,' he said, 'who has shown himself to be a good subject, who was ever put to death for religion.' This brought loud cries of agreement from the commissioners. 'But I have to say,' continued Burghley, 'that some have been executed for treason, when they actively supported the Pope's Bull against the Queen.'

'Yet I,' insisted Mary, 'have heard otherwise and read it also in books set forth in print.'

'The authors,' said Burghley dryly, 'do say many things against Her Majesty, but putting such lies in print does not make them true. We are concerned here only with what we can prove.' There was loud applause from the crowd, and some commissioners, for these sentiments.

Walsingham then stood up and protested that his mind was free of all malice where Mary Stuart was concerned. 'As God is my witness,' he said, very sincerely and convincingly, 'I have done nothing out of malice against Mary Stuart, neither as a private person, nor in public office.'

Mary accepted this statement in an extremely gracious manner.

'Be not angry with me, Sir Francis. Please do not give any more credit to those who would slander me than I give to those who would slander you.' Turning a brave smile on Walsingham, she gently dabbed at her cheeks. Drying her eyes, Mary cried out, 'I would never harm my soul by plotting with others the death of my dear cousin!'

Listening carefully to all these exchanges, Jacob couldn't but admire Mary's bravado performance. It was totally wasted on Walsingham however, he knew only too well how Mary had used her charm to bend her jailers to her will. Glancing across at Walsingham, Jacob could see from the sceptical smile that he was certainly unimpressed with Mary's tears and protestations. She had swayed the crowd a little, however, and the angry mutterings died away and were replaced by more sympathetic comments.

After this exchange, the Lord Treasurer announced that they would rise for dinner and asked all parties to reconvene promptly at two o'clock. When Mary and the commissioners had left, Jacob was about to leave himself, when a clerk approached him with a summons to attend Walsingham in his room.

On his arrival, Walsingham invited him to share the food that was laid out. 'Do join me,' he invited, for him, most jovially. 'I have not had the chance to thank you for your help in locating Babington.'

'Having seen his execution,' said Jacob, unable to keep the distaste from his voice, 'I wish that I had not.'

Walsingham was not offended. 'It was a very gruesome affair,' he admitted. 'The executioner went too far.' He gave a slight smile. 'The crowd would agree with you and the fellow that led the protests.' He took a leg of chicken and bit into it watching for Jacob's reaction.

Jacob helped himself to some food before he replied. 'I agreed wholeheartedly with everything he said.' And cut a large slice from the beef. He guessed that Walsingham thought he had recognised him as the protester, but was not going to give him the satisfaction of confirming it. 'You know how I feel about legalised torture, for that is what this was.'

Continuing to eat, Walsingham did not comment. He did however say that the Queen too, was horrified at the reports and had taken action to prevent it. Turning to the trial, he asked Jacob how he thought it had gone.

'I do not think you need me to tell you that things are looking black for the Scottish Queen and no doubt there is more to come.' Shortly after this exchange, Burghley sent a messenger asking for Walsingham to attend him, so Jacob took his leave and went for a stroll in the fresh air.

The afternoon session, after a further warning from the Queen's Sergeant about unruly behaviour, was largely taken up by the confessions of Mary's secretaries Nau and Curle. Burghley went to some lengths to establish that they had not been tortured to obtain them. Their signed statements confirmed that Mary had compiled the letter and approved of it before it was put into cipher. They also confessed that they had tried to dissuade their mistress from her dealings with Babington and that she resented it.

'I would point out,' said Burghley, 'that in your letter to Babington you suggested that there should be uprisings in both Scotland and Ireland. It is more than a coincidence that shortly after Babington received the letter there was unrest in both countries.'

He now turned to Mary's dealings with others.

'From your own letters to the Bishop of Glasgow, Mendoza, the Spanish Ambassador and Charles Paget, it is clear,' he said calmly, 'that you intended to deliver your son, James VI of Scotland, to Spain and transfer your title to the English throne to Philip II of Spain.'

There were gasps from the crowd and Mary shook her head in denial. 'You must take that up with those who wrote the letters. I did not write them and I have nothing further to say on the matter.' It was the only line of defence left to her and she could only stick to it.

Burghley gave a bleak smile. 'That was exactly my intent in putting them before this commission. There can be no doubt that *you* were the originator of these letters. Your own secretaries, who you say are honourable, confirm it.'

Again the smile. 'We can of course bring them to this place

and ask them to establish the truth of it ... *in their own words,*' he said, with heavy emphasis. There were nods of approval from many commissioners and applause from sections of the crowd. This is not going well for the Scottish Queen, thought Jacob. She still has not realised the extent to which her letters have been intercepted.

'We also have,' Burghley continued, 'copies of their replies to you and further letters you have sent. If you had not sent the first letter, surely you would have taken up the point. You surely cannot expect us to believe that you have never sent any letters at all. Besides, in the papers seized from your apartments at Chartley Manor, there are draft letters corresponding to these, *in your own writing.*'

Mary looked a little out of sorts at this, but decided that silence was the best course. She just shook her head sadly as if Burghley was being foolish.

He turned to his clerk who handed him another letter. 'And what of the pension you granted to Morgan, after you were informed that he prompted Parry to kill Queen Elizabeth.'

'It was not for that purpose,' Mary retorted hotly, stung into a reply. 'Morgan was a faithful servant. I disapproved of some of his efforts on my behalf, but I was in no way responsible for them.' There were scoffs of disbelief from the watchers.

'That is as maybe,' said Burghley, tartly, 'but neither did you condemn him for trying to do so ...' he paused tellingly, 'on your behalf.'

This rejoinder brought more approval from the commissioners and applause from the crowd. Jacob could see Mary's credibility was being seriously damaged. Shortly after this exchange, the afternoon proceedings came to a halt. The Lord Treasurer gave a stern instruction that all parties must assemble promptly at eight o'clock the following morning. After the commissioners had filed out, Jacob left immediately, as the only lodgings he could get were at the inn at Wansford some five leagues away. He would need to leave early in the morning. As for the trial, it appeared to have gone very badly for the Scottish Queen. Unless she could find some way to discredit Babington's letter, he feared she would be found guilty.

Chapter Thirty-Five
London & Fotheringhay, October, 1586

Jed had no wish to be present in Fotheringhay while the councillors and officials were coming and going from the castle. Although it was unlikely, someone, perhaps even Jacob Bell, might be present to identify him. Accordingly, he had spent the day scouting for miles around the village. The countryside was largely open fields and forest, but within a few leagues of the castle there were a number of small villages. Because of the huge influx of officials, almost all of the accommodation, for several leagues around, was full. On his return to Fotheringhay late in the evening, he was approached by the owner of his rented cottage. Coming straight to the point, he asked if Jed would give up the cottage in return for the whole of the back rent and offered a small bonus. It was obvious that because of the lack of rooms in the village, the commission was prepared to pay well for accommodation.

When Jed refused, the owner then asked if he would be amenable to sharing the cottage for the duration of the trial. Jed's first inclination was to say no, but when he learned that it would be one of the clerks of the commission and, furthermore, that he would receive a bonus of two gold sovereigns for agreeing, he changed his mind. After all, it would give him an opportunity to find out how the trial was going and possibly some other useful information. He made sure that there was plenty of food and drink available in the cottage. A well fed and happily inebriated man will tell you almost anything.

And so it proved. Master Titus Barr was partial to a good pot of ale, or several, especially when they were free. By the time he and Jed had toasted just about everyone they could think of, he was only too delighted to give Jed a detailed and confidential account of the trial.

Lying in his bed late that night Jed was unable to sleep. The disclosure of how all of Queen Mary's letters had been read out in court showed Jed just how much he had inadvertently helped his

Queen's enemies, by acting as their innocent courier. His only small consolation was that the commission had been brought together for only one reason - to convict Mary Stuart, by whatever means that foul fiend Walsingham could concoct to convince them.

At least his own presence here in Fotheringhay was not suspected. Even if it was, Walsingham and his men would never suspect he could enter the castle, let alone try to rescue the Queen. But something Titus had babbled about in his cups had given him an idea how he might effect an entry into the castle. He would need to do some careful planning and his chances of success, or even surviving, were slim. He had to try though. It was better than living with his guilty conscience. With that thought in his mind, Jed at last fell asleep.

Next morning, Titus Barr was nursing a very sore head. 'Let me be,' he moaned, when Jed shook him awake. 'I want to die.'

'That might happen a lot sooner than you think unless you get a move on. Didn't you tell me that the Lord Treasurer gave strict instructions that the commission had to reconvene by eight o'clock?'

'What of it?'

'Well, Master Barr, it is already fifteen minutes past the hour of seven. If you are to be there on time you will need to move yourself.'

I can't,' moaned the hapless clerk. 'If I move my head will split.'

Roughly pulling the covers back, Jed pulled Titus into a sitting position and held out a cup. 'Drink this,' he ordered. 'And don't fuss. Just get it straight down and you'll soon feel better.'

Titus looked at it blearily. 'What is it?'

'Never mind what it is, just drink it.'

Titus still hesitated, so Jed grabbed his head in an armlock and held his nose with the same hand. As Titus opened his mouth, Jed poured the drink down his throat and clamped his jaw shut.

'Aargh,' he moaned, 'you've poisoned me.'

Jed let him lie back and grinned. 'It won't do you any harm, it's just my mother's cure for a bad head. It's herb tea with a good dose of honey. I always keep some with me. I used to be a brewer and I had more than my fair share of bad heads.'

By the time he'd finished this little story, Titus's face had taken on a look of surprise. 'Why,' he muttered, 'it's working. My head's nowhere near as bad.' He sat up gingerly and then swung his legs out of bed. 'Thank you, Jed. It's not gone, but I feel well enough to move now. I'd better get myself down to the castle.' While he was talking, he was hurriedly putting his clothes on. 'Will I see you later? I'd like to buy you a drink in the inn tonight.'

Jed shook his head in disbelief. 'I'd have thought that after last night...' He might as well not have bothered, because before he'd finished, Titus was out of the door and running up the street. '...you might have had second thoughts about drinking but, if you insist,' Jed completed to the closed door.

When Mary entered the room everyone rose and bowed, which she acknowledged with a gracious gesture and sat down. At her request, a small table, with a jug of water and the blood-red goblet on it, had been placed alongside her chair. Pouring water into the goblet, she took sips, while looking round at the commissioners in a regal manner.

When she had returned to her apartment yesterday, Mary had been in a despondent mood. She had often in her embroideries depicted Elizabeth as a ginger cat stalking her as the mouse. Today, she had learned what all mice know instinctively. When a cat catches a mouse, they play most cruelly with it before they finally despatch it!

It had been a shattering blow to learn that all of her letters had been intercepted. Not only her dealings with Babington, which was bad enough, but her offers to Spain. When word got out about them she would lose all credibility with her relatives and supporters in France. Burghley and Elizabeth would not hesitate to ensure that copies were circulated in France and elsewhere.

Worse still, in the later exchanges with Burghley, she had been dismayed to see even the two Catholic lords on the commission were nodding in approval at Burghley's points. If she couldn't carry her friends on the commission, she had little hope with the rest. The interception of all her letters was going to make it almost impossible for her to continue to deny all knowledge of the plot against Elizabeth. The only solution was to find a way to discredit the Babington letters. It was not high treason to scheme for her release, only to be party to killing the Queen. She must try to persuade them that, although Babington told her about the plot, she never agreed to him assassinating the Queen. Unless she could convince them of that, her cause was lost.

The first part of the morning was spent in listening to her complaints, justifications and attempts to recover lost ground. Then she admitted that she had received letters from Babington and had replied to him. However, she insisted that the letter produced in court, purporting to be her reply, was not the one she wrote. With a sigh, Jacob realised that this argument would also fail.

When questioned why she had lied in the first place, she replied, 'In the circumstances of my position, I am being tried by a commission whose authority to try a Queen I deny. It is therefore up to that commission to prove what they can. Not for me to confirm it.'

'There can be no doubt that you wrote a letter consenting to the assassination of Queen Elizabeth,' retorted Burghley. 'Taken in conjunction with Babington's letter, there can be no doubt what you are referring to in your reply.'

Mary gave a dismissive scoff. 'I deny that the letter you have produced was written by me. Even supposing I had, it does not contain the phrase that says the writer agrees to the assassination of Queen Elizabeth. Therefore it is simply a spurious attempt to condemn me by association with another letter also not written by me.'

Walsingham interposed at this point. 'There are four people who know what was in the letter which was sent secretly to Babington. You, who say you did not write it, your two secretaries who both say you did and tried to persuade you not to send it, and the man who deciphered the letter. All three of those people can be brought into court and will confirm that this is a copy of the letter you sent.'

Mary simply shook her head and continued to deny that it was a true copy of the original letter. For the first time, she saw a glimmer of hope. They could not prove she wrote the letter, so if she continued to deny it, she might yet prevail.

Burghley now took up the point. 'This letter you say you did not write, contains not only the phrase you dispute, but a complete ratification of Babington's plans for rebellion, an invasion by Spanish troops and your own liberation.' He looked around the room at the other commissioners, 'She can hardly deny that. She says as much in other letters we have intercepted to Thomas Morgan, Charles Paget, Sir Francis Englefield and to Mendoza the Spanish ambassador at Paris. The drafts of these letters, *in your own hand*, were found amongst the papers seized from your apartments at Chartley Manor.' Oh! no, I thought they had been destroyed. Mary looked around anxiously at the nobles and it made her very uncomfortable that Burghley was even convincing her fellow Catholics.

'Is it likely,' Burghley continued, 'that you would agree to everything else in the plot and not the assassination ...' Mary tried to interrupt and deny this again, but he would not let her. 'No Mary Stuart,' he said assertively, 'I will finish the point before you may speak. You certainly wrote an agreement to the first three parts of the plot, that much we have established from the other letters. But if, as you say, you did not agree to the assassination, this was the only part of the plot not so far mentioned. Why would you insert a phrase that implies you agree, rather than the phrase, *Do not carry out the assassination! I do not sanction you to do so?*' Burghley sat down at this point to loud murmurs of approval from the commissioners and looked patiently at Mary Stuart.

Mary stood up and made her final appeal. 'You may think from all you have heard that the circumstances of my guilt are proven. But you have not proven the fact. I did not in any letter specify the work that the six gentlemen referred to by Babington were to carry out. There is, in my mind, a clear distinction in my letters between *intending to assassinate* and *leaving to God and the Catholics under God's providence*.'

She held her arms wide in appeal. 'I am an independent Queen and wrongfully held in captivity,' she said haughtily. 'Even an act of war is legitimate, if it is the only way to gain my freedom.' She drew herself up to her full height and regarded them with a regal stare. 'If I am not an independent Queen, then I am guilty. But if I am an independent Queen, then if the act should result in the death of Queen Elizabeth, it would be no more than a fortuitous event in a legitimate struggle to regain my rights.' This was said with all the conviction she could muster and no one in the room could have been in doubt that this is what she really believed. The reaction to her statement dismayed her. She had not expected the commissioners, to agree with this interpretation, but she had hoped that her friends would. The crowd certainly did not and began to shout loudly, calling for her execution and despite her outward calm, Mary felt very afraid for the first time.

Burghley was quick to seize the challenge. 'You cannot,' he said, with little respect in his voice, 'expect us to accept this view of your so-called rights as an independent Queen. Your own failings and shortcomings are to blame for the failure of your own and the Scottish Lords efforts to free you. You have never honoured attempts to negotiate with you. You were plotting to gain the throne even while we negotiated in faith. In the end, even your own son rejected the opportunity to set you free, because he did not respect your sincerity.'

There were loud cheers at this comment and Mary was visibly shaken as she felt deeply betrayed by James. She poured a glass of water into the goblet and sipped it delicately to disguise her feelings, as Burghley continued.

'The failure of talks to free you are due to your own failings, not those of Queen Elizabeth.'

Mary rose with a haughty expression. 'My cousin has hidden behind her Ministers and refused to negotiate with me face to face. How could we reach a resolution, when her chief negotiator has now revealed himself as my adversary?'

Burghley answered simply, but with immense pride, 'Yes, I am,' he cried in ringing tones, 'I am the adversary of all who would be the adversaries of my Queen.' The crowd cheered wildly and Mary sank into her chair as she saw the reaction of the commissioners to these words. All she could say was, 'I will hear the proofs in another place and defend myself.' It sounded weak, even to her own ears. Mary had come to believe that she would die a martyr, but that her son, James would take up her mantle and gain the throne of England. This is why she had adopted the phoenix as her emblem and the cipher of Mary of Guise, her mother, *In my end my beginning.* That event would be her justification.

After a few more formalities, the commission was told that the proceedings were ended. When it was announced that no verdict would be given until the record of proceedings, had been presented to Queen Elizabeth, in the Star Chamber, the crowd of onlookers went wild. They screamed for vengeance against Mary Stuart and surged forward. At a signal from the Queen's Sergeant, a large number of armed soldiers rushed at the front, with shields at the ready and swords drawn. More troops filed in at the back and, pushing their way to the front, began to clear the room. Mary sat numbly in her chair. After the way the trial had gone and the scale of popular anger, she did not imagine there could be any other verdict at the Star Chamber, but guilty of high treason.

Chapter Thirty-Six
Fotheringhay & London, October, 1586

When Titus Barr returned to the cottage, Jed was sitting in the kitchen, sorting out his riding tack. When Titus came in, he nodded and then continued with his sorting.

'Don't you want to know the outcome of the trial?' said Titus in surprise.

Jed sniffed. 'Not really. It's obvious what the verdict will be.'

Titus laughed. 'Ah, now that's where you're wrong. There was no verdict.'

Jed stopped what he was doing and looked at Titus in surprise. 'No verdict. Are they going to continue next week?'

'That got your attention,' said Titus, smugly. 'I thought it would.' Jed threatened to hit him with the bridle. 'All right then,' Titus said, with a laugh. 'They're going to meet again in the Star Chamber on the twenty-fifth of October. After the Queen has seen the record of the proceedings, which are on the way to London under guard as we speak.'

He gave Jed a friendly smile. 'Oh and by the way, thank you for sorting me out this morning, you saved my neck. I just managed to get there in time. You should sell that remedy of your mother's, it worked very well. I drank plenty of water and I only have a slight headache now.' He sniffed derisively. 'I'd have had one anyway, listening to all of the lies, evasions and complaints from Mary Stuart.'

Jed turned away so that Titus couldn't see the fury on his face at this dismissal of his Queen. You'll pay for that insult my fine friend, he thought, but not until I've finished with you. When he turned round again his face was smiling. 'You know what you said last night about helping you to clear up in the commission room after the trial finished. Do you still want me? I could do with the money.' Titus had said nothing of the sort, but having seen the state he was in that morning, Jed had seized the chance. He was sure that Titus wouldn't remember.

Titus frowned, he had only the vaguest memory of the night before. He had no memory of his offer, but Jed was waiting with his eyebrows raised and he did owe him a favour, so he simply said, 'Of course I do. One good turn deserves another. I've been put in charge of clearing up after the commission. Mind you,' he warned, 'you'll have to come and get a pass from the sergeant-at-arms tomorrow morning. There shouldn't be a problem. Unless you're a wanted man,' he said and laughed at his own joke.

Jed forced a smile, as he suddenly wondered if it was the same sergeant-at-arms who knew him from Chartley Manor. In that case, there would be a problem.

He need not have worried. The sergeant just looked at him without recognition as Titus explained he had been instructed by the Lord Treasurer to use some local labour to help with the cleaning up process. When Jed left he had in his hands an authorisation allowing him access.

All morning they had been packing the detritus of the trial into boxes. They filled many boxes with the papers and letters produced at the trial. There was furniture, banners and other decorations to return to various places, including the Queen's apartments at the Tower. In taking the boxes to some empty storerooms, Jed had gained a working knowledge of the castle layout. He deliberately made some wrong turns and explored further corridors to try to find out where Mary Stuart was being held. Titus had told him she was to stay at Fotheringhay after the trial, while her fate was decided.

On venturing into the west wing corridor, he was challenged by a couple of guards and was asked to show his authorisation. 'You took a wrong turn at the end of the corridor leading towards the kitchens.' the guard patiently explained. 'This area is out of bounds.'

As they were talking, a maidservant came out of a room at the far end of the corridor. Jed recognised her immediately as one of Mary Stuart's ladies he had often seen at Chartley Manor. He was sure now that this was where they were holding his Queen.

When the first cartload of boxes and furniture had been loaded, Titus mounted the driver's seat. 'Don't worry, Titus,' Jed said reassuringly, 'we'll have the rest of the boxes packed up for when you return.'

'There's no rush. I have everything needed for the Star Chamber. The rest can come back to London in due course. I doubt I'll be back before the end of the month.'

'In that case,' said Jed, 'when I've finished here, I'll go up to Sheffield. I have some business to attend to for the Earl of Shrewsbury, but I'll be sure to be back well before the end of the month.' He was fully intending to head for London, but he wanted to throw people off the scent in case his plan went wrong and he needed to escape. As soon as the cart was out of sight, he rushed to the cottage and, collecting the saddlebags he'd packed previously, mounted his horse and set off for London. It was an easy task to make a wide detour of the road and pausing on the brow of a hill a short while later, he smiled in satisfaction to see he was ahead of the cart. With any luck, he would be in London at least a day before Titus. Once there, he would put the second part of his plan into operation.

The house at Mark Street was in a state of turmoil as Maria supervised the task of helping Rico to pack. He was to join The Crystal as an ensign when it left for Venice in two days time. Jacob had gone to the Glass-Sellers headquarters with Roberto to organise shipping to replace *The Crystal* while it was away. By even the most optimistic calculation, they would need a replacement for at least six to seven months.

Maria was busy checking her list and adding a couple of items missed off previously, when Rico came in, 'What is it, Rico? I'm sorry, but as you can see, I'm very busy, so unless it's very important ...'

Rico nodded. 'I can see that, Mother, but there's a messenger at the door from father. He wants you to go to the Glass-Seller's office as soon as possible.'

Maria sighed in exasperation. 'What on earth can he want me there for? Did he say?' When Rico said the messenger didn't know, she gave an exasperated sigh. 'I suppose I'd better go in the coach. Please go and ask Bob Petts to get the coach ready for me, please.'

'Can I come with you?' asked Rico eagerly.

'I don't know about that, Rico,' said Maria wearily.

Rico persisted and Maria hadn't the energy to argue.

When Jacob arrived home several hours later, Jack Petts handed him an envelope that had been delivered by hand addressed to Master Jacob Bell. He thanked Jack, went in the office and poured a large glass of wine. He took a good swig and opened the envelope. He read the short note twice before its contents sank in.

His mind reeled. It must be a a hoax. Maria would be somewhere in the house. Throwing the letter on the table, he ran into the hall calling for Jack.

'Where are my wife and Rico, Jack?'

'I assumed they were still down at the Glass-Sellers,' Jack gasped as he rushed up.

'The Glass-Sellers!' exclaimed Jacob in confusion. 'Why have they gone there?'

'Because of your message, Master Jacob.'

Jacob's heart began to thump against his ribs. 'What message?'

'The one you sent by messenger asking them ...' Jack broke off. 'Oh no! They went off in the coach with Bob driving ...'

'What happened about the messenger? Did he go with them?' Jacob's mind was reeling. 'And where's Harry Heywood?' This couldn't be happening after he'd taken so many precautions to prevent it. He was beginning to get angry.

'I don't know,' said Jack dully, 'and Harry's gone to the farrier with your horse, it's cast a shoe.'

'What do you mean, you don't know what happened to the messenger, man?' he raged. 'It's your job to know. What the hell were you playing at?'

'I only saw Lady Maria get into the coach with Rico. Bob was already on the driving seat...,' he said and broke off, as Bob staggered into the hall from the rear of the house, his face and tunic covered in blood. He was very dazed and would have fallen if Jack had not rushed to help him. 'The messenger,' he gasped, 'as soon as we got into the stables he hit me over the head. When I came round I was lying in one of the stalls without my overcoat and hat and the coach was gone.' He saw Jacob's distraught expression and tried to stand up. 'I'm sorry, Master Jacob, but he seemed so genuine. What's happened to Lady Maria?'

'I don't know, Bob. That's why I'm asking questions,' he said trying to remain calm, but not succeeding. He turned to Jack again. 'What did you see when the coach drove off?'

'I only saw the back of the driver and he was wearing Bob's coat and hat. I thought it was Bob, but it must have been the messenger.'

'And you couldn't tell it wasn't your brother driving?' Jacob raged. 'I pay you to notice and keep my family safe. God knows where they are now thanks to your stupidity.'

He began to pace up and down thinking furiously. The guilt-stricken Jack, was mopping at his brother's wounds, with a not too clean kerchief, and asking him if he knew any more.

Jacob meanwhile had come to a decision. 'Leave Bob for now Jack,' he ordered brusquely, 'go and get Anna and then go straight round to the barracks and find Colonel Young. Ask him to come immediately. But before you go, describe the messenger. You too, Bob, if you're up to it.'

They both described the messenger, as a dark, swarthy man, tall and thin with a gaunt face. The description fitted. I had to be Jed Sutton and Jacob's worst fears were realised.

Hearing the commotion, Anna rushed in. 'What's happened to Bob?' she enquired anxiously.

'Please, no more questions for now, Anna. 'Just take Bob into the kitchen and see to his head. I'll explain everything later.'

Anna did as she was told and took Bob off to dress his wound and while Jack rushed off to find the colonel, Jacob reread the letter. It was simple and straight to the point.

I have your wife and son. Be at the packhorse bridge at Fotheringhay, in Northamptonshire, by noon on the day after tomorrow. Don't try any tricks or you'll never see them alive again.

Chapter Thirty-Seven
London & Fotheringhay, October, 1586

When Jacob arrived at the packhorse bridge in Fotheringhay shortly after noon, Jed Sutton was nowhere in sight. After Jacob had waited for almost a quarter hour, he suddenly emerged from underneath the bridge.

'No tricks now, Bell,' he said menacingly, waving the pistol in his hand, 'or your wife and son will die. I've put them where they won't be found easily.' He looked at Jacob with an expression of loathing. 'I'd be very happy for you try. But remember, it will be on your head. You will have condemned them to a slow and painful death.'

'How do I know you haven't killed them already?'

Jed smiled. 'You don't. Now, follow me.' He concealed the pistol in his doublet and then led him to the far end of the village where there was a small cottage, the last on the main street. He gestured for Jacob to dismount at the rear and then producing the pistol, indicated that Jacob should go inside. Once there, Jed pointed to the plain chair in the centre of the room. 'Put your hands flat down on the chair and sit on them,' he ordered. When Jacob had complied, he sat down at the side of the table, with the pistol in his hand. 'Now, I am going to explain your part in this and you're going to listen. You don't ask any questions and you don't make any suspicious moves. Do so and I'll shoot you. Nod if you understand.'

Jacob nodded and Jed explained his plan. 'I've been working at the castle, clearing up after the commission. I know where they're keeping Queen Mary and how many guards there are.'

He gave a sardonic smile. 'They've got very slack now that the trial is over and stay mainly in the guardroom gambling. They only patrol now and again, so it will be easy for us. 'I've made sure they won't be in any fit state to do anything. I found their beer supply and drugged it. They're always drinking in the guardroom at midday. With any luck, they'll all have some and get very sleepy and sluggish. It will be easy to overcome them, there's only three or four. And if there are any who haven't been drugged,' he shrugged, 'so much the worse for them. No one is going to stop me.'

Jed was always a bully and convinced of his own superiority, but there was a calculated desperation in his voice as he explained his plan. He's going to rescue Mary Stuart even if he dies in the attempt, thought Jacob. But I have a feeling he'll make sure he takes me with him. Thank goodness I guessed right, thought Jacob, but before he could continue with his thoughts, he had to concentrate on what Jed was explaining.

'We'll drive up to the castle shortly, in the cart. The guards at the gate are expecting me to come and remove some boxes. Some of them are quite large and need two to carry. We'll release Queen Mary, hide her in the last of the large boxes and carry her to the cart. They never check the boxes. Once she's safely on the cart, we'll wave to the guards at the gate and drive away.'

There was no doubt about it, Jacob thought, the plan is simple, but for all that, it had a good chance of succeeding, especially if the guards were slack now the trial was over.

Jed was obviously enjoying telling Jacob how clever he was. Jacob knew he must give Jed the impression he was totally concerned for the lives of his family. He had not come to Fotheringhay without making his own plans which, reluctantly, Colonel Young had agreed to go along with. Should Jed get a whiff of any double-dealing on his part Jacob would be killed out of hand. God knows what he would do to Maria and Rico.

'Will you let my wife and son go if I help you?' he pleaded, acting the part of the worried man.

Jed gestured for him to be quiet. Jacob could see he was enjoying the moment as he thought about it.

'Only once Queen Mary is free. What happens to you will be up to her to decide. Perhaps she will let you go as a reward for helping, although when I explain your part in her downfall, perhaps not.'

Jacob didn't believe a word of it, but as he started to protest Jed waved him to silence. 'I know all about the way the letters were intercepted. I was the brewer. You made me betray my own Queen.' Jed's waved the pistol threateningly at Jacob,. Jacob was in no doubt that what he said was true and for a moment, he feared Jed was going to shoot him. Jed's mouth tightened and he lowered the pistol. 'I swore that day I would make you pay and here you are,' he finished, triumphantly. 'But I'll have my revenge when my Queen is free.'

Jed tied up the cart by the drawbridge and showed their passes to the guard who, after a cursory glance, waved to the guard in the gatehouse and the portcullis was raised. When they reached the storeroom, Jed indicated a number of small boxes. 'No tricks now. Your wife and child will die if I don't get back to them soon.' Jacob was puzzled. Did that mean Jed had an accomplice watching them with instructions to kill them if he didn't return? He didn't think that was likely. Perhaps he was just goading. Jed gave a mirthless laugh at Jacob's expression. 'Never mind taxing you brain. Just get on and start taking these boxes out to the cart. They're to be stacked at the front, leaving room at the back.'

When they had loaded the small boxes, Jed indicated a long box. When they got to the gatehouse with it, the guard gave them a cheery grin. 'That looks heavy, it's a pity I can't leave my post, or I'd give you a hand.'

'Of course you would,' said Jed, with an answering smile. Jacob, as ordered, said nothing. They took three more long boxes, then as they came back through the gate Jed had a word with the guard. 'Just one more big one to come, but we might be a little while. There's quite a bit of straightening up to do before we leave.'

'Doesn't bother me,' said the guard. 'Take as much time as you like.'

Instead of going to the storeroom, Jed turned in the opposite direction. When they reached the west wing corridor Jed took out his pistol, held it in his left hand and drew his sword. Motioning for Jacob to open the door, he prodded him in the back, forcing him down the corridor in front of him.

There was no sign of anyone until they reached the guardroom door. Looking inside, Jacob could see two guards slumped over the table, and two more were lying on the floor, snoring loudly.

Jed moved him out of the way and looked in cautiously. He

smiled broadly. 'I must have put a bit too much sleeping powder in the beer,' he announced gleefully. 'We'll leave them to their siesta. I think that's all of them, but we must be careful in case there's a man guarding the Queen. He'll slit her throat as soon as look at her if our mission becomes evident.

'Mary Stuart's apartment is just round the corner.' whispered Jed and he took a quick look round to the left. Dodging back, he prodded Jacob forward, indicating he should turn into the corridor to the right. Puzzled now, Jacob did as he was told. He had only gone a few paces when there was a shout. 'Hey you! Where do you think you're going.' He turned round just in time to see the guard who'd shouted coming towards him with a pistol held threateningly in his hand. Before Jacob could react, the guard reached the corner and Jed, seizing him from behind, slit his throat. As he slumped to the floor, Jed waved his own pistol. 'You won't do anything silly will you?' Jacob was stunned. Why on earth was a guard still at the door? This wasn't supposed to happen. Colonel Young was to ensure all of the guards look as though they were drugged.

Jed waved him to the door and Jacob saw the key was still in the lock. Either the guard had been about to enter, or was just leaving. He hoped it was the latter, or it might mean his plan had failed. He wouldn't know until he entered Mary's cell. Jed prodded him with his sword and with a grin, put his finger over his mouth, telling Jacob to be quiet. The door had a small grilled opening and keeping one eye on Jacob, Jed looked in. He motioned for Jacob to have a look, but all he could make out was the figure of a woman sitting at a table with her back to him. He couldn't see the rest of the room.

'When I tell you,' Jed whispered, 'we'll rush in together. Make sure you keep out of my way while I despatch the guard, if there is one. I want to catch him by surprise.'

Quietly turning the key in the lock, he pushed Jacob in first and looked around wildly for the guard. While he was distracted, Jacob thankfully picked up the sword that he had arranged with Colonel Young would be placed behind the door. At least that part had gone to plan. Before Jed realised what was happening, Jacob struck the pistol from his hand.

'What trick of the devil is this? How did you get that?' cursed Jed. He darted towards the table drawing his sword. 'You must be careful, Your Majesty,' Jed said respectfully. When she did not move, he touched her shoulder lightly to gain her attention. The figure fell off the chair. 'It's a dummy!' roared Jed. He lunged wildly at Jacob, nearly catching him unawares, and they circled each other warily. 'You'll never find out where your precious wife is now Bell,' he taunted, 'you've just sealed her fate.'

'It was a risk I was prepared to take,' said Jacob, with a grim smile. I'll make you tell me, he thought grimly.

Jed laughed, weaving his sword as he circled warily. Jacob was watching Jed intently, looking straight into his eyes, which were always the give-away to a person's thoughts.

He needed to keep Jed off balance. 'You know I'm the better swordsman. You will have to get past me and that's not going to happen until you tell me what I want to know. I will make you tell me where she is even if I have to cut you up into little pieces.'

As expected, this drew a response from Jed who lunged wildly again. Jacob parried with ease and inflicted a cut on Jed's arm. After several more attempts, each more desperate than the last, Jed retreated behind the table, bleeding from numerous cuts. They were not serious, but they hurt. Jed circled round the table as Jacob prowled round the other side.

'Tell me what I want to know and I'll stop cutting you,' promised Jacob, moving nearer the long side of the table. Just at that moment, Colonel Young called from the corridor. 'Need any help in there, Bell?'

'No thanks, colonel,' said Jacob, but the slight distraction was all Jed needed. In one fluid motion, he put both hands under the table and, with a Herculean effort, heaved it at Jacob.

Its weight knocked Jacob off his feet and as he fell, the fierce pain in his right arm told him it was broken. His sword fell from his useless hand and seizing his chance, Jed picked up his pistol and, head down, barrelled through the door into the corridor. Jacob's one thought was for Maria and Rico. Gritting his teeth he pushed the table out of the way, picked up his sword in his left hand and rushed out after Jed.

The soldiers had been caught completely by surprise. Jed had smashed the colonel into the wall and the pistol had fallen from his hand. He lay stunned while another soldier lay groaning with a sword thrust through his stomach. As Jacob reached the guardroom door he saw that one guard was lying dead inside and a sword had been thrust through the lugs on the outside, barring the door. Two of the soldiers were battering the door in an attempt to get out. There was no sign of Jed, but he could hear soldiers shouting in the distance, so knocking the sword out of the lugs as he passed, Jacob set off in pursuit.

Reaching the end of the corridor, Jacob could hear someone shouting to the guards at the gate to close the portcullis. Coming into the outer courtyard he could see that Jed had nearly reached the gate. Only one guard was there, the other had gone to close the portcullis. As he came out of the gatehouse Jed shot him in the chest and he lay spread-eagled in the entrance.

Seeing the fate of the gate man, the guard leading the chase fired off a shot at Jed, who vaulted over the prone guard just as the second chasing guard fired at him. This time as he ran on he was limping. He'd been hit and blood was running down his leg. Ignoring it, Jed sprinted past the portcullis, so the guard began to raise the drawbridge. It had already been raised about three feet by the time Jed reached the end. Running at full pelt Jed leapt off the end and crashed awkwardly on to the far bank.

He lay still, obviously stunned, but the chasing guards were hampered by the half-raised drawbridge which the guard was now desperately lowering again. As it came down, Jacob could see that Jed was on his feet, stumbling towards the cart. The soldiers had reloaded and fired at Jed, but he was out of range. They stood waiting for the drawbridge to come down further and, seizing the moment when their full attention was on Jed, Jacob rushed past them and jumped off the end on to the bank. He landed with a jolt that wrenched an involuntary cry from him. Stumbling and almost falling, clutching his broken arm he expected at every stride to pitch on to his face. Just before he reached the cart, he tossed his sword into the back, just as Jed whipped up the horses. Using his momentum and all of his remaining strength, Jacob threw himself on to the back of the cart.

The pain was so intense he passed out. When he came to, the

cart was jolting along at high speed and Jacob was sliding towards the back. Jed was urging the horses on to even greater speed. They made a skidding turn that threw him across the cart. Just when it seemed he must be thrown off the back, his left hand found and grasped a rope. The cart raced on along a narrow track hemmed in by trees and Jacob clung on for dear life. The cart bucked and swayed and he tried to catch a glimpse of Jed, but the boxes were in the way. On the other hand, they also shielded him from sight. He was almost sure that Jed didn't know that he was there, or surely he would have done something..

After another wild, skidding turn to the right, the track became narrower and Jed started to rein in the horses. It was no easy task, as they had the bit between their teeth. The pace eventually slowed almost to a walk, there was another turn to the right and then the cart pulled into the rear of a dark, tumbledown barn.

Jacob tensed himself, ready to launch himself at Jed, but he never so much as glanced towards the back of the cart as he went to the horses. He could hear him calming the horses as he tied them to a rail and then there was the sound of a door opening and light streamed into the barn. Jacob ducked down again and the door was dragged back into place and the barn was dark and still.

Raising his head cautiously, Jacob looked across at the door to the barn. There was no sign of Jed, nor could he hear anything except the horses, so he eased himself down on to the floor. Fortunately, when he had thrown his sword on to the cart, it had stuck fast into one of the boxes. Pulling it out with some difficulty, he made a few practice parries with his left hand. He had always practised exercise routines with his left hand, but it was weak compared to his right.

He crept carefully from the barn and made his way to the farmhouse. It looked very neglected, but at least the roof didn't look too bad. The door at the front had been boarded up, so Jacob moved round the side. He could faintly hear Jed's voice coming from the room at the side.

Peering through a gap in the shutter that barred the dirty window, he could see Maria tied to a chair and gagged. She shrank back as Jed caressed her face, whispering in her ear and her eyes showed her disgust at his suggestions.

'Leave my mother alone!' cried Rico, who was also tied to a chair, but had loosened his gag. Jed walked across and slapped him hard across the face raising a red weal. The blow left Rico stunned and Jed turned his attention back to Maria.

Rage hammered in Jacob's head. The door at the rear was broken down and he moved quickly and silently along the passage towards the room where Jed was talking. He could see that the door had been locked and barred, but was now open a crack.

'Well my fine lady,' said Jed, his voice dripping with sarcasm, 'I'm afraid your husband wont be joining us. Now that is a real shame, because I had such plans for you all. However, before I explain them, I must trouble you for a strip of your petticoat to bind this scratch on my leg.'

There was the sound of cloth being torn and Jacob resisted the temptation to rush in. He inched forward. He hoped to kill Jed before he was aware of his presence. This was no time for niceties. In his crippled state, he was no match for Jed.

At last he could see into the room. Jed was using the cloth he'd torn from the hem of Maria's petticoat to bind up his wounded leg, but he was also leering at Maria's now exposed thighs. Tensing himself, Jacob crept forward and prepared to lunge as Jed straightened up.

Jed was looking directly at Maria and warned by her involuntary look of hope, threw himself to the right just evading Jacob's thrust. As the lunge took him forward, Jed lashed out and hit Jacob on his broken arm. The excruciating pain left Jacob temporarily helpless. Jed was on him in a flash. Blow after blow rained down on him until finally, barely conscious, he was sent plummeting into Rico's chair, sending both of them crashing to the floor.

Seeing them both lying still, Jed turned his attention to Maria who was struggling vainly to free herself. Jed slapped her hard across the face and checked her bonds. 'No you don't lady,' he said with a smirk, stroking her thigh. 'I'll just deal with these two, then you and I can get better acquainted.'

Through pain-filled eyes, Jacob saw that Rico's chair had broken in the fall, his bonds had come loose and he had almost managed to wriggle free. Gritting his teeth, he managed to get up and picking up his sword with his left hand, he shouted at Jed, 'Come on then, what are you waiting for?'

Jed turned towards him and seeing Jacob standing unsteadily, but his sword at the ready, Jed moved towards him. 'You're a game one, I'll give you that,' he said, with grudging respect. 'You don't give in easily.'

Jacob shuffled awkwardly around so that Jed had his back to Rico. Drawing his sword Jed advanced cautiously towards him. Injured or not, Jed was obviously taking no chances. Meanwhile, Rico had freed himself and was preparing to launch himself at Jed. Using what strength he had left, Jacob slid his sword across the floor towards Rico. Caught in two minds, Jed tried to stop it, but his bad leg hampered him and Rico snatched it up and took up the *en garde* position.

'Oh this is priceless,' Jed chortled. 'I couldn't have organised this any better myself.' He shot Jacob a look of pure hatred. 'I'm going to kill this whelp of yours in front of you for starters. Then I'll finish you off and use your delectable wife like a Winchester goose. Several times.

'When I'm good and ready I'll kill her,' he said with a leer, 'unless she satisfies me a great deal. I might keep for a while in that case, until I get tired of having her and then I'll kill her.'

He looked at Rico who was still standing ready and then, swinging around, battered Jacob to the floor with the flat of his sword.

'Well then,' he said, beckoning Rico to come to him, 'now it's just you and me, so let's have the first course.'

Making a few practice swings, he suddenly feinted to lunge and Rico jumped back nervously. Jed laughed and circled round. Suddenly he lunged for real, but Rico parried. After Rico had blocked his slashes a number of times, Jed changed his tactics. He started to bait Rico. 'I'm going to enjoy undressing your mother. She's still ripe for plucking. I think I'll tie her to the table on her back with her legs wide open. She might enjoy being dominated.' Rico's face darkened with anger, but he still watched Jed cautiously.

'Don't like that idea, eh? Well what if I tie her face down. I could tickle her up with my belt first. A few cuts across her arse could really get her going. I'll be licking and pumping her nick until she screams for more.'

This last description was too much for Rico. His face purple with anger he rushed at Jed slashing wildly as he attempted to stop his foul mouth. Which of course was what Jed wanted. All that Rico achieved, was a cut in his side.

Maria had been watching in horror as first Jacob was battered to the ground and now Rico was fighting for his life. She struggled violently to free herself, and blood began to seep from the grazes as she tried to force her hands free. When she saw the blood staining Rico's doublet, she began to rock the chair back and forth, all the time keeping her terrified eyes firmly on her son, her cries muffled by the gag. At last, the chair fell backwards but, in better condition than Rico's, it failed to break and still she couldn't free herself.

Fortunately, Rico's cut was not deep, but it continued to bleed. Jed started his foul suggestions again and Jacob, coming to his senses and hearing him, realised his purpose. 'Remember your training, Rico,' he shouted. 'Remember the mantra. Say it to yourself.'

Rico began to mutter and rapidly gained control. When Jed continued to goad him, he simply ignored him. Jacob was relieved, now he had a chance. Suddenly their positions were reversed. Rico began to drive Jed back and Jed suffered cuts to his arms and a wound in his side. Now it was Jed who lost his temper. He began to batter at Rico's defences, using his strength advantage. But although he drove him back, he could not get through. Redoubling his efforts, he locked swords and using his superior strength, forced Rico on to one knee. With a cry of triumph, he stepped back, raised his sword and brought it down in a killing stroke. Rico, anticipating this move, plunged forward under the stroke and, with his whole body weight behind his stiffened arm, drove the point of his sword upwards. The razor sharp blade, slicing through muscle and tissue, rampaged up under the rib cage and impaled Jed's heart.

Chapter Thirty-Eight
Fotheringhay & London, October, 1586

Jacob let out the breath he had no memory of holding and then looked to see how Maria was faring. She was still struggling with her bonds in the fallen chair. When he tried to stand up to go to Rico he sank back with a suppressed groan. Every movement sent pain lancing through his chest and he thought he might have a broken rib. He had twisted his right ankle when he'd been smashed into Rico's chair and his right arm was broken too, so he had nothing to brace against. From his own experience of a first kill, he knew Rico would now be in shock. Using his good leg and arm, he managed to slide over to the wall. With a struggle he sat up, bracing his back against the wall and looked towards Rico.

Dragging his eyes away from Jed's body, Rico came back to reality and rushed to his father. He was doing his best to keep control of himself, but his face was wet with tears.

Jacob did his best to comfort him as Rico helped him to his feet. 'It's never a good thing to kill another human, but in the heat of battle, it is sometimes necessary. This was necessary.'

He raised Rico's head and looked with compassion at his son. 'I am so proud of you. I couldn't have done what you have just done when I was your age. In time, you will come to terms with this terrible experience, but now I need you to be very brave.'

Rico gave a smile and dashed the tears from his eyes with the back of his hands. Taking a deep breath, he straightened up.

'That's well done, Rico,' said Jacob, with great pride. 'I'm afraid my arm is broken and my ankle is twisted, so I'm going to need your help. We must release your mother. Help me to get to her.'

Leaning on Rico, he hobbled across to Maria. She gave a cry of relief when Jacob removed the gag. As soon as she was free, she hugged them both. 'Oh, thank God you are both safe.'

Then she realised that Jacob was wincing in pain. 'You're hurt, Giam. That evil man! I hope he rots in hell.' She glanced over towards the body, but Rico distracted her.

'Father has a broken arm, Mother,' Rico explained. 'We need to do something about it.'

It was exactly the right thing to say. Dragging her eyes away from Jed, she managed to control herself. Now that she had something to do as a wife and mother she busied herself.

Sending Rico to look for some clean water, she removed the remainder of her torn petticoat and used part of it for a sling for Jacob's arm. After a short while, Rico came back with a bucket, half-full of water.

'There's a well at the back of the house,' he said, 'and I've found the coach in the back of the barn. The horses are there too.'

For the next few minutes Maria was busy tending the various wounds suffered by Jacob and Rico. Fortunately, none of them were deep, although Jacob's ribs were very painful, so she strapped them tightly with the last of the petticoat. When she had finished, Jacob suggested that she and Rico went to have a look at the coach and sort out the horses. When they'd gone, he hobbled over to Jed and pulled out his sword, cleaning the blade on a piece of torn petticoat. Jed's eyes were still staring at the ceiling and Jacob drew his fingers over the lids and closed them. Looking down at the body, Jacob examined his feelings.

Try as he might, Jacob could find no compassion in him. Jed was a man with a cause to fight for, but was a brutish evil man. Even in the relatively short time that Jacob had known him, he had been responsible for several deaths. Jacob's only feeling now was one of relief. They would all be able to sleep better at night now that he was dead. Looking around for something to cover the body, he couldn’t see anything. In the kitchen was a broom and he found he could use it as a crutch. As he came out of the kitchen, he noticed a flickering light coming from the other room. Taking out Jed's pistol, that he had thrust in his belt, he cocked it and cautiously pushed the door open.

The room had been used as a bedroom, but there were some barrels covered with a sheet and on the table was a lighted candle. There was no one in the room and Jacob went to the straw mattress and picked up a sheet. The candle puzzled him. There was a sort of thick black cord near the base of it and the flame had almost burned down to it. 'Oh my God!' he shouted as he realised what it was. The cord was a fuse and, no doubt, the barrels were full of gunpowder. That was what Jed had meant about his wife and son dying. He hurried towards the table and carefully moved the candle away from the fuse. Having pulled the fuse out of the barrel and secured it again, he examined the candle. It had not long to burn. It was fortunate he had found it and he crossed himself fervently.

With a sigh of relief, he picked up the sheet again and went back to Jed's body. Covering the body up he heard the sound of the coach pulling up. He went outside and found Maria sitting on the driver's seat with Rico beside her. 'Get in Jacob, we will take you back into Fotheringhay.'

'Are you sure you can manage to drive the coach?'

'Well, you can't and Rico never has, so it looks as though it will have to be me. I've driven a chaise on many occasions. Help your father in, Rico and we'll find out if I can.' Rico smiled for the first time since the fight and did as he was told.

'What about the cart horses?' asked Jacob when he was settled.

'Rico's given them some straw, so they'll be all right until we can send someone for them, so let's go.'

Maria drove the coach cautiously along the cart track to avoid hurting Jacob. Despite her confidence, the coach was much more difficult to control than a chaise. Fortunately, the horses were well trained and as they moved down the track, her confidence increased. The first turn was the worst, the coach needed far more room than she thought and the turn was narrow and sharp. Somehow, she avoided the ditch and carried on. The trip to the main track leading to Fotheringhay seemed to be far longer than she remembered.

Once they had turned on to it and were heading for the village, she was able to go a little faster. They had barely travelled a mile, when they were stopped by a patrol and one of the soldiers rode off to fetch Colonel Young.

'I see you've been in the wars again, Jacob,' he said cheerfully, when he arrived. 'You seem to be losing your grip.'

Jacob gave him a rueful smile. 'It certainly seems like that.

Perhaps it's time I thought about retiring from this game.'

'I'll keep you to that,' said Maria, with some force and Jacob could see that she meant what she said.

Jacob then gave the colonel a brief outline of what had happened. When he got to the fight, he proudly explained in detail how Rico had saved their lives. 'I doubt very much I could have done it at his age.'

The colonel was impressed. 'Nor I. Still, he did have some good fencing instructors.'

'What about you, colonel. You were slumped against the wall outside the cell.'

'I was lucky. When I went down, I was only winded. Two of my men were not so lucky and two more will be out of action for some time. Jed Sutton was a very strong man,' he said, with more than a little respect in his voice. 'I don't know how he managed to get out of the castle.'

'Well thank goodness it has all ended well for us in the circumstances,' said Jacob. He handed the fake warrant to the colonel. 'You'd better take this and do what you think is best with it. On second thoughts, you'd better destroy it. It was never used, as Jed had already arranged for authority to enter the castle.' He gave a sigh. 'It just shows how difficult it is to stop a determined man.'

'I couldn't agree more,' said the colonel. 'He might have succeeded, if we hadn't been expecting him. It was a good idea of yours to have the sword put behind the door and Mary Stuart well away from her old cell.'

'That's may be true, but I certainly didn't expect Jed to get away.'

'Neither did I,' said the colonel ruefully. 'I had not time to react when he burst through the door. I thought you had everything under control.'

'So I did until he threw the table at me,' he said, rubbing his arm.

'Ah well, all's well that ends well. I will make sure that Walsingham knows of your part in this.'

'Except that,' said Jacob with a laugh, pointing to the fake warrant.

'Certainly except that,' agreed the colonel. 'As I've said in the past, it has been a pleasure to work with you again. You still have the knack of ensuring I don't get bored.'

Chapter Thirty-Nine
London & Fotheringhay, February, 1587

Lord Burghley slumped into the seat of his coach and curtly ordered the coachman to drive on. He was exhausted after yet another long and frustrating session with the Queen. Of course, there was only one topic on the agenda: should the Queen ratify the sentence of public execution announced on Sunday, 14th December.

There was no doubt that the return of the Earl of Leicester from the Low Countries in November had prompted the publication of the verdict. He was strongly in favour of doing away with "this Queen of murderous intent." Not for him the niceties of a formal execution. He would have had her poisoned, or killed and had been urging this course on the Queen for over a month.

Leicester's entreaties to the Queen had led her to hope that one of her subjects would take matters into his own hands and, in so doing, relieve her of the necessity of making a difficult decision. When this convenient assassination had failed to happen, she had suggested sending a letter to Sir Amias Paulet and his assistant Sir Drue Drury, sounding out their disposition to taking the law into their own hands in accordance with the Bond of Association. Davison, Walsingham's assistant, had advised against this course of action, but the Queen had commented that it had been suggested by a wiser person than herself. Possibly Leicester, thought Burghley.

When Paulet wrote to her, saying, *My good livings and life are at Your Majesty's disposition and I am ready to so leave them this next morrow if it shall so please her ... But God forbid that I should make so foul a shipwreck of my conscience or leave so great a blot to my poor posterity to shed blood without law or warrant.*

This noble sentiment did not spare him from the Queen's bitterness. She railed to Burghley against Paulet's daintiness, his disregard of the Bond of Association which he had signed and stormed against *the niceness of these precise fellows who in words would do great things, but in deed perform nothing.* Burghley thought it was a foul blot against the character of a great Queen. Even now this avenue was closed to her, she was still procrastinating. So yet again, Burghley was leaving Windsor without a signed warrant.

As he told Walsingham later the same day, 'Never in all the years I have advised my Princess and lately Queen has she dallied and procrastinated so much over a decision. I am at my wit's end. Whether she will sign or no,' he complained, 'I am sure that even Her Majesty does not know. It will become a matter of her whim. Woe betide any of us who, even though acting in good faith, misinterpret her wishes.'

The very next morning she had changed her mind again and sent for Davison, as Walsingham was indisposed. As Davison went down the corridor, passing the guards, he saw at the far end a figure leave the apartments and head towards him. The man, on seeing Davison, took the corridor to the left. Davison was sure it was Leicester. 'Good morning, My lord,' he called, but the man did not answer. By the time Davison reached the corner, there was no sign of him.

He was shown in to the Queen's retiring room where she was seated at her vanity mirror, adjusting her hair. Although it was already after nine o' clock, she was still wearing her housecoat over a negligée.

The Queen indicated a warrant on the table. 'It is time this matter were dispatched,' she said. 'By God's wounds, it is a shame that it has not already been done. Those craven, lily-livered lords profess they would give there lives for me, yet are afraid to upset their self-serving consciences. I have done for my part, all that law or reason could require of me.' She handed him the warrant. 'You must take it to the Lord Chancellor,' she commanded, 'so that it may receive the Great Seal. On your way, I desire you to stop and see Walsingham, who is lying sick at his house and communicate the matter to him.

'The grief thereof,' she added, with a flash of wit, 'will go near to kill him outright. You must, however,' she charged him, 'keep this matter secret.'

Davison took the warrant from her and then hesitated. 'Your Majesty, the Lord Chamberlain knows of the warrant, so does the Lord Treasurer and you have instructed me to tell Mister Secretary.' He didn't know how he was supposed to keep it a secret if so many people knew of it, but he dare not say so out loud.

The Queen simply dismissed his implied question with a curt, 'I have given my instructions, do your part.'

Giving a deep bow, Davison hurried off to carry out the Queen's orders.

Once the Great Seal had been affixed to the warrant, Davison was instructed to call on Robert Beale, Walsingham's brother-in-law, and a stout defender of the Puritan cause, both in court and in the Commons. Beale was to go to Greenwich next morning to appear before a meeting of the Privy Council in Burghley's chambers.

Eleven of the councillors were there, including Burghley, Leicester, Howard, Hatton and Davison. Burghley presided and explained the position to Beale. He impressed on him the need for great speed and secrecy, the danger facing the Queen if his errand became known and gave him detailed instructions on how to proceed.

They arranged a cover story that Beale had a commission to investigate hues and cries in Hertfordshire and the surrounding area. Beale was also provided with letters for Shrewsbury and Paulet, which had been drafted by Burghley, written by Davison and signed by all of the councillors. They had even sent them to Walsingham to sign on his sickbed.

Beale was instructed to proceed with all speed and the councillors vowed to keep their actions secret from the Queen, until the execution of Mary Stuart had taken place.

It took Beale three days to find Shrewsbury who was visiting his various estates. He briefed him on his mission and together they went to Fotheringhay to meet with the others. On the evening of the seventh of February, Paulet and Drury led Shrewsbury upstairs to see Mary.

Mary was reading the Bible. One look at Shrewsbury's face was enough to tell her why they had come. Closing her Bible, she laid it to one side and regarded them with a tranquil expression. Not even reacting as Paulet tore down her cloth of state from over her desk, for the last time.

'Do not fear to tell me,' she said when Shrewsbury unrolled the warrant and hesitated. 'I have been waiting for this moment ever since the trial. When is it to take place?'

'The execution will take place tomorrow morning,' said Paulet brusquely, 'shortly after eight o' clock.'

Shrewsbury then read out the full warrant and she listened in silence. She did not speak for a while and then asked a question that surprised them all.

'Am I then to be quietly murdered as was King Richard II in Pontefract Castle?'

Drury was an honourable man and much kinder than Paulet. He also knew Elizabeth's firm intention that she should be quietly done to death. He too had received the same letter as Paulet which he had answered in similar vein.

'You may have no fear of that, madame,' he said kindly, 'you are in the charge of a Christian Queen.'

'Then, gentlemen, I thank you for such welcome news. I will be very glad to go from this world. I have tried, without success, to reach an accord with Queen Elizabeth. All of my overtures have been rejected: I can do no more.'

She stood up and crossed herself in the name of the Father, the Son and the Holy Ghost. 'I am ready and very happy to die and to shed my blood for Almighty God, my Saviour, my Creator and for the Catholic Church, to maintain its rights in this realm.'

Mary then asked if she could have her own chaplain to comfort her, but Paulet refused angrily. When she asked if she could be buried in France. Shrewsbury told her that the Queen would not sanction this. Mary made a final request that her servants should be set free after her death and that she should be allowed to reward them. Having no instructions to the contrary, this was agreed.

She then stood up and addressed them. 'Now, if you will excuse me, there is much to do in the time remaining.'

They bowed and left her while her women began to wail. 'Enough of that caterwauling,' she exclaimed angrily. 'There will be time enough afterwards when I am not here to admonish you.'

This set them off again and she shooed them out saying, 'Begone until you have learned to control yourselves. Send in my secretary. I have much to do.'

Having issued various instructions, she ate a little, prayed for about an hour or so and then, gathering her strength, she began to order her affairs. First she wrote her will, stating that she died in the true Catholic faith and asking that requiem masses be said in France for her soul and that her servants should be allowed to attend. She instructed that her debts should be settled and that any remaining money should be used to reward the servants. Her cousin, Henri, Duke of Guise, was named as her principal executor.

When this was done, she included a letter of farewell, setting out her position as a martyr for the Catholic faith. She saw this as her new role, for whatever little life she had left and she must make sure she played her part to perfection.

Penning a final letter to the French King Henry III, her brother-in-law, she lay down on her bed and tried to sleep. Unable to do more than doze, she managed to keep still until six o' clock, when the candelabra was lit. Composing herself, she made herself ready and when the maidservants brought in the clothes they had been preparing all night, she began to dress.

In accordance with custom, she would be expected to undress to her chemise. Accordingly, she chose the deep red one. The colour of Catholic martyrs. She fortified herself with some wine from the blood-red goblet made for her by Jacob Bell and remembering his other gift of the red Murano necklace, asked her maid to fetch it. It will go well with my black dress and provide a little colour, she thought. It may even reflect on my face, which I'm sure will be very pale.

Having carefully put on her make-up and wig, she called her servants all together in her presence chamber. As one last spark of spirit, she had her cloth of state erected over the chair and began to pray.

Barely had she begun, when a loud knocking was heard on the

outer door. When it was opened, there stood Thomas Andrews, the Sheriff of Northamptonshire, together with the Earls of Shrewsbury and Kent. Mary's last hour had come.

Mary turned to her servants and instructed them to remember what she had told them. Picking up the ivory crucifix, she was about to go with the earls, when one of her servants reminded her about her illuminated Latin prayer book. With a nod of appreciation, she picked it up in her other hand. Kissing the crucifix, she went over to the door.

Stepping forward, she crossed the threshold and started on her last journey. With the Sheriff of Northamptonshire in front and the earls flanking her they went down the wide stairs to the Great Hall on the ground floor where the executioners and a large crowd awaited her coming. A scaffold had been erected in the centre, twelve feet square and three feet tall, draped in black linen. The only items on it were a disrobing stool, the block, a cushion for her to kneel on, and a bloody butcher's axe that had previously been used in a slaughterhouse. At the first sight of the block and axe, Mary's iron resolve almost cracked, but squaring her shoulders, she continued her measured pace.

The Queen entered the Great Hall full of grace and majesty, as if she were coming to a ball. Jacob, who had been asked by Walsingham who was still very ill, to attend as a witness in his place watched Mary carefully. There was no change in her expression and he could only admire her spirit as she faced her end.

Drawing up before the scaffold, she summoned her major-domo and Jacob heard her say, 'Please help me mount this. It is the last request I shall make of you.' He proffered his arm and together they mounted the five steps to the dais, followed by her two maidservants. She thanked him for his assistance and reminded him of the details he was to convey to her son. Turning to the Earl of Kent, she addressed him directly. 'I beg of you to allow my chaplain to attend me.' Much to Jacob's surprise, he saw she was wearing the red Murano bead necklace he had presented to her at Sheffield.

'I pity you greatly,' the earl replied, 'to see you thus the victim of the past superstitions. Better that you carry the cross in your heart, than carry it in your hand.'

'It would be difficult,' she replied bravely, 'to hold a thing so lovely in your hand without feeling a thrill in your heart. Every Christian, at the hour of their death, should carry the true symbol of redemption.'

When the earl then offered her the comfort of a Protestant minister, she rejected it angrily. Then falling to her knees, she prayed that Queen Elizabeth would spare her ladies-in-waiting. She then said a prayer for the conversion of the Isles of Britain and Scotland to the Catholic faith.

Having completed her prayers, she stood up and motioned for her ladies to start to undress her. She took off the chain of red Murano beads and her crucifix and placed them on the disrobing stool. The executioner tried to take them, but she handed them over to her servant saying he would receive three times what they were worth.

One of the two executioners stepped forward to help and touched her arm and she cried out, 'Nay my good man, touch me not.'

He knelt down and begged her pardon and she said she forgave him and all who were responsible for her death, as freely as she hoped her sins would be forgiven by God.

The executioners and her two servants then helped remove a black outer gown, two petticoats, and her corset to reveal the deep red chemise - the liturgical colour of martyrdom in the Catholic Church.

As she disrobed, she smiled faintly to the executioner and looking around at the crowd of between four and five hundred witnesses, she said, 'Never have I had such assistants to disrobe me, and never have I put off my clothes before such a company.'

Having been stripped of all her apparel saving her petticoat and kirtle, her two women beholding her made great lamentation. They crossed themselves and prayed in Latin. She, turning to them, embraced them and said, '*Ne crie vous, j'ay prome pour vous',* and so crossing and kissing them, she bade them pray for her, rejoice and not weep, for now they would see an end of all their mistress's troubles. They were to stand back quietly, pray to

God for her soul, and bear truthful testimony that she had died in the bosom of the Holy Catholic religion.

Mary's clothes were collected and taken to be burned on a bonfire just outside the Great Hall to prevent supporters keeping them as relics.

Her other maid now approached Mary and, at her signal, tied a kerchief around her eyes and knotted it at the crown.

Jacob gave a sharp intake of breath as the final moment arrived and like many present he made the sign of the cross.

The Queen quickly knelt down on the cushion placed in front of the block. Without faltering, she felt for the block, positioned her neck on it and held her arms stretched behind her back.

As she muttered a prayer, the executioner struck her a great blow but, to Jacob's horror, he hit the back of her head. He struck again and although the head was almost completely severed, he was forced to saw through a piece of tendon. He then picked up the severed head by its hair and, showing it to those present, cried out, 'God save Queen Elizabeth!'

At that moment, to Jacob's amazement, the auburn tresses in the executioner's hand came apart and the head fell to the ground, revealing that Mary had very short, grey hair. Although only forty-four, twenty years of captivity had taken their toll.

As he rode home. Jacob mulled over his part in Mary's downfall. There was no doubt that he had helped Walsingham to forestall Mary Stuart's plotting, more than a little, but in the end, it was the Scottish Queen's ruthless ambition that had brought about her end. There was much to like about Mary and he, like many others, had been touched by her charm. He had even had qualms about working against her, but in the end, he saw her for what she was - an ill-starred, overly-ambitious woman who would stop at nothing to gain the English throne.

Later when describing the scene to the incapacitated Walsingham in a visit to his home, Jacob was full of admiration. 'She walked to the block like a Queen and like a Queen she died.' He struggled to find the right words, as Walsingham waited patiently. 'Nothing in her life became her more than the leaving of it.'

Walsingham nodded in agreement. 'Whatever I thought of her

machinations, I confess to some admiration and sympathy for her end. Even though it was of her own choosing.' Walsingham sighed.

'I have no wish to trample on the grave of an undoubtedly very charming, attractive and unfortunate woman,' he continued, with the utmost sincerity, 'but we ought not to forget why she was executed. She was perhaps in herself, the greatest menace that ever threatened the safety and welfare of England during my Queen's reign. The English can breathe more freely now she has gone.'

But this was not the end of the matter. There was still the wrath of Elizabeth to face. And face it they did. On the evening of the tenth of February, the Lords and Privy Councillors were called into the Queen's withdrawing chamber. The exceptions were Lord Burghley who had fallen from his horse the previous day, hurting his leg quite badly and Leicester. The Queen rebuked them in the most extreme language that many professed they had never heard her use before. In particular, her greatest ire was directed against Davison and the Lord Treasurer, Burghley. After enduring the most virulent tirade, she ordered that Davison should be immediately committed to the Tower. As Leicester was told in a letter from her secretary the next day, *if the Queen continues this morning in the mood she was in yesternight, I think Your Lordship happy to be absent from these broils.*

Burghley was also informed of the Queen's extreme anger and displeasure towards him. He had expected it. The following morning he penned a letter to the Queen. He entreated the Queen not to blame Davison, she had placed him in an impossible position. Once he had shown him the warrant with the Great Seal attached, as instructed by her, what followed was out of his hands. Burghley made a dignified defence of his own actions and those of the Privy Councillors. He begged her not to allow her grief to affect her health. Long experience had taught him that, so far as Mary was concerned, Elizabeth would never take the straightforward course. She favoured Mary's death for her own safety, but was loath to be answerable for it.

He, Burghley had taken that responsibility on himself, even if he had taken the precaution of having the whole Privy Council sign the letter instructing Beale to serve the warrant. He had absolutely no regrets at the course he had chosen. Even if it should be his total downfall, it was a small price to pay. Had Mary Stuart been spared, she would have continued to plague Protestant England for as long as she lived.

Chapter Forty
London, July/August, 1587

At the beginning of July, Jacob received a letter from his father. The Doge had asked him to pass on the enclosed letter for handing privately to Queen Elizabeth. He had not sent it through normal diplomatic channels, as he was afraid it might come to the notice of the Spanish spies in Venice. Jacob went straight round to see Lord Burghley at his London home. From him, he learned that the Queen was back at Greenwich, but that Burghley was still feeling the sharp edge of her tongue and anger. In short, he was very much still out of favour.

This was amazing to Jacob. Burghley had been her mainstay since the time she was a princess in Queen Mary Tudor's court. It is doubtful whether she would have survived if it had not been for Burghley's advice and support.

Burghley told Jacob to go immediately to Greenwich and seek an audience. 'In her present mood, she is likely to turn on anyone, even on such as yourself, if you delay.'

Promising that he would try to advance Burghley's cause if the opportunity was presented, Jacob set off for Greenwich. He had to wait for almost three hours before he was called into her privy chamber. Jacob could see that she was looking drawn and tired. Nevertheless, she greeted Jacob warmly. 'We are pleased to see you, Jacob Bell. Welcome and take your rest. I hear you have a private letter from the Doge.'

Taking the packet out of his doublet, he handed it to her. 'I have ordered some refreshments for you, Jacob Bell. Please help yourself of the repast, while I read what the Doge has to say.' She waved to the chair beside the table. 'Sit yourself down, man,' she ordered with a smile and a touch of her old spirit, 'and make no more of it. I may have questions for you when I've finished reading.'

Having eaten all he wanted, Jacob sat and sipped a glass of wine, while the Queen read the letters. One of them seemed to upset her a little and she glanced sharply over in his direction, before re-reading the letter. She placed it on her lap and studied Jacob for several minutes, while he wisely sat waiting patiently.

With a sigh, she picked up the letter and waved it in Jacob's direction. 'Are you privy to what the Doge has written?'

With a shake of his head, Jacob replied that he had not read them. 'The Doge did discuss them in general terms with my father, but was there something you would like me to clarify?'

It was the Queen's turn to shake her head. 'Not clarify, but give me your honest opinion.'

Jacob bowed. 'I'm sure Your Majesty is aware, that this is my chief fault. I always try to answer honestly, even if it is not to my advantage to do so.'

'It is what I have come to value in you, and so apparently does the Doge.' She regarded him shrewdly. 'Have you told the Doge of Lord Burghley's part in the Mary Stuart execution?' She regarded him intently as he replied.

'No, I have not communicated with him on this matter. The last time I was in Venice, he asked me for my opinion of Lord Burghley and I gave it.'

'What did you say?' asked Elizabeth eagerly. 'It must have been complimentary, or the Doge would not have written as he does in this letter.'

Jacob did not hesitate. 'I told him that Lord Burghley was the most astute councillor any monarch could have. His grasp of the affairs and needs of the realm he put before any thought of himself.' He looked calmly into Elizabeth's eyes. 'As for the present, I do not know his part in the execution of the Queen of Scots. What I do not doubt, was that whatever he did, it would be in the interests of his Queen and country and not for his own advancement.'

He paused and the Queen could see his hesitation. 'Fear not for yourself, Jacob Bell, tell me the truth.'

'Then, Your Majesty, you do yourself and the nation a great ill in preventing this great man from being at your side to advise you. As Walsingham said to me before I left, "How many more people would be forced to die in order to further Mary Stuart's ambitions, while she escapes the consequences of her machinations".' He gave a sad smile. 'He also told me with the utmost sincerity, "I have no wish to trample on the grave of an undoubtedly very charming, attractive and unfortunate woman, but we ought not to forget why she was executed. She was perhaps in herself, the greatest menace that ever threatened the safety and welfare of England during my Queen's reign. The English can breathe more freely now she has gone".'

There was silence in the privy chamber for some time and Jacob began to think that despite her assurance, he had gone too far. Fortunately, the Queen was simply overcome by her own thoughts and touched by the words of her Moor as she called Walsingham. She stood up and Jacob did so too. When she held out her right hand, Jacob bowed low over it. When he straightened up, she regarded Jacob with a most warm smile. 'I can always rely on you, Jacob Bell, to get to the heart of a matter. You have served me well.'

Taking his courage in his hands, Jacob told her what was in his heart. 'Thank you, Your Majesty. I regret to say, however, that I will no longer be able to serve you in my capacity as an agent for Walsingham. I believe the threat to your personal safety has largely receded now that the fulcrum of it all has been removed. I cannot therefore put my family in any more danger. We were fortunate to survive the fanaticism of Jed Sutton and I will not put them in that position again.'

The Queen stood with her legs apart, her hands on her hips and threw her head back and roared with laughter. 'You will not, eh! Jacob Bell, you are absolutely priceless. It was a fortunate day for England when you were cast so precipitously on to our shores. You have my blessing to retire from my secret service.' She waved a finger admonishingly at him. 'And tell your wife to come and visit me as soon as she can.

'And now, you ungrateful, outspoken wretch,' she said, thrusting her jaw forward, 'begone from my sight lest I change my mind and throw you into the Tower.' For a moment, Jacob hesitated wondering if she was serious. She certainly sounded it. Seeing his indecision, the Queen sat down shaking with laughter, while Jacob made a shamefaced exit. He couldn't believe the Queen had fooled him again.

At the beginning of the month, one of the Queen's messengers arrived at Mark Street with an ornate letter from the Queen. The whole family was invited to attend a banquet at St. James's Palace, on the fourteenth of August, followed by entertainment. Jacob was instructed to be at St. James's Palace an hour before the banquet began at five o'clock in the afternoon.

The invitation created huge excitement in the household. It was decided that the three eldest children, Rico, Eleanor and Maria Jane could attend and Anna would look after the other two at home.

The matter of clothes now became the sole topic of conversation, particularly amongst the girls. Jacob had continued to patronise the tailor first introduced to him by Walsingham, who, delighted to make a new outfit for him, promised to have it ready for a fitting the day before the banquet, so that any alterations could be made immediately. Maria decided to wear the outfit she had worn for the ball in Paris. It was a fashion that was becoming popular in London and Maria had not worn the dress since. As she said to Jacob, 'I will have to wear the Paris dress again, there will be far too little time to have a new one made. And, I hope you don't mind, but I'll wear my rubies this time.'

Jacob chuckled. 'I rather thought you might. I can't see many at court wearing Murano bead necklaces.'

When the family arrived at St. James's Palace, they were met by the Queen's equerry. As instructed, they had arrived an hour before the banquet was due to start and the equerry led them into the Great Hall. There were a number of tables already laid out, with a head table and central throne set under the imposing cloth of state.

The equerry led them to the table on the right of the Queen's throne with Jacob at the top right and his father directly opposite. Maria was on his left and the children alternating down the table. This still left a number of spaces and when Maria asked Jacob who was joining them, he confessed he had not the slightest idea. Not long afterwards the mystery was solved, when Roberto, his wife Elizabeth and the children joined them. When Jacob had a word with Roberto and Elizabeth, he found that they were just as mystified as Jacob about what was going on.

Just then, the equerry asked Jacob to come with him. Excusing himself, Jacob followed him and was surprised to find they were going to the Queen's privy chamber where a number of Privy Councillors were present, including Lord Burghley, Walsingham and Leicester. Jacob acknowledged their greetings and bowed low to the Queen.

The Queen then nodded to Burghley who stepped forward. 'Master Bell, we have an important question to ask of you and would be pleased if you would give it some serious thought before you answer.'

Jacob promised he would, totally perplexed.

'Very well then,' continued Burghley. 'In a recent interview with Her Majesty, you indicated that you no longer wished to be directly involved in the activities that have put your family at risk. Is that correct?'

Jacob agreed he was correct.

'Would you explain your reasons, please.'

'Firstly,' Jacob said, 'I was extremely fortunate to survive an assassination attempt by Sutton, thanks to the brigandine so kindly given to me by Her Majesty.' He turned and bowed to the Queen who acknowledged his thanks with a graceful gesture.

'Secondly, I was also lucky to rescue my wife and son who had been kidnapped by Sutton. This was despite all the precautions I had taken.' He was interrupted by a dry comment from Walsingham.

'Modest as ever I see, Bell,' he said, with a trace of a smile. 'I would rather believe it was your spirit, pluck and determination.'

Jacob returned his smile. 'As you will, Sir Francis, but to come to the final reason.' He looked around at them all. 'The death of Mary Stuart has removed the largest threat that existed to Her Majesty.' He held his hand up as Walsingham was about to protest. 'By your leave, Sir Francis, I know there are many malcontents but I also know that your network of spies has them well watched. The strongest threat to this realm is not a plot, but war. War with Spain.'

He paused and saw that Burghley and the others were nodding in agreement. 'I am not a soldier, therefore I believe that for all those reasons, I should no longer act for Sir Francis Walsingham.'

The Queen and Burghley then exchanged glances and Jacob saw her nod to Burghley, who turned and addressed him again. 'Thank you, Master Bell. There is one other question that we would like to ask.'

'Ask away,' said Jacob, who in truth was feeling a little euphoric having resigned from the spy business. 'I will answer to the best of my ability.'

'Our question is,' Burghley said, pausing dramatically, 'are you still committed to remaining in England and developing your glassmaking interests, or do you plan to return to Venice for good?'

Jacob gasped in surprise. Of all the questions he was expecting, that certainly was not one of them. 'You catch me unawares, My lord,' he said, with a rueful smile. 'I am not sure what reason prompted that question, but to answer it fully. I have no intention to return to Venice on a permanent basis. England is now my home. It has been good to me and to my family and friends.'

He looked across at the Queen who was getting to her feet. She gave him a beautiful smile and Jacob thought how radiant she looked at that moment.

'Well gentleman, we have our answers. Let the festivities begin,' she said gaily, as she swept out of the room with her smiling councillors following. As Jacob made to follow, the equerry appeared at his side and bade him wait a few moments.

He asked Jacob to remove his sword and passed it to a waiting squire who hurried off with it. Just then there was a fanfare of trumpets and the equerry motioned for Jacob to follow him.

As they reached the doors to the Great Hall, the two gentlemen pensioners on guard saluted him and turning, opened the door. When Jacob entered the hall, he found that Lord Burghley and Sir Christopher Hatton were standing inside facing him with delighted smiles on their faces. As Jacob stepped inside, they fell in at either side of him and asked him to wait.

There was a loud fanfare of trumpets and all of the guests in the hall stood up and turned towards him. Jacob was bewildered, but he had no time to ask questions as he was ushered towards the waiting Queen by Burghley and Hatton.

As they moved towards the top table, with people bowing, or giving a friendly greeting, Jacob had another surprise. The throne had been moved to stand in the open space in front of the table with the cloth of state hanging over it and the Queen was sitting in regal splendour watching his approach. They stopped a few feet away and bowed deeply to the Queen. She acknowledged with a graceful wave of her hand.

The knight herald then stepped forward and there was another fanfare. When it ended he addressed them. 'Who sponsors this supplicant?'

'By Your Majesty's leave, I, William Cecil, Baron Burghley and I, Christopher Hatton, Knight,' they intoned in turn.

There was another fanfare and four heralds appeared in red and gold livery with a tabard sporting the sovereign's arms on the front and a large Tudor rose on the back.

The first carried a red velvet cushion which he placed in front of the throne and bowing deeply, backed away to the side. The other three approached the cushion and stood slightly to one side nearest the Queen, facing her. On one cushion was a pair of ornate spurs, the second carried what looked to be a shield covered by a cover of cloth of gold, and the third carried an elaborately decorated sword, scabbard and belt.

The herald motioned Jacob forward and indicated he should kneel on the cushion. Jacob did so, totally bemused. The Queen's chaplain now stepped forward and standing in front of Jacob, prayed that God would look into the supplicant's heart and cleanse it of all evil. He then made the sign of the cross over him and stepped back.

The knight herald turned to face the audience and opening out the scroll he carried began to read.

'By order of Her Majesty, Queen Elizabeth, in this year of fifteen hundred and eighty-seven, I do hereby announce that for services to the Queen in the field of Diplomacy, for bravery in the face of enemies of this realm, for services to the Crown by the establishment of a thriving glass industry in this realm, she is pleased to convey on Jacob Bell, Master Glassmaker to Her Majesty Queen Elizabeth, the accolade of Knighthood.'

Taking the sword from the herald the Queen stood in front of Jacob and raised it above his head. Jacob bowed and the Queen tapped him lightly on each shoulder with the flat of the blade, calling out loudly, 'I dub thee, Sir Knight. Arise Sir Jacob Bell.'

To loud cheers and another fanfare, Jacob stood up dazed and proud as the Queen handed him the shield, sword and belt. Lord Burghley took the spurs and fixed them to his shoes, while Sir Christopher girded the sword round his waist. They both embraced him warmly and then turning round to face the crowd, proclaimed loudly, 'We present to you, Sir Jacob Bell.'

What followed was like a dream. Faces coming and going, well-wishers shaking his hand and all the time he was looking around for Maria. The crowd was all about him and he tried to move towards where she had been sitting.

Suddenly, the crowd parted and there she was, with tears of pride streaming down her face. They embraced and kissed with the crowd roaring their approval until, remembering where they were, they broke apart.

Maria's cheeks were burning as Jacob offered his arm and said, 'Come with me, Lady Bell. I would like to see my family and dear friends.'

The rest of the evening passed in a blur. First there was music and then they sat down to a supper, with beer and ale, wine and all manner of meats, tarts, pies, larks, chicken, sallets, custard and sauces for the first course and pheasants, partridges, plovers, lark tart, connyes, butter and eggs of various sorts for the second.

When they were all almost too full to move, there was the Queen's favourite pastimes, music and dancing. Jacob was given the ultimate sign of the Queen's favour by being singled out to dance with her.

Later, the Queen sent for Maria to join her and when Jacob glanced over, they were in deep conversation and he wondered what they were discussing. Although they glanced at him occasionally, as far as Jacob could see, their attention seemed to be more on Rico.

That worthy of course was enjoying himself immensely. He had a fine athletic build like his father and was schooled in all of the social graces. At first, he danced with his sister Eleanor, who was also receiving a fair amount of attention from the young bucks of the court. They were preening and showing off outrageously in an attempt to get her attention. Later, she too was surrounded by admirers and they were too busy to dance together again. Not that he was allowed to, being in great demand with the Queen's ladies, particularly a black-haired minx of a girl who seemed to be about fourteen or fifteen. She had hardly taken her eyes off Rico all evening and somehow contrived to dance with him more than the other ladies.

Eventually, of course, all good things come to an end and it was time to return home. Lord Burghley had a brief word with Jacob and asked if he could visit him in the early afternoon, as there was something he wished to discuss with him.

By the time they finally arrived home they were totally exhausted. Jacob and Maria fell into bed and were asleep before they even could talk about the momentous events of the evening.

Chapter Forty-One
London, September, 1587

After the events of the previous night, Maria and Jacob were late up so they had no time to discuss the events of the previous evening. Except for a mischievous curtsey and a cheery, 'Good morrow, Sir Jacob,' from Maria. Jacob's reply to which was to hug Maria and kiss her soundly. When he finally let a breathless and glowing Maria go, he bowed deeply and said, 'And good morrow to you too, Lady Bell.' It is doubtful that matters would have rested there had it not been for a discrete knock at the door.

'Are you awake?'

Jacob recognising Rico's voice, said they were.

'Can you come downstairs, please?' came the request.

'We'll be down in a few minutes,' Jacob promised and they hurried to finish dressing.

'I wonder what the problem is,' said Maria as they went down the stairs.

When they reached the wide atrium they were astonished to see all of the staff and the family lined up to greet them. Maria linked her arm with Jacob's, snuggling close to him as they stopped on the bottom step.

At a signal from Rico the men bowed deeply and the ladies curtseyed. 'Good morrow, Sir Jacob and Lady Maria,' they chorused. As Jacob went down the lines greeting everyone, they all applauded. Walking back to the stairs when they had acknowledged everyone, Jacob stood on the bottom step again and faced them. Holding his arms up to get silence, he addressed them. 'On behalf of Lady Maria and myself, I thank you for your greetings and courtesies. However, this is the last time I expect you to use my title when we are in our own home.' He smiled as he looked around. 'I give fair warning, however, that anyone who addresses me as Sir Jacob from now on will be dismissed immediately!' Maria tugged on his arm and looked at him with an amusing pleading expression. He looked lovingly at her. 'Oh well then, except for when we have visitors or we are outside.' He gave a friendly smile. 'To be serious. I would like to keep things as they are. Master Jacob will be fine for when we are at home. Lady Maria will still be Lady Maria, or mother,' he said, smiling at the children. 'I'm certain that she will decide for herself and let you know if she wishes you to use anything different.'

He looked around expectantly. 'Now we must get on. Rico will be leaving the day after the morrow, so there is much to do.'

As the servants went off to their work, Jacob and Maria went into the study. 'Have you started to get used to this knighthood yet?' he asked seriously.

'It has started to sink in that it's for real. The attitude of the servants left no doubt in my mind.' She gave a sigh. 'It's going to mean some changes,' she said ruefully. 'Even the children can see that.'

'I know,' replied Jacob, 'but I meant what I said to them all. I want to revert to plain Master Jacob, or father. I don't expect this Sir Jacob business to make any difference to our lives.'

Maria shook her head doubtfully. 'I'm afraid it will never be quite the same, but,' she said with a chuckle, 'we'll try to see it doesn't go to your head.'

About an hour later, Jack Petts knocked on the door and entered. 'Lord Burghley to see you, Sir Jacob,' Jack said, stepping aside. Burghley entered, carrying what looked like a sword wrapped in cloth. Jacob assumed it was his old sword that he had left at Saint James Palace.

'The servants are taking to your new status very well, Sir Jacob,' said Burghley, with a friendly smile, placing the parcel on the desk and taking the proffered seat. 'Have you recovered from last evening's festivities?' he asked, with a warm smile. 'You seemed a little surprised at the proceedings.'

'Stunned would be a better description, my lord' said Jacob, with feeling. 'I had no idea what was going on.' He gave a shrug. 'Of course, it became obvious that I was to receive an award, but a knighthood,' he shook his head, 'that was never in my mind.'

Burghley took a scroll out of his doublet. 'In that case, I don't expect you will have expected this either.'

Jacob examined the scroll as if it was about to explode. 'What is it?'

'Why don't you have a look and see?' said Burghley. 'Open it, Sir Jacob, it won't bite you.'

Unrolling the scroll Jacob began to read. At first, his expression did not change but, reading on, he raised his eyebrows in total surprise.' Looking up at Burghley he waved the scroll at him. 'Is this another of the Queen's jokes?'

Burghley laughed. 'Not at all, Sir Jacob. That is your warrant of appointment as a member of the Privy Council. As the head of the Glass-Sellers Association, you are particularly well placed to advise the Queen on matters relating to business and also as her Special Advisor and Envoy for Venice.'

He stood up to go. 'Don't look so surprised, Sir Jacob. You have contributed much to England since your inauspicious arrival. Besides, it will make a change to have someone else on the receiving side of the Queen's moods. You have led a very sheltered existence with Her Majesty, so far.'

Jacob could think of nothing to say and just watched as Burghley picked up the parcel from the desk. 'Is your son, Ricardo here?' he asked.

'Yes, he is getting ready for his much delayed departure for Venice on *The Crystal.*'

'Ah yes, of course. He is going as an ensign I believe. Could I have a word with him?'

When Rico arrived, he bowed to Lord Burghley, who stood up holding the parcel across his extended arms.

'Her Majesty has asked me to present this to you, in recognition of your brave action in saving your parents from the would-be rescuer of Mary Stuart.' He handed it to Rico, who stammered his thanks and unwrapped the cloth. His face lit up when a bejewelled ceremonial sword and scabbard were revealed. As he studied it, Lord Burghley smiled and said, 'Examine the blade, Ricardo.'

Drawing the sword from the scabbard, he looked at the elaborate engraving on the blade and saw there was an inscription, *To Ricardo Giacomo Bell - For valour - Elizabeth Regina.* He gasped and showed the sword to Jacob, who read the inscription and turned to Lord Burghley. 'How did this come about?'

Burghley laughed. 'Walsingham of course. His reports to the

Queen are very detailed and he seldom misses anything out.'

'It's very kind of the Queen to remember Rico. I hope Colonel Young has also been rewarded.'

Lord Burghley smiled. 'The colonel has done very well. The Queen has awarded him some of Babington's London property, which will bring him in rent of at least a hundred pounds a year.' With that, he took his leave.

Reluctant though she was to admit it, Maria was dreading the departure of her eldest son. Her only consolation was that her father would have Rico living with him while he was in Venice. That was not the problem, it was the time he would be spending at sea that worried her. As they reached Somers Key to go on board *The Crystal*, Jacob sensing her unease, tried to reassure her. 'It won't be for ever, Maria,' he said. 'Captain Roberts is an excellent captain and will take very good care of him.'

'I know that, Giam,' Maria said simply, 'but he's my first-born. It's a great wrench for a mother when children fly the nest for the first time. Men don't feel it the same.'

'I do feel it,' said Jacob, 'but since his fight with Jed Sutton, Rico has changed a lot. I'm very proud of the way he's coped and moved on. He's no longer a boy. He's a man.'

They stood and waved at *The Crystal* until it was out of sight and then returned home.

For Jacob and Maria, sleep was a long time coming that night.

'I've been thinking about what you said at Somers Key, regarding Rico,' said Maria. 'He has grown up a lot these past few months, but the sea is so dangerous.'

'It is,' agreed Jacob, 'but there are dangers everywhere and *The Crystal* is one of the finest ships afloat.' He shrugged. 'There would be dangers if he stayed here. The storm clouds of war are gathering pace all across Europe.'

'I know,' said Maria, 'the broadsheets are full of dire predictions. I thought now Mary Stuart is no longer a source of plots, we might have been allowed to live in peace,' she said, yawning sleepily. 'I'm too tired for such a deep conversation, I can barely keep my eyes open. Good night, God bless.'

She kissed Jacob and snuggled down on the pillow and was soon asleep. But Jacob was still mulling over the situation. The French religious civil war was dragging on, with no sign of a solution. Spain was becoming more aggressive and his contacts abroad said they were building up a very strong armada of ships. Their purpose could be for only one thing. Invasion of England. Jacob knew from his close friendship with Admiral John Hawkins that he had been getting the Navy ready for this day. The ships were in fine shape now and the Admiral's new concept of fast, manoeuvrable gunships, rather than floating castles, could tip the balance. That true pragmatic, Lord Burghley, believed that God was on the side of the fleet with the most effective artillery and he had been fully behind Hawkins as he overhauled the rotting naval ships he had inherited.

In France too, the outcome of the struggle would have a huge effect on England. Should the Duke of Guise prevail, Catholic France would become a very active enemy of England. The execution of Mary Stuart their cousin, had seen to that, even if the poor relations between the Guises and Elizabeth were not enough. The defeat of King Henry III and the Huguenots would leave England isolated as the only major Protestant force remaining in Europe.

Ah well, he thought as he settled down to sleep, I'd better make sure I play my part. My new ship will be even more powerful than *The Crystal.* I think I'll name it *The Maria.*

Epilogue

Opening the furnace door, Jacob tossed another shovel-full of coal into the furnace. After all the fuss over his knighthood, he had escaped into his private workshop and was preparing a new glass mixture. He intended to try out a new design that had been held up by the events of the past few months. Carefully removing the cover of the melting pot, he examined the molten mixture. Deciding it needed a few more minutes, he put the lid back on and, going back to his desk, re-examined the sketches of the design.

A few minutes later, there was a knock on the door and Roberto came in. 'You have a lady to see you, Jacob.'

'Oh, who is it it?'

'She wouldn't give her name, but said you would remember her, as your late night guide from Chatsworth. It didn't mean anything to me, but perhaps it will to you.'

For a moment Jacob was nonplussed and then he remembered Mary Stuart's lady-in-waiting who, on his first visit to Chatsworth, had led him in secret to meet her mistress. It seemed a lifetime ago. 'Did she say what she wanted?' Roberto shook his head and Jacob said to show her in.

When the lady pushed back the hood of her cloak, that had largely obscured her face, Jacob recognised her immediately. She curtseyed and produced a parcel wrapped in cloth from under her cloak. 'My Mistress, Queen Mary, instructed me to bring this parcel to you, Master Bell.' She blushed and curtseyed again, 'Forgive me, Sir Jacob. I should have used your new title, but I forgot.'

Taking the parcel from her, Jacob told her an apology was unnecessary. 'My title is of little importance in these circumstances. Are you to wait while I open this?'

'Oh, no, Sir Jacob. I am just carrying out my mistresses last wishes, before I travel to France. My ship leaves in the hour and the coachman will be fretting if I am over long here.' She pulled the hood over her head again and gave a deep curtsey.

'With your permission, Sir Jacob, I will be on my way.'

Jacob wished her a safe journey and after she had left, he sat at his desk looking at the parcel. The Scottish Queen's servant and the package she had brought, raised all sorts of emotions in Jacob. Particularly the sense of guilt he had tried so hard to suppress. When eventually he opened the parcel, he found it contained the ruby-red necklace and the blood-red goblet, he had made for Mary Stuart and a short note that simply said, *lest they fall into the wrong hands.*

He was unprepared for the extreme sense of revulsion that rose up in him. Driven to action, by his feelings and the note, he swept them both up and striding to the furnace, removed the cover from the paele and cast them into the molten glass. The necklace sank below the surface immediately, but the goblet sank slowly, losing its shape as it melted into the mass, suffusing it with its ruby colour. Putting the lid back on to the paele, Jacob strode to the corner and quickly fashioned a sand mould into the rough shape of a cube. When it was ready he poured the quiescent, molten red glass into it.

When the mass had cooled, he removed it from the mould and securely wrapped it in the cloth it had come in. Putting on his working cloak and hat, he walked quickly down to London Bridge. On reaching the middle, he went along the outer footpath on the south side of the bridge and finding a suitable spot, studied the muddy brown water of the rain-swollen Thames, eddying in swirling whirlpools around the piers below him. Checking to see that he was unobserved, he took out the parcel and consigned it to its final resting place in the deep turgid water. As it sank from sight, he let out the breath he had been holding in a long sigh. It felt as though a heavy load had been removed from his shoulders. Straightening up, Sir Jacob Bell, Privy Councillor and Glassmaker to Queen Elizabeth, turned and strode off for home without a backward glance.

Historical Notes

As always, I have tried as far as is possible to be true to the historical facts, but this is a novel and not a factual account of what really happened. However, where historical characters are involved, I have kept as close to actual events as possible. Most of the actions of major historical persons are based on my research into the contemporary accounts of events and State papers covering the period.

The Elizabethan era was a very turbulent one. There were many plots against Queen Elizabeth, all with one common source, that of the claim of Mary Stuart to the English throne. Within the scope of this book, I refer to three plots, the Parry Plot, the Throckmorton Plot and the Babington Plot. Although they bear the name of certain individuals, they were inextricably linked, being part of a continuing plot to invade England, dispose of Queen Elizabeth and put Mary Stuart on the throne.

What is not commonly understood, is that none of these plots were instigated by the persons naming them. The major players, Henri, Duke of Guise, Thomas Morgan, Charles Paget, Gilbert Gifford, John Ballard and other dissident Catholics in exile, stayed well in the background. In order to help the reader to make sense of this, I have dealt with all three plots separately in these notes.

The Parry Plot

It is not easy to ascertain the real truth of the so-called Parry plot. Doctor William Parry was charged with having conspired to murder Queen Elizabeth. Accused by Sir Edmund Neville early in February 1585 with proposing to murder the Queen, he admitted as much at his examination. He later confirmed this confession in letters to Elizabeth, Leicester and Burghley. As further proof, he produced a letter from Cardinal Como, the Papal Secretary, urging him to put his *holy and honourable purposes into effect* and granting him plenary absolution from the Pope. There are several copies of this letter in the British Museum.

Although this seemed to confirm the prosecution case, Parry insisted he had never intended to kill the Queen. In the past, he acted as a spy for Walsingham and confessed to plotting the assassination of the Queen in order to obtain information. He had used similar strategies with dissident Catholics, including Thomas Morgan, in France, and had met Cardinal Como some years earlier. These he had confessed to the Queen, was pardoned, and rewarded with a seat in Parliament. Later, he was paid a large sum of money by Thomas Morgan, Mary Stuart's agent in Paris, to carry out the assassination.

Unfortunately for Parry, when he involved Neville he had no remit from Walsingham at all. Whether, as it was reported by a number of sources that Parry did in fact attempt to kill the Queen, but lacked the courage, there is no conclusive evidence one way or the other. Parry was found guilty and executed, but the truth of his guilt will probably never be known. I chose to use the story that he did attempt an assassination, but the events in the *Prologue*, are purely my thoughts on how it might have happened, not what did happen.

The Throckmorton Plot

Walsingham first got wind of the so-called Throckmorton plot from a spy in the French Embassy. He informed Walsingham that the chief agents for Mary Stuart were Francis Throckmorton and Lord Henry Howard who only visited the ambassador's house at night. In view of this report, Walsingham set spies to watch Throckmorton's every move. He was already watching Lord Henry Howard.

After six months, he had enough information and had him arrested and all of his papers seized. Among the papers the searchers found a list of Catholic noblemen, a plan of certain harbours suited to the landing of foreign forces and a number of scurrilous pamphlets against the Queen.

Throckmorton denied everything in front of the Privy Council despite repeated offers of clemency. He was eventually sent to the rack, but revealed nothing. However, when taken to be racked a second time, he confessed all without further "persuasion". He gave a detailed confession naming all the parties and set out how the Duke of Guise intended to invade England at Arundel, sending Charles Paget into England to survey the port. This came as a complete shock to Walsingham, as previous attempts to invade England were all based on an army entering from Scotland. In fact, the Duke of Guise was planning to invade both from the North and the South and was negotiating with Spain for them to send an army into the East of England. Had the invasions actually taken place, the Privy Council were in no doubt that they would have succeeded.

The plot that bears Throckmorton's name was not his. He was only an agent acting according to instructions received from overseas. Many of the men named by Throckmorton fled the country at the news of his arrest. After months of delay, Throckmorton paid the penalty for his treason at Tyburn. Walsingham knew only too well, the main plotters were still carrying out their designs in France and that Mary Stuart was heavily involved in proceedings. Proving it was another matter.

The Babington Plot

With the demise of Throckmorton and the failure of the Duke of Guise's invasion, matters took a different turn. As a direct result of the Throckmorton plot, Walsingham advised the Queen to takes sterner measures with Mary Stuart. Accordingly, she was removed from the household of the Earl of Shrewsbury and subjected to a far more rigorous regime. As the months went by, this regime became more and more strict, until under Sir Amias Paulet, Mary was totally isolated from the outside world.

Walsingham then managed to enlist Gilbert Gifford as a double agent. Working with Phelippes, who was deep in Walsingham's trust, they came up with an elaborate scheme to encourage Mary to send out letters. By allowing letters previously withheld from her to be delivered by this new method, they built up Mary's trust in the scheme. She became convinced that the means of getting them in and out were absolutely safe. In reality, the brewer who provided a secret compartment in his barrels of beer was in the pay of Walsingham. Every letter sent in and out, was seen and copied by Walsingham's cipher man, Thomas Phelippes. In the *Blood-Red Goblet,* I have substituted Jed Sutton for this brewer.

Eventually, Mary sent a letter to Babington which was the key to her downfall. Babington's reply detailing the plot and Mary's reply, taken together with Babington's full confession, were the prosecution's case against Mary. Much has been written about the legality of putting a sovereign Queen on trial. Elizabeth herself had many doubts and refused to allow it for a long time. Only fear for her own safety after the plots to assassinate her came to light, and extended pressure from Parliament and the Privy Council, caused her to change her mind.

When eventually Mary was found guilty of high treason, Elizabeth dithered for many months in making the decision to sign the order for her death. In the end, having finally signed it, she tried to retrieve it, but the Privy Council had ensured it was carried out before she could rescind it.

As a direct result of the execution, Davison, Walsingham's assistant, was sent to the Tower and never regained his position. Lord Burghley, her closest advisor since the beginning of her reign, was in disgrace and banned from court for many months.

Walsingham was accused by the Catholics of orchestrating Mary's downfall by forging letters to convict her. The facts, as determined from the State records, do not support this view. Phelippes did add a forged postscript to a letter - it is a matter of public record. However, the rest of the letter was confirmed by Mary's secretaries as being genuine. Also, copies of letters written in her own hand to the French and Spanish Ambassadors were found amongst her papers. These confirm the views expressed in the letter to Babington. Namely, that Mary Stuart supported the invasion of England by Spain and condoned the assassination of Elizabeth.

During the period of Mary's captivity in England, many men who became enmeshed in her ambitions to gain the throne of England and restore the Catholic religion, paid the ultimate penalty. Some of them, including Babington, in extremely barbaric ways.

The closing scenes in Mary Stuart's life are extremely touching. They have invoked the admiration and sympathy of later generations as nothing else in her life has done. She went to her execution like a Queen and died like a Queen. Sympathetic to her end we may be, but she was almost certainly the greatest menace to threaten the peace and security of England during Elizabeth's reign. The nation in general celebrated the removal of this bosom serpent from their midst and as a result breathed more easily. Now they turned their attention towards Spain, an enemy that threatened them overtly with an Armada.

Postscript

When Elizabeth I died in her seventieth year, some sixteen years after the execution of Mary Stuart, she did not officially name a successor. The story that she named Mary's son, James VI of Scotland as her successor on her deathbed is, just that; a story. It is a myth, unsupported by any solid evidence, since by then, Elizabeth had lost the power of speech. James VI was proclaimed King, by a group of Nobles and Privy Councillors, at the gates of Whitehall Palace.

The Proclamation document was truly remarkable. It stated that James was rightfully King of England, because he was lineally and lawfully descended from Margaret Tudor, eldest daughter of Henry VII and sister of Henry VIII. This statement completely ignored Henry VIII's will barring Mary Stuart from the succession. Instead, it was recognition of Mary Stuart's claim, that she was the lawful successor to Elizabeth. This was a victory, far more conclusive than even Mary could ever have hoped to attain. It meant that since that time, every British ruler has been descended from Mary Stuart and their claim to the throne is derived from her and not Elizabeth Tudor.

Despite Mary Stuart's eventual estrangement from Bess of Hardwick, the wife of the Earl of Shrewsbury, her jailer for many years, their families became inextricably linked after Mary's execution, when Elizabeth Cavendish, Bess's daughter, married Charles Stuart, Earl of Lennox. Another redoubtable woman of the Elizabethan era, Elizabeth, Countess of Shrewsbury, or Bess of Hardwick as she was popularly known, left a strong legacy. She was famous for her building projects and two of her houses, Chatsworth and Hardwick Hall in Derbyshire, are very popular with visitors today.

Bess had high hopes that Arabella Stuart, her granddaughter, would one day take the throne of England, but this was not to be. However, a descendant from her line became our present Queen Elizabeth II. Among Bess's other descendants are many titled families, including the Dukes of Devonshire, Norfolk and Somerset, Baron Waterpark and the Earls of Lincoln, Pembroke and Kent.

Although women in the 16th century had few legal rights, the fair sex certainly produced some of the most influential people of their times in Elizabeth I, Mary Stuart and Elizabeth, Countess of Shrewsbury.

Peter Cooke, Yorkshire, November, 2010.